A Ghost Spell:

A W-C's Haunting Return

By Cordelia Malthere

Wilton Town's Spooky Tales

Book Two

Published by Malthere Publications Limited

Find out more about the author and her books at
http://www.cordelia-malthere.co.uk

If you want to become a published author visit
http://www.malthere-publications.com

ISBN:978-0-9931450-8-7

Graphics by White Tiger Designs

Dedication

To the unjustified victims of the November 13th 2015
attacks in Paris
Innocents caught in a storm of bullets and blasts,
You will live forever in our hearts
For blind hatred never goes anywhere
If it can make the heart of humanity bleed,
It will never make it stop
For Hate has no place in religion, society,
nor a decent man or woman's heart who can
call themselves humans

To my Ma,
Who has implacable,
And impeccable,
Stubborn ways,
Who will never read any of my stories,
Fearing that because there is a ghost or two in them,
That they will never end well.
I can assure you they do.
For this one has a very happy ending,
But will you ever know it?

To my dear Sandra Dean,
Who was ever so puzzled by Zachary Wilton-Cough.
This sequel is the answer
To all your questions:
No one would let that boy turn bad.
For the answer is Love.
And it will always be so.

Foreword.

Welcome to Wilton Town's Spooky Tales. The readers who have already visited the cemetery of Wilton Town, will know that this instalment is the second story released about that whimsical imaginary town. They will know all about the richest man in town, Abraham Wilton-Cough being shot while protecting his customers in his bank, the very first bank of Wilton Town which he created. They will know about that anti-hero, his great pride for they would have followed him from grave to grave up until his deathbed.

Anti-hero or not, Banker or not, proud or not, Abraham Wilton-Cough is a very much loved character. So much so that he had to have a second writing outing, right from his fans point of view but also from his Author's aims for him. I wept penning A W-C last lines which only implies that his character had grown on me so much. Confession for confession the death of my own father had happened shortly prior to me writing 'Hair Rising, Heir Raising, Erasing,' which speaks about a father dying of an untimely death, leaving three children and a wife, reconsidering his entire actions during his life on his deathbed. If there are many parallels which could be clearly drawn out from my personal story to the one I am writing, I must say that Abraham Wilton-Cough is an entirely different kettle of fish from my father. He was inspired by the Dickensian's Ebenezer Scrooge mainly, with a sprinkle of some traits of my own father here and there.

Here you will find Abraham Wilton-Cough raising once more from the dead as a Ghost setting out on another journey in order to destroy once and for all what is causing his unrest. You will find him using any means to rally the living to his cause. He is a Spirit with an aim and he is not alone...

No, not only does he come well accompanied, you will see him gathering followers. You will recognised most from the first tale about Wilton Town. Some characters, who were just mentioned previously, take centre stage like the good yet curious to a default Doctor Vincent

Valdi while others are introduced like the immortal White Witch Whilhelmina.

Teeming with characters from the Past, Present and Future, Wilton Town has many tales in its chest to share. They may lay in a ruined cottage by the edge of the forest or in the cemetery yet for its inhabitants to rest in peace, their stories have to be told.

Spooky: maybe for some, as soon as you speak of Ghosts and Ghouls, some will not read a book terrified by it already. If you don't believe that statement, speak to my mum who will not read any of my books until I create a rosy story of some sort. Then she will read just that one. It would probably go like this: 'Once upon a time Winnie the Pooh shared his honey pot with little red riding hood and they went all Mills and Boon over it. Nine months later the Hundred Acre Wood was full of cute Teddy Bears running everywhere.'

Joking apart, I would rate the level of spookiness in my tales as rather mild. If we had a chilli/chilly chart for scary stories, it would not reach the high end of 'scaryville chill units' of the pure horror type. It would be very mild to medium in some parts, one line or two here and there.

Tragicomedy: definitely. Like the first tale about Wilton-Town this one bestows emotional moments but also lots of humorous scenes throughout. Just like life, tears and laughter are paving the journey into Wilton Town's Tales but sprinkled with just a tad of spookiness.

Enjoy the journey from one's grave to someone else's body...

Spirited away.

Cordelia Halthere

Chapter One

A Ghost's unrest

-Well, well, well, I must be cursed, I can't sleep in peace anymore, not when I know who is playing that tune, the 'Toccata and Fugue in D minor'.

The ghostly hand of Abraham Wilton-Cough rose from his corpse, tried to push the coffin lid open with no success. His desperation grew with every second of struggle as he vociferated for himself,

-I just want to see my boy Josiah! He is becoming a church organist like I feared. With the new will I left behind, he should have shown more ambition... I have visions of concert halls full of people to see him play.

Suddenly a tiny light appeared within the darkness of his coffin, right in front of his nose. It was bright enough to startle Wilton-Cough and make him swear,

-Bugger! Money can't buy you everything these days. Spend it on a bug free coffin, top of the range coffin-wise, they said, and it doesn't do what it says on the tin. I have a bloody glow worm in here! Just wait for his less glowy brothers to get in and I am just an happy meal.

Becoming stronger the light landéd on his cadaverous nose, where it sat and crossed its legs and arms across its chest and looked very much like an angry Angel although a very tiny one. The little voice coming from it was very powerfully upset,

-Pray Abraham, first, what is wrong with Josiah becoming a church organist? Explain yourself. Second, I am not a bug nor a glow worm. Third, apologies are in order for your corpse not to be eaten by an army of worms, right now. Last but not least, you are a ghost and whatever will be chewed off will not affect you for you are spirit matter.

Pulling his other hand from his cadaver and checking its consistency out, or rather inconsistency, Abraham repeated as if he was digesting the information,

-Ghost... Spirit matter...

He raised his ghostly head from his corpse, shook it negatively, making the tiny Angel slide from the bridge of his nose, before he stated strongly,

-I do not like the sound of that. Plainly speaking, that means my soul is not resting properly, now is it? I thought I redeemed myself.

The small Angel cocked an inquisitive eyebrow while sneezing loudly within the dust cloud her fall raised from the deep velvet of the corpse's black jacket. She corrected with confidence, standing upon his chest and dusting her shoulders,

-No Angels would take that away from you that with the few minutes you had left, Abraham, you did redeem yourself pretty well. But, alas as much as your skeleton is gathering dust, your lively bones gathered sins by the bucketful. I know full well for I am the result of one of them you tried to totally ignored under the thick carpet of your stubborn mind. However what causes your unrest this time around, is a pure technicality...

She was interrupted by Wilton-Cough's fearsome sneeze which had the strength to push the light of her to the far end of his coffin, while he apologetically acknowledged her small entity,

-I know you! You are my big fat tiny mistake! You are Abigail, the result of my old bone diving into the poor and totally drunk Widow Bates. Sorry for just waking up from the dead, my mind, stubborn or not, is trying to adjust back to reality. Last time I saw you, you were, well, awesomely tall, fearsome and all...

Coughing, spreading her tiny wings, tidying her pristine white toga, Abigail landed back upon the dead skeleton. She scolded with her nose up in the air,

-Last time you saw me, Human, was a premonition dream, kind of a glimpse of the future set in the present. You see me now as a spiritual Angelic form. I am still to be born to Amelia. Give or take, I am due in a couple of weeks on human terms, however on Angelic ones, I come when it is needed. As for you, you laid in there for the past five months. Know that your sleep was far from peaceful and you were bond to wake up soon or later. Every time I paid you a visit, your spirit was doing the twist and turn within its skeleton and never tried to reach for Paradise. A lot of souls are true grave dwellers yet yours is still in there for another reason: the technicality.

Hearing the technical word a second time, Wilton-Cough grew extremely worried. He expressed his anxiety,

-I do not like the sound of your last word either, my soon to be born Angelic creature. Do I have some more redeeming to do for you to pester my grave? Are you going to take me on a punitive journey where I will have to learn to repent all over again? For frankly, last time was gruelling enough. Besides I think I am a truly sorry arse down here. Did you happen to sneak upon my two boys too? How are they doing? How is my Angie? How is everyone coping after my death? Do I dare to just ask, am I being a little missed if only just for a fraction of a minute?

The tiny Abigail climbed inside the ghostly hand of Abraham. Within his very pale palm, she enjoined him with a compassionate yet sad smile,

-Come, dear old Soul, do not fear any journey, emotional or not. As an Angel, I will only let you alone whilst I know, once and for all, that you can rest in peace. As you clearly are not at peace, I will endeavour with all my might to make you be so. As your daughter, there's only one place I will accept you to be, and I can tell you now, that it is not seeing your ghost, tossing in his grave, roaming cemeteries, and be one of the restless souls burning in Hell. No, the only place for you Pa is Paradise. Let me make sure of it. Follow me I will explain en route all the technicalities.

Abraham Wilton Cough saw himself float out of his coffin, passing through the layer of earth and the heavy stone covering his grave. He could not believe, he was outside in the hilly graveyard, in front of his tombstone just as much as he could not believe the words he read upon it. He asked, his tone deeply dipped with sudden shyness to the Angel standing on his shoulder,

-May I beg you to share some of your light on those words for me?

Abigail went to fly by the stone to light it with her Angelic glow, obliging him straight away. She commented,

-It's pretty dark out here. Late March, a couple of weeks to Easter, the nights although warming up can still be very pitch black, breezy and chilly.

The ghost pointed to the engraved eulogy with an apologetic grin,

-I didn't mean light as for light, little Abi. I meant did my family really mean what is written there? I remember seeing another inscription altogether back in my prophetic dream.

Landing on the top of the headstone the miniature Angel scrutinised her father. Tall, rather slender, with a sorrowful air about him, she just knew she was facing a rather lost soul in need of plenty of reassurance. The great pride and vanity of the living human that was Wilton-Cough had totally vanished in his floating ghost. She could clearly hear what sounded like music to any Angelic ears, the beat of an humble human heart drumming his care about love, the world and the beings within it. Abigail, highlighting one particular word with her special glowing powers, replied with certainty,

-'Beloved' this is the most important one in your whole inscription, and I can tell you it is meant for you as a father and as a husband.

As for heroic if it can be justly contested on the ground of your motives, nonetheless the fact is that you gave your life to protect others. No other souls did that on that fatal day, for they were all hiding behind you and the safety that you gave them. None of the lives you saved will ever dare brand you as a coward, for you are their true hero. Even when shot, you tackled that armed robber out off your bank, ordering the people within to close the doors behind you, lock themselves in. They saw the robber ran away empty handed with his threat of killing everyone dusted to a prompt end. They saw you collapsing in the dust and carried you home to your wife and children. You, then, passed away from your far too damaged guts and wounds, in your bed, surrounded by all who love you. Let me repeat this, 'who love you'. Abraham, you did enough to be entitled to a little love, trust me.

Wilton-Cough tried to hug himself full of emotion yet his arms dived straight through his own chest. He stated, with a goofy smile on his lips,

-Oops! Just forgot I am a big bad ghost.

Winking, Abigail flew through him then teased while correcting,

-Ghost, yes, you are. Big and bad, I am afraid you aren't. One can go through you as if you were just melting butter, and you can go through things likewise. Isn't it a beautiful ghostly technicality to grasp? Let me tell you about the others. Follow me.

As the tiny light went forward, illuminating the cemetery path ahead of them, Abraham followed, floating above it, full of wonder,

-Where are we going?

Flapping her minute white feathered wings in front of him, his Angelic daughter replied,

-Where your heart wants to go. Did I not catch you trying to open your coffin just to check on one of your sons? So this is what we will do. This is the big technicality I was alluding to, my dear Soul, you started to care an awful lot. Hence you can not rest until you are sure that all you love are alright. So together, we will make sure they are. Fancy that journey? You will get to peak and haunt until your heart is fully reassured and content enough to rest.

Filling with excitement but also dread, Wilton-Cough mentioned in an almost sad whisper,

-Will Josiah ever be happy to see me? I doubt it very much so.

-Well, he will not see you for a start. You are very much invisible to him and most humans. As you are a ghost, maybe it is better that way, don't you think? You don't want to freak him out, surely. He just turned thirteen last February...

Abraham repeated with a bright smile, and tears dropping like dew on the path below him,

-Thirteen! He just entered his teenage-hood. Bless the little fella! I just missed that big time and all, being dead. I wanted to take him fishing with me for that very birthday. I planned it all. It was just going to be me and him and no one else. I rented a cabin by a lake for a week. I figured that it would be enough for us two to communicate properly for once. But I wasn't very sure of it either, because when I followed my father on hunting trips, I just failed to understand him. I hated hunting and I didn't know if little Jo would have loved fishing either. However I thought it was worth a try. Well, it was not to be. Death took me away and we parted with lots to say to one another and no time to say it anymore.

Abigail went to hold tightly a finger of her father as she encouraged him,

-Ghosts have ways to communicate, many, we need to find the right one for you. Like you can feel my hold upon you, right now, don't you, Pa? You have some sort of physicality that we can work upon to allow you to express yourself to any you feel you had an unfinished conversation with. I will help you throughout. It may be as tough as learning the ABC at first. Grasping the ropes of communicating from the Spirit world to the one of the living is not easy, yet can be done and has been accomplished before. Do not lose hope.

When her last words expired in the darkness of the starry silent night, the church bell rang nine times filling the air with a certain ceremonial aura. Wilton-Cough stated seriously worried,

-Nine o'clock: what is my boy doing in a church at that time of the night when he should have been in bed since eight? Did Father Odell convince him to become a church organist?

The Angel leading the way through the graves towards the illuminated church scolded him,

-Again what is wrong with Josiah becoming a church organist if he wants to? He bestows free will at the end of the day. It is only an hour.

Forming a fist around Abigail, enclosing her carefully yet firmly, Abraham vented out, rushing to get by the side of his younger son,

-In my books, it is still an hour past Josiah's bedtime. If I was not allowed to impress upon my son to become a banker because of free will granted to all humans, I do not think any religious cleric with their specific and so diversified agendas and politics can justify impressing upon my child to become their tool of propaganda. After me and my forceful psychological ways with my son, the only wish I have for him is true freedom to make up his own mind, not more skillful, powerful, dutifully imposed brainwashing. I wish him to reach his own freedom, just be who he was born to be as a human, not the cast and mould others imposed on him.

Abraham Wilton-Cough in his anguish burst through the doors of the church swinging them both open. He stood there, invisible to all but his Angelic daughter who commented from his tight fist,

-WOW! Someone understood the Angelic lesson about free will all too well. If you want some wings Pa, carry on fighting for it. Free will will be endangered in the future, and we will need all who understand it to protect it to save humanity as a whole. Food for thought.

But her father was far from listening to her, he scanned the church with scrutiny and when he saw Josiah seated in front of the organ, he just glided to him silently. He ignored Father Theo Odell who went to close the two main doors, looking worryingly outside before stating,

-Such a calm Spring evening, how can such a burst of wind occur? There is only a little breeze out there.

Josiah upon his stool responded to the priest, with an all knowing air,

-Mrs Bates said that the hail we had yesterday forecast a week of funny weather. She describes it as nice one minute then winter like the next. She recommended my Ma and I to do like French people do in April. They have a saying that tells them to not uncover in April, something like: 'En Avril ne te découvres pas d'un fil.' So I put my best jumper on. Although I can still feel the chill in the air. It's very sharp. There's definitely a breeze in here.

The tiny Angel warned Wilton-Cough with a knowing wink,

-Your son is feeling your presence, sharp and cold. It is simply ghost's features that you have now, which you will have to get used to. You are not warm and cuddly anymore although you never were.

Abraham sighed deeply,

-I wish I had been when I had the time to properly love my family.

Watching Father Odell putting all of the wildly flickering candles out one by one, Abigail told,

-If you can make a connection, do it now, Pa. We managed to freak a tad good Theo Odell. He is calling it a night in his own silent way which he will announce to your son in less than five minutes.

In response the ghost tried to hug his son, but his desperate attempt failed through him, chilling Josiah to his bones, who pestered,

-It's gone right breezy in here.

Father Theo replied,

-It's getting late. Like Mrs Bates says early Spring can be a tad chilly and we must be aware of them. Time for you to head home to a nice warm chimney fire. Mrs Amelia has made her nice little lemon cup cakes and she brought them to your mum's tea party tonight. I told her to keep one for you with all her might. So your mother and her would have hidden one from the greedy crowd of neighbours, and it is waiting for you.

The boy frowning his young eyebrows, confided,

-I wanted to practice one last time for tomorrow's big competition, Father Theo. I know Mrs Bates is nice enough to do me plenty of cup cakes almost forever, but winning that big thing is not something that will be every Sunday. It has just become a yearly event. Pretty please, can I have one more go?

Watching the determined Josiah furrowing even further his young brows, Father Odell conceded,

-One last go and off you go before your mum gets worried.

Little Jo hit the first notes from the Toccata, dismissing out loud genuinely,

-Mama knows I haven't access to such an instrument apart from here. Although we have a very nice piano, it doesn't have the belly gusto of an organ. I also want to be fully talented and know by heart all the keys I can stroke to impress anyone.

Putting the last remaining candle by the child upon the organ, the

Priest replied,

-Play, lil'Jo. You will never fail to be listened to by anyone with your musical gift.

Josiah started playing again with his utmost concentration, biting his lower lip as he did so, then he confided,

-Thank you Father Theo to let me stay so late. I have got to get it right tomorrow to make Mama and Papa proud. I want to win the competition to tell my Pa, he was right to finally encourage me to play.

Father Odell sat upon a small stool by the organ. He opened a book of prayers while commenting with a welcoming yet slightly sarcastic grin,

-Do you believe your father can pay attention to your music from Hell?

The child without stopping his tune corrected strongly,

-You mean from above and Heaven, Father.

A jubilating Abraham standing by his son vented out to his Angelic daughter, his folded fist slamming the ivory keys of the organ,

-Go on, Jo, correct his assuming arse! How dare he? How can he think of my soul as dwelling in Hell when I am right here? Bless you, my Josiah for wanting to make me proud after I am gone.

When the sound of the keys he pressed with anger resonated throughout the church, the squeezed Abigail within his fist scolded the ghost at once,

-They can't hear us talking, Abraham, but whatever was that punch they did hear its sound. Please do not scare any human as a ghost, Dad. For I will have to drag you to Hell. Please, learn to behave.

Father Odell coughed, closing the prayer book worryingly. He put all his attention to the child before him and his skillful little hands which were carrying on playing the Toccata like nothing had happened before he advanced,

-Do not be upset, please, Josiah, I meant wherever your father is. My tongue slipped a tad.

Josiah told chillingly,

-I am not upset Father Odell. But a spirit in this church is. I just saw about four keys being punched down at the same time on my left. That's where the draft comes from. I can swear I can see a flickering light by me. Do you think it could be my Pa?

Unnerved the Priest stood up, and announced,

-No, I think it is grand time for you to go to bed. You are clearly overworked by that competition and hallucinating.

The tired child became teary, pestering against Father Odell's statement,

-I can swear upon my Pa's grave that it was not me being upset.

He remained playing ignoring the scolding Priest, who advised,

-Swearing upon anyone's grave would do no good. Worst it can make souls unrest and come forward.

In a sudden daring temper, coming from the belly feeling that he was damn right and that he saw what he saw, Josiah stood up, stepped away from the organ and pointing at the long set of ivory keys, shouted,

-I may be tired but I didn't dream. I swear on my Pa's grave, I saw the keys moving on their own!

Wilton-Cough, seeing the passion in his son, told full of

compassion,

-Someone has got to prove him right. I am the only one that can.

Before Abigail could do anything to stop the ghost, he hid her within his top hat, thinking that would be a suitable prison to restrain her tiny disapproving Angelic self from dragging him to Hell, then he punched the keys of the organ once more. But this time, it was slow, controlled and meaningful. After a D major, a A followed by a D minor. Seeing the three keys going down one by one, the little boy staid mesmerised in front of the organ spelling out,

-D-A-D. Dad! That's Pa!

Witnessing the organ playing on its own just as well freaked Father Odell beyond belief. Becoming as pale as his white collar he told off the child, scaring him in the meantime,

-Right! Did I not tell you to not swear upon a grave? We have your father's spirit forward. Run and let me exorcise his soul. I hope he was not a Hell dweller, that's for sure. Run and let me deal with your ghostly father.

Abraham saw Josiah leaving the church with no further ado, legging it. Managing to lift the top hat enclosing her, and throwing it on the ground, Abigail warned him,

-Pa, exorcism doesn't sound good, that's drastic shit for a soul. Leg it out of here too. Fast.

The ghost followed the path of his son swinging once more violently the church's doors open, exiting it with some fracas.

Standing in the following darkness, as the only candle left was blown out by the gust of wind that ensued, Father Theo Odell whispered,

-I will be damned.

Then noticing a fine yet weathered black top hat at his feet, and recognising it all too well, he picked it up. He scrutinised it carefully, then when his thumb felt the thread embroidered letters, the A, the W the dash followed by the C, embedded in the ivory silk lining of the inside of the hat, the Priest wondered for himself,

-Good old Abraham Wilton-Cough, what is your soul questing now? Why are you awake? Gosh, you are the last soul that I would have bet upon to stand by your children in the After-life. You are following one, one which you least favoured during your life. Why? I would follow the eldest if I were you and worry about him greatly. Let's check your grave.

Turning upon his heals, Father Odell went by a back church's entrance, clutching Wilton-Cough's top hat close to his chest, then went running to his Presbytery to fetch some tools, swearing all the way,

-Oh Lord! Why Abraham? Why? He was not the easiest man in Wilton Town to deal with. Why? Did I not bury him properly? Oh Lord, oh Lord, oh Lord!

Chapter Two

Running Directions

A confused Josiah ran as fast as he could down the hilly graveyard repeating to himself wildly,

-Was it Dad? Was it Dad? Was it Dad?

Stumbling upon a prominent pebble on his path, the young boy fell forward. Hurt, his knee badly scratched and bleeding, he stood back up, looking at the damage and pestered,

-Blast, Great Auntie Jo will pull my ear hard and tough on that one, for that was one of my best new attire.

He tried to fix the tear in his clothing vainly, desperately stating after a few seconds,

-Right, no hope I won't be able to hide that one from no one.

Josiah didn't notice three creatures rising from a grave not far from his fall. Winking at each others, their noses humming his fresh blood in the cool breeze, they whispered together in the darkness,

-Yes, you cannot hide from anyone.

Hearing the eerie voices, Jo went awfully quiet, scrutinising his spooky cemetery surrounding carefully to know where they were coming from. Seeing three pairs of bloodshot yellow eyes transfixed upon him, the child stood still swallowing his greatest fear in a gulp. However a great gust of wind chilled him to the bone passing through him accompanied by a vivid flash of light whilst he could hear two persons talking straight to his mind. He could recognise the voice of his father in one of them, ordering him with a sense of emergency,

-Run my Jo, run. Those are Ghouls. They will eat you alive if you are not careful. Just leg it to Mum, Son. Just leg it and never look behind. I will make sure they don't follow you.

Josiah seemed to wake up from his fear by the chill passing through him. When he saw the human like creatures crawling towards him, he just did what the voice of his father told him to do. He ran as fast as he could without looking back, far too scared to make sense of anything.

However arriving at the gate of the graveyard and closing it behind him, Jo looked back at the spot where he fell, and saw the three monstrous creatures being thrown about in the air by an invisible force. A tiny light passed by him very fast telling him off in his mind,

-No time to enjoy the fight, Josiah. It's spiritual against physical, it will not last long. Beside it is unequal, one Ghost against three Ghouls. Like your Pa said, just leg it, he will keep strong for your sake as much as he can.

The youngster totally confused followed the tiny light showing him his way home despite the night and his tears. When he arrived exhausted at his own doorstep, he could not see any Ghouls following him, he could only see the tiny light shining on the brass handle enjoining him to knock on the door.

A little voice in his head reassured him,

-You are going to be safe, now. You made it home, Josiah.

Taking his breath back and regaining courage the child knocked on the door a fair few times strongly. Wiping his tears, he saw the tiny light leaving his side and flying fast down the road, taking back the direction of the church. The door opened and his worried mother welcomed him home,

-Oh my Jo, look at the state of you. I was worried sick. What time do you call this, little Wilton-Cough? You know what your Pa would have done and said? Lots of ear pulling are going amiss... Don't just stand there, step in and you'd better come up with some good explanations for Aunt Josephine, Mrs Bates and I were getting ready to fetch you wherever you were.

As Josiah entered, he could only acknowledge that the three ladies in question were wrapped up in their shawls ready to go out, with the elderly Aunt Jo carrying a lantern scrutinising him from head to toe attentively. Aunt Josephine started sternly,

-Right, you look like you ran into some trouble young man. You are visibly shaken, shivering uncontrollably like you've just seen a ghost, and I can clearly see that you cried. You have some explaining to do. Come with us. A strong brew will warm those bones of yours.

She grabbed his young hand then almost dragged him to the cosy drawing room. Pushing a hand decorated footstool by the fire, Aunt Jo ordered,

-Sit down, child, and take your muddy shoes off. Mrs Bates, if you would not mind tending to that fire and revive it a tad. Angie, get me his slippers then fetch him a cup of tea. Your boy is visibly shaken by something.

Josiah did as he was told for there was no contesting old Josephine Cough. She was a tough cookie of a woman who had travelled far and wide. She could tell bedtime stories to keep you awake at night full of wonders of the big wide world. She was that formidable character who gave up travelling to come back to Wilton Town when she heard the sad news about Abraham. Auntie Jo loved her only nephew, Abraham Wilton-Cough who she almost brought up. Since his death, she had been a very regular visitor at their home, helping Angela coming to term with her loss.

The effect of her orders was immediate. Soon settling down, yet his pulse still high, his hands holding shakily his cup of tea, the youngster looked at the inquisitive eyes of the three women surrounding him with their caring attention wondering if he could confide to them. He took his bet and tried,

-I didn't see a ghost Aunt Josephine, I heard one. It was Pa.

He could not have stun the entire room more if he wanted too. Amelia Bates was the first to venture a comment,

-I think you have caught the flu, a fever or something. We should call Doctor Valdi right away, Angie. He went every night to that windy church for the past two weeks, hours on end, it can not be right.

The teenager defended his actions vividly,

-It is right! There is a musical competition tomorrow which I intend to win. One has to put the effort in to win the prize. Not only will it give to mum a bit of cash, it will send me to a music Academy in Paris. It's an opportunity I can't miss, Mrs Bates.

Coming to the defence of her son, Angela confided, while bringing him a plate with a couple of egg and cress sandwiches which he took with a thankful look,

-We can not blame Josiah for his ambition. He takes that from his father. Like him, he is a hardworking type that will push himself to his own limits at any time. Tell me, Jo, do you feel unwell? Shall we call Doctor Valdi?

The boy shook his head negatively while tucking into a sandwich. He answered with his mouth full,

-No Ma, it's not necessary. Besides I am not ill. Father Odell heard Pa too. He is not ill, spooked, yes, but not ill. He saw the organ keys stroke down the notes, D-A-D just like I did on their own. He told me to run away, that he will have to exorcise Pa.

Aunt Josephine stood up, stating strongly,

-Well, sisters, either we have two souls hallucinating together, or we have our Abraham in danger of being exorcised. We have to get to the bottom of this. Angela, get Doctor Valdi to check your son then tell Vincent Valdi to make a call on Theo Odell later on this evening. Mrs Bates and myself are going to check out what is going on at the church right now. Look after the wee one, Angie, we will be back.

Taking the lantern firmly, the old lady disappeared from the room with the widow Bates in a hustle and bustle of black laced petticoat. Left alone with her son, Angela took a good look at his knee. She asked very concerned,

-Did Pa's Ghost do that to you?

Just the fact that his mother acknowledged that he had encountered a Ghost rather than quizzing the possibility of the matter made Josiah put his plate down to hug his kind mum silently. Then he took her hands within his as he recounted what happened,

-No Ma. I did that to myself. I fell in the graveyard running from the church. We heard Pa playing the big organ. It was a tad scary and Father Odell scared me much more saying that he hoped Pa wasn't coming from Hell. He advised me to run and that's what I did. But then I fell pretty badly. Still stunned, checking my attire, I heard voices in the dark. I saw creatures crawling out of graves coming towards me. I froze still. My heart was racing but not me. I could not think anymore. But I felt Pa, Ma, going right through me. Waking me up to react. He spoke to my mind. He told me to leg it. He said he would stop the creatures from following me. When I reached the cemetary's gates, I looked behind. I could see the monsters being lifted off the ground and thrown back down. A voice in my head told me to not stay there, which was not Pa this time. It guided me here as a flying tiny bright light. It said things about Pa being a Ghost fighting Ghouls, that the fight was unequal for he was one and they were three. Ma, I don't know what to make out of it all, apart that I felt Pa, throughout, I did, and I know it's him, and he fought for me.

Angela smiled to her youngest son in a comforting manner. Tidying one of her stray black curls back behind her ear, she posited in earnest,

-Well my dear boy, I do not know what to make of it, either. But all is not lost we will find out together soon enough with Aunt Jo going to the church. I trust her to make sense out of it all for us. We do not need Doctor Valdi in here to quiz you further. He is far too Cartesian to understand you, but I will give orders for him to go to Father Odell, for if he heard a ghost like your father too, he will also be in need of help. Let's clean that grazed knee of yours.

Josiah saw his beautiful mum swinging the tiny brass bell by the chimney. A girl of about his age presented herself in the drawing room, shyly asking, her eyes bowed onto her own feet,

-Mum? You want me?

-Yes, I do. Fetch me some warm water, strong vinegar, a couple of clean muslin cloths then just run to warn Doctor Valdi to go to his friend Father Odell immediately. If Vincent asks anything just tell him it is a ghostly issue, that will make him run fast and forward. Vicky, don't call me mum or mistress, just Angela will do. Off you go.

The blond servant bowed and left the room with a silent nod. Alone with her son, Wilton-Cough's widow's emotional blue eyes gave a long look at her husband's portrait above the mantle piece. She loved the proud posture of her husband in that painting. She remembered with a tender smile like if it was yesterday when Abraham unveiled his portrait and his first reactions to it: 'For sure that's a likeness of me, and a very good one. When I intended to pay the artist a penny less for the inconvenience of all that posing I had to endure, now I can clearly see that it was worth it. I will even pay the fellow a penny more for his good work and all the imprecations he had suffered from me while making it.'

She whispered half for herself, but also half hoping that her husband could hear her,

-Oh my Ab, my proud Ab, why are you awake? Why?

Her son, taking her pale hand within his, answered softly,

-Maybe Pa wants to tell us something. He certainly tried to communicate with me.

Touched by the firm conviction of Josiah, Angela started to wish to encounter her ghostly husband for she herself had kept a lot of words from him in her breast, that she just wanted to share to him. If it was not too late to do so. If it was possible to communicate beyond the grave, then for Abraham she would be brave enough to attempt it. The young maid of Aunt Josephine interrupted her reverie by stepping into the room with all the necessary to tend to Josiah's knee.

Angela welcomed her with further instruction,

-Thank you Vicky. I don't want you to walk to Doctor Valdi's clinic, my dear girl, but run there. If there is an exorcism to be done on my husband's spirit I want him to stop it as soon as possible. Vincent Valdi is the only one Father Odell will listen to apart from God. Just run for me. As soon as I have my boy fixed I will go there myself. If anyone is unwilling to speak to my ghostly Ab, I am prepared to do so and find out why my dear husband is not resting in peace.

The young girl nodded her agreement before running, trying to come to terms with the strange oddity of her mission at her every step and how to formulate it to Doctor Valdi without him deciding on the spot that she was just plain insane and good to be put in an asylum. It was a tough call, and gosh she surely regretted to have left Victorian England to follow with devotion Josephine Cough wherever she went.

Chapter Three

Apparitions

Abraham Wilton-Cough on the verge of exhaustion welcomed the tiny Angel flying towards him at the speed of light. When she settled on his ghostly shoulder, he asked wildly, delivering another good punch that sent one Ghoul in a grave,

-How is my Wee-one? Is he safe? Is he coping? Did I scare him too much?

Abigail, holding as strongly as she could to his fighting Spirit's spectral collar replied impressed,

-Your Wee-one is in a better position than you right now, safe with his mother. As a ghost you've got to get used that you are spooky naturally. It's a matter of fact. Josiah will get over it. He is much stronger than he looks. Now, the immediate question is how are you doing, yourself?

Giving a glance at his opponents who were climbing again out of their graves with fierce look on their faces, the ghost stated,

-Not bad, considering I stood my ground and they didn't, but not good either, I am running out of energy badly and didn't resolve yet how to get rid of those three once and for all. I think I left my grey cells in my coffin which is a pretty daft thing to do in this instance.

His Angelic daughter giggled,

-I admit you did pretty well on your own. We just need to put a lid on those buggers. Ditch them in a hole, and I will spell a good tombstone right up to keep them in.

Abraham winked with relief at the tiny Angel,

-That's sound like a plan, Baby, let's do it.

He went to push back one ghoul in a grave, knocking it almost unconscious, giving him enough time to put the massive marble stone slab in place to close the grave. Abigail jumped on the smooth surface immediately, ordered,

-I will deal with that one, Pa. Knock the other ones for me before you are fully depleted of strength.

The Ghost obeyed the Angel while confessing,

-I do not understand where do I get my strength from, Abi. I can kick arses more than I did during my mortal life. Yet I am just immaterial matter. How does this work?

As Abigail glowed over the tombstone like a beacon, she revealed,

-You are an angry soul. Your strength comes from your heart. You are worried about your eldest son, Zachary, turning into one of them. Your entire heart and soul want to prevent it. It has caused your unrest. You have to deal with that matter before you can start to rest properly. You want to save your son. This is the bottom line. This is what kept you awake.

Abraham knocked out another ghoul before blaspheming out loud,

-Blast, you have to become a monk then to be allowed to rest in peace! Forget having any children for they will make you turn in your grave: I knew something was wrong all along since I woke up.

When he finished his sentence, Wilton-Cough saw Father Odell running towards them, brandishing his crucifix up, shouting madly, more times than it could be counted,

-Vade Retros Satanas!

He shook his ghostly head in desperation,

-Here comes Trouble with a big T! Let's make sure Odell doesn't end under hungry Ghouls's nachos in his hunger to exorcise me.

Giving a quick glance at the Priest running with his open bible in one hand and a small cross in his other one, Abigail stated,

-I agree with you Pa. If he is prepared for you that man is unprepared to face Ghouls. We will have to drag him back to the security of the church. With me at once. Use any anger you have within you, it will allow you to push that physical human just like you did with the Ghouls to keep them at bay. But be warned, his little crucifix will hurt you, burn you, sting you and will make you reminisce of your faults when you were alive. Forget about the damage it inflicts you just think of bringing that man to safety. I will go 'blinding light' on the remaining Ghouls to prevent them to follow you both. Please be fast, for those creatures deprived of sight can still rely on their powerful sense of smell so make sure you do not make the tiniest scratch on Father Odell's skin. Think of Ghouls as hunting monstrous bloodhound and you will get it right. You can do it, Pa.

While Wilton-Cough gave her an anxious look, he saw her Angelic self getting brighter and brighter, spreading an amazing blazing blinding light all around the nearby tombstones. He muttered to himself,

-Right, I guess it is just a get on with the task with no arguing with it then: Angelic ways... Let's save the bloody Priest who wants to exorcise me to Hell. If anyone complains that I never turned my other cheek, I am about to show in my curriculum that I did not scratch the living being that wants my soul in a burning fire for eternity. Swell, I am overwhelmed, let's get burnt with his tiny cross while I save his arse.

Abraham just went rushing towards Father Odell. He past right trough his body to give him the sense of his presence, then he took hold of his black robe and started to pull him. A struggle ensued yet Wilton-Cough although regularly hurt by the crucifix managed to drag the Priest back within the safe haven his church could provide to anyone. Holding Theo Odell against a pillar by the entrance, he whistled to his Angelic Daughter his success. She came rushing in, speed of light obliging, and was right by her father's shoulder when she ordered,

-Slam the damn doors shut, Pa, the way you do it best. How's Father Odell?

Dropping the Priest from his grasp, Wilton-Cough went to close the church entrance doors, with a short comment,

-Heart racing madly, chilled to the bones, I guess that amounts to being Ghost-handled. Yet, check him out, I've been good: no scratches.

Abigail, going towards Father Odell unnerved him greatly for she was still her full blinding bright self. He vociferated as fast as he could as many 'Vade Retro Satanas' in a single breath without choking believing he was facing some sort of true evil. He opened his holy book wildly to start the exorcism of whoever he was in the presence of. The little Angel warned her father,

-Hide behind the tabernacle, Pa. This man is on a mission to remove whatever spooks him from his vicinity. I am angelically safe, you are humanly not. If he proceeds with what he has in mind, your soul will not face a stairway to Heaven but a straight down slide to Hell.

Her father glided to the safe spot. Wilton-Cough thought wildly while crouching behind the altar, out loud for his daughter's sake,

-Surely if that Priest has the power to send me to Hell, he must be able to sort out the Ghouls problem in Wilton Town and save one of my sons from becoming one. That would be a better use of his mighty 'blaspheration' rather than attacking my poor damned ghostly self with it.

Getting even brighter than she already was, inundating of light the entire church, Abigail transformed herself into a full size Angel. This time, she was entirely visible to the human Priest. Going behind the tabernacle, standing by Abraham, putting her hand on his shoulder, she rendered his Ghost visible as well. Her commanding voice emanated from everywhere at once, filling the space between the walls of the church of a vibrant aura. It revealed,

-Father Odell, there will be no exorcism of Abraham Wilton-Cough necessary. For before you, I present you a caring soul, a Ghost on a mission. Be a Father to your flock, help him out, for the souls of the children of Wilton Town are at stake, past present and future. Consider yourself called upon by high above Theo to free this town from its curse. Time for you to become the soul's shepherd, you were born to be.

Father Odell in great awe, fell on his knees, totally speechless. He just considered the beautiful Angel facing him which held protectively the shoulder of a rather sad looking Abraham. Knowing how the man was during his life, remembering all too well his proud demeanour and stance, the Priest could tell that it was an altogether different kettle of Abraham Wilton-Cough that he was witnessing. He was just a shadow, a tall one, yet with eyes scrutinising him with an heartbreaking great sadness and a demanding anxiety. Something was up bothering that soul beyond belief, beyond the grave, causing its unrest. Theo could only acknowledge that fact upon his vision of the Ghost.

He wanted to reply but completely mesmerised by the apparition, he remained silent, holding the bible close to his chest.

A repeated banging at the church's door brought the Priest's attention back to the living.

Chapter Four

Haunted Hearts

The great light subsided to become just the tiny orb floating in the air behind the tabernacle while the ghostly apparition of Abraham Wilton-Cough could not be seen anymore. However Father Odell felt by the coolness of his surrounding that the entity was still very much within his church.

The great entrance doors opened to what it seems was a stampede of petticoats. But at a glance the priest saw only two women invading his sacred space, but he sighed for these were two heavyweights of the gentle sex to reckon with. Not in the sense that a heavily pregnant Amelia Bates and a somewhat getting corpulent since settling into town for good, Josephine Cough was just fatter around the edges than others, no, it was very much meant in the boxing context match in the mind of Theo. He feared facing the two articulate and most argumentative females in Wilton Town, both at once. He knew what would happen already, for he experienced it many times, they would talk so much over him that he would not be able to place a word, reasonable or not, valuable or not.

It started to his anguish with old Josephine Cough, swearing,

-What the hell is going on in here, Father? The cemetery in your care is attacked by grave robbers. Amelia and I kicked out two pasty faces from it. Very abhorrent and stinking young lads they were. You should be out there dealing with that pressing issue, a riffle in hand, shooting their feet and dragging the robbers to their mothers or the prison by their ears with right scolding summons. What was that big light about? You haven't exorcised my nephew, have you? Have you? For if you have, I will box your own ears right and proper!

Terrified at the sight of the elderly woman making a straight bee line towards him, with one hand holding a lantern and one lifted up in the air, ready to slap, Theo told as fast as he could,

-I didn't, I promise, I didn't. I wanted to but I couldn't.

When the old Cough was by him, and despite him standing up, she slapped him twice harshly, venting,

-Wanted to! How dare you wanting such thing as a Priest? You should help him rest not send our Abraham to Hell. This is for Angela Wilton-Cough and this is for my disappointed self.

Nursing her own hand afterwards, Josephine demanded inquisitively,

-So it is true that you believe having heard Abraham, just like my great nephew did. We will clarify that matter quickly enough if you hallucinated together or not. I ordered for Doctor Valdi to check on you both. The wee one is a bit overworked by his will to win that competition tomorrow, so it could be logically explained for him to have an hallucination. As for you Father, the matter needs investigation. As you have no mother to look after you, nor any servant, I decided to do you that favour. I called the Doc and will pay any bill. We can't have a tired beyond belief Priest in our town, hallucinating at night so much so that he lets the cemetery at the mercy of petty thieves.

Amelia, coming by Mrs Cough, leaning on her, partly exhausted, readjusted her bonnet,

-Oh my, oh my, what a run! I never thought I could kick anyone so hard my entire life. It was exhilarating. Maybe you and I should patrol the graveyard for a couple of weeks to give a break to Father Odell?

Theo rejected that at once,

-Not in your state Mrs Bates. You should not have ran either. I am sorry to have caused concern to you both, Ladies.

He stopped talking to turn around and inspected in a sharp glance the darkness behind the tabernacle. The tiny light was still there yet just above an extinguished candle giving a realistic vision to all eyes within the room of a lit candlestick. Feeling a cold breeze going through him, Father Odell confided,

-I appreciate you calling Doctor Valdi out of concern, Mrs Cough, but we have a spirit situation here. I have the Ghost of Abraham Wilton-Cough in my church. Of that I am sure of. I saw him, Josephine, the shadow of himself. His soul is here, right now, floating around us. If you feel the chill passing by you, it will be him. I am tired but not that tired to not recognise your nephew when I meet him in any shape or form.

-Seen, felt? Check him for fever, Amelia. The man is not even questioning his vision.

Stepping away from a diligent Widow Bates, Theo argued, pointing to the bright orb above the candle,

-I have no fever, I swear upon this bible before me. Look, can't you see the light, it's the Angel of Abraham. Maybe his Guardian Angel, she illuminated the entire church a minute ago by her glowing presence. She spoke to me. She gave me a mission.

By the great entrance, Doctor Vincent Valdi coughed to warn of his presence. He had been there standing quietly, observing for long enough, to be worried about his friend. When the priest saw him walking with a firmly determined steady pace towards him, he gave a desperate gasping plea,

-I can swear that I saw what I saw and heard what I did... Pray Vincent, I am fine, don't sent me into any mental institutions. I will pray less at night and sleep more, I promise.

Half giggling in a sarcastic manner, the Doctor announced sternly,

-I will be the judge of that, my dear Theo. When you see Angels in

candles, talk to them, and hear ghosts, one has the right to be
worried. Besides I am paid by two of your parishioners anxious
about you and your sanity. Mrs Wilton-Cough faced with her
overworked younger son, tonight, raised my alarm bell via the little
servant Vicky. Just for science sake, you must admit that the two of
you hallucinating together was too beautiful to miss and get
unreported. First constatation, my friend, you are not your usual
'doubting Thomas'. You have thrown your scepticism out of the
window to believe in Ghosts. Such faith is exquisitely interesting.
Come, convert me: talk to me about the big Ghost you've seen and
his big guardian Angel?

Sensing the outright mockery in Valdi's tone, Father Odell could
have blushed under the scrutiny of his best friend. He knew he had
always failed to sway Vincent away from his Atheism. It didn't
matter how many beers they would have at the bar together, talking
about the inhabitants of Wilton Town, their dilemmas and
challenges, and them arguing and finding solutions wracking their
brains together on a daily basis, Vincent Valdi could not be
perverted away from his own way of seeing the world through his
own human heart. What chances did Father Theo have at that
moment to convince his friend of his own sanity and on the
existence of Ghosts were pretty slim to say the least. That was not
even mentioning the Big Angel, he truly saw. The fear of going
straight to the insanity ward, made the Priest sweat profusely despite
the cold air surrounding him.

All of a sudden, Theo heard another voice than his in his mind: the
one of Abraham Wilton-Cough warning him,

-Do not be scared Father, I am going to help you and try to
convince Doctor Valdi of my after life existence. Please do not fight
it.

He had no time to give his answer as he felt invaded throughout by
a thousands icy cold blades penetrating his flesh. An instantaneous
paralysis prevented the Priest to react against the Ghost invading his
entire body. He opened his mouth to scream in fear of what was
happening to him but the voice coming out was not his. It was the

guttural one of Abraham Wilton-Cough who shouted to the Doctor,

-Start believing in something, bloody Cartesian, for I am right in front of you. Don't you remember my pestering, swearing and curses against any treatment you inflicted upon me? Let me refresh your memory, let me go skin deep so you know at once when you are face to face with a Wilton-Cough. You will never forget to have met one for eternity.

Vincent Valdi dismissed the threat by taking the wrist of the Priest and checking his pulse in a concentrated manner, answered strongly,

-Right, this good impersonation of Abraham Wilton-Cough if to the point perfect doesn't impress me, Theo. My concern for your mental welfare has just reached its limit. I need to assess you thoroughly and take you to the next level.

If Theo Odell feared the worst, it was because he didn't take into account the ghost using his body to get a word out to come again big time with another helping plan. He felt the entity leaving him, with his mouth just announcing in Abraham's voice,

-Let me take you to the next level of believing, Doc!

If Father Odell felt immediate relief, feeling his entire body as his own once more, he grew worried for his friend and watched his reactions closely. He did not have to wait long to see the effect of how being invaded by a Ghost felt like on the face of his best friend. Vincent's dark brows rose in great pain and surprise. His blue eyes asked a thousand soundless questions at once. While his voice vociferated in the exact intonation of Wilton-Cough, his suddenly paralysed body flew off the ground to be pinned violently against a wall,

-Do you remember the man that you could not save despite your best efforts? Do yo remember my thoroughly damaged bleeding guts? Let me give you the feel of my agony, you were there observing it helpless. The only thing that you could do was trying to alleviate the pain of a dying man.

Valdi, feeling thoroughly and excruciatingly physical distress, especially throughout his guts, paled, and just whispered,

-Wilton-Cough!

Before shouting loudly trying to regain control once more over his entire own body,

-You made your point powerfully clear, Ghost, I believe in your after-life existence, so just stop twisting my guts right now. I am ready to listen to whatever you have to say and whatever Father Odell has to say for you.

The Doctor fell immediately back on the ground, where he landed on his feet with quite a fierce look upon his face. He went to the small group who had watched what happened to him in complete disbelief and utter terror. He recalled them all from their stupor by stating,

-Right, we truly have Abraham Wilton-Cough present in a ghostly form. Straight talking and acting as usual with no double measure, as harsh as he can be, if you don't want your inner organs going into a mushy peas pulp feeling, we have to pay attention. My first question is why is he just here among the living?

The Widow Bates answered to him with some certainty and conviction in her voice,

-Well, Mr Wilton-Cough did not have a pretty death. He had an untimely one. Being shot and dying from the wound for a few hours, very painfully so, was far from a peaceful death in your own bed. It is common knowledge that the way in which you are dying make you either rest in peace or unresting.

However the old Josephine Cough corrected,

-Abraham is a Wilton-Cough, he would know how to handle a

bullet wherever and whenever with bravery. He was shot protecting people. This is a big fat redeeming factor for the fact that he was a notoriously shrewd and fairly harsh businessman. Something else must cause him to be a Ghost. He tried to contact his little boy. Maybe he still has something bothering his conscience, something he still has to say to Josiah. Come, Father Odell tell us what happened. Feel free to talk in front of us and Doctor Valdi without the fear of being branded insane. Abraham took care of convincing us of his ghostly presence pretty well.

Amelia agreed with her, wrapping her black shawl tighter around her shoulders,

-Pretty well... That's an understatement I almost peed in my petticoat. I can feel him observing us. The temperature in this drafty church is gone Arctic, clear sign of being haunted. Better your place than mine Father Odell, I don't fancy flying against any walls anytime soon each time I cross that Ghost. Can anyone remember the volatile temper of Wilton-Cough?

While all nodded positively looking at each other with certain anxiety, Vincent Valdi went to check the candle closely. He invited his friend,

-Theo, tell us what you experienced. Be precise, detail everything even if you think it might sound stupid. Your exactitude will determine us to decide if we have a Ghost haunting your church that needs exorcising badly or not.

They all failed to notice the widow of Wilton-Cough entering the church at that precise moment. She stood still at the Doctor's words, silent tears appearing at the corners of her eyes. Angela's soft voice burst the almost complete darkness by her gentle sob begging,

-Please whatever you do, do not exorcise my Ab. I need to talk to him. I have something important to tell him. Maybe, just maybe he will be able to rest after that.

Chapter Five

Loving Angie

The first to notice and reassure Angela was Theo Odell who told,

-Your Ab is a ghost on a mission, I will not dare exorcise him away. I have been ordered to help him by an Angel, and this is what I will do.

Abraham Wilton-Cough, full of emotion at the sight of his wife, glided to her as fast as the wind. He slammed the door shut behind her to protect her from being followed by any Ghouls before embracing her with all his might. But the only result was an anxiously spooked Angela, chilled to the spine, who asked nervously, to the darkness surrounding her,

-My Ab? Is it you?

Abraham's sorrowful sob answered her in a low whisper, almost inaudible,

-Oh my Love...

She felt fingers holding her hands for a split second before a cold caress gently and slowly stroked her face, accompanied by an ordering voice invading her mind, one she knew all too well, yet one which had now the softest and saddest undertones,

-Please, don't cry, my Angie. I want to see sunshine in your eyes once more, not rivers, please don't cry for me.

But Angela couldn't stop the tears from forming pearls at the corners of her blue eyes, as the conviction of the presence of her husband dawned upon her. He was there, by her, she had no doubt about it. It was her proud Ab. She was about to wipe her tears with a tender smile drawing at her lips, when she realised that something had been deposited in her hand. She inspected the small token, which was a cravat pin. She recognised straight away the object with its red garnet engraved AWC.

Worried that her friend had not moved from the doors, Amelia went to her, asking her at once,

-He didn't freak you out, did he?

Receiving a sudden bear hug from the Widow Bates, Angela seemed to wake up within its warmth and replied,

-No he didn't. My Ab was so very gentle. I think he tried to hug me at first. My body went abruptly cold down to my every single bone.

Vincent Valdi watching the two women walking together up the aisle, giving an assessing glance to the frail Angela Wilton-Cough, commented,

-I am glad he was gentle with you, Mrs Wilton-Cough for he has been a bit frighteningly gutsy with some of us. So much so that, for the sake of Father Odell who has his church haunted, I rather have him resting nicely in his grave...

He watched his surrounding with scrutiny before saying louder,

-If he doesn't mind me saying and being honest. Your wife has not eaten properly since your death. She lost her appetite. She nibbles. Hence there's no more fat on her bones. Make those hugs scarce if you don't want her to join your grave.

Then addressing himself back to Angela, he demanded,

-What gave you the certainty that it was your husband and not any other entity? After all this church is surrounded by a massive grave yard.

The Widow of Abraham showing him the cravat pin, stated,

-There is no mistake to be made: my Ab left a token of his identity.

Bringing the top hat of Wilton-Cough to the altar, Father Odell confirmed her saying,

-My resident Ghost is none but Abraham Wilton-Cough, Vincent. He is leaving proof behind him, with his initials on, with items he wore day in and out, with objects he was buried with. If we dig up his grave now, I am sure those would be missing in it.

The Doctor examined the two garments carefully, checking their tangible physicality. He recognised them. Just touching them, he had flashbacks of the tall banker wearing them. He remembered his presence and eagle eyes, vividly, so he proposed,

-Let's confirm that, Theo, let's dig him up and have a bet. For science's sake, we have a spirit able to do so much. You are all my witnesses, here.

Josephine Cough barked,

-Let's not do that. Vincent, for science's sake you are asking for your intestines to become mushy peas again. I am warning you that my nephew might not enjoy for one bit being dug up. And I didn't enjoy watching you being guts stirred against a wall...

However Amelia objected, handling the items on the altar,

-Somehow, how did those get here? We last saw those when we closed his coffin. It would be the very proof that we are not hallucinating together. If Doctor Valdi wants to write upon the existence of Ghosts scientifically, I dare say, it should be encouraged. It would prevent many doctors telling many patients that they are just mad, seeing things and hearing voices...

Taking back the top hat closed to his chest, Father Odell, cautioned,

-I would rather let that grave be undisturbed and not take any bets on it if I were you Vincent. You have all the evidence before you.

Angela, looking at the cravat pin with affection told,

-I would not mind seeing his body. If his cravat is without a pin, I will know for sure, I am not just tired and wishfully hoping that I can talk to him once more. I will know for sure, my Ab is back as a Ghost.

Valdi gave a winning smile to his friend, announcing,

-Three against two, Theo, we win hands down whether you like it or not. Go and get the shovels. Before you even try to argue about disturbing a grave, it will not affect Wilton-Cough for he is dead and hovering about in your church, haunting it. Your first send off was clearly inefficient to make his soul rest. We are only going to give you a second chance to do it right. If you succeed this time around, I may in the future let you bury me the godly way.

Looking at the Doctor who took the lantern from Josephine Cough, presented his arm to the pregnant Amelia and headed the march to the graveyard, Father Odell shook his head disapprovingly. Lost for words for a few seconds, he stood there watching the group leaving his church. A breeze twirling by him, chilled his bones right and proper. The top hat flew out of his hands to land on the altar. The cravat pin levitated to write on the black velvet. Theo read the words,

-Move! Get the shovels and use them as weapons. There are Ghouls out there. Save the women. Meet you at my grave. AWC.

The Priest saw the doors of his church slammed opened once more. The air surrounding him became much milder. He had no doubt that Abraham did leave his sides to protect his Angie, but also his unborn child. How could a Ghost protect them, he had no idea but if Abraham's Angel asked him to help Wilton-Cough, that's what he would do. And Abraham's message on his top hat was as good as an order to him. He ran to get his bible first, then as many shovels as he could carry, for he trusted Mrs Bates and the old

Josephine to know how to make use of them if in trouble. For Angela, he had no such faith. She would be the helpless one out there. He carried his load as fast as he could to join the others in the cemetery.

Chapter Six

Digging up for Answers

Around the grave of Abraham Wilton-Cough, the three women stared at it and at Vincent Valdi who was examining it very closely. He announced to them after his inspection,

-The results my dear Ladies are clear. This tomb has definitely not been disturbed. It is as pristine as we left it five months ago. Now, the truth will be in its contents. If you are squirmish about digging the grave please turn around and let me do the hard work. I am used to doing autopsies and forensic work.

Josephine Cough barked at him, holding the lantern to provide the Doctor with enough light for what he was doing,

-Squirmish does not apply in my case, Valdi. What applies is disagreement to open the grave of my nephew purely and simply. If you start touching his corpse with your assessing fingers I will certainly react. We are only there to confirm that Abraham is here, dead and buried. You can only assess if his heart has a pulse on my watch if you do not want a kick of that lantern. So be assured that I will be watching you with my eagle eyes with no squirms at all.

Amelia standing by her, posited,

-I am all for minimal inspection too: just a confirmation that Mr Wilton-Cough's body is all there and to seal the whole thing up once more with many prayers for his restless soul. His body was disturbed enough by the bullet he received.

Giving a quick glance at the pregnant widow, Vincent advised,

-I would not try to be brave in your state, Mrs Bates. I can promise you I will do the minimal if you turn around and do not feel suddenly sick all over Wilton-Cough's body. He has been five months in there: his sight will not be the prettiest nor the handsomest one. I think it would only be best, but I just appeal on you, knowing you have that deep curiosity for everything around you. I will look after you if you dare to watch and faint.

The Widow nodded at his advice before telling,

-I will dare and try not to faint, nor be sickly, nor be a nonsense. Thank you Doc to be on the looking after.

Seeing the chubby Amelia blushing slightly under his stare, shyly putting her crooked spectacles on, he smiled to her in a reassuring manner. He just knew she would watch everything with a deep genuine interest and try to be brave to quench her strong thirst to know everything that was going on around her. Ignoring his feelings for her that were increased tenfolds since he knew she was alone, and in a pregnancy hiccup, Vincent rejected bluntly,

-No need to thank me, Mrs Bates, my daily duty is to look after you all in life, my dear townsfolk.

Then turning to the pale Angela, he added,

-Mrs Wilton-Cough, how are you feeling about the whole matter right now? If you have second thoughts, please say so right now for only your voice and order will stop me to do anything to your husband's grave.

Under the moonlit sky, the beautiful Angela gave him a tearful look, grabbing her own flanks. After a long silent minute, she was able to express herself with a voice full of emotions,

-I want to see my Ab in the flesh, in his grave, with his garments missing, just to be fully sure I am not his mad Widow loving him so much that I hear him and feel him. Show me his body so I know his spirit is here and has been talking to me for sure. I just need to see his cravat pin missing. That's all... that's all...

She felt a great chill coming over her as the ghostly Abraham tried to hug he as soon as he arrived at her side. The invisible Wilton-Cough shaking his head with sad disapproval commented to Abigail on his shoulder,

-Opening my grave is far from necessary, but if I can blame them for their irrational needs for further proof, my heart cannot do so for my Angie. After all I did to prove I am here, I fail to understand them. What makes me more angry is that their insane desire will put them at risk. My poor Angie is putting herself in danger by standing here. What can I do?

His Angelic daughter replied with slight sarcasm and a sad smile,

-Against human stupidity, not much I am afraid, as a ghostly spirit, you can't even start to pull your hair over it like Angels do. What is pretty much left to you is a capacity to haunt them and poltergeist objects but that may lead to transform their common state of being unwise to collective hysteria, and we do not want that really.

Annoyed Wilton-Cough vented out,

-Great! Are you suggesting that there is nothing I can do to stop them, that I must watch them dig up my grave with passivity, Angel? Damn that!

He glided as fast as he could to the running Theo Odell, passed through him chilling his every bone to warn him of his presence, before shouting in his mind,

-Father, their intention is still firmly to dig my body up, please do something! Scold them! Tell them off!

The Priest answered out loud to his unrest, acknowledging Wilton-Cough fully while hurrying towards his grave carrying all the shovels,

-Abraham, I do not have any overcoat on and the night is cool enough, so start behaving like a good Ghost that don't go through people, especially if you want them to do things for you but also to stay in my good books to not get exorcised. I will see what I can do in terms of scolding. Trust me when I say this: I do get your sense of emergency beside your Angel told me to help you and that's what I will do.

Abigail which had followed her father, smiled happily at Theo's answer and winked,

-Pa, I think we succeeded in convincing at least one Human. This one sounds on board. If you keep speaking to his mind, we might get him to influence the others to help us on our mission.

She lit the path of the running priest while Wilton-Cough glided by him with more satisfaction.

When Doctor Valdi saw his friend arrived with the shovels, he grabbed one strongly, with his determined eagerness to dig only for Theo to object,

-Vincent, I want you to reconsider the matter. Please do not desecrate his grave.

It did not stop the Doctor to push the large stone slab covering the tomb and to reject,

-Theo, we talked about it. There is nothing sacred here.

An offended Wilton-Cough interjected in the mind of Father Odell,

-Nothing sacred! It's my grave, he is talking about! Has he got no respect for the dead? Hit him with the spade!

Pestering out loud the Priest complained,

-I will not be violent for you. It's out of the question. I will not hit Vincent with a spade.

Looking up at his friend, with a concerned scrutiny, and the shadow of a mocking smile on his face, the Doctor demanded,

-Are you alright Theo? Speaking to yourself about kicking my arse is a tad worrying. Care to explain yourself?

Father Odell argued as strongly as he could for the first time in his life,

-For Christ's sake, Vincent, I do not need a sanity check! We have a Ghost here, speaking to me, and he is well pissed off about your grand plan to dig up his body. The cemetery is consecrated ground. Everyone has a right to have his tomb undisturbed.

Valdi started digging anyway to the consternation of the Priest and the unrest of Wilton-Cough. He replied,

-Not Wilton-Cough. As you can speak to Ghosts, Theo, tell your one, that the mere fact that he is one necessitates further investigation scientific or not for it will also satisfy the heart of his poor widow.

In desperation Abraham invaded Father Odell completely, with the resolution of pushing the Doctor out of his grave, and batter him. However the strong pacific will of Theo, fought to keep his body's control but also Angel Abigail went to the rescue of the Priest, preventing her father to succeed. His spirit stuck, Wilton-Cough started howling within Theo Odell.

The three women witnessing the internal struggle of Odell, and upon listening to the long lament of Wilton-Cough coming from him, felt devastated. In turn, they all started crying. If the old Josephine Cough's tears were silent, the ones of Amelia and Angela were not as the two friends sobbed in the arms of the other.

Vincent Valdi's active shovelling made him reached the coffin. The Doctor opened the lid before he turned and scolded firmly,

-Wilton-Cough stop traumatising Theo: out of his body now! If you want to incarnate, I have your corpse right here. Look at the distress you caused to the Ladies. You always had your ways in life, can't you learn to give way in death.

Throwing himself out of Father Odell, frustrated and furious, the Ghost went to incorporate his own cadaver, which he levitated only to attack Vincent with the shovel, giving him a right kick to the shoulder that made him tumble down. His angry self gave Wilton-Cough the strength to re-use his old larynx, tongue and mouth as his ghastly voice resounded,

-Learn to not do the same as I did in life, you fool! How many will you hurt by not listening to them and having just your own way? This graveyard is sacred to the dead and Father Odell. Be a good friend to him and listen to his concern when he expresses them. Don't become the arrogant fool I was, who knew better than anyone else. There's a lot to learn from others, trust me.

Wilton-Cough realised that all around him were as pale as his own cadaver, in state of utter shock and completely silent. He looked at his almost skeletal hands still holding the shovel as a weapon, suddenly conscious of his hideous decomposing corpse. He threw the shovel away from him. His eyes burning him of tears he could not have, his voice trying to sound softer, Abraham apologised,

-I am sorry. I didn't mean to frighten you all like that. I am sorry to be so upset at being dug up. Maybe I wanted you all to remember my guts as they were back then. Maybe it was me wanting to keep the last bit of pride I had left, a tiny bit of respect. But mainly, chiefly I want you all out of the cemetery at night, for it is not safe. Go to the presbytery, I will talk to you there for they are things you need to know.

His spirit left his old corpse which fell on the ground. Angela ran to him, completely distraught, repeating,

-It's me that is sorry my Ab, it's me.

Stroking the face of her dead husband ever so gently, she checked his untidy cravat which missed his pin. She gave a sad smile to all before announcing,

-This is not how I prepared him, Father, do you remember when we closed his coffin?

Theo Odell recovering from the invasion of Wilton-Cough went to her to consider the cadaver,

-His hat is missing too. The experiment is over, Vincent, I hope it convinced you enough this time around. But I also hope you learnt the lesson 'my' Ghost taught you, for it sounds like a valuable one for you to learn so you stop getting hurt. Now help me putting his body back respectfully into his grave.

Despite the pungent smell and sight, Angela was redoing the cravat of her husband to the exacting standard he had in life. Undoing her tight bun, she took her pretty hair pin to fasten the cravat properly, saying softly,

-This is better. This is my gift to you to help you keep that last bit of pride. Know that I will always love you. From the day I met you to the day you passed away, and forever, my love is yours Abraham Wilton-Cough.

The spirit of Abraham, watching her every precise move, her long raven black curls now flowing freely upon her shoulders, the gentle care of her touch on his ugly corpse, confessed, ever so touched, to the tiny light by him,

-My Angie loves me truly, despite, despite...

Abigail went to nestle on the Ghost's neck, finishing his emotionally charged failing sentence for him,

-Everything. Yes and forever, I can confirmed that. So your soul better get to move on to Paradise one day and not be stuck upon Earth, because you will need to be there to receive her loving one. I advise you strongly to stop invading the body of the living in a hurtful way in order to do so. You can find your spiritual voice in many other ways to pass on your message, which are less physically damaging for humans. Any Angels can teach your spirit that helping mankind doesn't necessarily mean violence to resolve issues. We need to find you a way to communicate less intrusive. Although I think Vincent Valdi is paying respect to your body now. Hit of a shovel, hey!

Abraham saw the chastised Doctor helping Father Odell placing his corpse back in his coffin with great care. They buried him again with all the women helping them. But when he saw Theo opening his bible for all to recite prayers, his spirit intervened in a physical way despite any Angelic advice. He went to close and throw the holy book away from Odell's hand, invaded his mind with a warning,

-I already had prayers, Father, with all your due respect, I am dead and you are all still alive. Attend to your flock, arm them with shovels and make them run to safety. The graveyard is full of Ghouls lurking in the dark and they love flesh and bones. Trust me when I say run.

Doctor Valdi, seeing the bible hitting the tombstone, asked worryingly,

-Are you possessed again, Theo? Is it Wilton-Cough? Does he need to be exorcised?

Father Odell, grabbing a shovel, stood up, while answering strongly,

-It's him, warning me to protect you. He is not the problem, he is the helping hand. Take a shovel, all of you, lets run to my home.

Picking up the bible as well as his shovel, the Doctor enquired,

-What's the problem then for we reburied him alright?

Theo replied with as much emergency as he could have in his tone,

-Get it out of your head that the problem is a ghostly Wilton-

Cough. The problem are flesh eating Ghouls, all over the graveyard.

Chapter Seven

Ghouls and Crosses

Valdi repeated with circumspection,

-Ghouls: this is the stuff of legends. Theo, you are not believing in them, are you? Wilton-Cough is possessing you, I swear.

However as he finished, Amelia grabbed a shovel and lifted it as if it was a sword, scrutinising a particular area of the graveyard. She whispered worryingly in a warning manner,

-I swear I saw something move by the grave of Clara Pendleton...

Josephine Cough armed herself with a shovel before illuminating with her lantern the spot pointed by Mrs Bates. The Doctor paying attention to the grave in question ordered,

-Keep quiet everyone, I can hear something coming from it.

An anxious Angela asked Father Odell as she hid behind him, taking reluctantly a shovel and holding it awkwardly,

-Could we have done a mistake with the young Miss Pendleton? She was only buried a couple of days ago... Maybe she was just unconscious and we took her as being dead...

Theo realising at the way she was holding her shovel, that the frail Angela would certainly need most protection corrected her posture so she could look a tiny bit more fearsome as well as her doubts,

-I do not have a tendency to bury my parishioners alive Mrs Wilton-Cough. Beside I rely and trust on the expertise of Doctor Valdi to call out the time of death. He never made a mistake as far as I know. Now, Angela, if something or someone attacks you, you must attack back with that. Be liberal with the kicks, God will forgive you.

Vincent Valdi putting himself in front of the pregnant Amelia and pushing the old Cough to be closer to him, confirmed,

-I know how to make the deadly call, Mrs Wilton-Cough. I can assure you that Clara's accident left her no chances whatsoever. She was trampled by those coach horses right and proper. Big fat well fed ones. Arriving at the scene, Theo and I could do nothing for her but catching her last expiring breath and words. We also took the decision for her poor broken body to not be exhibited in her coffin. She was dead alright and not a sight to be seen. Theo, there's definitely something out there. I can hear chewing noises. I thought we managed to trap all the foxes roaming your cemetery, but being Spring I would bet on an impregnated vixen.

But Josephine Cough contradicted the Doctor straight away sternly,

-Bet is over, Vincent, we have a Ghoul down there and it's eating Miss Pendleton alright. I can only agree that she is not a sight. Ladies, hold your shovels firmly against your breasts, I think the best thing to do right now is to follow my nephew's advice, let's take shelter in Theo's presbytery.

As all saw in the trembling light of the lantern the terrible spectacle, as all heard the sound of a tibia bone being snapped in two and its internal marrow being sucked, they did not stood still for long. They followed to the letter the immediate short order of Theo,

-Run!

Father Odell made all the Ladies goes first while he closed the run with Vincent Valdi, telling him,

-Ghouls, stuff of legend, right! Wilton-Cough would not pester me for no reason, Vince. He was not a man suffering any non sense in his life time, remember.

Watching the creature taking notice of them, humming the air around itself, muttering between its blue lips,

-Fresh flesh.

The two friends swore side by side, as the Ghoul dropped the corpse of Clara it was scavenging to go for them,

-Holy fuck!

Everyone had much fear in their guts during their run for their lives. Josephine who led, encouraged,

-Keep running Children, I can see the presbytery from here. It's just a big long slope, almost going straight to it.

A Ghoul jumped across the path ahead of her, grinning, showing off a full set of deadly nachos. If Amelia and Angela behind her screamed out loud their inner fear, the old Aunt Jo kept running and swung her lantern as if it was a medieval spiked ball mace. She hit the Ghoul out of her way, who landed in an opened grave with the lantern, which caught fire.

Father Odell, passing by the grave burning like a furnace and the Ghoul burning alive, howling in the darkness, confessed out loud,

-Jeez! Miss Cough, that was not a real grave, that was my holy wine storage for the mass! I had to hide it there because it kept being stolen.

Amelia Bates in front of him commented,

-It's still holy, Father, in a different kind of consuming way. Can we throw the other Ghoul following us in that burning Alcohol?

It was Doctor Valdi who replied to her firmly,

-I will see to it, Amelia!

He stopped running by the burning pit, ready to tackle the pursuing

Ghoul. This made Theo backtracking his steps to stand by him. Shoulder to shoulder, the Doctor and the Priest, shovels lifted right up, confronted the carnivorous creature. It was a pretty violent affair where Odell's bible and shovel went up in the air to turn into ashes in the burning furnace. Left with only his hands to fight, Theo turned to the crucifix on his neck, to make an impression on the Ghoul pinning him down on the ground. If it burned the flesh of the monster with a cross, it didn't got rid of him. Seeing the smoking crucifix mark on the cheek of the Ghoul, the yellow teeth about to take a dig upon his neck, the man lost all hope for his own life. Yet a tremendous shovel hit came. It was enough to throw the creature away from him. It was Valdi getting rid of the Ghoul. He recognised all the swearing words of his best friend, from the bloody to the bleeding and the bleeming, passing by the bastards and the sons of a bitches and when it was over a burn in hell you are not touching a bit of him, made him sigh with relief. A strong hand made him stand back on his feet. Another held his chin in order to inspect his neck, and he heard the conclusion of Vincent,

-The beast did not have a dig. You are alright, Theo. Keep your faith in check. Your crucifix although too small did some damage. It burns their flesh up. Go and get the massive one by the altar while I protect the Ladies.

Seeing the second Ghoul burning in the grave on fire, its face distorted by convulsions, the Father did as he was told. He ran as fast as he could towards the church, his mind questioning the seriousness of injuries that a larger cross could do.
But as he entered the church, a quick glance back made him realise that the Ladies hurdled by Vincent, and his friend were surrounded by half a dozen Ghouls. He had to hurry. Making the sign of the cross, as he arrived by the altar, he repeated,

-For what I am about to do, forgive me, Father. Oh my, oh my, oh my.

He stood there for an instant, trying to figure out which of the crosses Valdi had been referring to, the large gold one on the altar or the super-size wooden one on the wall. He swore out loud, before grabbing the gold crucifix to put it in his belt like if it was a sword,

-For Christ's sake, there is no time to make such decision. The Lord will forgive me.

Climbing upon the altar, he took the large cross from the wall before jumping to the ground with it.

For a split second Theo Odell felt like a knight Templar on a crusade. Hearing the feminine voices of the Ladies shouting their distress, he ran to their rescue, voicing a loud wish,

-May the Lord be with me.

Maybe the Lord was truly with him as he stepped out of the church, or maybe it was Angel Abigail shining behind him so strongly, but he was such a sight, brandishing his cross like a sword, ready to fight, that Vincent and the Ladies, all thought they were having a vision.

The Doctor spat on the ground by him swearing as he pushed another Ghoul in the fire,

-Holy Jesus! That's what I call reinforcement.

Josephine Cough hitting with a shovel the Ghoul that had jumped upon his back commented,

-Dear me, now I think I have seen everything and I can die in peace.

Amelia striking repetitively the Ghoul attacking Angela,

-As long as he knows how to swing it. I will keep my faith in him.

Coming to Angela's rescue too, physically removing the Ghoul from her and fighting with it fiercely, Vincent vowed out loud,

-If he gets us out of here, I'll go to church.

During his violent tackle, he was thrown the gold cross by Father Odell who was making good use of his large wooden one. Theo had managed to pull Amelia and Angela safely behind him on the path. He ordered them,

-Make a run for it. To my presbytery at once. I will make sure no Ghouls follow you.

Valdi seized the crucifix and placing it right between him and his assailant, he saw the creature release his hold upon him, but also that its flesh was blistering and burning where it had touch the cross. Vincent's face lit up with a very cruel smile,

-Now, we are talking! I can get use to this.

Taking the cross by it's head, the Doctor fenced with it, pushing the Ghoul right to the edge of the pit of fire, burning the creature, each time he touched it with the tip of the crucifix. At the end of his last offensive, the creature had made one step backward too many which sent it in the flames. Very pleased with himself, the Doctor saluted the death of its opponent by bowing his head to it,

-Alleluia! Burn in Hell.

He turned to see Father Odell protecting Josephine Cough with all his might or rather his mighty cross. Swinging it on one side then on the other, he had kept the two remaining Ghouls at bay. Grinning evilly, Valdi pushed one Ghoul by the point of his crucifix. The creature jumped forward in the path of the larger cross, and was hit by it forcefully. It sent the Ghoul on the side of the path where it combusted itself.

The Doctor stated with a joyous grin,

-Magical! Let's do the other one, Theo.

As Vincent repeated his trick with the tip on the other creature, which made Father Odell finishing the beast up in one revolving swing, he corrected his friend,

-Not magical, Vince, Spiritual, they are gone and dusted by the holy Spirit. Let's put the slab back on that grave to contain the fire.

The Doctor agreed helping Theo moving the large stone,

-This will not contain the flames, it will extinguish them by the lack of air which is all the better.

Standing up, he went to Josephine and examined her arms,

-Scratches and bruises, Miss Cough, you are a true warrior. Without you at my side, I would have been overwhelmed. I will look after those in the presbytery. Let's make sure Amelia and Angela managed their run to safety.

Josephine Cough holding proudly her shovel, leading the march, confessed,

-May I be forgiven Father for having enjoyed the fight?

Theo Odell giving a knowing smile to the Doctor reassured,

-Vince, you and I may all be forgiven.

Chapter Eight

To Love Beyond the Grave

When the three entered the main room of the presbytery, they saw the two widows trembling in the arms of one another trying desperately to comfort themselves from their terror. Father Odell went to close the shutters in every room while Doctor Valdi went to the two Ladies ordering,

-Miss Cough, I need a bowl of hot water, strong alcohol and some clean cloths. Mrs Bates, Mrs Wilton-Cough, did anyone of you have been hurt or suffered any injuries? If so show me.

The old Josephine obeyed straight away, while Amelia replied trying to recover her breath,

-Angela has a bleeding shoulder. As for me, I just sprained my ankle legging it. Something quite painful but I will survive.

Questing a chair for her and inviting her to sit down before turning his entire attention to Mrs Wilton-Cough, Vincent demanded,

-Angela, show me where you are hurt. Describe to me the pain.

The widow removed her black shawl to reveal the top of her black dress ripped badly. Her entire right shoulder up to the base of her alabaster neck was thus exhibited with the damage. Valdi swore at the sight,

-Ouch! That looks painful. One of those bastardly bloody beasts had more than one good bite on that shoulder.

A loud punch on the nearby table made them jump of fright. If they could see nothing in that part of the room however they witnessed a chair levitating and placing itself by Angela. Vincent commented,

-That would be your husband, Mrs Wilton-Cough, probably upset to see your injuries and wanting you to take a seat so I can tend to you.

When Josephine Cough entered the room, she made a bee line to the Doctor and stated at the sight of the bleeding shoulder,

-Gosh, Doc, you have your work cut out to make sure that wound does not get infected. Hope this will do. If you need more help, I am your self appointed nurse.

-Your help is most welcome, Miss Cough. Amelia has a sprain in need of attention, could you kindly apply compresses of very cold water on it. I will be a while with Angela. Just to let you know, we have your ghostly nephew within the room. He sounds a tad 'bangingly' angry about his wife's state.

Going to Amelia and kneeling by her to attend to her ankle, Josephine could not help commenting,

-I bet he is. He has been 'banging' about his Angie all his life. If my nephew was not a very friendly person, not talkative and rather secretive with anyone, he confided a lot to me. From a young boy which was not much liked by his parents who spent his school holidays travelling with me, to an adult man who wrote to me regularly asking for my advice, passing by the young man who was making efforts then to be sociable by attending my parties, I was a surrogate mother to him. His main subject of conversation with me since he saw Angela for the first time was her. Her blue eyes simply and truly stole the heart of my nephew.

Despite the pain she felt, having her shoulder being cleaned thoroughly, the widow of Abraham smiled tenderly, her thoughts diverted by the memory of her proud husband, she asked almost begging,

-Did I manage to please him a little, Aunt Josephine? Did I make him happy?

The Aunt of Wilton-Cough scolded her as she stood up to get the cold water and compresses,

-Don't be a non-sense Child, of course you did. My nephew only ever spoke very highly of you. I will show you his letters. In those you will find the individual he was hiding from all, his true self, a rather shy, awkward, and insecure one, so unloved by his parents that he truly thought he didn't deserve any sort of love. My nephew was always scared to be hurt because he had been in his early years, so he built his big uncaring and proud pretence which impressed so much on others that they were doing whatever he said without a question.

When she left the room, Mrs Bates commented, looking at her black and blue ankle carefully,

-Angela, you have to fill me in about the content of those letters. Abraham Wilton-Cough certainly did fool the lot of us, for the proudest man in town was him. However we saw the man Josephine is talking about on his death bed for a very short window of minutes, an hour at most. I think my ankle may be broken, Doc.

Vincent Valdi with a confident smile argued, as he considered all the teeth marks upon the slim shoulder before him,

-Right, you are clean now, let's start the harshest part. I am going to apply the alcohol. Here, take a glass before I do so. Trust me when I say you will need it. In my honest opinion, your husband was a proud but most importantly brave man. He achieved a fair few things in this town, taking on the creation of its first bank and being a serious but tough lender, allowed a lot of people to build their dreams. If Wilton-Cough didn't see any value in me as a Doctor when I first came into town, I would not have my practice today. He also helped me with the economics of it. The first time I was paid by a patient with a chicken, he laughed at my face when I brought it to him as part repayment for my loan. However he gave me a stern lesson that day. Next time, he said, I was to sell any chicken or animals and bring their value in coins to him or the cleverest option was to keep them by the side of my practice, make money out of their produce, from eggs to milk passing by manure, to make ends meet and also to feed myself, as for him, being paid in chickens left unchecked meant I would starve. That day he told me he would keep the chicken not as payment but as a token of my good will to repay him properly in the same kind he gave me. He softened the blow by inviting me for dinner that very evening at his home to enjoy a 'Poule au Pot', or the very chicken I gave him. Like anyone, I feared your husband, Angela, but in his rough, tough way, even in death, he has taught me valuable lessons to remember. I wish to be as brave as he was on my own deathbed. I wish to be a Ghost as loud as him to give my caring messages to humans.

Accepting the glass of rum, Wilton-Cough's widow was thankful to hear the respected Doctor's opinion of her late husband. She drank silently as he reassured Mrs Bates,

-You can not stand on a broken bone, Amelia, it will give under your weight. It does look bad from what I see from here, but it is just a sprain. I dare say I will have to bandage that one, and order you to not move for a good week or two.

-But I need to attend to my shopping, cleaning and what's not...

-I will do all of that for you for the time being. You are due soon anyway.

Blushing thoroughly, Mrs Bates didn't dare to argue. Since revealing to the Doctor, her shameful situation, he had been most attentive towards her with a care that was going well beyond his duty. If he was like Father Odell, a beholder of her secret, Vincent did adopt a staunchly protective and supportive attitude towards her. She loved the way the two friends had masterminded the well thought out plan to preserve her from public shame and attack. Valdi had been kin to ingrain in every mind in town that the poor Widow Bates was becoming fat with grief. Sometimes he was spreading the rumour with sensible explanations during his visits to his patients: -Now, Miss Elliott, you do not want to be comfort eating like the grieving

Widow Bates. Sometimes he was ruthlessly teasing Amelia in front of many like one morning in the waiting room of his practice: -I believe it is your turn, Mrs Bates, I am eager to hear all about your biscuit diet.

But by word of mouth, by the natural love of gossip of many, and by the persistent comments of our two friends, the rumour was suitably fuelled up to become a 'home' truth in Wilton Town: the Widow Bates was fat with grief. No one in town would have put a bet that she was in fact pregnant up to her eyeballs, thanks to the protection of a forgiving Priest and an understanding Doctor, with their cunning ploy to defeat the common hatemongers. Valdi and Odell were determined to ensure that the kind and only too human Amelia would stay safe under their watchful eyes especially since she became so devastatingly and this time, truly, alone.

Turning his attention back to Angela, seeing her jerk a tad at the application of alcohol, Vincent proposed as Theo entered the room,

-Mrs Wilton-Cough, do you want to bite into a cloth? It may help a tad for I have to do this and you have to stay put. The teeth that dug into you chew on dead bodies. I can not start describing the damage they may have caused on your skin and muscles tissues for their straight filthiness.

A concerned Odell offered coming to them,

-I can hold your hand if you prefer Mrs Wilton-Cough and maintain you for Vince to do his mending work. I am so sorry to see you in my home in such a state. Know that your husband is not resting, that he is with a guardian Angel of some sort, to warn us about the Ghouls.

Angela, her eyes moist with retained tears, turned to Theo,

-Thank you, Father. I would rather hold your hand rather than anything else. I came here with the strong intention to speak to my Abraham. Knowing that his soul is with us tonight, even pain is not strong enough to gag me. Please, hold me still and help me be strong to not miss the opportunity to tell him how much I love him.

When Father Odell obliged the widow, a knot was forming in his throat for he had heard her confession and regrets many times, for he knew almost by heart, that as Wilton-Cough grew to become a tough proud overwhelming man, Angela was ceasing altogether her loving conversation with her husband. She'd rather be silent than speaking to a brick wall for so many years. He saw the head meet the tail at the death of Abraham Wilton-Cough, when his great pride folded, when all was left was a man. He was there to receive and witness the final will of that man but also the struggle of his wife hanging onto his lifeless hand all night long, desperate for her Abraham to wake up just to be able to hear that she loved him.

A moved ghostly Wilton-Cough invaded the mind of the Priest, apologising,

-For what I am about to do, I am sorry Father Odell, please forgive me to borrow your body once more.

Theo did not have time to react to the invasion. He shivered thoroughly as he saw the tiny orb of light landing on his shoulder. Watching the minuscule Angel within it, shaking her head in sad desperation, before she went ramming and disappearing inside him, the Priest warned everyone,

-Abraham is in me again. If I sound forceful from now on its him, only him...

A voice in his mind intimated to Theo,

-I won't let him be forceful.

While another, the broken by emotions one of Abraham, expressed himself out loud,

-I can be gentle, I promise I can, just let me hold my Angie's hand using yours.

A resigned Theo Odell could not feel his own hand anymore. Everyone witnessed the awesome glow surrounding it. It seemed to shine from the inside out. For Angela, holding the ethereal hand, she recognised the pressure applied to hers as the one of her late husband: the strong solid grip, the one she knew too well, the one which was always so reluctant to let her walk on her own anywhere.

The embodied Father Odell knelt by Angela who had tears silently streaming upon her pale face. When he spoke, it was solely the voice of Wilton-Cough,

-My sweet Angie, don't you think that I know full well how much you loved me. If it went without words, I always knew your love was there. For else how could you have stayed with a man like me? You were my beacon of forbearance and patience. At night, stroking your beautiful raven hair, when I wondered why you were still nestling upon my chest, I could only come to that conclusion that it must be love. When I passed away, my spirit floated above my corpse, I saw your tender lips repeating your love and devotion for me over and over again. My love I heard you, the gift of your love is the most beautiful thing I ever beheld. I know I have it for eternity, and you have mine, Angie for my heart and soul belong to you. Please don't cry, for I am here with you and will always keep an eye on you from beyond.

With his other hand, he gently dried the tears of his wife, scolding,

-Now, you need to be strong for you, our two boys and I. Promise me to look after yourself better, my Angie, for it pains me to see you so fragile. Eat and live for us two. I will be there to make sure you have endless tea parties where I would gaze in awe at your beautiful and welcoming smile. I will be your shadow, my Love, following you everywhere like a ghostly puppy, and the day you finally enter Paradise I will be there to welcome you, and I know I would wag my tail to and fro if I had one.

It was too emotional for Angela who forgetting herself went to hug tenderly the Priest showering him with kisses all over his face. Theo burst out, regaining his own voice,

-That's enough! No more abuse of my body you lovebirds!
Abraham out before I cry out for rape! Mrs Wilton-Cough, I am
not really him, he is just using me. Too much using!

The Priest tidied his black robe with indignation while his friend
laughed his heart out, teasing,

-I guess a proper loving hug is not something you could get used to,
Theo. Wilton-Cough, leave this giant virgin of a man alone. That
was too much effusions for him.

Tidying her dress just as well, the widow apologised, confused and
blushing,

-I am so sorry. I don't know what took me. It is just if my Ab was,
well alive... I would... I would...

Father Odell finished her sentence strongly,

-Hug him tight, yes I know. Let's look after your shoulder, Angela.
No more moving and hugging. You have to stay as still as a statue.
Miss Cough, if you would be so kind to do the holding of her hand
this time around it would be most appreciated. I think your dress
will be in less trouble than mine if Mr Wilton-Cough decides to use
you as a Ghost's puppet.

The old Josephine scolded whilst obliging,

-A hug has never done anyone any harm, Father. Your attire should
not make you less human. You must understand that our Angela
was simply moved. For I was moved, myself to hear what my
nephew had to tell his wife to comfort her. Now there are plenty of
ways for the dead to communicate with the living, I am too well
travelled to not know a fair few of them. My dear Abraham, if you
listen to me, no more intrusion of anyone, let us finish the mending
of your Angie then I will teach you to talk to us in a civilised way.
You will be able to tell us all about your unrest.

Chapter Nine

Spirited Spiritism

All were seated around the large round table in the presbytery's drawing room. The clock stroke eleven. Josephine Cough ordered with a solemn air:

-To all present, please let us join hands. Clear all your thoughts to only think of the spirit we are about to communicate with: Abraham Wilton-Cough.

As all joined hands together, Vincent Valdi, looking at the upside down water tumbler in the middle of the table, grinned and blinked before observing,

-Are all the gimmicks necessary, Miss Cough? We heard your nephew well enough without all those props.

The old Jo squeezing his fingers strongly acknowledged,

-Well, Doc, to be honest they are used to give respect to one another, the dead but also the living. Do you want my nephew to talk straight through you, smashing you against a wall, because he can do so? I do not think so. Besides we have sensitives ladies present at this table and a Priest who feels he has channelled our Ghost quite enough against his will. This is positive communication: it goes through without hurting anyone's feelings. Shall we get on with my props or do you want to be the only prop, for I will not leave this room until I know fully what my nephew want to say?

Daunted the Doctor nodded his agreement,

-I like the materialistic props better, Miss Cough. I would love you to teach me all about them another time, for I am genuinely intrigued by them in a pragmatic sort of way. Let's go ahead with whatever you learnt during your travels. It sounds safer right now, not straightforward, but much nicer when dealing with the spirit of Wilton-Cough.

Josephine Cough presented,

-We have in front of us written on pieces of paper forming a circle the letters of the alphabet. In the middle of that circle is the glass. Please my dear nephew who are with us in spirit, use the glass to point to the letters and form your words and sentences. As you levitated a chair, your corpse and even Doctor Valdi, you should be able to push that glass about. If not you can use some of our joint energy to do it.

To the great curiosity of all, the glass moved slowly at first but then picked up in speed in the direction of the letters. If its noise gliding against the grain of the wood of the surface made Theo Odell shiver, but also worried about scratches on his table, it didn't intimidate an excited Amelia who read out loud what was indicated,

-I-T-S, that must be it's, R-I-D-I-C-U-L-O-U-S, L-E-T, let, ME, I-N-V-A-D-E, invade, T-H-E-O, I-T-S, it's, F-A-S-T-E-R, faster. It's ridiculous, let me invade Theo, it's faster!

In a common voice all the participant replied out loud,

-No!

Angela with begging eyes, looking at the direction of the glass, pleaded,

-Please my Ab, be patient with us, be a good Ghost.

Interjecting strongly, Father Odell scolded,

-He will have to be a good Ghost, because if he invades my body again, I will exorcise him for good.

The ghostly Abraham shook his head in frustration, before

confiding to Abigail sitting on his shoulder,

-I think I managed to upset the patient Theo. But I always apologised whenever I used him a little. I wish it was not so complicated to be a spirit.

He then pushed the glass towards the S then the O, twice to the R and finished by Y.

His Aunt Josephine stood up, clapped her hands in a commanding fashion, then stated,

-Right, my nephew dislikes this method as ridiculously not fast enough for him. I will not have him apologise for it either. I have plenty of tricks in my old bag. Lets find a method suitable for everyone.

Her injection pleased Wilton-Cough endlessly. He smiled to his angelic daughter, swearing,

-I would have loved to have that woman as my mum a thousands time better than my own! Jeez, pardon me for saying it. But for the sadness of it, it is only true. When my mother would not give me a hand to cross a street, it was because she would be in a carriage with who knows, while her sister Josephine would be by me, holding my hand firmly while shopping for all I needed to go back to boarding school. Aunt Jo was the one I remember standing at the school's gates to bring me in and out of school without fail, giving me a long hug and if it was not for a 'Make sure you write to me every week', it would be a 'I am taking you to Norway, we haven't seen the Aurea Borealis yet.' Or whatever place she fancied to drag me along with her. She gave me a bit of a childhood in her odd ways.

From his shoulder, the little Angel replied, waving her finger and pointing it to a quill which was brought by Josephine Cough to the table, along with a bottle of ink and paper,

-Focus, Pa. Your next task might be less tedious and long winded. Look, there's hope at hand, she has a quill. We can throw the glass scheme away, here comes proper writing.

The frustrated Abraham threw the glass off the table with glee upon a nearby mirror which cracked in thousands of little pieces. The glass fell on the marbled mantelpiece still intact, not broken at all despite the throw and its impact. This had Father Odell standing up to deliver a stern sermon, not at all amused,

-Which part of good Ghost did you not understand, Abraham Wilton-Cough? If your patience has notorious limits, I can show you right now the extent of mine and send you straight to Hell! Do not poltergeist my home, I will not allow it.

The tiny Abigail shook her head in desperation, telling her father off,

-When I said throwing the glass scheme Pa, it was a figure of speech. You were not intended to take it quite as literally as that. How am I supposed to guard a spirit like you? You are simply impossible.

Giving her an apologetic goofy smile, Abraham, looking worryingly at the fear he caused on every faces of the living, confided sheepishly,

-Oops, my bad. Please do not give up on me, little one. I promise I can listen and learn to be a good Ghost. Beside I really don't fancy going to Hell.

A curious Doctor Valdi went to inspect the glass and the mirror, without hiding his amazement to the others,

-That was such a powerful throw, such velocity, yet look at that humble water tumbler: intact after such impact. Well, correction upon humble, that's crystal. Theo, I am surprised that you bestow such a set of glasses especially after all your sermons every Sunday to the community about charity and helping the poor. You do know what I think about double standards. Anyhow, especially made of this material, that tumbler should have shattered into tiny pieces just like the mirror did. Mirror? Theo, I did not know you were that vain. Let's do an experiment and throw that intriguing glass about the room and see if it ever breaks.

As he was about to drop the tumbler on the floor, his friend rushed with fear of seeing his home being wrecked further to stop him however he was beaten by Aunt Josephine Cough who had already retrieved the glass from Vincent's hands. She sternly advised the Doctor,

-Let's not do that, shall we? It could have terrible consequences.

Father Odell was readily eager to agree,

-Yes, let's not do that. If you want me to sell those glasses, Vince, and give the proceed to the poor of Wilton Town, having the full set is a good idea, value wise.

Vincent gave him a mocking smile, before questioning teasingly,

-Is it you being all of a sudden charitable, Theo, or are you in the 'protecting that neat presbytery of yours' scheme? Come, Miss Cough, apart from treading on shards of glass, there is no 'terrible' consequences to be had.

Correcting him, Josephine Cough went back to her seat, keeping the glass by her in an almost protective fashion on the table,

-Indeed, if shards of glass were not bad enough to tread on, Doctor Valdi, and can do quite substantial damage to our feet, there is another greater risk. Believe it or not, I do not care, but I am not prepared to challenge that one presently, now that we all know that Spirits and Ghosts do exist. I have been told that once a glass has been used by an entity, where the glass break, the entity stays. During my time, and spiritism sessions done in Europe, in fashionable circles, I witnessed the different Masters of seances being very particular upon the matter. You seemed shocked while inspecting this glass, Vincent, for it defies your logical interpretation of the world. Mine has been challenged many times over, so much so, that I am not sure of anything with a one hundred per cent certainty for everything, everything, mutates and changes, from grains of sand to that translucent glass, from lava to rock and fertile slopes, from an ocean that disappears leaving behind just the largest desert one can cross upon Earth, everything changes, Valdi, and the truth one day is not the one the following day. I accepted that fact of life, from walking on four to two legs and reaching the stage that I will need my third leg soon, it made me an eternal learner for you can never reach the stage where you know all. Be contented with that fact and you will be contented with the ever changing life. Take your seats back, Children. We need to get that new session under way.

If Father Odell sat quietly, happy that his home did not become the 'Palace of throwing glasses about', Vincent Valdi took his seat by the elder woman watching her attentively as he questioned,

-Josephine, I want to know whatever you saw. I will never be able to stop questioning everything, but I guess that's just me. Can you bear it and educate me about your travels? I would love to have a beer session with you at 'Ye old Grizzly Bear'. Tomorrow night? Theo, are you coming? Now, why did that glass not breaking did not startle you for one bit, Miss Cough? Please, share with us your experience.

Putting a strand of her salt and pepper hair back into her bun, Josephine acknowledged with a kind smile,

-Well, I saw a glass used in a seance being thrown outside a window, three storeys high, right on to the pavement of a Paris street, and it didn't break. The session had been pretty scary, with death threats from the Spirit to one of the member participating, a very gentle yet stunning brunette of a Mademoiselle called Laure, so much so that the Master of the seance reacted by terminating it. If the Spirit is evil, you mustn't let the glass be ever used again, he said for anyone drinking anything from it would be inhabited by the entity. Breaking the glass is said to release the spirit, but he will remain where it is broken. In the instance I am talking about, the Master ended up throwing the glass in the nearby river Seine as all his attempts to destroy the glass were unsuccessful. To us, he only explained that the entity he dealt with was demonic. In our case, however we only have my nephew...

-Only! I definitely don't want Wilton-Cough haunting my home forever. I intend to sleep at night. Let's break that glass in his grave where he is suppose to rest as soon as he told us what he has to say.

Vincent had a cocky grin at the reply of the Priest before teasing,

-Come, Theo, Wilton-Cough is a wonderful guest. Your mirror needed a makeover, it wasn't pretty enough.

His friend gave him a killer glance before the old Josephine recalled them,

-Children! May I remind you that his Spirit is present in the room, and although we cannot see him, he, on the other hand can see us and hear us. I suggest you two, not to try his patience too much. Let's concentrate.

Mrs Bates, fiddling with the bow of her bonnet with some anxiety, agreed with her,

-Yes, let's do so, Gentlemen, for if Mr Wilton-Cough frightened a fair few alive, he definitely does so dead.

By her, Doctor Valdi took her hand reassuringly, before telling Aunt Josephine,

-I am ready when you are Miss Cough.

-Right, hand joining again, concentration, and think of addressing the Spirit respectfully when asking him any questions. This time, I will let my hand be guided by my nephew for him to write his answers. Abraham focus on my hand only. Now tell us if it is the nasty Ghouls that we encountered in the cemetery that woke you up?

Wilton-Cough smiled confidently behind her, whispering to Abigail,

-Now, we are talking.

He seized his Aunt's hand, moulding his own onto it with precision, so that her grasp of the quill was identical to his during his life. From the way, Josephine went to dip the quill in the ink pot to the position it adopted onto the paper, Angela recognised the mannerism of her husband, it was perspiring in the energetic tapping of the excess of ink upon the pot, and by the curve position of the arm. When the quill started to move in a fast pace, writing in a neat, legible cursives, she confided out loud with a sad sigh,

-That's my Ab's writing.

Aunt Jo, considering the paper that was filling with lines, confirmed it too,

-My nephew always had clear cursives.

To which Vincent Valdi commented with a sarcastic smirk, recalling the ways of Wilton-Cough,

-Yes, that would be him, he taught me to stop writing like a Doctor, he told me if I wanted to be paid correctly, my invoice should be precise and to the point, so no one could argue with me that I wrote a one and not a ten. Beside the clear cut money matter of it, he said there was another advantage for me as a Doctor, for the patient I sent to the chemist would get the correct medicine, therefore will be most likely to survive and ultimately pay me for my services. Make no mistake, I did follow that sensible advice to the letter. I made sure a chemist would never have to guess what I wrote.

The ghostly Abraham had finished writing his answer, and smiled with proud satisfaction to the Angel on his shoulder,

-See, I am glad to hear that I have been useful to someone, I prevented Valdi to kill any of his patients by impressing on him to write most correctly.

His daughter blinked at him amused, replied,

-Do you know that the possibility of killing his patients by mistake is a recurrent nightmare of Valdi and only started since your advice?

While he saw Josephine reading out loud his answer, the Ghost argued with Abigail,

-Well having nightmares never harmed anyone. Look at me, Angel, I am the deadly proof of it. I improved greatly by having one on my death bed.

When his Aunt asked him,

-If it is not the Ghouls that woke you up in 'per-se', what did, Abraham?

Writing again with application with the help of his Aunt's hand, Wilton-Cough attempted to answer her. His long reply was read by Josephine,

-The knowledge that there is a curse upon Wilton Town which will affect one of my sons in the future caused my unrest.

Father Odell acknowledged to the group,

-The Angel that follows Abraham, appearing to me, said just as much. She asked me to be a Father to my Flock for the curse affected the children of Wilton Town, past, present and future.

With a deep air of concentration, Josephine Cough tried to remember out loud,

-In my childhood, I heard some elder saying such a thing that there was a curse upon the town. I do not remember the particulars but upon their strong advice my younger sister Juliette was given an exorcism when she was just an infant. When I asked my father, why, he replied that it was due to the ancient curse. I was only about five then, and it impressed me greatly what they did to Juliette, so I asked if they did the same thing to me when I was little but my Pa said it wasn't necessary for I wasn't born during a full moon.

Full of interest, Vincent Valdi posited,

-I noticed a concern in this town, since I arrived here, which I always associated to local superstition, for women that if they delivered at night their children, often asked me if there was a full moon or not in the odd belief that the child would turn out bad if he or she was born during one. I always reassured the ladies that it was just pure, utter non sense. Let's ask Abraham Wilton-Cough if he knows anything about that. How does the curse affect the children born in Wilton Town?

Josephine saw her hand moving rapidly as it wrote Abraham's reply to the Doctor's question, which she duly read,

-To be honest, like you Vincent, I have been a great sceptic all my living life, all I know now, being a Ghost, is that my son Zachary will become a Ghoul if we do not stop that curse upon the town. Like me, and my Aunt Jo, you were there at his birth, it was a night of November with a very full blue moon. You were exhausted for having delivered three infants before my boy that night. I was so happy to hold my first child and so worried about his first hours of life with me and Angie being parents for the first time that I insisted for you to rest at mine. I prepared myself the guest room which would allow me to keep you nearby to attend to my Angie and my boy if the need ever occurred that night. But Auntie Jo was such a nurse to Angela and I kept Zach in my arms warm all night, unable to put the boy in his cradle for a minute, that I had no need to disturb you. How is my boy?

Valdi recalled the night in his memory, so did Angela and Aunt Josephine, yet all grew pale. He was the first to break the heavy silence with his confounded disbelief,

-If that answers my question right, we have a massive problem on our hands. For in my twenty years as the Doctor of this town, I delivered many babies during a full moon. If all of them are cursed to become Ghouls when will they do so and how? Did Juliette Cough became a Ghoul or did the exorcism performed on her as a child worked? It could be interesting to excavate her to assess her body. If it has that nice pale blue flesh and bleeds, we will know we have a Ghoul and that exorcisms are vain on the curse, if she is a skeleton or decomposed, we have a possible solution at hand. But could it work on fully fledge Ghouls? We could capture one and try it out. Are you up for it, Theo?

Father Odell nodded positively, before answering,

-We need to do something to save all we can. The answers to your questions may bring about a solution to that damned curse. I have a cadastral map of the cemetery in my desk. Abraham, we will try everything to save Zachary. Since your death, your eighteen year old has been a bit troublesome to all of us. He follows the wrong crowd in town and whatever we tell him, he replies that we are not his father and have no right to tell him what to do.

Angela Wilton-Cough admitted, half sobbing,

-I have no control over Zach since your death. He refuses to listen to anything I say. Tonight he went out with his friends, and I will not know where he will be until he decides to come back home, usually at dawn. And then I will see him, collapsed on his bed, sleeping through the day to only get up at night again.

Tapping her shoulder in a comforting manner, Father Odell, told the Ghost,

-We do not know how to get through to Zachary, all our attempts failed even the straight talking ones of Josephine Cough.

This unsettled Abraham Wilton-Cough deeply, he seized the hand of his Aunt and demanded,

-Where is he now? Has he turned to a Ghoul? He swore to me to be loving! Yet I blame myself. I put down my Angie so much in front of my boys, that one decided to disregard her while the other took determinedly her side. I divided my own household. Let me repair the harm done, let me get through to him. Lead me to him, he will hear his father once more, forcefully maybe, but trust me, if it prevent him to turn totally bad, I will do it. I do not want any of my children to turn into heartless gits of the type I was.

Reading his words, Josephine, feeling a tad emotional, fed all the information she had the knowledge of to her dead nephew,

-The boy has not turned a Ghoul yet, Ab. He is just a belligerent teen going through adulthood a tad too fast since your untimely departure from the living. He refuses all responsibilities apart the one of spending his own inheritance. I have it on good authority that he spends his nights playing poker with his friends at the 'Crying White Doe Hotel' between Wilton Town and Cabrel Town. An old school friend of mine works there as a bar tender and she keeps a tab on the lad for me. She informs me of his losses, troubles and wins and I have been settling his bills so it doesn't affect him without Zachary knowing anything.

The sensitive Angela almost crumbled at the news, blinking to her Aunt,

-You never told me where Zach went...

Father Odell confided to the widow,

-We kept that information away from you, Angela, to protect you. You were already so distraught by his attitude and also by the grief of losing Abraham. Miss Cough has a connection in the Hotel, where Zachary goes to play poker. It was important for us to keep a concerned spying eye on your son. We also all tried to work on the owner of the Hotel, secretively and independently trying to encourage her to stop holding those poker sessions. She only replied that ceasing them will open the boundaries of Wilton Town and that many parents will never see their children again. She told me that she had a duty to keep those children within Wilton Town, that I should consider gambling as a lesser evil in that matter. Whilhelmina White also warned me that if I should mobilise the community against gambling at her place, starting my 'goodie-goodie' war, I would spread more evil than good far and wide. When she finished casually mentioning that I would probably not survive long enough to regret having started a cross exchange with her about her livelihood, I took my leave respectfully and just headed as soon as I could back to Wilton Town, fearing that my steps could be caught by dusk.

His friend, half teased,

-Somehow, pardon me for saying this Ladies, Theo, you must have been getting on her tits right and proper. I know Whilhelmina fairly well. If I play poker once in a while in her establishment trying my theories on probability, I also meet her path as she forages for the same medicinal herbs as I do. We do share our knowledge of them and recipes. I dare say that she is a medicine woman, and I worked with her to deliver children almost daily but also we have a shared understanding to help the elderly and the sick at the edges of the town. When I cannot visit a patient because of too many emergencies at a particular time, she would have made the call. I consider highly Wilhelmina, as a benefactress in our community. Look, her Hotel is homing a few of the elders who have got no child to look after them. I can not believe she is capable of death threats. You must have dreamt them.

A slightly disgruntled Theo retorted,

-Just like I dreamt the Ghost of Abraham and his Angel. You'd better start believing in me a little. Miss White has no appreciation for me and has no problem indicating so in a manner that I find right down intimidating.

Despite their arguments a thoughtful Wilton-Cough made Jo tapping her quill on the ink pot recalling them. Before he wrote down,

-The White knows something about the children of Wilton Town, I would bet on it. Valdi come with me to her Hotel. Let's bring my Zach back to his mother. Theo, no need to check the cadastral map, my mother was buried in the crypt of the Cough below the church. Aunt Josephine can show you the exact place. Check on her state. When I come back with Valdi and Zach, we will capture a Ghoul together to see if exorcism can work on them. Angie stay safe with Mrs Bates.

When Josephine read out loud the paper, she stated,

-This sounds like a plan.

Doctor Valdi stood up and saluting everyone told,

-It does. I would be interested to find out if Whilhelmina has some knowledge about the curse. Let's go Wilton-Cough.

Throwing his cape on his shoulders, he left the Presbytery, while a ghostly Abraham followed him, slamming the door shut behind them.

Chapter Ten

Record the Past to Solve the Future

Left in the room, Angela considered the written paper with attention, while Josephine went to warm her hands by the fire, stating with a sad smile,

-Even dead, my nephew manages to order us about. Maybe he will achieve where we failed with Zachary. Gosh, his strong Spirit grabbed my hand so tight that I am chilled to the bone. That won't be good for my arthritis. Do you think the assumptions of Abraham about Miss White are valid, Father?

Going to his desk and opening it to get the cadastral map, Theo replied with honesty,

-Maybe it is very unchristian of me but there is something unsettling about that woman. I tend to be very kind and compassionate with all my parishioners but if I manage to fake sympathy towards her, she still makes me cringe and gut feelings or not, I would not be surprised if she knew something unworldly.

Mrs Wilton-Cough agreed with him,

-I am not blaming you, Father. What you said made my blood curdle. Knowing that my eldest son is at hers every night, let alone gambling, upset me greatly. I will join you in being a tad unchristian, I wish my Ab to poltergeist her hotel and drag my Zach back to me, walloping his ears with a sound telling off. Well for a start on being unchristian, we can not beat Miss White who never goes to church every Sunday.

Sensing her niece in law's uncommon anger, Josephine Cough brought to the table a silver platter with a carafe holding a golden spirit glistening by the candlelight and offered,

-Our wait to see them coming back with Zachary may be long. I tended to the fire but this will help us to keep warm and you Angie, to numb the pain in your shoulder. Please my Child, do not hold any grudges against Miss White. If you have any, just lay them at rest. She is an elder in this town. Although she is no Christian, I can assure you that she has her own religion. Her hotel has its own chapel where she lead a service every Monday.

A very circumspect Father Odell scanning the map and an old manuscript commented,

-I will have a full tumbler Miss Cough: I need all sustenance if I have to perform a few exorcisms tonight. One can only wonder what her religion can be? Monday, the day of the moon, could it be witchcraft?

Amelia Bates couldn't help joining in the conversation,

-Well, it could not be too far fetch, for I remember being with my mum, who was pregnant with my last brother that did not make it, at the market. We crossed Miss White's path and she scared me like no other that day. She told my mother that she had only days to live and that her child will accompany her to heaven. She was ever so precise in her predictions that I will never forget them. The fact that they did happen to the day and on the hour, disturbed me greatly. I went to see Miss White a few days after the funeral to ask how did she know about someone's death. I was only about eight at the time, and the 'Crying White Doe Hotel' impressed me by its grandeur. Miss White invited me in a cosy parlour, offered me tea, biscuits and cakes like if I was one of the wealthiest kids in town, although I was not. She also talked to me as if I were an adult. There were no 'dear' or demeaning tone in her voice whatsoever. She explained to me that any human had a body which wears and tears, that work, food, wealth, health and lots of other factors came into play affecting the longevity of any. She took the example of my mother, hit by poverty, working far too hard, not feeding herself adequately, having children after children almost every given year, with her health declining in the dye factory, breathing chemicals, and concluded that she just saw a worn out being. She told me that having delivered all of the little Elroy children, she knew that having another would be the death sentence of my mother, yet that my god fearing mum sealed her fate. The last Elroy was not to be and she gave her life for him, leaving a eleven strong brood that needed plenty of mothering. If that conversation made me understand things better, and made me come to terms with my mother's death, I was still baffled by the accuracy that the woman did predict it in the market place.

Sipping pensively, Theo asked almost with an absent mind,

-Pray, how old was miss White when you were eight?

-She must have been in her thirties, it is hard to tell because of her hair which was so blonde that they always looked almost white at anytime.

Josephine downed the content of her tumbler at once, before confiding, in a sheer moment of enlightenment dawning upon her,

-I met Miss White as a child too, about the same age as you were Mrs Bates and I would have said she was in her thirties just as well. Thinking of it, she doesn't look past her fifties now. I always remember her living on the road at the boundary of the town. Father Odell, you came into Wilton Town five years after Vincent, therefore fifteen years ago, how would you describe Miss White then?

A paling priest replied,

-In her thirties, give or take. What are you trying to imply Miss Cough?

Filling her tumbler with more brandy, Josephine told in a fashion which chilled everyone in the room with fear,

-That the woman is ageless. She should be well over a hundred by now, or even dead and buried and isn't. That something simply unnatural is going on and yes maybe Abraham was right in betting that Miss White must know about the curse.

Going to an oak chest, and opening it Father Odell asked,

-Josephine, do you happen to know if miss White was born in Wilton Town or did she come here? I have ways to find out. In this book, a report about all inhabitants of this town is kept, and I maintained the tradition which was started by the founder of Wilton Town himself, Noah M Wilton. All the priests of Wilton Town had that obligation from then on.

The leather manuscript, Theo took from the chest and brought to the table, smelled of old worn out shoes. He opened the massive book proudly as Josephine confessed,

-From memory, she has always been there in Wilton Town. She has no known relative apart from a daughter, called Mina which no one ever sees, who must have left Wilton Town ages ago.

Undeterred by the lack of information, Theo Odell told with some assurance,

-I can work with that. Either way, their births in this town or arrivals will be reported here. Give or take a hundred years and their surname as White, we will find an entry for them. Mrs Bates, I will look at all the entries on the right pages, please would you scan the left pages for us?

Sitting by him, Amelia was only too happy to make herself useful and forget that all were drinking but her for Doctor Valdi had cautioned her against it in her condition.
Putting her index upon the left page of the manuscript, she applied herself to her given task,

-Sure, Father. White, White, White...

While they were occupied scouring the large logging manuscript, Aunt Josephine told everything she knew to Angela about her son

Zachary's night escapades. The clock struck the time, and all realised that a very long hour had past since Vincent Valdi went with the spirit of Abraham to chase for Wilton-Cough's eldest boy. Refilling the glasses, Aunt Jo asked anxiously,

-What is the score on Miss White and her daughter, Father?

Theo, who had been scribbling on a piece of paper with a carbon pencil, reported,

-There is no births for her and her daughter being reported nor any arrivals. We have scanned three hundred years so far in the life of Wilton Town. But, but...

His voice sank. Amelia Bates took over his notes and presenting them to Josephine announced,

-Miss Whilhelmina White has been living in Wilton Town the entire time. We have many entries registering her as a Godmother to many children throughout the decades. She was there, well here, in this church, for their baptisms. The last time, she stood here was in November, eighteen years ago, to the joint baptism ceremony of the four boys that were born during the same night. She was the appointed Godmother of Hugo Phileas. He is one of the naughtiest teenagers in town and the best friend of Zach unfortunately as you know, Angie. Now, we have an entry here for Miss White, three hundreds years earlier, at the baptism of Clara O'Neill, which was the great great grandmother of our Clara Pendleton who only past away lately, the very one we saw her body being devoured by Ghouls. This research confirmed our suspicions about Miss White. If she is eternal, she cannot be human.

An anxious Angela enquired,

-Could she be a Ghoul?

Father Odell dispelled her anxiety straight away,

-No, she is definitely not. According to Valdi, and having fought against many Ghouls tonight, she does not fit the description. She has no pale blue skin and yellow voracious teeth. She is something else altogether but what? It is a mystery.

-Out of curiosity Father, did you track her existence back to the creation of Wilton Town?

Looking at Josephine, Theo answered her, as he immediately went to the first pages of the manuscript,

-We did not go that far back in time, but your question makes me just as curious as you are. Let's check the first entries. Amelia, check the left for her name.

Within minutes, the Widow Bates smiled with excitement pointing at a page,

-There, Father, here she is with her daughter. She is in the list of who arrived in Wilton Town with Noah M Wilton.

Theo, his interest piqued, shared out loud for everyone,

-This list has been penned by Noah himself. It is not only a nomenclature, he is very thorough in describing whom he calls his followers. Miss Whilhelmina White: very interestingly the words describing her are in French. Ladies, are any of you fluent in that language? Why did Noah write most of her entry in French, while for the others, they are in English?

An intrigued Josephine went by him, proposing,

-I can have a go, Father. I travelled to France many times. I am not fluent but I know enough to maintain a good conversation in a 'salon Parisien'.

The Priest moved sideways, leaving to Aunt Josephine the opportunity to make sense of the entry. They did not have to wait long as Miss Cough told them,

-Well 'fille-mére' describes the fact that she has a child despite not being married. Noah even reported why. He says Miss White was abused and raped at the service of the owner of the land that they all comes from whom he describes as a tyrant. He mentions that she was a multi tasking servant but he employs her for the new community as 'une blanchisseuse', this means laundress. However he emphasises her importance as a renown 'sage femme', that is not meaning that she is a wise woman but a midwife. One can see that in the wilderness he was taking his followers, that that particular skill of Miss White could become rapidly essential. That could also explain why so many parents throughout the ages chose her as a Godmother to their children. Worryingly, it clearly indicates to us that Whilhelmina White's connection with the children of Wilton Town dates from its creation. Now let me translate that part. It is in French, but it will take time for it is in reversed writing.

Amelia asked full of curiosity,

-What do you mean Jo?

-I mean by that that Noah was making it very difficult for us to read that particular part. It's an easy way to code a text. Leonardo da Vinci used that method a lot for his notes, yet put a mirror by them and be amazed at the genius of that man from anatomy to art passing by his inventions and creations.

Theo Odell turned around and took a large slab of his broken mirror on the wall then presented it to Miss Cough,

-Please carry on reading, what does that part says? Be careful with that piece of mirror Miss Josephine, the edges are so sharp that I managed to cut myself.

Giving him in exchange her pretty handkerchief, Aunt Jo smiled to him kindly, obliging him,

-Who has got sparks of genius, Father, if it is not you? Amelia, look at his cut, wrap it if necessary with that and maybe apply a little brandy upon it. So let us see what Noah wanted to keep a little more secret than the rest...

All waited patiently by her, all ears, and so silent that you could have heard a fly in that room, but as it was, just the crackling of the coals within the fireplace, just the spring wind whistling against the shutters, and the muted, repeated, 'Ouch' of Theo pierced the profound silence.

Having looked inside the mirror blade attentively, finely, Josephine revealed with satisfaction,

-Well, I dare say for Noah M Wilton, he probably wanted a certain secrecy to protect himself and Miss White if anyone came for them from their old country. He says that during the havoc and the mini revolution, he created, he freed all prisoners, that Whilhelmina was one them, one who followed him by gratitude, ready to devote herself to whatever he wanted to create, but one who had been condemned to be burnt at the stake as a convicted witch. To all prisoners that followed him, he clearly tells that he gave them the benefit of the doubt and the chance of a new life to redeem themselves. Only three of that prison crossed seas, rivers, mountains and forests to dream the same dream of Noah: Miss White and her daughter, and a certain Isaac Cough, my very own ancestor. I never knew Isaac to be a convict, only to be an illustrious creator of this town, a blacksmith, an educated one. Let me check what Noah says about him. Interesting he used French and reversed French writing again. Right, Isaac's crime is to have brutally murdered a Tax man in desperation. At the time he was freed, he had been sentenced to be hanged. Right, that is a bit of news for me. What we have to take from this is that Noah M Wilton was protecting his skin and his convicts by writing in a different language about them and their former convictions and sentences. As for Miss White and her twelve year old daughter Mina both had been accused as witches and sentenced to burn to death. As it is not a very nice end, I have no wonder why they followed Noah M Wilton anywhere he would go with his strong axe. He established himself like the protector of those who followed him regardless of their pasts.

When Josephine became silent, all looked at each others, digesting the informations. Suddenly all the shards of mirror still within their frame fell on the floor. Theo Odell reacted by closing the large manuscript at once, anxiously ordering,

-Let's not dig into the past anymore. I certainly do not want any other Ghost than Wilton-Cough as resident in my presbytery, especially not the one of a convicted murderer that could play with those slabs of mirror and stab us all. Isaac, if you heard us, don't be upset, just rest in peace. I will pray for your soul.

His unrest was met by Amelia Bates who commented,

-I hope your bribery will work, Father. To any Ghost, I will match Father Odell's proposal. I will give you as many prayers as he does.

A bewildered Josephine Cough told them off,

-My ancestor would not kill anyone like that for no reasons. Besides, lets be honest and pragmatic, I wish Vincent was here to support me, that mirror was so chattered that it was only minutes away for the laws of gravity to take hold of all its broken pieces and make them fall behind us. Besides, Theo, you, taking a shard of that jigsaw precipitated the mirror to fall apart. Children, stop being scaredy-cats.

The Widow Bates pouted before defending herself,

-Come Miss Cough, you must agree with us that we have seen and heard much today enough to scare us for an entire lifetime. You have been acquainted with the Spirit's world while we have not. Just knowing that Miss White is a convicted witch, with her strong connection with the children of this town makes her the perfect culprit responsible for the curse. The fact that she never ever passed away makes me shiver. It goes beyond anyone's comprehension.

Finishing her brandy, Josephine corrected her with an implacable certainty,

-It does not Amelia, trust me when I say that some do comprehend those matters pretty well and down to a T. Back in the days of Noah, anyone who knew a little about those, like myself, would be branded as a witch and burnt without the blink of an eye, nor any doubts. Just her knowledge of herbal medicine which was pinpointed by Doctor Valdi would have put her into deep trouble in Noah's lifetime yet it is the same knowledge used by chemists and Doctors nowadays. Now, we mustn't repeat the actions of our forebears which made so many flee their country of birth to settle in the wilderness. They left tyranny behind to live in a fair society where their children can thrive. They left the barbaric, uneducated, inhuman and pre-medieval dark age laws behind to embrace a loving humanity and the world. So we have to be fair, it is our duty as descendants of whom built Wilton Town as a place where freedom and fraternity ruled to make it a safe haven for all. So I will correct you, Miss White is not the perfect culprit for the curse upon this town, let's give her justice, and just say that she is a clear suspect. Let's investigate to make sure she is clear of that crime. You have seen Ghouls and Ghosts, what is an eternal witch? Maybe just that, let's learn to cope with it. Let's be strong together. We have a curse to beat together. Father, I hope you are recovered from your fright for we need to inspect the corpse of my sister.

Theo, pouting in the exact fashion of Amelia, confessed,

-When I harboured the slight hope that we would forget about that dreary task...

Miss Cough scolded him sternly,

-Father, how unchristian of you! After all the promises of help you gave to the spirit of my nephew.

-Well, I am just a man behind my robe, Josephine, who does feel fear and have weaknesses just like anyone. Let's be honest, who would be thrilled to exhume a body apart Vincent? Right let's arm us with some crosses.

After bringing a couple of very large crucifixes, he pestered,

-I do not know what Valdi did with the gold cross of my tabernacle. I could only find my one by the entrance. I hope he didn't lose it in the cemetery. But the one of the refectory is large enough to give you ample protection, Miss Cough. Just use it like a sword.

As Josephine took the cross and tried it out, doing some fencing moves in the air around her, Father Odell put a couple of large manuscripts on the table by Angela and Amelia, he opened one of them and ordered,

-Ladies, the night shall not be fruitless in our fight to protect and save the children of Wilton Town. You two, are my soldiers, for they are many ways to engage in battle, one of which is tactical. On the map here we have our battlefield, full of Ghouls who, we must not forget, are the cursed children of the town. Your mission is to determine the graves of those lost souls, and mark them for me on the map with that pencil. As we never met a Ghoul during the day, that must be where they sleep from dawn till dusk, in their respective graves. The process to localise those cursed children is easy enough yet tedious. This is the register for every single birth, this one is for every death, and this book here tells who is buried where on the cadastral map. Here is to use the books efficiently. First page, you see in the births, Ladies, there is that little symbol by every entry. This is when we say thank you to the meticulous superstition of my predecessors, which I carried on dutifully not even knowing what it was all about. Can you guess what it is?

Abraham's widow advanced uncertain,

-It's a big black dot, well circle.

-Have another guess, look at this one and that one.

It dawned on Mrs Bates what it was. She readjusted her glasses on her nose with a bright smile, as she revealed,

-They represent the stages of the moon! Look Angela, black moon, growing crescents and there full moon, and plenty of little suns. So, if I understand you right Father, if we pinpoint all the children born during a full moon, find their times of death, we can then look where they were buried, we would have found all the cursed wee ones of Wilton Town.

Holding her hand with appreciation, Theo confirmed,

-Yes, Amelia, this is the principle of it. Now, if my theory is correct that their graves is where they sleep during the day, and providing exorcism does work on them then we will have a possibility to save their souls tomorrow. In the worst case scenario, I am sure this gathered information will be useful to us in another way. For example just knowing how many Ghouls we are dealing with in this town alone will be extremely valuable. Make note of all the children not dead but born during a full moon, just as well. God will reward you for your efforts, and I will be forever in your debts.

When he left the room armed with his cross, followed by an approving Aunt Josephine, Amelia and Angela were suitably spurred to do their bit to solve the dreaded curse of Wilton Town.

Chapter Eleven

To Forget and to Forgive

The church was peaceful and enveloped in a shroud of silence that neither Father Odell nor Josephine Cough were willing to break. Not that they had anything to say to each other, but because they were worried of any Ghouls which could have hidden in the church. Complete silence makes any noise stand out, like the ruffle of skirt and petticoats on the stone slabs, or the anxious heavy breathing of a priest wondering what he will find in the crypt he has not stepped in for a good decade.

The lantern carried by Aunt Jo provided them just enough light to perceive any shadow nestling by the pillars. A peculiar one, most immobile with its arms open and extended forward, cloaked like a ghost prompted them to walk closer together. Bathed in the moonlight procured by the huge stained glass windows, the dark shadow on the floor seemed to belong to someone awesomely tall. In preparation, a cold sweating Theo put his cross upside down, holding now the lower tip, ready to strike, along with his breath. As they reached the dreaded pillar, the Priest jumped in front of Josephine protectively, brandishing his crucifix like a sword, shouting out lout,

-Vade Retros Satanas!

As none moved, Miss Cough lifted her lantern to highlight the corner of their combined fear for the past minutes, and only saw the statue of the Virgin Marie. Her tight lips formed a smile as peaceful as the one displayed on the statue, as she whispered,

-False alert, Father, please do remember the emplacement of the statues in your church. If we had encountered a gargoyle one, I may have fainted.

Ashamed, Theo signed himself in front of the statue, stuttering a prayer,

-Please, forgive me, dear Marie, I didn't mean what I meant. We are trying to save the cursed children of Wilton Town. But they are so hungrily ugly, that they are frightening the living daylight out of us. Please I beg you to let me love them and live long enough to break the curse plaguing them. I am trying desperately to be what the Angel demanded, a Father to my flock. Please, forgive me.

To their joint amazement, the marble effigy cried blood tears. Father Odell signed himself repetitively, fearing he had caused the upset, yet swore like a butcher of Wilton Town,

-Holy fuck, I did upset the Holy bloody Virgin! I am so so very sorry, Marie.

Impulsively he went to hug the statue with a most humble and sorry heart, however still holding his massive cross. The marble arms enclosed his shoulders in a cold and very tight almost suffocating embrace, then tapped them with the gentlest and softest of touch. The voice that wrapped his mind and engulfed his soul into paying full attention, was full of sorrow, but also full of hope,

-I am with you, Father, for I am a mother. Make one of us, mothers, dry her tears. Put the town's children back to bed, make them rest.

It lasted for a split second before the statue towered Theo again, completely still within the majesty of its sculpted marble. The Priest gave a very lost look at Josephine Cough behind him, asking her anxiously,

-Did I hallucinate? I swear the holy Virgin talked to me. She said that she was with me.

Having witnessed it all, Aunt Jo reassured him at once, before pointing to his cross shining like a beacon, illuminating the entire church,

-You did not dream, Father. Otherwise I am a victim of the same hallucination. I believe that she is with you. Look at your crucifix glowing like it never did before. What else did the Virgin tell you?

Father Odell, signing himself before leaving the side of the statue, walked more confidently towards the crypt, his faith renewed a thousand fold. He confided,

-Well, it sounded important but also like a riddle... All I know is that I have the duty to resolve that curse. Word for word, she said that she was with me, for she was a mother. She asked me to make one of them, referring to mothers, dry her tears, to put the town's children back to bed and to make them rest.

Following him, Josephine nodded and commented,

-The mother she is talking about might be her own self for we saw her statue cry those blood tears. She might indicate that as a mother to all, knowing that the curse afflicts the children, she needs them to rest to dry her tears.

Theo deposited his large cross by him to open the large double trap door on the ground. Their creaky noises revealed how ancient was the crypt which they were about to enter. The carved lintel slab had macabre drawings surrounding the engraved word 'crypt'. The Priest confided,

-I hate this part of my church. I hardly go there. The last time I did was about ten years ago. As for the riddle you might be right Miss Cough, but my mind keep thinking if she was referring to a mother of Wilton Town, a very distressed one, who knew what did happen to her children... Like Wilton-Cough is unable to rest knowing that the curse will affect his eldest son one day, this mother cannot stop crying. Would that mother be alive? But I swear during my fifteen years in this town, I would know about such a mourningly distraught parishioner. Or maybe she is dead and buried, a howling Ghost that need to be appeased just like your nephew?

As he engaged himself down the narrow and uneven stairs, fighting with his bright cross the multitude of webs and spiders surrounding them, Aunt Josephine replied,

-This is a possibility, but yes definitely a puzzle compared to the 'we just have to wipe Marie's tears'. You certainly failed to do the housekeeping around here, Father. You bestow the best collection of live spiders that any well respected entomologist could dream of. You should show it to Doctor Valdi, he is already an avid collector of beetles and butterflies. From my trip to Mexico, I brought him back a blue Morpho butterfly which he was so thankful about. Just leave Vincent in the crypt, he will not only sweep it clean for you, but it might also keep him silent for a while. Pray, why would you not step in here more often? The family crypt of the Cough has been paid with a great deal of money. Their expectations would have been care and maintenance in return at the very least.

Theo was so appreciative to have a strong character like the Aunt Cough to go inside the crypt with him, that he welcomed her advice and criticism with an honest smile,

-Just wiping the Virgin's tears would be a large endeavour enough for it would encompass all the cursed children therefore solve the plea of any particular mother, Josephine. I must confess that I have been deeply negligent of this crypt. I promise you to bring Vincent to help me tidy it. I must say I love his incessant chat and even sarcasms. His constructive criticism tends to keep me on my toes. I consider that having my best friend as my harshest critic is indeed a blessing in disguise. I would not be surprised to see that your suggestion about the spiders could happen to be very true. It would give me great pleasure to lead Vince here, and witness it. The reason I am not going down there alone is simple. I keep hearing noises by any of those tombs. Sometimes I imagine they are whispers and voices in the dark, and other times I rationalise them like there must be a colony of rats living here. Back in the days, I got three cats from the streets and put them in the crypt for the night with the intention that they would eat the rodents...

He paused as they reached at the bottom of the stairs a long hallway with on either sides a series of arched entrances, all grilled.

It looked more like a prison than a crypt to his own eyes, as he continued,

-When I came to release the cats in the morning, none of the animals responded to my calls at the trap doors. I thought I would see them sleeping in the crypt, digesting their rat feast. However, when I went down, I found them all dead, all having been eaten away in such a gruesome manner by what I imagine was ravenous rodents that I left the place, closed it to never return until tonight. Here, look at those very slim bones, Miss Cough, that skeleton belongs to one of those poor street moggies.

He pointed to another pile of slender bones then another one further down the hallway and commented,

-These are the carcasses of the other two or what is left of them. The rats must be dead by now...

A suitably daunted Josephine, now understood full well the concern of Father Odell and his dread of his crypt. Somehow she shared it, seriously expressing her doubts,

-I am dubious that rats will die because one closes a door, Father, they have ways to enter and leave a building that defy almost gravity itself. But I rather think that you have Ghouls down here, and the street moggies were just an happy meal for them. Let's be fast and do our duty without further a do.

Taking a set of keys hanged on the wall, an anxious Theo ordered,

-Let me make sure that all the grid doors are locked. Wait for me by the Cough's crypt.

Feeling like a conscientious jailer Father Odell went through the entire hallway. Only a couple of the iron gates had to be locked. Somewhat reassured, he gave a sheepish smile to Josephine as he returned by her side, explaining,

-I am trying to reduce the chances of us two ending up like those poor cats...

-Good thinking, Father. I can only approve entirely for my old bones haven't seen China nor Japan yet.

-Well for the moment they have to do a trip to the unknown. I will lock us in by precaution.

Theo opened and closed the rusty iron doors then turned to look worryingly at all the stone tombs within the confined crypt. He vented,

-Somehow the Cough have been a very prosperous family. Let us pray that only your sister Juliette was born during a full moon.

Josephine went by the marble sarcophagus of her sister. Her lace gloved fingers removed the dust from the golden grooved letters revealing to its glory the engraving:

'Here lay, Juliette Wilton-Cough, born Cough, the most beautiful woman in the entire county. Ashes to Ashes. Dust to Dust.'

She remembered disapproving of the epitaph written by an embittered Terah Wilton-Cough. Of course she did not expect the cuckold husband to say something along the lines of 'to his beloved wife' nor Abraham to lie and put an untrue to a 'loving mother' for she knew full well that Juliette was neither. Josephine recollected the night of the funeral when almost for the first time the hardly talking Terah opened himself to her in a statement about her sister. She could still hear him word for word:

-Truly, what your sister had in beauty, she lacked in heart and even compassion. I just buried the ugliest soul I ever met, and wished to have never encountered. I have no doubts that Hell will have her for eternity.

Lost in her thoughts, she didn't notice Theo by her, who had started to work out a way to open the tomb. He startled her by his question,

-Why was Juliette buried in the Cough crypt rather than the Wilton part of the cemetery?

Josephine replied with a sigh,

-Terah Wilton-Cough would neither allow it nor consider it. Their union was a bitterly unhappy one. If you never met my sister, Father, know that she wasn't a very pleasant individual. Full of her own self, pride and vanity, she made life a hell for a lot of people around her.

-That is a bit bitter right before we lift the marble slab enclosing her. Come, you must have some good sisterly love to remember. Think of a good memory, Josephine.

Miss Cough shook her head negatively and very sadly answered as she gave him a hand,

-In all honesty Father, I have none. My youngest sister was capricious and crying to get everyone's attention from the start. Then as she grew older and bolder, started steeling my dresses and pretty things, if she wasn't maliciously ruining them. Consumed by jealousy, let alone envy, she stole my bow of the time, only to break his heart soon after. He killed himself over her, and the whole affair broke my heart forever. She is part of the reason why I remained a Miss my entire life. She is part of the reason why anywhere but Wilton Town always seemed a better place for me. She is the reason why my nephew Abraham had so much trouble showing sentiments and expressing his own heart for she gave him no maternal love whatsoever. It is terrible to admit but none does regret her.

When their effort to lift the stone remained fruitless after a good few minutes of struggle, Father Odell proposed,

-Lets use the cross as a lever. Could the curse be responsible for the temperament of the individuals affected during their life I ponder? Maybe the folks tale that Valdi heard repeated over and over is valid and has some foundation. Think about it, Josephine, your sister born during a full moon was not amiable, but if we take the example of Zachary and the three boys born the same night as him, all are hard to deal with. Maybe I am trying desperately to find excuses for the way they are or were. Maybe I just want you to find the strength in yourself to forgive your sister in your own heart before you see her remains. So when we put the cover back over Juliette, you will be able to lay all your bitter regrets with her and at rest.

Josephine was touched by that impromptu sermon of Theo. Despite remaining silent, tears appeared in her eyes which she tried to contain desperately. The Priest enjoined her further as he put all his weight to counter lever the cross in order to push the tomb lid up,

-Come Josephine, it is in your heart. It is in the heart of all of us in one way or another. You can do it. Forgive your sister Juliette once and for all. Free yourself from past grudges. Don't let yourself carry them into your own grave.

Maybe it was the emotional night that they all had, maybe it was the persistence of Father Odell, but as the old stubborn Miss Cough put her own weight onto the cross to help opening up the tomb, she finally surrendered and told out loud with some reluctance, as if she was speaking to Juliette herself,

-Alright, I forgive you to have been a bitch of a sister, a vulgar heart-breaker, and an appalling mother to Abraham. The possibility that you have been cursed grants you my forgiveness.

Theo shook his head in slight dismay at her speech, while the slab was finally pushed enough, leaving a gap large enough for them to inspect the sarcophagus but also wide enough for a Ghoul to arise from it. Swallowing his fear, he ordered,

-Let me check inside, Aunt Jo. Just hold your cross to be ready to hit if something attacks me.

The curiosity made Josephine stand right above him in her

defensive position, yet after a few seconds she reassured,

-Nothing is moving in there, Father. Shall I get the lantern?

He nodded positively despite his fear still clenching his throat. Once he was given the lantern, he could see clearly within the sarcophagus and announced,

-Juliette Wilton-Cough is not going to strangle us, she has been eaten almost completely away. Only her skull and dress are left with specks of bones. As I face her ravaged skeleton, I can safely say that she is no Ghoul at all. But...

Theo stopped talking, daring to take a piece of bone from her cadaver, he considered it carefully by the light, before he shakily stated,

-There are teethmarks all over her bones. She was eaten by them like the young Clara Pendleton.

His loud statement sent shivers down their spines as they realised, that Ghouls were definitely residents within the crypt, but as they entered unlocking the door to the family one of the Cough's, it dawned on them that they were locked in with at least one which had not eaten any flesh for the past ten years.

Aunt Josephine rallied her spirits straight away, seizing the bone from Theo's hands and throwing it back in the tomb, she recalled him strongly from the utter fear she could see drawn on his face,

-Father, my sister being just bones is the hope we were looking for. Exorcism must have worked on her just like Doctor Valdi postulated. We also know we have a Ghoul in there in one of those tombs. Let's get out right now in one piece. If we lock it in, we will have the ready experiment to see if exorcism works on a live Ghoul.

The Priest didn't wait to be told twice. Standing up, he rushed for the door, trying to open its lock with a massive rusty key, which would not turn as fast as he wanted to. Josephine was right there behind him holding her cross in a fashion which would have made any to be very worried to get rat arse kicked by it and facing her in her family crypt, she protected the efforts of Theo to get them out of there fast, covering his back.

The minutes it took to open the grid were far too long for anyone's taste. Theo blatantly struggled to open it with his trembling hands. The impatience reached Josephine when she started hearing screeching, scratching sounds that did not come from the rusty key unwilling to turn in its lock. She shouted,

-Father, hurry! How difficult is it to open a door? I can see some slabs moving.

Theo vented his despair,

-Twenty family crypts mean twenty keys on the same ring. I tried ten so far... Keep strong for me Jo, keep strong for us.

Aunt Josephine understanding their dilemma went to fetch the larger cross, slamming shut the sarcophagus of her sister doing so. She scoured her family crypt with eagle eyes and hammered with the heavy crucifix any cadaverous hands she could see lifting their tomb slabs. It bought Father Odell enough time to find the right key, and when he heard the right noises of an opening grid, he rushed in to grab the old Miss Cough out with her big cross. Once out with her, he locked the Cough's crypt with a great sense of relief.

As both caught their breath back leaning on the door, they held their hands in deep silence. Aunt Jo spoke first,

-My bones are going to see China after all.

-They will, and mine are going to perform the mass tomorrow. But before yours leave Wilton-Town, you are one woman that the town needs to resolve its curse. Are you up to stay with me as I try to exorcise those caged Ghouls belonging to the Cough family? I may need support, and yours is the best I can ever get.

Suitably flattered, Josephine gave the large cross back to him, and answered with a positive strong nod,

-You can count on me. Let's try a good exorcism on the Coughs, it looks like they need one. What do I have to do?

Father Odell put the massive crucifix back in her hand and replied, then he entered the Cough's crypt again as fast as he could to retrieve the lantern and his refectory cross,

-Stay by me as I perform the exorcism. If you ever see me struggle just talk to me like you did earlier. If I can not cope with it, drag me out of this place at once, leave the crosses down there but not the lantern for I do not want my church burnt down to the ground by evil Spirits.

When he came out with everything, he slammed the grid close and locked it. Aunt Jo, putting the lantern by her told him firmly,

-You've got it, Theo. I will stay. Try it all out. I counted three Ghouls in my family's crypt. Let's see if we can get rid of their curses that way.

Father Odell went on to perform the exorcism. Him and Aunt Jo could see lots of ghouls appearing like prisoners at the doors of every crypt, moaning, screaming and crying the further he went on with his prayers. It lasted hours. But in the end, to their utter disbelief, amazement and relief they witnessed the collapse of the Ghouls and their transformations to the corpse they were supposed to have been without the curse. An exhausted Theo leaned on Aunt Josephine Cough as he crossed the threshold of his presbytery, yet happy internally to have resolved the situation in his crypt. However, he was utterly worried for his friend Vincent Valdi as he was not back with the Ghost of Abraham nor Zachary. A look at his clock warned him that it had gone just past two. He hoped everything went fine at the 'Crying White Doe Hotel'.

Chapter Twelve

Wishing in the Spirited Night

Walking the country lane, Doctor Vincent Valdi was glad to have cleared the cemetery fairly fast. He was not one easily spooked as he was very used to go miles into the deep night in order to attend to his patients but then he never had been conscious of Ghouls being out and about, like he was now. By him the Ghost of Abraham Wilton-Cough glided, invisible to his eyes yet Vincent could see that little glowworm floating ahead of them, the one which was qualified as the Guardian Angel of the passed away Banker by his friend Theo.

The Doctor wasn't one to contest the validity of the facts anymore, however he wished he had that glowing orb which was moving too fast for his own liking captured in a jar. First, it would be a reliable lantern then, one that would move at his own human pace, and then it would give him a chance to examine the creature to his heart's content satisfying his deep curiosity, because that tiny light somehow was defying his conception of Angels if he ever had one as an Atheist.

But he could only admit that his conceptions and assumptions had been thoroughly turned upside down that night courtesy of Wilton-Cough whom he could feel by his side in the very cold air, almost like a freezing breeze, on his right. Vincent addressed the ghost in the darkness,

-How does it feel to be a Spirit, Abraham? Is that light in front of us an Angel attending to you?

Wilton-Cough gave a quick glance at the inquisitive living man by him. He pestered for himself,

-Trust Valdi's mind to ask too many questions when mine is

preoccupied by retrieving my Zach and he should do so too.

Before his Angelic daughter could stop him, Abraham went to invade the Doctor's mind, scolding and warning,

-I haven't got pen and paper to talk respectfully and peacefully to you, Doc. If you want to engage the conversation as we walk to the hotel, it will be a straight invasion of your mind, I am afraid. Let's focus on walking and retrieving my son.

However Vincent felt that this invasion was more mindful of his being than the one he experienced before and proposed,

-Look Abraham, we will fetch your son back. Rest your spirit about it. Now, Zach doesn't respond to my plain talking or anyone for that matter, and yours coming from pen and paper will not be as effective as if you use me and my body over there to impress on him. This might get his attention, and allow you some physicality to do a straight talking he will remember and may react to. What do you say? Stay with me, and talk to me on the way. For fair to say, I had my share of frights tonight and the way to the hotel is long and traitorous. I will not mind you in my mind for one bit.

As Wilton-Cough decided to remain within the offered living body, he told Valdi,

-Doc, you've got yourself a deal. I must say it is a very thoughtful proposition and I thank you for it. Now I never thought of you as a scaredy cat, just as an inquisitive git my entire life. If it can reassure you, I saw you fight those Ghouls earlier and you did really well. Just look at that strong healthy body of yours, I can feel it. When I was in my prime myself, I would look pale, slim and lanky, compared to you. It is all that walking you do and a bit more, for I remember seeing you helping the elderly and the sick with their farms and fields. You are a generous hardworking man, Vincent, but not only that a brave one too and you mustn't fear the darkness surrounding us.

A smile appeared on the Doctor's face despite the coldness

spreading throughout his every limb. He acknowledged,

-I never thought you had a good opinion of me, Mr Wilton-Cough, I am gladly surprised. May be it is just the allowance of co-habiting within me a little while which affects your better judgement for I know I have a fairly high opinion of myself. I can tell you I am no scaredy cat either, in my trade I have seen many a thing yet tonight I did feel fear mainly at your hands, because I am truly sorry to have been unable to save you. I felt so helpless in front of how damaged you were the night of your death. I know I could not stop the inevitable to happen, the only thing left was to make you as comfortable as you could be in your appalling state. Allowing you to share my body to talk to your son is in fact my own way to ask for your forgiveness upon my limitations as a Doctor unable to perform miracles.

Seeing through the eyes of the younger man the dark and narrow path snaking before them steadily up the hill, Abraham soothed,

-You are readily forgiven in my heart, for you were not the bastard who shot me through the guts, you were the one that tried to do his utmost, knowing that saving me was impossible. Whatever you did that night allowed me to keep my life long enough to speak properly to my family the way I should have always have done but never did. No, my opinion of you is not partial to sharing this strong body of yours, I gained it during my lifetime by observing you and it has not changed by my dreadful death whatsoever. I only shook your guts a little earlier on, not by a personal grudge I hold against you, for I have none, but because I needed you to start believing in Ghouls and Ghosts. In my fight against the curse that is hanging above my eldest son's head, I need clever living beings on board. Of my acquaintances, you are one of them. By the way, call me Ab, drop the Mr, for you saw the inside out of my guts enough to be allowed to do so.

Climbing the ragged path with a steadier stride, regaining at every step his usual confidence one, Vincent Valdi confided with slight bitterness,

-Thank you for clearing that one up for me, Abraham. It relieves me that you don't hold that type of grudge against me for your opinion good or bad, somehow, always mattered a great deal to me, despite, well my opinion of you having sank a fair deal in those past months. Tell me about your observations. Can you posit yourself as an excellent judge of characters?

Wilton-Cough gave a desperate look to Abigail who he saw landing on the strong shoulder of the Doctor. He did not like the turn of the conversation, beside he was not one who enjoyed talking a lot, full stop, a bit like his taciturn father Terah, who preferred his woods and hunting to company. However unlike him, Abraham hated sports of all sort and it was his accountancy books which was his favourite company, but not so silent they were, for they talked to him about the life outside of his office and bank, about Mrs Pendleton living far above her means not by vanity, but in the hope that faking having a status would attract a fiancé to at least one of her three daughters. His books told him about Wilton Town and its inhabitants more than they would themselves. It was about petty cash which went down to the nitty gritty. What did they tell him about Vincent Valdi? A lot. He reluctantly started,

-Well, my observations came from my accountancy books at the bank but not solely, for as a staunch lender I didn't mind doing errands to reclaim borrowings. For you, I can say in all honesty that you are a fine fellow. Worryingly in my books, I could see you being as poor as Job, yet you were meeting your repayment deadlines with punctuality. Making your accounts, I realised that after the repayment you had barely anything left to have a decent living. During your dreariest months, I invited you at my dinner table every week at least once under any pretence, something which would boost your ego and not make you feel that I was doing it, in fact, by charity. But I realised very soon that your generosity as a Doctor, accepting sometimes not to be paid at all, was repaid a thousand fold by generosity too. Passing by your door once for a minor ailment, I took a basket full of eggs, bread and a jar of jam, which was at your doorstep to your desk. I read the scrambled note in the basket on the way, which moved me, it said simply: Thank you for saving me from the scarlet fever, from mum and I, Tom Hugh. It happened during one of your hardest month financially as far as I remember, and I started leaving food on your doorstep like everyone from then on, but without a note. I saw you working in fields during my errands, wondering what you were doing there, but it was just the extension of your help to your patients. I witnessed many making their repayments to myself on time because of it. Sometimes I must confess with some annoyance, for I would not have minded seizing a good farm here or there, give or take. But I was not able to do so since you stepped into this town, and you have my entire appreciation for it, for if it was not for your strong indomitable generosity, I might be in Hell right now. In my eyes you are a fine man, but watching Mrs Bates looking at you tonight, I dare say she would call you so herself. She knows her people down to a T. Now, can I posit myself as an excellent judge of characters, who can? Apart maybe Amelia Bates? I am no judge, Vincent, how can I be one? I regret many things I have done far too much.

As he reached the crest of the hill, the Doctor looked down at the dark forest in the valley below they had to cross before reaching on top of the hill opposite them the dominating hotel. He felt a humbleness in Wilton-Cough which he had never grasped during his life. They were having it seems a proper heart to heart, and he was willing to push it to know just exactly how a Spirit felt like beyond his grave. He started with slight emotion,

-The carefully wrapped sausages at my doorstep without a word on it, it was you.

-Someone had to beef you up for your long journeys on foot in the countryside. Beside, I appreciated that you were one of my good customers, which was strict upon yourself rather than telling me you could not repay me. You would not beg for more time or ask to repay lower amounts like others would. You had that stamina which I wished all my customers had.

Vincent starting the descent voiced sternly despite his slight pride at the Banker's words,

-Well a little more charity here and there could not have hurt you for you were a rather brutal and tough lender to your customers, even if they had less stamina than me to carry on proudly their daily poverty and dilemmas. I had many patients who could not sleep at nights fearing repossession, scrutinising the road with the anxiety to see you in your buggy coming to strip them from the little they had left, some who were too sick to work yet slaving over their piece of land, clinging to dear life by only a shoe string. Yes, my heart only told me if I wanted to be able to cure some, I had to help them thoroughly and that did involve working in their fields, making sure they had food on their table and would stay out of trouble with you, Wilton-Cough. Tell me the truth. Are you proud of that now?

The Doctor felt a very heavy sigh coming from deep within his body generated by the Ghost of Abraham who confessed,

-The truth is I had no regrets or almost none until the long painful night that took me away from the living. It pains me to say and admit that I was quite a despicable man. The regrets, the terrible regrets, flowed upon me wave after wave as the realisation of my deeds sank my soul to rock bottom, stripping it from all pride, as I was about to expire. I cannot explain my agony to you, Vincent, but it opened my eyes to much before closing them for eternity. The time even ever so slim you brought to me that night, I will forever be indebted to you. You may not have saved my body but you gave a chance to my soul to make amends before it departed.

As they approached the forest, Wilton-Cough stopped talking to the mind of the Doctor, taking in the sight of the ancient oak trees and elms with majestic branches which almost seemed to scratch the starry night sky. He knew those woods very well, for they did belong to the Wilton family since his ancestor, Noah M Wilton claimed them. He revealed to Valdi, whilst warning him,

-Those woods are haunted. From a child following my father during his hunts I fear them for we saw strange things out there. You crossed them many times to play at that place, Doc, did you encounter anything peculiar? I sold those woods at the first opportunity I had from inheriting them. Whilhelmina White came forward to purchase them with a very handsome sum I would never have expected. I remember her coming to my office at the bank with her proposal which did annihilate any others I had for the very same woods. She meant business from the first foot she put forward in that office. I was not a man who admired beauty in women, apart for the one of my Angie of course, but I liked it when they showed a bit of character. Mrs Pendleton for example, with her big dreams for her daughters, bought my attention to her purse by her steadfast character who would not accept a no for an answer. Instead of giving her more credit, I compromised by giving her a job, a regular income she could rely on. As a receptionist at my bank, her strong organised personality shone through. As for Miss White, I remember the way she stood in my office, wrapped in white arctic fox fur, not taking her hat or gloves off like any other ladies asking for terms would in a polite almost begging manner. She promoted strongly her motives for her hotel, solely, with just a few words: a wood by it would offer the opportunity of a romantic stroll, a good walk or a great hunt, all of which would attract more customers to her hotel. She did offer me the full price for the woods but also a life supply of firewood for my home and bank. We struck the deal. I was thinking then that I had more than I could ever ask for, for that piece of haunted woodland. She knew what she wanted, and I was just too happy to give them away at any price.

Vincent entering the woods told with some confidence,

-I always loved those woods. I see them as a giant natural chemist that gives its medicine for free. Miss White let me used those to my heart's content. Gosh, Abraham, how could you part with your ancestral land so easily? Haunted, humbug, just another local legend. The first Ghost I can acknowledge in here is you within me.

Making the Doctor shake his head negatively, Wilton-Cough replied strongly within his mind,

-Local legend? I was a wee boy when I saw the Crying Doe with my dad. We were not allowed to kill her he said. So I knew I was not dreaming because he saw it just as much as I did. Even more so, he told me that his own father did let her go many times. If my father and my ancestors were fond of hunting, him for sport, them by necessity, I never developed that inclination. First, I lacked the skills despite my father's every effort. Secondly and more importantly, something that may surprise you, I was a sensitive boy who would cry at the death of any animal. Being forced to kill one to just have a little consideration and respect from my own dad made me lose my own self respect. Call it clumsiness or the shaking hands unwilling to fire despite the orders behind me, I missed the clean shot but did hurt the deer. Devastated I threw the gun away in tears, while my father told me to get a grip and went to finish off the animal with his knife. That event made him believe I was no good and a rather useless boy. His keenness to show me his passion, which was hunting, or to make me follow him anywhere disappeared almost instantly for the following day I was sent to boarding school. I already didn't have the attention of my own mother, now I had lost the attention of my father almost overnight. This ancestral piece of land wasn't synonymous with happy memories for me, on the contrary, so as I had no use for it, it made sense to get a large lump sum for it. With money, at least I could do plenty even buying people and force their attention. I didn't need anymore then to be good at some sport, I became an expert in calculation. Somehow money got me the attention of everyone, who would beg to be allowed in my office. During my life I had everyone in town, not a soul missing, stepping in my bank crawling to be in my good books and worth my consideration. So I did get my own back from my neglected childhood. However my distorted vision of things was such that I did fail many times to recognise genuine love as true love. In my mind I could not be loved for myself, but just for my titles, my fortune and all I represented in this town as its richest man. This explains why I was such an overbearing bastard to my Angie and as my Angel is my witness, I regret every single minute I spent with my family and her. If I could go back to the past, I would correct my attitude, maybe from the start when I was asked by my own father to man up and be insensitive. I should have given the gun back to him and tell him straight that it hurts me to see a beautiful creature being killed for the sport of it. I should have listened to my heart then and stood my ground. Maybe my old man Terah would have had more respect for me because of it, rather than me trying to please him and failing miserably, causing so much unnecessary harm to the poor deer. I have regrets sown all over my heart so much so that it is no wonder why my soul can't rest.

Vincent felt fairly emotional at the confession of Wilton-Cough. The narrowing path was leading them into the heart of the forest and he could imagine a little Abraham eager to be loved following the footsteps of Terah the Hunter, a man who had a reputation to be notoriously hard to please, a reputation which irremediably fell like a legacy onto his son's shoulders. He asked into the darkness, conscious that if anyone would see him now, they would think he was mad for talking to himself, or as it was the case to a Spirit,

-Abraham, confession for confession, I did admire your great pride. Somehow a lot of men would have wanted to walk in your shoes. I remember you walking out of my surgery practice one day and the patient waiting there, having looked at you pass by, starting polishing his shoes with spit and sleeve desperately trying to get the shine you had on yours. Although you were born into money, there was an aura about you of self importance which most of us did not have. Words from you inspired respect, despite them being either right or wrong. Men admired you, for you represented to them power and what it was to have it aplenty. Yes, like you, they thought it bought you the beautiful, sweet and charming Angela who gave you two boys. However, my admiration did crumble before your death when I had Amelia Bates in my surgery revealing your infamous night together and its result which I could only confirm. I could not have fallen from my seat higher. I was ready to believe her to be a broad day light liar but she produced the dirty handkerchief, yours, with your initials on, one which I saw many time, when you complained to me about the stench of my patients and you mocked that it was smelling like I would only be paid by you that day. I could not comprehend. How a man like you with a wife like yours could do something like that to your 'just widowed' neighbour, let alone putting her in a well compromising position. At least you admitted it on your death bed, yet I cannot reconcile myself with the matter, can you explain it to me?

A very deep and heavy sigh came from his chest from Wilton-Cough who replied,

-I cannot reconcile myself with it either. I love my Angela more
than I can say. I have been a jealous prick with her day in and out.
Yet, yet, I am the one who did falter, big time, and I do not even
remember any of it. I was so drunk that night and upset. Harry
Bates had been a school mate at boarding school, one that was
always looking out for me, and if I lost any marbles on the
playground, he would retrieve them for me by nightfall with his
fists. If I ever did acquire a friend, a true one, it was him. Maybe the
currency then were my skills in 'Calcul' for I was doing all of his
mathematics homework and I had tried desperately yet vainly to
explain them to him. He was physical whilst I was more intellectual
which made us pair together to go through boarding school
unscathed. I was simply shell shock at the announcement of his
early death, although, him, being a soldier did not raise his life
expectancy a great deal, it rather shortened it totally. By any mean, I
took on board the entire cost of his funeral, of getting his body
back from abroad, of giving him a decent burial. His wake was
meant to be in the town hall which I hired but Angie decided to
invite everyone back at mine. I am not fond of big crowd and
parties so when the mood turned to celebrating a hero, I was crying
for my schoolfriend in the darkness of my kitchen. Amelia stepped
in to refill her glass. She was so upset and so much so on the verge
of collapsing that I offered to walk her back home. She accepted,
and I remember us talking about Harry, his demeanour, his ready
smile, his strength and stamina to see something done. Then I
remember giving her my shoulder to cry on as I was about to leave
her bedroom. Next thing I know, I woke up on top of my bed, fully
clothed, with my dreaded cuckoo clock announcing to me that for
once in my life I was late for work for it was noon. I did notice my
handkerchief missing in my jacket. I had flashbacks of part nudity,
of a woman's legs with boots laced to the top opening, of me
crawling back home holding on the iron gate railing linking our
street houses to just collapse on my own doorstep. What can I say
Vincent? Apart that I was a total mess who did a massive one which
was completely out of character. I am as upset if not much much
more as you are about it. On my death bed, I had a delirious
nightmare tormenting me about everything, I saw their
consequences in the future and... and... I am so, so utterly sorry for

everything.

His voice faltered to become a low sob. Vincent Valdi feeling his chest moving painfully confided to the ghost,

-At your deathbed, I was struck by your courage during those hours of physical pain but also by the admission of your faults. Those did require as much courage as your slow and painful agony. I must admit that you did get back a bit of my consideration then. I cannot pass by your grave to go and see Theo without removing my hat to your memory. Theo and I had been keeping an eye on your family, Angie and the two boys but also the pregnant Amelia. Angela hasn't been eating very well since your death grieved her deeply. Theo took a liking to Josiah who plays the organ in his church like no other. We tried to monitor Zach as much as we could, Aunt Jo, pushing all of us to do so. I, for helping keeping the shame of Amelia secret, started to have deep caring feelings for her. I must say I was fond of her prior to that for her wit, humour and great attitude about life.

This revelation pleased Wilton-Cough who stopped his internal weeping all of a sudden to enquire full of curiosity,

-Are you going to do something about it, Doc? Are they charitable feelings or more? I must say Amelia was the most annoying of my neighbours but I wish her all the best nonetheless. As a customer at my bank I remember her coming with the pay of her husband but also an old black sock with a hole in it at the tip which she had tied with a knot which was full of her parsimonious savings every three month. She would ask me to monitor all those so she would get just a little at a time every week to live with adequate commodity. Mrs Bates never lived beyond her means, she lived well within them, for her sock was full of coins not spent every time. Her main expense was newspapers so she could check remotely on Harry but also to know all there was to know at anytime. Despite our mistake together, I am far for believing she is a bad woman but more that I was the bad man in the whole affair.

Pushing some heavy branches from the path, Vincent stated,

-Yesterday's thunderstorm did some damage, that was a very young oak that fell. That will make nice firewood for Miss White's hotel. My feelings for Mrs Bates are more than charitable, I must admit. Amelia is a very intelligent woman and her curiosity about everything tend to match mine. Each time I met her, I had a proper conversation with her going from A to Z and back to A. By her, time is flying, and half an hour is gone before I even noticed it. I can see myself as an old Doctor, having scoured the country side, exhausted, sitting by a fireplace with a nice cup of tea in my hand, and Amelia by my side, fiddling with her glasses, mending my socks, while telling me what happened in the world while I was away to look after my patients. It might not be anyone's idea of bliss but I do cherish that vision somehow. I can see us together for a very long time so much so that I started to save for a stone to ask for her hand properly. I am just waiting for the appropriate time to come along our paths when I can take her hand and just give her all my love, care and protection. When your little one, your mistake comes along, Amelia and that little baby could do with my working hands helping them day in and out.

Wilton-Cough was jubilating at the news, making the Doctor clap his own hands together,

-That's perfect, that's brilliant! My daughter will have you as an adoptive father. I could not wish for a better man to look after her first steps.

A suspicious Valdi scolded out loud,

-Abraham talking to my mind doesn't need to involve the use of my hands, with that insane clapping of yours, we will definitely have woken up any Ghost if they live in those woods. A girl, for all you know and the way Amelia carries herself, it is more likely to be a boy. Beside, the genetic on your side, the Wilton-Cough's one, has always been prolific in heirs and they have been solely boys for generations.

The Ghost popped out of Vincent Valdi, took the little orb of light from the Doctor's shoulder into his spectral hands carefully and presented,

-Vincent, this time around a Wilton-Cough will not have a boy, for my mistake is a girl. She is going to be a beautiful little girl. Her name is Abigail and her Angelic Spirit is before you.

As he realised that he could talk, despite his voice being slow and chilling, as he saw his cadaverous hands appear along with the rest of his floating body, Abraham continued his revelation to the Doctor. He had no doubts that it was the result of holding the Angel,

-Her Spirit has been the guardian of my Soul and my little companion on this journey to defeat the curse of this town. Meet my Abi, Vince, like you, one day she will be a Doctor, a valuable member of the community, one that saves lives. If you are to be her adoptive father, she will follow your footsteps... It's in your future...

Awestruck Vincent stood still. Not only could he see clearly the Ghost of Abraham, but within the orb of light he was holding, he could make out the silhouette of an individual ever so tiny. He asked with a sudden shyness, full of curiosity and questions.

-May I hold her? How do you know all that Abraham? How do you know for sure?

Wilton-Cough gave an emotional and heavy sigh before replying,

-You may hold my Abigail. I was shown part of the future, the one which I influenced and created by my life and deeds, on my death bed. No one may not know for sure because everyone can change the future by their very acts. However this tiny mistake of mine is to be. Contrary to mine, Abigail will live an inspirational and exemplary life.

Taking the orb with the utmost care Vincent Valdi examined it thoroughly. Not only it felt warm to the touch, it radiated waves after waves of something he could hardly describe, which made him feel good, more than good. From the cold possession of the Ghost, his chilled body was now being embraced by something totally different, extremely warm and kind. His wondering heart was soothed when he was given vision after vision within the ball of light, accompanied by an ethereal voice, who told him,

-Of course you can hold me, for those hands are going to help me enter the world. They will be there when I first stand up to make my first steps. They are the ones holding mine to teach me to write. They are the ones taking me to school and picking me up from it. They are the ones that will applaud at my every diploma. They are the ones leading me to the altar. Your hands will be my guiding friends. I will be a Doctor because you are an inspirational one.

Lost within his emotions, Vincent felt totally humble but also numb. He had seen his future linked to the Spirit, he was holding. His entire belief system shattering once more at his feet, he lifted the orb to nestle it back upon his shoulder before enjoining the Ghost of Wilton-Cough,

-You convinced me, Abraham. I believe that a Wilton-Cough will have a daughter after all and a welcomed change it is. I can tell you what, I can't wait to look after your Abigail. She is going to make me a very proud man, a very proud adoptive father. Come back inside me before anyone sees you or you catch a cold.

Abraham disappeared once more inside the dashing Doctor, thinking that he could not have a better father for his tiny mistake. However he decided to tame the jubilant smile of Vincent back to his habitual smirk. He announced cockily,

-So you've seen a bit of future too. It's powerful isn't it? It did churn my guts up and down just like the bullet did when I knew what would happen. Although I didn't smile after my premonitory nightmare, like you are right now. Maybe it is the difference between a good man and a bad one. Did she show you the brood of adopted children Amelia is going to welcome with open arms? All the tiny mistakes of Wilton Town are going to appear on her doorstep after my one. Father Odell and your brainchild of a plan worked a treat apart for its later implication to the big heart of Amelia who never had children with her Harry and was desperate to have a large family of her own. You can blame it on her blood but her grave will be flowered for it centuries later. I can only admit that her epitaph put mine to shame for she was cherished to her death and beyond.

Stepping into a large clearing where a slight mist was hanging above the tall wet grass, the baffled Doctor admitted,

-I did not see any brood. How many children are we talking about? Are they all adopted? Aren't some my own? I didn't see graves in my future. Does the one of Amelia bear my name?

Before Wilton-Cough could tease Vincent some more, his Angelic daughter replied in a solemn manner,

-The answers to your questions are within your heart. What do you want them to be?

Readjusting his leather hat and cape against the sudden breeze, Valdi thought hard and strong out loud, pouring his heart out by the bucketful,

-After holding so many children during their births and having none to behold against my chest to call my own, I do not mind adopting a brood. If Amelia wants a large family, I would not have the heart to go against it, I will just work harder for it. I fancy myself becoming a father to any child. I reckon and hope I would be a good one. As for Amelia's grave, I have no wish to see it for it will truly upset me if I ever did. But what I do wish is for her name to have changed from Elroy to Valdi passing by Bates and for me to not have let Amelia down in her hour of need.

This truly silenced Abraham, while Abigail seemed to fly away far from them in the depth of the night sky, with her voice surrounding them,

-Let's make sure that your wishes come to pass.

As she disappeared, the Doctor left alone in the now complete darkness, with only Abraham to talk to, went to dig out a small lantern from his satchel. He lit it with the words,

-That's better! You can never rely on spiritual light to never leave you, can you? You must always come prepared for a blackout. Right, we walked through the thickest part of the woods, now there is just that last leg of it climbing up until the hotel.

Wilton-Cough looked around him worryingly, happy that he was inside the strong body of Vincent Valdi in the sudden darkness yet pestered,

-Where did my Angelic daughter go to? She can not leave us like that, in the middle of that bloody forest. Let's move on before I chill your bones too much with my fright. Make small talk so I keep my cool. Bloody Abi! You know she is going to make your wishes come true. You are going to end up with a flock of children before you know it, you damn good fool! Well, if your heart is well hanged... You will have what you asked for.

As the Doctor advanced within the tall wet grass, he asked with anxiety,

-Oh, my! Do you think she went to get all the little children to come to pass?

The Ghost confirmed for him,

-I think she did. Well, keep your heart open and your chest broad enough to hug as many tiny mistakes as you can, for Amelia and you are decidedly going to be their future parents. Can you see what I see in the mist? Look! Stand still for a second, on your left. I think we are being followed by the Crying White Doe.

Gazing sideways, Vincent saw the white almost ephemeral animal. Fragile, it barely touched the grass with its hooves. Silent, it stared at him with huge tender black eyes, which had tears of blood running from them. Valdi stood still in the mist like if he was shot in his heart with an arrow by the vision of the White Doe. He could barely breathe, just watch but he turned to shed the light of his lantern upon her, to only see her vanish in the darkness of the woods. His trembling lips asked humbly to Abraham's Ghost,

-This is the first time I ever saw the Doe. Please, tell me again what does the local legend say about her. I swear I felt sheer pain at the sight of her. Just for a moment, just for a second, my heart seemed to stop beating. I was a prisoner of her sorrow until she disappeared. Abraham, please, tell me more.

-I am afraid I can't tell you a lot, like you I have been fairly practical all my life and never paid too much attention to legends. Especially to some which unsettles me. I can only remember my father recounting that the White Doe has been haunting those woods since the time of the first settlers. He told that she cries rivers of blood every night for her own children ate her heart.

-Children, you mean fawns. As deer are herbivores there is a big impossibility here. If they have done so she would not be alive and walking. I hate the stupidity of legends.

-Well, you saw the Crying White Doe like I did. Try to explain her then with a bit of imagination! I am only repeating what I heard as a kid. My father did say children, I swear. The Doe could very well be the physical manifestation of a Ghost.

Arguing in the darkness with Wilton-Cough, the Doctor was stepping away from the woods as he climbed the hill in large steps. The path became neater and tidier the more they approached the large hotel which stood majestically on top.

Chapter Thirteen

The Crying White Doe Hotel

With all its stained glass windows lit up, with a lively music coming from inside, at first glance 'The Crying White Doe Hotel' appeared more than welcoming. A light breeze made the emblematic panel by the entrance swing with a rusty noise on its hinges. Wilton-Cough pointed to it to the attention of Valdi,

-Look at the emblem for the Hotel, Doc. You haven't got a pretty painted picture of the Crying Doe, no, you have a heart, with two chunks of it missing on either side, with what are very realistic bite marks which you could normally find on an apple. Hey, pretty gruesome for a local legend but you must admit that I paid attention to whatever was told to me as a child. Do I win the argument about the eaten heart of the Doe which is why she is crying blood tears?

The Doctor took a good look at the panel, making it stay put for a fair few seconds. He commented in a whisper,

-The observation skill in that painting is staggering. It is an anatomically very correct and precise depiction of a heart. It is not the one of a doe, deer or stag either. It is a proper human heart. I admit that you raised your intriguing case, Abraham. This would explain on little details that always intrigued me: all the shutters in this hotel have a symbolic heart cut out in them, which is fairly pretty usual so far, but all of them were incomplete and missing a chunk or many. It must be related to the story of that eaten heart. I never paid attention to that panel before, I am afraid, only to the slate by the door.

Hand written neatly, in a somewhat very ancient style of cursives, it stated that the Hotel was full and had no rooms available for the night, but that all were welcome to spend it at the bar and gaming tables. A pretty lantern above it, and a matching one of the other side of the door made the entrance not only well lit but also very welcoming.

Abraham moaned inside Vincent's mind at the sight of the slate,

-How to attract a pretty crowd! Miss White never asked for money, no wonder. She always came to me with a purse full whenever I was selling some of my ancestral lands. How many lads did she pick pocket the money from with her alcohol and gambling tables? Well, it is the last night my boy spends in here.

Trying to make the offended father calm down a little before entering the Hotel, the Doctor scolded out loud before he was about to knock the polished brass ring in the mouth of a brass effigy of a stag's head,

-Now we can hardly call that pick pocketing, especially on weak minded lads, it's a trade, and a winning one.

The door opened as his hand was still mid air and just an inch away from the knocking brass ring. Whilhelmina White stood at the door, dressed in the most elegant fashion, with her thin red lips wearing a condescending smile. She welcomed the night visitor presenting her pale, well manicured hand to hold,

-If it is not Vincent Valdi, let me express my surprise on the time of the night compared to the one of your customary visits. Speaking to yourself on my doorstep, Doctor, are you unwell or mumbling another theory to win at my gambling tables?

A tad unsettled by the door opening without him having to knock, Vincent took his hat off politely in order to try to give himself some sort of countenance. He ventured,

-Please do accept my apologies for my late coming. I had a pretty troubled night so much so that it is fair to say that I have a lot on my mind hence my fairly constant mumbling tonight. I hope I do not disturb nor intrude for my nocturnal arrival was noticed before

I could even knock.

The beautiful woman scrutinised him from head to toe while stating,

-You do look unusually pale, Vincent. Have you been working all day non stop again? I have just the right infusion for you on the stove to make you chill and relax for a while. I was alerted of your venue by seeing one of my deer leap out of the forest.

As he held her hand ever so briefly the Doctor enquired, his interest picked,

-Do you mean the White Doe? For I swear to have seen her in the woods.

The smile of Whilhelmina wickedly widened as she teased,

-You were the last person on Earth, I would have thought would give credentials to Ghost stories, Vincent. It must be your tiredness. Your hands are unusually cold. Did you stay out all night? Your pulse is fairly high. Let me settle your fears at once. Come with me.

She stepped down the white marble steps of the entrance into the courtyard, turned around and enjoined again,

-Follow me. Let me show you something Vincent which will reassure you that you haven't seen a Ghost tonight.

The Doctor followed her determined steps wondering what did she want to show him in the Hotel's well kept garden, pondering about her acute senses. He could swear he didn't leave his hand long enough in her one for her to get a pulse. Wilton-Cough added to his worried mind,

-Watch her closely, Doc, I bet she is one Lady that knows everything there is to know about this town. Query, ask and let's find out together. Make sure you don't try that potion of hers, we want you awake for me to be able to talk to my Zach.

When Whilhelmina turned to face him again she confided in a
concerned voice,

-Vincent, what happened tonight? I swear I never seen you so
affected by something. Your face and demeanour which are usually a
depiction of happy contentment are the opposite right now.

Valdi catching up with her in the neatly gravelled alley, confessed,
trying the respectful friendship he thought he always had with Miss
White,

-Well, the evening was so far very eventful. I simply paid a friendly
visit to Father Odell which turned out very sour...

Whilhelmina boasted straight away, not letting him finish his
sentence, moving her cream feather boa upon her shoulders, with a
beautiful smirk,

-Let me guess, let me guess, Theodore went all religious on you and
you wanted to strangle him just a tad for the sake of your
arguments.

Watching her every move suspiciously, more than he ever did
before, finding that she was a very handsome woman despite her
supposed age was a ghostly Abraham within Vincent. Miss White
was attractive and she knew it. She appeared confident and mature,
with a stunning natural elegance. But the Ghost could only see that
his host Vincent Valdi wasn't affected whatsoever by her beauty for
he knew her very differently. He knew the woman that would cross
a muddy field because it was the season for a particular herb she
was after. He knew the woman that would cease to be self
important to get stuck in helping him giving a hand to a farmer
whose cow had trouble delivering her calf. Valdi had respect for
Whilhelmina, hence he defended her strongly against the claim of
Father Odell, however he also knew that Miss White had a strong
dislike of priests in general, and if it affected Theo in particular,
Vincent was ready to have a word with her. Because for Valdi Theo
wasn't a black robe, he was a good man but most of all his best

friend. Therefore the Doctor corrected Miss White's assumptions,

-I would never wish to strangle 'Theophile' for any of our petty arguments. Despite how dreary he can be sometimes, he is my best friend and I value him more than I can say. When I can not bring hope to someone on a verge of dying, he can. He soothes souls while I am trying to achieve that just for bodies. Earlier on, he was with the little Josiah Wilton-Cough letting him train on his church organ for tomorrow's musical competition. The mother came to pick up her son to take him home. It was well after nine. Both were attacked in the cemetery by grave robbers, a fair few of them, I would say. Theo and I hearing the mayhem intervened. The fight was intense, Whilhelmina, it was not an easy one at all. Whilst Theo was able to bring the little Jo back home, I had to tend to Angela Wilton-Cough in the presbytery. She is in a very bad state, with the most despicable wounds on her shoulder. She will only truly be alright if infection doesn't settle in her injured shoulder. She needs proper monitoring constantly. I have Josephine Cough on board and I came to fetch Zachary to do his part for his family. First tell me, is he messing about at yours as usual so I didn't come all the way for no reason?

Miss White's face turned to an array of expression, but the one that came forward and stayed in her features in the end was of utter compassion and concern. She asked,

-I may be of use for the shoulder's injuries of Mrs Wilton-Cough, yet I would need to see them for myself. I have many unguents which may help against infection. Truly, I am sorry to hear those bad news. Only the other day I saw that sad Widow at the arm of Josephine Cough at the market. She was just skin and bones with a look of absolute sorrow on her face. She was not acknowledging anyone in town who saluted her, like when I did say hello, no, she had only eyes for her own shoes and to not trip on her black dress. Her son Zachary is here alright. Doctor, your trip was not in vain. I think I will only see him disappear from my establishment when he has finally spent his entire part of his inheritance. He is on a winning poker hand at the moment and I only hope that his selfish teenage self will be able to act with sensitivity upon the family emergency you bring to him. If it may help your incentive, I am willing to walk down to town with you two to offer my nursing help to Mrs Wilton-Cough. If Zach proves to be too uncaring to bother going back to his home earlier than dawn, I will close my game room for the night upon him.

A little taken aback by the proposal, Vincent accepted it without listening to all the cautions that Wilton-Cough was presently blasting into his mind by the bucketful. Valdi trusted Miss White as the best nurse in town, while his internal Ghost distrusted her to just even lay a hand on his Angela. He just answered,

-If you could do so, it would be most helpful but also welcomed. I would appreciate if you showed me the unguents for I would probably know which one would be most efficient for her type of wounds. Do you happen to know something about the legend of the Crying White Doe?

Looking at him most inquisitively, while inviting him to follow her through a tunnel made of climbing white roses still in buttons, Miss White replied,

-Of course I do, most probably as much as any locals, but I do not believe it for one bit to be true. However, to tell you the honest truth as a shrewd business woman I play with this myth in order to bring customers to my hotel even if just the random curious traveller. There, let me dispel that myth for you Vincent, we are arriving at the 'folie' in my garden. Pray describe me the type of injury Mrs Wilton-Cough sustained in the attack?

The Doctor saw what appeared to be some mock ruins, beautifully tended, with different kinds of ivy running along the crumbled walls covered by lush moss, and within them three white deer were grazing peacefully the green grass. Whilhelmina had a bright 'I told you so' smile at her red lips before she explained,

-Albino deer. I have also a white stag. I quested far and wide to gather and buy those particular animals. They are rather shy but can be glimpsed in the woods regularly which helps feeding the local legend. They graze the slopes of my garden in the early hours of the morning. Like that it keep the grass short, neat and tidy like a beautiful British lawn, effortlessly and on the long term most economically. Their red eyes captivate the wild imagination of my guests. It makes them look supernatural but those deer are just an investment to increase the value of my property, and most importantly, the prices of the bedrooms.

Approaching the animals, Vincent inspected them but also the ruins. Somehow the tangible explanations of Miss White didn't stack up for him or they did to a certain extent for the deer before him were real and very much so albinos. He could swear on his own mother that what he had seen in the forest was that mystical Doe for she didn't bestow red eyes but black ones. What he had in front of his eyes was just an attempt to convince him otherwise, he had to admit to himself it was a very good attempt. Wilton-Cough was praising in his mind,

-Isn't she clever? Makes money sense to get those when you have a Hotel named 'The Crying White Doe'. It renders it picturesque with a quaint charm. This was a shrewd move.

As if Abraham had spelt out what was wrong with what he was witnessing, the Doctor ventured in the ruins by the remain of a door, while he stated with a cocky smile addressed to Miss White,

-The one I saw was crying. Maybe you should get a veterinarian... Your garden 'folie' looks very real, like the shell of a house.

Whilhelmina suddenly turned upon her heels and engaged herself back in the tunnel of roses, with just a few words for explanation,

-You are probably right on both accounts, Doctor Valdi. Let's get back in, I am starting to feel chilly out here.

However Vincent stayed a little longer looking at the vestige of a fire place. The supposedly shy deer were domesticated enough to come towards him which only confirmed to him that they were not the one he had seen in the woods. Something shining by the blackened stone slab of the ancient fire place caught his attention. He dug out the object from the crevice between the stones. As he started to walk back in order to catch up with Miss White, he considered what was a rather pretty rosary made of ivory beads all carved to represent white roses which finished with a very ornate ivory cross. At the centre of the cross, was what had been shining so strongly at the light of his lantern, which made Abraham ask him widely,

-Put that crucifix closer to your eyes, Doc. If it is what I think it is, you are rich. Yes, this is a diamond, a nicely carved one, in a lovely heart shape. Turn it around. There are letters on the other side. Look T O. Do you think it could have been lost by Father Odell the last time he visited the place?

Vincent whispered,

-I don't think it belongs to Theo. I never saw him with a rosary. This has a very old style to it. This probably would have an antic value. Being in the property of Miss White, it is hers. It is our duty to give it to her.

This provoked an immediate soliloquy from a pestering Wilton-Cough in his mind which made him swear out loud,

-Jeez, stop, just stop for one minute.

Seeing the woman smiling ironically at him at the end of the rose tunnel who demanded,

-Am I walking too fast for your taste, Vincent? I would appreciate if you minded a little your manners at mine. You are not your usual polite self.

He didn't know if it was the blond almost white curls escaping from the bun of Miss White which moved in the breeze like grass snakes, her pearly white teeth or the blood red lips, but for the first time in his life, Vincent felt slightly intimidated by Whilhelmina White at that precise moment. From gut instinct, it dawned on him that

Theo with all his scrupulous exaggeration may have been right in confiding that he had receive warning threat from the woman. The Doctor apologised readily,

-Tiredness, I am talking to myself again, Miss White, it may be due to a virus before I know it but let's hope it is not the case. I am sorry if I did offend. A good glass of rum, while teaching a rough gambling lesson to Zachary will appease my mind altogether. I found that in the ruins of the house in your garden. Is it a trinket of yours?

His presenting hand was met by a receiving one which dropped the rosary on the ground almost straight away. Miss White bit her lips as she put her hands closed together upon her chest in a protective fashion. She shook her head negatively trying to regain a little composure from her unexpected reaction,

-It's not mine. I am sorry, I am shivering. Whatever it is, give it to the church's charity schemes of Father Odell. Let's go inside and share a glass of rum.

Picking up the rosary, the Doctor presented it again this time with the light of his lantern,

-I would not dispatch that little rosary easily without a good look, Whilhelmina, I believe that the stone in it is a diamond. Do you recognise it?

With marked reluctance as if she was shown dirt picked up from the ground, Miss White's vert-de-gris eyes glanced at the crucifix and beads with some curiosity. She would however not touch the item at all, letting Vincent moving the object in his hands for her observation. A wave of sad emotion filled her face as she answered,

-This is no trinket, Vincent. It doesn't belong to me but to one of my very old customers from years ago who has passed away without any children to be spoken of. She loved to sit by that former fireplace in the old ruin of the little cottage which I transformed into a garden 'Folie'. Tristina Ogin was more than a customer, she was a very dear friend who would come to me to share her pain, troubles and sheer sorrow. I tell you what, give this rosary to your friend and tell him to pray for the soul of my friend. Ask Theophile to sell this item and use the proceed to repair the damage in his cemetery done by the grave robbers. Despite not being religious whatsoever myself, it was heartbreaking to see Tristina lose her religion entirely almost overnight. If as you said, your friend can soothe souls, I can only recommend hers to his prayers.

Putting the precious rosary safely in his satchel, then tapping the flap twice, the Doctor assured,

-I will do so. You can count on me to relay this to him. I must apologised for my somewhat mumbling and rambling I can't control tonight. I have so many questions I ask myself sometimes, that at times they burst out in the open. Please would you be so kind to answer some of them? Nothing tedious, it is just about the beliefs in our patch of the wood, well Wilton Town to be exact and its entire district. Being a Doctor, I have heard many folks stories which I dismissed readily, however twenty years on, I consider them now, not as trash to be discarded as stupidities, but as ancient tales worth being recorded like treasures to pass on to new generations within this town and beyond. I have decided to write about those old stories, and I am gathering any versions I can get in my endeavour. I dare say any version is not better than another but all of them are priceless altogether. Can you tell me your version of the Crying White Doe story without me adding a begging pretty please...

As Miss White led the way back to the entrance of her hotel, as she gathered her cream satin skirt together to walk faster, she ventured,

-This new venture of yours impresses me, Vincent. It will make you be the first Anthropologist in Wilton Town. Well, what can I tell you about the Crying Doe. The story starts like this: Once upon a time, a long, long time ago, Noah M Wilton saved a lot of people from bad circumstances. He made them cross oceans, countries and they settled finally in a large forest, the remnant of which you see patchily surrounding Wilton Town. They were a bunch of people who went through a lot, and I mean a lot, together. When they settled here in the luscious green surrounding them, they all thought they did reach a bit of Paradise on Earth, that everything will be alright from then on. But it did not worked out that way. From the first step, they walked into that new land, the sky stopped shading tears. In all that greenery, none of the settlers realised they would be facing a severe drought. They established pretty cottages here and there, the home they always dreamt to build but never could in their former country and Noah with his huge axe and dreams helped them through and through to ensure all had a roof above their heads. But his help failed short almost there, because he could not feed all of them from the forest, despite hunting tirelessly and clearing as much lands to grow crops onto.

Reaching her door, she opened it before inviting,

-Come on in. Follow me. So the crops they had were not suitable for those new lands. Therefore it took time for the settlers to manage to grow something adequately. Well, it took years of relying on hunting to escape the famine which seemed to be settling with them, slowly but surely. As people were watching each other almost dropping dead like flies, something terrible happened out of their desperation. In the midst of the night, when darkness would hide their shame, they would dig up the family members they had buried that very day and start eating them. No one of the inhabitants would admit to such practice but it went as far as planning to kill their own mother in the mind of two children.

The Doctor followed Miss White into a cosy drawing room. Being shown to a comfortable crimson velvet armchair, he sat deeply interested by the tale, commenting,

-It sounds like a realistic historical account so far. I have heard about the foundation of Wilton Town which was less than rosy.

Bringing a kettle from the stove and pouring its nicely scented content into a tea pot, Whilhelmina confirmed,

-You can say that, Vincent. Whatever is denied nowadays, the truth is that the ancestors of many in this town ate their own dead in order to survive. But where the reality of the past and the legend arise is the point where one family took cannibalism a step too far. Mr Ogin was a very pious man but he also had an umbrageous personality and violent temper. He clashed with Noah Wilton and all others so many times for they were disgusted by the way Ogin was treating his wife so much so that Ogin established his cottage far from all others, right at the edge of the town. There he believed that no one would hear the almost constant tears of his battered wife. Proud, during the famine, this farmer tried desperately to grow something, anything, and refused altogether any charity and help, putting in danger his own family by his stubbornness. His two boys were miniature version of him, with the only difference that they were not god fearing whatsoever.

Valdi intervened, while watching his host putting a couple of cups of tea in front of them on a small table,

-I think that difference is not important at all.

Miss White corrected him strongly as she brought a bottle of rum and a couple of tumblers,

-Well you would be wrong, Vincent, for it makes a hell of a lot of difference, especially in this story, for the two boys Ogin were born without any scruples. When their father passed away as much from starvation as exhaustion, their mother brought Noah Wilton to help burying him. At her return, both found her boys feasting on the body of Ogin with piles of clean rib bones at their feet. If Noah condemned strongly what he witnessed, he promised to himself to feed all in Wilton Town from then on. He went far and wide bringing deer, bears, badgers, hares, to everyone especially the two sons of Ogin, Tarquin and Terrence, then age twelve and ten. He did hope that his help would prevent the horrors that he saw in the cottage at the edge of the town on the over side of the forest.

Intrigued by the last mention the Doctor took a sip of rum before asking,

-Could their cottage be possibly the one in your garden Whilhelmina? You mentioned that your friend's surname was Ogin. Was she their descendant? Did Noah succeed in curbing people from eating their dead?

Miss White gave him an enigmatic smile, before sitting in the armchair opposite him, however she replied,

-Far too many questions, my dear Doctor. Yes, I would like to think that the ruin in my garden is the one of their cottage, and to my curious guests, I am saying that it is. Don't you think that it adds a bit of drama and character to the place. As for Noah Wilton unfortunately, he suffered an accident while hunting, his leg was almost entirely gored by a boar. Despite it, he carried on, with an amputated leg, walking on a wooden one, he went back to hunt for his community. After just about a week, he returned to the Ogin cottage with a doe for the family to eat, a white doe. But what he found were the children eating the heart of their mum. The legend says that her heart was still beating in their hands, that the two boys committed the unthinkable, murdering their own mother. Their joint culpability was proven to Noah as they fled into the forest at his sight never to be seen again. A devastated Wilton deposited the white doe to carry back to town the body of the murdered wife of Ogin. It is said that the tearful Noah didn't see that he dropped the doe on the partly eaten, still beating, heart which had been left behind by the murderous children. Since then it has been regularly reported that there was a crying white doe scouring the woods. The White Doe is believed to be inhabited by the desolate spirit of the poor mother, crying blood tears for her lost children, searching for them yet also condemning them for eternity with her entire damaged heart.

Abraham Wilton-Cough jubilated within the mind of Valdi,

-What did I tell you about the eaten heart, Doc! I knew I was right, I am always right. Well may be you could ask her about Ghouls and see how she does react. I did find her rather unusually interested by my Angie's injury. I bet she knows something about the grave robbers in Wilton Town being Ghouls. One thing there is to say for her, is that she sounds too shrewd and smart so far. She didn't answer to all of your questions either. Make her drink a little more to loosen her tongue.

Finishing his glass of rum, and following the dead Banker's advice, the Doctor commented out loud,

-It is a very interesting story. The lines between what could be history, reality and facts are slightly blurred. It could also be linked to another legend that I did encounter many times as I delivered children since twenty odd years in this town, something which I discarded as housewifes's tales. May I help myself to another glass of rum and may I bother you a little longer with those tales. I must say your account of the Crying White Doe legend is the most thorough I ever heard. More rum for you?

Miss White gave him a suspicious glance before fetching her tea pot and serving her infusion to both of them,

-No, not for me, but help yourself, Vincent. As I can still see your hair standing on your wrists, you must still suffer from your slight hypothermia, a little more will do you good. From who did you hear about the Crying White Doe before? I must say I got to know the story a little bit better in order to use it for my business, to make it look like the very bespoke place where it did all happen. Come, you are welcome to bother me with those housewifes's tales of yours, as you and I share the burden of helping the delivery of many children in this town, I bet I would be able to answer you adequately. You should try this infusion, blood oranges, cranberries, cinnamon, put a spoon of honey or two, and you have something that will warm you up right and proper.

Looking at a large portrait above the mantle piece, of a lady with the exact features of Whilhelmina White but in a dress of two centuries ago, the Doctor could have sworn it was the woman before him. He enquired as he poured another glass of rum for himself,

-You probably would be able to, for my twenty years of service in this town do not compare to yours. I will try your infusion for I think I caught a ghost of a cold 'en route' to the hotel. To answer your question, it was the old devil Abraham Wilton-Cough who mentioned the Crying Doe story to me first, as vaguely as you can imagine he would. However he got it from his father who was an inveterate hunter spending his time in the arms of the forest rather than in the ones of his beautiful wife. I did find him a rather credible source. So I have heard about the eaten heart by bad children. I am wondering if this relates to mothers worrying that if their children are born during a full moon, they believe they will turn out bad. Were Tarquin and Terrence born to be bad? I heard of a curse on children, Miss White, in this very town. Were those two cursed from the start, from birth? This is of course if we ever have to believe any legend, local or not.

The poised hostess looked at her guest with an unfathomable look which made Valdi gaze down inside the tumbler and focus on the golden robe of the rum swirling in it instead. She poured herself a glass of rum slowly and silently, then told sternly,

-Vincent, I believe that you have seen something tonight which makes you buy into all those old folks tales, and your inquisitive mind is trying desperately to search for an answer and a little truth in the matter. I can oblige you within my own limits. I am your elder and indeed I have seen and heard more than you. The two Ogin children were not born in Wilton Town nor during a full moon. They grew accustomed to the violence perpetrated in front of their eyes by their father against their mother. For them truth was dad and dad was always right and whichever interpretation he had from his religious books. We are speaking of a time of course when no schools were in place in this town to educate its children. They were not cursed from the start, no, they were cursed when they committed their crime, by the very heart of the mother they killed. She believed in hope until she set foot in Wilton Town, and saw the famine unfold. She thought that her children were perverted by the inhabitants who dug up their dead to eat them. She cursed before her own death the survivors of the famine and their children that none should rest in peace.

Slightly unnerved the Doctor drank his entire glass in one go while he could hear Wilton-Cough pestering madly in his mind repetitively,

-I told you she knew something, I told you. She speaks as if she was there. Look at her portrait. It's her, make no mistake, it's her. That painting is genuine, I can tell you from close as well as afar, but get me closer to have a proper look at the paintbrush work. Remember as I was very astute when I came to pick up the goods in properties to recover my loans by force, I can tell a fake from a genuine piece. I knew my antiquities and that portrait is definitely two hundred years old. Where do you think she gets her medical knowledge from? Maybe she has been there all along. There's something with her that, that, is just wrong. She is as beautiful as I first met her and saw her, ages ago. She should be in her grave by now and she isn't.

Shifting uncomfortably on his armchair, Vincent decided to take his cup of tea in order to walk towards the painting. By it, he aimed to regain some countenance which rising fear was making him lose slowly. As he stood below the portrait, he demanded,

-One woman cannot curse an entire town. She must have just vented her own despair at her situation, just spelling out her own grief and anger. Seeing your dead husband being scavenged upon by your own children before you have time to fetch someone to bury him decently must have been a total shock for her. This must have prompted the curse before her own death but how did she go about it? If she knew something, couldn't she prevent it from happening, like moving her entire family in the vicinity of the town where the entire inhabitants could monitor her beastly behavioured children? Living on the edge of society is living on the edge...

Whilhelmina sipped her tea quietly observing his every move before she answered after a fair few minutes correcting the Doctor,

-One woman can curse an entire town. Her words were not lost in the wind nor her true sorrow. Her entire plight was answered too late, maybe by minutes, I dread by only seconds, by the good Noah who had appointed himself the saviour of everyone. Yet, fate reminded him that he was only too human and could not carry the burden of everyone on his generously strong shoulders. He failed that lone mother and some said her entire family and as a result the town that he built was cursed. I do not defend this mother's choices, but she may have stayed on the edge of the town because she knew what was happening in town during the night when the inhabitants were feasting on their dead while poor Noah, having passed laws against the practice but not able to applicate them on the ground, spent his nights in the woods hunting to feed his people. One can understand her for remaining at the edge of the town. I dare say I live on the edge of it myself and that should not constitute a reason to condemn me.

Letting the Ghost within him consider the portrait at leisure, Valdi replied firmly,

-I dare say who spoke of condemning you or condemnation here? In the highlight of what you mentioned in the story, if the Ogin family stayed in town, the barbaric practice of that father battering his wife would have kept being opposed to and argued upon by Noah Wilton and the others. Their majority would have prevailed in the mind of the youngsters that violence was far from being the law, and that their father and attitude was far from being right. Moving his family to the edge of the town allowed the father to perpetrate his own rules in his home with devastating consequences. Civilised rules, although they were only starting in Wilton Town, would have kept that family in check. Condemning the entire town for letting two violent despots growing up without their peers by your tyrant of a husband in your own household, I dare say that is a bit of a mis-justice. What did she do in her grief, Miss White? What type of curse did she think would put to right what happened to her? Have you ever seen a Ghoul, Whilhelmina? For I have seen many tonight, enough to cross me deep down for a long while. I need to bring Zach home. Let me teach him a lesson at the card table that he will remember. By the way, this infusion is truly invigorating. I will never condemn goodness nor kindness but always wrongdoings. In the balance, have I been alright all my life to put you in my heart among the good people that this town count?

Whilhelmina White stood up and went to refill the cup in the hand of the Doctor. Staying by him, she considered her portrait before offering him a smile full of apologies,

-So my inner suspicions were right, you are a man who had his fair share of fright for the night. I am sorry for you to have encountered creatures that only belong to the darkness. You are one individual I hoped the curse of Wilton Town would not affect in any way.

Somehow feeling the boiling wrath of Wilton-Cough rising within him, not knowing if he would be able to contain it, Vincent Valdi was fairly emboldened to demand for answers more strongly, he exulted,

-Fair share of fright for life, Whilhelmina, not just the night! The creatures you are talking about do not belong whatsoever to the darkness, they are the condemned children of Wilton Town. What did Tristina Ogin do to them? You can be sorry for me for I will not sleep until everything is put to right, until that curse is gone, until all in this town can rest in peace. That woman did not deserve her plight but none of those children did either! Think of the distress I have seen tonight, the injuries done to a sweet individual who has nothing to do with those grudges of the past. Think of all the souls not resting in peace, if the White Doe is crying, I can assure you that she is not alone. I expect to be a father one day, Miss White, in this very town and I will make sure no children are cursed, not mine nor anyone else's. You are a mother, look at your daughter standing behind that curtain in that painting, hiding in the shadows, when will you let her rest in peace? Where is she tonight? Why is this child a recluse in your magnificent home? Very accurate portrait, you face the light in all its beauty while your child dwells in the darkness, cursed like all the others in this town. Miss White, help me, answer my questions, for if you are sorry for me, I am sorry for you and all the others. How long have you been alive? 1615 is the date under the signature of the artist but you are much older than that, are you?

Throwing his cup of tea within the fire, he seized one hand of

Whilhelmina before she could step away from him. Turning it around, he forcefully opened the fingers to reveal her palm at the light of the flames. There, he saw the burnt mark of the crucifix of the rosary fairly embedded within her pale skin. The hand within his trembled. The vert de gris eyes transfixed upon him seemed to lose all confidence. Her stunned silence met the charitable answer of the Doctor who closed back all of her fingers to hide her mark,

-I have cauterised so many times that you can never hide the smell of burning flesh from me as it happened. I am sorry for this incident outside. It was far from being intended. So my suspicions were right, you are a woman with a profound knowledge because you lived for quite an eternity. You are one individual I hope could help breaking the curse upon Wilton Town. In those twenty years I known you, I grew a respect for you, and I will not start treating you as a creature of darkness now, keep my respect and help me on the mission to rectify the situation that afflicts so many. If Tristina was your friend we need to put her soul to rest and we can do so together with my own friend, Theo.

Throwing her tea pot within the fire, Whilhelmina reclaimed her hand, wrapped her shoulders tightly within her cream feather boa, before announcing,

-I will help you, Vincent, I am game. You will not hurt me for what I am?

Winking at her, the Doctor presented his hand to shake,

-Good. You are enlisted on our mission. As long as you are not hurting my human throat and respect my life, I will not dispatch you in a little pile of ashes and respect your eternal one.

Bursting in imprecations in his mind Wilton-Cough warned him, as Miss White took the offer with a rather subdued demeanour and shook the presented hand,

-Heaven's forbid! You are shaking the hand with a vampire! What are you doing, Doc? Think! How did she survive for so long?

Valdi, who had guessed that much so far and more, ignored his internal ghostly guest to focus on his hostess who asked rather shyly,

-What can I do? Where do we start?

He answered with great certainty,

-Why do you think I am questing for Zachary Wilton-Cough tonight? He is one of the cursed children of this town. Show me to him. I need to talk to that teenager, and pray, do not intervene at any point. You will understand with what loom above his head that it is only for his own good, not only that, the good of many in the future.

Miss White gave him a polite bow before leaving the room, worried to have let the intelligent Vincent Valdi in her establishment for the night, yet her heart feeling at his service. How many humans had guessed what she was before? None. During twenty years she had watched him tirelessly helping everyone with a generosity which compelled her to share with him what she knew about medicinal herbs and plants. His selflessness reminded her of the one of Noah M Wilton begging her to amputate his gored leg so he could walk again and carry on helping. She led the way to her gaming tables thinking that one more human had spoken right through her own sorrowful heart.

Left alone for a minute or so within the drawing room, Vincent Valdi pestered back to the Ghost of Abraham,

-Trust me a little, would you? I am the one who is going to look after your daughter for Christ's sake! I know what I am doing. By enlisting Miss White I may have brought in the strongest person to help us getting rid of the curse. Let's talk to your son and let me deal with Whilhelmina. She has a pulse, hence a heart which is still beating. She has not turned properly, she is a human stuck in limbo, for eternity.

Chapter Fourteen

A Game of Consideration

Miss White showed the Doctor into a large and lively room. If he was used to the place, however the ghostly Abraham wasn't as he moaned,

-This is where respectable goes out of the window. She is running a saloon. I tell you what I would not be surprised if her bedrooms are used to do funny business too.

Valdi ignored him totally as he followed his hostess to the bar to see her order,

-Georgia, the usual for Mr Vincent, on the house, and a Sangria for me. Any trouble tonight?

Cleaning energetically the glasses with a white cloth, the corpulent woman behind the counter replied,

-You've got it, Miss. The old town milkman has lost everything on the poker table tonight. He looks so devastated that I fear that if we let him go into the night, he will do the nasty one on himself. So I made him sit in the corner by the musicians whose noise covers the sound of his sobs. I also offered him a bottle of strong whisky, I will pay for it with my wages, in the hope that he will finally collapse and sleep everything off safely on our couches. Apart from him, everything is in order. Doctor Valdi, I dare say, this is not your usual hour. I know there is a Spring breeze outside, but you look more dishevelled than normal.

Vincent took the tumbler of rum presented to him and put a silver coin on the counter. He winked at the barmaid, with a bright smile,

-I thought I would adopt that hairdo for you, Georgia, to look just dashingly Sicilian like my ancestors and to see you blush just once in my entire life. This is for old Scott Snow's whiskey bottle and to get him another one if needs be. Keep an eye on him for me and keep him here. I will fetch him tomorrow morning and have a good talk with him. I know he is out of work but I also know how to find him one quickly. Father Odell needs help with the up-keep of his cemetery. I am pretty sure he will be very generous to the person who will present himself for the task. If the poor lad has lost his home, the presbytery will be his welcoming new one. Who was heartless enough to do that to old Scott? Keep an eagle eye on him for me, Georgia, and I will deal with him for you. How is my boy doing in there?

Doing the sangria of Miss White pouring a liquid with the colour of blood rather than the robe of wine from a dark bottle without any label, Georgia Marlow confided,

-Well, your boy was the heartless one, Mr Vincent. I know you showed him the trick to not lose so easily, but Zach has been on a winning hand all night. One traveller left the gambling table and hotel penniless without a word to say. We still have two regulars in there, the hard core ones, but they are desperately losing, and give or take a few minutes or an hour and I doubt we will see them again. The lad has never been the brightest one around, but whatever you showed him about mathematics and probability maybe have sinked in once and for all. It is that or he inherited his father's calculating skills. But I can assure you that tonight that young Wilton-Cough is scaring many wallets in town not unlike old Abraham used to do.

Whilhelmina White, taking her glass of sangria, told her barmaid,

-Give Mr Vincent back his coin, I am taking the tab for Scott Snow for tonight. They have trouble in town with grave robbers. They attacked Mrs Wilton-Cough. Father Odell and Mr Vincent fought them off although Angela has been injured. The fight explains the un-kept state of our Doctor more than the breeze, Georgia. He came to bring Zach back to his mum. Although first aid was already applied to Angela by Vincent, I will go to town with them to check on her. I am going to leave you in charge of the hotel while I am away. Keep Mr Snow in. When everyone has left at dawn, bring him a pillow and a cover to make him more comfortable. See that Mina goes to bed on time, leave the shutters open in that effect if you have to. Doc, follow me, lets make sure that boy of yours doesn't scare all my customers away. How dare you teaching him your mathematical gambling skills, he is a Wilton-Cough, you know? I am running a business here. I rely on people coming back.

Following her, Vincent gave a quick glance to Snow who was hiding his face within his large hands then the twelve year old Mina, as pale as her mother if not more, standing by him playing with a joyous energy the fiddle. The young girl had a wild untamed look about her, despite the lovely red velvet gown she was wearing. Her jet black hair flowed freely upon her hips at each moves of her sharp bow. Her vert de gris eyes met his for a fair second when he could have sworn that they were the exact copy of Whilhelmina's. He listened to Wilton-Cough expressing himself,

-Old Snow has never been good with his finances. However we are not going to leave that man penniless, Doc, we will give him back his meagre fortune. We will teach a tough lesson to my son. If you know a good hand at cards, I know a very mean one. Together we will teach a rough one to Zachary, we will fleece him right and proper. That boy is losing his inheritance tonight. It is time for him to learn how to earn money the proper way, working for it. I trust you to employ him and make him work for you, any way you want to, hard or not, to make him learn how to earn his keep. Pay him, week by week with small amounts of the inheritance we will have taken from him tonight. With me being able to check everyone's cards at anytime by popping in and out of you, I dare say Doc, that you will have the winning game of your lifetime.

Vincent Valdi, with a very wicked smile on his face, entered the saloon's doors into a snug little room where three gambling tables were. His confidence was sky high. Only one table had three players left. Zachary didn't bother to acknowledge him while the other two nodded respectfully. As he took a chair, he announced himself,

-Gentlemen, I am here to salvage the fortune of Mr Snow.

To which Zach Wilton-Cough commented sharply,

-You can't, Doc, he hasn't got any to salvage.

Abraham jubilated as he warned Valdi's mind,

-Game on, Doc, let's teach my boy a lesson he will remember! I will do the talking using all the intonation of your own voice, if needs be I will use my spectral one through yours. Just focus on the cards, Vincent, make us win the jackpot, the entire inheritance I left him. Zach will learn some manners. We will make him enter the school of life together.

Not flinching for one second, like if he was striping Zachary Wilton-Cough's soul bare, the Doctor's blue eyes had a glow of confident joy when they looked into the ones of the teenager. With a potent Ghost within him, he was ready to teach the insolent Zachary a lesson or two as well. He couldn't hide his rising smirk as Abraham replied to his son using his voice to pitch perfect,

-Fortune does not lay in the money you bestow but in the friends you have, Zachary. Mr Snow happens to have the good fortune to be very much loved in Wilton Town. Let me tell you that he earned that love by his hard work as a milkman, waking up before everyone to deliver the milk your own mother gave you at breakfast. If you think you can milk the milkman just like that without anyone reacting to it, you are making a bit fat mistake for I will cream out of you every single cent you took from him. Gentlemen, if you want to join me, you are welcome, this is my stake for Mr Snow.

Putting the entire content of his leather purse in a somewhat grand gesture on the table impressed enough the two other men, for one to put the gold pin of his cravat on the table within the coins and for the other to add a couple of silver coins to it. His stance met their approval, as they were sincerely hoping that the luck of the damn boy would turn from then on.

Miss White added to the pile the rank of pearl at her neck in a graceful move before going to sit on a Louis the fifteen chair by the fire place, with for only encouragement,

-Pray, Gentlemen, save the night, save Snow.

As she spread an elegant fan in one hand and started sipping her sangria with a very amused smile upon her face, Zachary took offence,

-Miss White, you can not prefer one player against all others. It is not fair. Beside it is not my fault if Mr Snow was totally appalling tonight.

Whilhelmina teased fluttering her eyelashes shamelessly,

-My dear Darling Zach, I love all my players equally and if one can't play anymore at my tables, I simply call out: where was the fair play? We all know you learnt a clever technique from Mr Valdi so he is here to teach you how to use it with a little more fairness. Think about it, if you are my only customer, where is my business? Of course I want everyone to have a fair few cents to spend in here. Can you consider now to give his livelihood back to Mr Snow and be fair yourself?

While the deceased banker commented to Vincent's mind,

-Miss White is growing on me. However I don't think she could pull the stunt I did when I presented my guts to the bullet aimed to my customers to save my livelihood... She seems a little more clever than I was. Look at her pearls, all the genuine article, you'd better not lose them in this game for that shows her trust for you and your so called technique. I wonder how fair she will be if she sees them lost. Do you want to try her friendship a little? I can get everything back for I know a mean game, and if you appear to lose a little my boy will show how bad his soul is at. I will know then what work we need to do upon him to make sure he is not as despicable as I was.

Valdi wrote a yes with his finger on the table to the attention of

Abraham, while everyone paid attention to Zachary's reply,

-Of course not! The old fool lost and that is all there is to consider.

Taking the cigar out of the youngster's lips to extinguish it in front
of him, the possessed Valdi corrected,

-What is to consider is that the old fool is back with a fair amount
to gamble and has not lost yet. Lesson in consideration, I hate
smoking and will not tolerate it at my gambling table, beside it is not
good for your lungs and at the end of this game you will not be
able to pay for my services when your cough chokes you to near
death.

The eighteen year old, putting his cards down in a very annoyed
gesture, took another cigar from the pocket of his smart jacket,
flashing that he had about three or four in there and was about to
light it, as he replied aggressively,

-You are not my father, Valdi. How dare you teach me lessons!

Before he knew it the tall Vincent was by him, took all his cigars at
once and threw them in the fire in a manner which left Zachary
stunned yet standing for a confrontation. The youngster could not
recognise the kind family Doctor he had always known. When Valdi
turned back to him with a sternly threatening voice, he bit his lower
lip to not reply and to just listen, the way he did, when his father
was angry and very much alive,

-How dare you, taking lessons from me only when they are
convenient to you, young man! Sit down, the lesson has only started
and the subject is called sensitivity. And if you don't like it and if
you decide to show none to the good people of Wilton Town, I can
change the title for you. I will call it insensitivity with my fists, and
drag you back home to your dear mother black and blue. Let me tell
you that you will feel very sorry for having been responsible for Mr
Snow's ruin.

Zachary obeyed straight away, feeling at a disadvantage, for not having his friends by him, because he had won all the pocket money they could play with that night. However he was promising himself that he would pay them a fair amount to give a good fists lesson to that daring Doctor. His mind relished in the idea of seeing Valdi battered to a pulp in an alleyway of Wilton Town for who was he to talk to him that way. As he saw the Doctor resuming his position opposite him on the table, Zach barked, pointing to the burning cigars within the fire place,

-You will pay for those dearly, Doc. They cost a fair amount of money, you know. I don't get the cheap stuff.

Unphased Vincent replied, as Miss White distributed a new hand to everyone, fanning herself wildly, while winking at her two most regular customers,

-If you draw a habit of them, you will pay for those dearly too, Zach. They will cost you your life. You know the little precious thing everyone likes clinging onto regardless of who you are. Life is not cheap my dear boy, it is costly, and you seemed to have the wrong type of currency set in your heart. I think a lesson of humility as well as sensitivity will not go amiss here, don't you? I will strip you so bare of everything, then I will make your working sweat earn your every cent, that you will finally feel something for a poor sod like Scott Snow.

Looking at their new hands the two other players understood that something beyond them was going on at the gambling table and took the hint of Whilhelmina with her fan going flat and close in mid air that they should let it happen and not intervene whatsoever. Beside it, they were enjoying the interaction for Zachary Wilton-Cough had been an insufferable young man in town since the death of his father. It was probably about time for the kind indulgence of everyone about him grieving to draw to a close. They were only too happy to see the respectable Doctor Valdi doing the overdue task in front of their eyes. They had no doubts that his intervention would work like his every remedy, that it will apply wonders to the overbearing Wilton-Cough boy which was bothering them so much since a few months.

Zachary did not feel one inch of sympathy in the entire room for being so staunchly scolded in front of everyone by Vincent Valdi. He resented it greatly but as he picked up his cards, he found a matter to smile again. He challenged right away,

-Let's see what you can come up with for the old fool you are so protective of, Doc. But let me tell you one thing that is clear from the onset, the richest man in town will always be a Wilton-Cough. Aren't you called Valdi? You have the wrong surname about you. Your ancestors did not create this town.

Picking up his cards, Vincent considered them carefully while the ghost of Abraham went to have a good glance of all the cards in hands around the table. He came back to Valdi with a thorough mind feedback,

-My boy has a very good hand compared to yours but all is not lost. Mr Sutton has enough to make everything hold to an happy outcome. Carry on the staunch demeanour throughout. Stay stern and do not give him an inch of sympathy, Doc, my son's soul is at stake. I can tell that he has been listening so far, for his lower lip has a slight bleeding dent. We are on the right track. Let's reply to his proud little arse. Your first card has to be the Ace of Diamonds. You will think you are losing but will recover ever so fast from that move. Your ancestors may not have created that town Vincent, but you are contributing so much to it, that I wish I could call you my son, you would have made me the proudest father on earth.

Somehow this stirred Vincent Valdi to feel extremely good and proud. He barely remembered his own parents, for they passed away like Wilton-Cough killed by bullets, on a coach attempting to pass the Alps during the Napoleonic wars. He was only a toddler then, and the soldiers decided to spare his life or their bullets. Whichever it was didn't matter, orphaned, he only bestowed a mother figure in his aunt who went to quest for him. The Sicilian village school teacher that his aunt was, never married. His lack of father figure made him wonder if it was that which made him appreciate so much any validation or advices from Abraham

Wilton-Cough. Since he arrived in Wilton Town aged twenty, he considered the Bank director as the most respected guide he could ever have about life in town. He pushed his thoughts away to concentrate on the game and his cards as Abraham used his voice again to give a sharp answer to his own son,

-It is all very well to have a lineage, but the pedigree doesn't always make the dog. The puppy I see in front of me is an aimless scoundrel who could not build his own town even if he tried his hardest. What is your aim in life, young man, if you even have one? Come on, impress me: expert gambler? Smoking expensive cigars? Sleeping during the day? Showing off your money to hide that you have no skills at all and that you are certainly not the cleverest one around? Your own father built the first bank of this town. He aimed to provide money for people to start up on their own dreams, whatever they were, a milk business, a surgery practice, a farm, a factory. Even your own brother Josiah shows dreams and ambition, participating in a music competition tomorrow. We believe in his talents and Wilton Town has a budding performing musician in him that we will all be proud of. But you, Zachary, what can you bring to the name of Wilton-Cough? Grief? I tell you what if your father was sitting in my place, he would be less than happy, less than proud to see you here and as angry as I am now to see you breaking the promises you made on his death bed. If a hand on your heart is just a gesture for you without any further meaning, or true intentions, he would disown you right here, right now, for you haven't got the faintest idea of what it is to be a true Wilton-Cough.

Feeling that he had a strong hand, the boy tried his hardest to not be affected by the earful he was receiving. However he was very self conscious that he had left school too early but that he also had absolutely no clues at all of what to do next. Having no particular talent which made him stand out from the crowd, like his younger brother which he could not deny was a born artist, he relied on his father's inheritance to get through. Valdi was indeed making him be as uncomfortable as one could be, beside referring to his own father made his stance hurt. If he was a nail, he thought, he would have been hit right on the head. Zachary played while arguing,

-What is stinging you tonight, Doc? I swear I never saw you so cross in my entire life. You'd better come up with some good cards for I will show no mercy to you if I win. That ace will get you nowhere with me tonight. You know, you know, I am only so young, so what?

As Mr Sutton laid his card, he looked in the direction of Valdi, still very impressed by the way he was talking to the young lad, eager to listen to the conversation yet feeling emboldened enough to have a say,

-So what, being young is not an excuse. It never has been, Zach. When my dad passed away, I was only fourteen but it didn't stop me to start running my father's business for the sake of my mother and younger siblings. I remember your father teaching me how to keep on top of things and how to balance my books to keep him off my back. Your father, Abraham, believed in hard work, not easy money coming from the sky. What are you going to do after spending your part of inheritance? What the Doctor said is not coming too early neither too late because you truly need to think about it.

The teenager gave him a heated look while he barked,

-Well keep minding your own business, Sutton, for I still have the winning hand in here.

Abraham Wilton-Cough was so cross within Vincent at that moment about his son that he could have gone all poltergeist about the room but he did not have to do so for the fan of Miss White hit the back of Zachary's head, a gesture which came along with her strong scolding,

-Mind your manners in my hotel, young Wilton-Cough for I do decide who can come here or not. Mr Sutton made a very valid point to you and does not deserve such an answer for it. Everyone in this room contributed to the town with their time, effort, hard work and businesses more than you can ever say for your own self. We can speak of our own deeds and not boast about our whatever remote great grandfather's ones as if they can make us own the town. The winning hands around this table are ours, not yours, for we are all hardworking at building our own luck, much more than you can say for your own self right now. What do you want to do with your own self apart ruining my customers, pray? What would you get from it?

It was the possessed Doctor that replied to her questions, as Abraham's ghost was only too happy to have everyone involved in the gaming room. Despite that it highlighted to him that his eldest son had been a pain to them all to a certain extent. He would not return to his grave until his problematic son's case was resolved. He started quite sternly,

-Let me tell you Miss White: the boy will get the short term joy of having influenced the life of someone. The more he does, the more he will feel triumphant that he is someone. But undoing someone, bringing their ruin about doesn't hide the simple fact that he is no one, not at this moment anyhow. He has nothing to bring to the table but cards. He has nothing to bring to this town but the ruin of the people he has contempt for. His contribution to this town so far is not even nil, it is negative. What does he get from ruining a man that worked very hard his entire life, the momentary feeling that he is someone? Come on? Look at him, nails dirty for not even washing himself, too busy to go in and out of bed to go gambling his inheritance! A bed bug dweller! Look at you, Mr Sutton, at least your hands are still dirty from the earth you sowed your seeds in which will become the flowers on every window sill in town. You have a useful growing successful business. As for you, Mr Brand, our town barber, you still have the bandage on those fingers I put this morning, for you slipped shaving young Tom Hugh. You preferred cutting yourself than that young man's cheek who was getting ready for his first job interview, Tom who is someone in this town, who aged sixteen, applied to work as a clerk for the best lawyers office in town. His aims are resumed to looking after his mum, pay for his law studies and become a lawyer. This is a fine example of a young man doing something about himself. So to answer your question, Zachary, what is stinging me tonight, is you. You, purely and simply, but I will tell you more, I am angry at your stupid arrogance. If only you had something to show for it, we can bear a fool or two in this town, but what have you got? Nothing for yourself that inheritance didn't give you. I am still waiting for you to answer my questions, my dear boy. I will break it down into easy chunks for you: What are your aims and dreams?

Zachary felt put upon the spot. All eyes were turned to him, scrutinising his every move and all he could do was biting his bottom lip fairly hard. He wished he was in his bed under a pile of covers to hide himself from everyone but he was here, at the 'Crying White Doe Hotel' shifting uncomfortably upon his chair, with a mind that could not find any answer to give. He tried to hide his total discomfort by playing what was good move which made every players put some money from their stash into his. But despite that, he could not smile nor think. His profound silence made the Doctor repeat his torturing questions,

-What are your aims and dreams, young man? We are waiting for your answers. Do you think we don't deserve them? Do you think that we are only good enough to take money from, and be abused by your disrespectful manners?

His proud shoulders slouching, his lips shivering uncontrollably, Zach gave a desperate look to his torturer. For a split second he could have sworn that he could see his father in front of him. It didn't know if it was the demeanour of Vincent Valdi or his staunch stance or his every word, but it reminded him of his late father. He could only start to imagine if he had his real father at the table. He could only acknowledge that he would be in deep trouble right now. He could not shake his vision off and apologised all of a sudden,

-I am sorry. I am sorry, Doctor, to appear so rude to you all. I don't think of you like the last bit you said. I, I...

His voice failed him. He was struggling to think again and put his own words together in a coherent sentence. Zach felt so hopeless at that moment that his hand reached for the glass of alcohol next to him, just to give him a bit of an air, or just a bit of confidence back. But the strong hand of Vincent Valdi stopped him and made him put the glass tumbler down. The unusually cold fingers of the Doctor kept his hand within his as he told him in a concerned fashion,

-My boy, your lip is bleeding and if you drink this it will sting you right and proper. Miss White, would you mind bringing us a glass of water? So at long last we had a bit of an answer from you but not the important one. Do you want to think about it?

Whilhelmina left the room. The cold friendly fingers left Zach's hand and the teenager felt a warm feeling inside him, one that made him believe he could express himself openly. Mr Sutton by him handed his handkerchief in a kind gesture,

-Just wipe and keep some pressure on your cut for a minute or two.

Accepting the folded handkerchief with a nod, Zachary's eyes went to find the ones of the Doctor before confiding,

-It's not that I don't want to think about it Mr Valdi, nor that I can't think about it either. It's, it's that I truly do not have any answers because, because, I honestly do not know what I want to do.

The glass of water was silently deposited by his side but the teenager acknowledged,

-Thank you Miss White, it is much appreciated. I have a bad habit of biting my lips. I thought I grew out of it but obviously I haven't.

Vincent played a strong hand with a very winning smile, which made him get a very fair amount from everyone. He commented,

-That would be your first lost of the night Zachary but not the last. So we have finally a little truth and honesty from you. It is a start. Now, not knowing what to do is one thing that can be resolved by knowing what your dreams are, but also what do you like to do, what you are good at and so on. Please do not reply by professional gambler otherwise I will demand from Miss White to officially ban you from this place.

Disappointed by his loss, Zach felt annoyed by the comments to which he objected,

-You have no such authority, Doc!

But a smiling Miss White posited,

-Yes, he has. Being a respected Doctor for twenty years, I will always consider Mr Valdi's advice but also act upon them. Just reassure us on your gambling habit a little for I am seeing you without fail every night here.

The teenager frowned at her statement,

-Who cares if I am here or not?

The Doctor replied strongly,

-Your dear mother for a start and everyone who knows you. Not knowing what to do is one thing and wasting your time totally is another, like sitting here, dressed up like a peacock with a vile attitude towards anyone. Come, give us a smart move. I am winning here. So what happened to school? You could have stayed there a little longer to learn a skill or two. It would have given you the opportunity to have a bit more time to reflect on what you truly want to do with your life.

This made Zachary frowned further his eyebrows and drink a little water before he confessed,

-I was no good at it. I kept on with school to please my Pa. But, I have difficulties memorising things and before I knew it I was far behind everyone else and awfully scared to sound stupid so I dropped it all. This may not have been my smartest move because I do not think I am ready like the others, like the Tom Hugh and so on to tackle the big world. When I had my father, he was so full of direction that I just knew what I had to do. I didn't have to think of what I wanted to do.

Vincent Valdi was impressed by how much more Abraham Wilton-Cough had managed to get out from his eldest son in the space of a few minutes, while all had failed to get through to the eighteen year old since a long while. Zachary was finally talking to them. Whatever the young man confided to them only told the tale of an individual fairly lost probably since the death of his father. The Ghost used a more considerate tone as he acknowledged,

-Welcome to the school of life, my son. Now, you have to think for yourself. It may be hard, it may be difficult, but you cannot delay from it any longer. You have been wearing the patience of all of us for far too long. Hiding your insecurities by giving yourself an attitude, or a grand air is not the clever thing to do. However what would be a good thing to do is to sit down and talk openly with someone. I for example, am more than willing to listen to you. I may offer you advice and then it is up to you to follow them or not but it will engage a proper conversation, an ongoing one, which will allow you to think in a more positive way about your current situation. A smart move could be to talk to your teacher and ask him to teach you individually in the evening and pick up where you left your curriculum. Just admit your understanding difficulties and memory issues to him from the onset and see what happens. Those private lessons would be tailored to your own needs, give you more time to reflect but also remove your current anxiety. It is not because your Pa passed away that you have to grow up straight away and play, very badly I must say, the man. Not mentioning your money for your tuition will be better spent than in here.

Winning again handsomely the Doctor offered a beautiful and encouraging smile to the teenager, as he asked,

-Ready to up the stake, Zach? I have all your winnings on this table, show me the warranty you got from Mr Snow. So what do you think of my proposal?

Reluctantly taking a folded piece of paper from his jacket, the teenager showed it to Vincent, upset by his loss so far and truly wanting to beat Valdi hands down. Zachary harboured the secret desire to see the confident smirk of the Doctor disappear however he could only admit that he was touched by his proposal. He advanced,

-The game is not over. I am ready to up it with this warranty. I will win everything again and more. As for the proposal, thank you but I do not want to be a bother. I have my friends to talk to. But I might consider the tuitions. It could give a little reassurance back to my mum.

Staring at the teenager while having a long sip of rum, Valdi remained silent. This unnerved Zachary but not the other players who took their new cards. When the Doctor took his cards, he proposed,

-For the slight consideration you are willing to show to your mother by taking on private tuitions, I am willing to show you some. Give Mr Snow his warranty back and assure him that you will not make him accountable for it instead of playing with his money and I will give you back all I won from you. This is your last chance to show consideration.

Zachary folded the piece of paper neatly and put it back in the pocket of his jacket in a move which showed his complete displeasure. He argued angrily,

-Why would I do such thing? Do you want me to hand that back to the old man and look like a complete fool after the game I played? Do you want me to lose my face in front of everyone? He lost and that is all there is to it. There is no consideration to be given. His money is mine and I will play with it right now.

Wilton-Cough expressed himself right away within the mind of Valdi,

-Go full on, Doc. You know what to do to cure this lad from his insensitivity. Let's teach him humble pie. Remove everything from him and let him start from scratch. He has got to learn to be considerate and it seems that only the hard way will crumble his pretence. Teach him what it is to truly lose face and earn the one he can show proudly. Game on, use whatever technique to correct my boy before it is too late.

The Doctor felt as much as the Ghost within him the incentive he was on. He grasped the sheer disappointment of Abraham at his son's refusal to give the money back to old Snow, for it clasped his own heart into a sad squeeze just as well. He was ever so willing to follow the stance of Wilton-Cough on Zachary however staunch it sounded. He truly believed it could be the right answer. His gambling skills would strip the lad in no time at all of his fortune and at the end of it, Zachary would have nowhere to hide anymore. He played while Abraham spoke,

-Very sensitive of you, my boy. So you do prefer stripping a man from his livelihood to avoid losing your face in front of him. Which face are you talking about? Your ugly one, the one that shows that you are tough when you are not. Fine, we will play with the stake of what you took from Mr Snow. For a lesson of consideration, I am warning you that you will be stripped of any at the end of the day.

Looking at his cards with slight dismay, Zachary boasted,

-My face is perfectly fine, Doc. It is a winning one. Why would I spoil my winning feelings, pray? You will not be able to strip me of anything now that I learnt your tricks. They work.

Wilton-Cough commented with a wry smile,

-Of course they work however I didn't show you all of them. All the better for acknowledging the abuse you did of the few given to you, you do not deserve to know the rest. One must applaud you however to have managed to understand something for once with the ability to apply it. So you see, you managed to show us a bit of brain. So I guess all is not lost for you if you apply those brain cells to more tuition. However to make sure they function properly day in and out, I would engage proper conversation with your elders, adults, rather than with the cream of the scum you call your friends. Their bad reputation is rubbing off on you and all present in this room can tell you frankly that we don't hold you in very high esteem for it whatsoever. However if you decide to bother me you may run into the chance of earning a little respect from me more than anything else.

Surprisingly he met a rather shy and honest reply from Zachary,

-I rather know that I am not the smartest one around. Will you take offence if I can not entertain you with brilliant and well educated conversation? Sometimes even with my friends I stay silent in the hope that no one perceives my pathetic lack of intelligence or that I have no clue at all of what is being said around me. The manner you taught me your technique last time along with the practice of it made me grasp it completely. I don't think I am an idiot but sometimes, but sometimes...

His voice emotionally broke down to a complete silence as he realised that all eyes were upon him, that he had the attention of the entire table. Valdi took a sip of rum before encouraging,

-Your honesty shows that you are far from being an idiot, young man. Admitting your lack or maybe imperfections are a first step towards improving and I can assure you that if you spend some time with me I will not berate you but encourage you. You seem to have some mathematic abilities about you which is something.

Nodding positively, Zachary acknowledged,

-I owe that to my Pa. When he helped me with my maths homework, I understood them better. Somehow it clicked. Numbers make sense to me but not so much any of the rest.

Putting some cards down to another brilliant win, Vincent demanded,

-Here we go, Zach show me the good. Gentlemen, thank you.

Miffed by it, the teenager told as he put the paper down with a pout,

-I didn't see it coming. It's not fair.

Taking the paper presented on the table with a satisfied smile on his face, Valdi ordered,

-Yes, you will learn I am afraid that life is not always very fair whatsoever. So what have you got on offer to tempt me to another turn. I can tell you straight that only your entire inheritance will do. Gentlemen, what are your stakes? Here, Miss White, will you give this to Mr Snow for me to end his misery and tell him to burn that paper. I wish you could also advise to him, that if he has nothing left to spend for the evening to just fold and go home rather than writing such warranties. You can take back your pearls Whilhelmina.

Grinning brightly the hostess took the warranty and held it like a precious paper close to her breasts,

-Consider it done, Doctor. You are almost forgiven to have taught a Wilton-Cough to play better at cards.

She left the room in a ruffle of satin skirts brushing the stately oak floor, to an offended Zachary who vented,

-I wanted to win that back!

To which Valdi replied strongly,

-Tough! You lost it totally and forever. How dare you not showing any sensibility to others? Does it make you feel good? Your lesson is not over yet. I need you to write me a proper warranty for your whole inheritance if you want to remain at this table playing with us tonight.

An upset teenager stormed out of his chair to walk crossly back and forth from his place to the fire place, moaning and mumbling but also terrified to take any decision involving his inheritance. However he knew one thing and one thing only, and that was he, Zachary Wilton-Cough wanted to teach a tough lesson to that impudent

Doctor who was patronising him so much. It reminded him so much of his dad however that he secretly liked it and he could only admit that he was willing to spend some time talking to Vincent Valdi. He sat back to his place throwing his own verbal gauntlet,

-I will play but I need terms, good enough to put this much at stake. First that my mum should not know about it, ever. Second that you put yourself as much as risk as I. The sum in front of you is not good enough to be close to tempt me. The content of your wallet is a meagre incentive compared to my inheritance. There is a total unbalance here. I need something as substantial as your surgery practice as a warranty. I can tell you what will happen to it right now, if I win, I will dismantle it and sell everything separately so you can not retrieve any of it. It was built because of the loan my father gave you which you may have repaid, yet I see it as a proper match of stake. I let you take what my father gave me if you win, and you let me take what my father helped you get if I win. Isn't it fair? Tell me, isn't it?

The Gentlemen turned to Vincent Valdi anxiously waiting for his decision. They could see at the way the teenager and the adult were staring at each other that all blades were out and they truly hoped that the good Doctor could cut the mustard on that one, for if the worst happened they would be fairly lost without his surgery practice in town. They saw Miss White re-enter the room with tears of joy on her face who asked eagerly,

-What did I miss? I can tell you what you missed, Gentlemen. Scott Snow gave me a hug to remember. It was, well, a big bear hug which took my breath away. I warned him to not put me in that state of anguish any more, and he promised to do so with a big tearful kiss on my cheek. I am still keeping him on my sofa for the night though for he is far too drunk for me to let him make his way back to town.

Mr Sutton informed her,

-Well Whilhelmina, the stakes are flying high again tonight on your tables. At the moment the debate is between the inheritance of this young man against the surgery practice of our good Doctor.

Miss White sat down on her chair by the fire place in an exaggerated fashion, mimicking that she was about to faint. Fanning herself vigorously, she scolded out loud,

-Gentlemen, I dare say that you are determined to be the death of me tonight. Pray why are the stakes so high? Why can't you play nice with each other?

The Doctor gave her a dark look which reminded her that he didn't want her to intervene on what he was about to do as he replied with a stern determination,

-I am teaching someone an overdue lesson, Miss White. One that his father unfortunately could not give him.

She nodded but turned to Zachary Wilton-Cough to demand,

-What about you, Zach? Do you find it reasonable to ask from our Doctor his practice? Do you know he is the only Doctor we have in Wilton Town?

The teenager felt bad but was still very adamant, enough to argue,

-We are speaking of my inheritance here, Miss White! I am not the cleverest chap around, what would I do without money? Mr Valdi is a very skilled and smart person who I am sure could recover from such a loss while I, I don't know if I could.

Whilhelmina wanted very much to discourage the young lad from taking the risk yet she remembered Valdi's instruction to her so she turned back to the Doctor for more reassurance to demand,

-I need a security for Zachary Wilton-Cough from you, Vincent, to allow this game to happen in my hotel.

The Doctor's eyes went to stare for a second at the golden robe of his rum before he replied firmly,

-The only insurance I am willing to give is to not let down that young man. I will help him find a job, failing that I will employ him. Is this enough security for you, Whilhelmina?

Miss White nodded positively however she tapped her fan on her youngest gambler in the room asking him,

-The answer to that belongs to you, Zach. Will this amount of security suit you?

The eighteen year old thought about it very silently for what seemed to all an eternity before he gave his answer,

-It would suit me if only, I mean, at the condition of my family not knowing why I suddenly try to find some work. As long as this secrecy is kept as a firm term from all present here, I am willing to go along with that. It's a matter of keeping a little bit of pride, you know.

The Ghost of Abraham smiled internally within Vincent Valdi only acknowledging that his son had pride issues just like he did, he commented to the mind of the Doctor,

-Bless, that is one apple that didn't land far from the tree. We have to consent to that for the boy is ready for the kill. Let's get on with it and seal the deal.

He then spoke out as the very convincing Doctor, who on his side was willing to argue that he had no security at all being offered to him, but only the hope that his clever techniques would not fail him this time around,

-You have got yourself a deal, Zachary. We will keep whatever happens here tonight a total secret. Gentlemen, Miss White, do we have a common agreement?

While he received a positive nod from the other players, Whilhelmina told while bringing paper and an ink well to the table,

-Let's write those warranties then. Doctor Valdi, if the worst happens to you tonight, I want you to know that this very room will be close to all future gambling but open for you to use as a practice for this town.

To which Mr Sutton added,

-I will help you furnish it with the equipment needed, Doc. You can repay me if you want but I will not mind if you don't.

Not wanting to be left out, Mr Brand joined in,

-Same here, Doc, I will participate for the furniture with the same closes as Mr Sutton.

This pleased Vincent endlessly for he never knew he had gathered so much respect in Wilton Town but Wilton-Cough's Ghost shared to him,

-I think you have made a strong impression on that lot, Vincent. You can definitely qualify Miss White as your friend, and I must agree with you with the good opinion you have gathered about her. I have started sharing it. This was a very decent thing to do to give you such security. Hey, what are we living for if not for those moments when people make you feel truly appreciated. Keep it up, Doc, keep it up.

Valdi thanked everyone who gave him his security before taking the quill from Miss White and writing his warranty, his heart not quivering any more about the terms. He had more confidence to engage in the final round in order to comply with the lesson schemes of Abraham Wilton-Cough for his son. He also felt sure that this was the right thing to do to the eighteen year old in front of him. He could feel within himself the love of the deceased father for his son. It was strong and so warm that he wished he had known his own father. He was now, himself, feeling so much for the teenager that he knew he would get involved in Zach's life and watch over him ever so more closely. Lending his voice again to be totally controlled by Abraham, he heard him enjoin,

-Right, Zachary, time to write and sign your warranty.

The boy looked lost and gave him a querying glance as he confided,

-How do I write one of those, Mr Valdi? I am sorry to be such a non-sense.

Everyone in the room but Zachary had very kind condescending smiles drawing upon their lips apart from Vincent who showed his warranty with his advice,

-Build your one around this model or just copy mine changing the words surgery practice with your inheritance and swap my name to yours in places.

As Zachary nodded, he started writing with attentive care his warranty letter, but just copying almost word for word. The Doctor couldn't help but noticing the great similarity between the writing of Zach to the one of Abraham. It was clear and concise yet, if it was neat, they were very subtle changes compared to something written by Abraham. The most noticeable was the amount of pressure and ink used. If Abraham Wilton-Cough was not afraid of forming bold characters and letters, his son was, as his marks were so thin that they could have qualified as mere scratches.

Before he could control his own body back, Valdi felt his hand reaching out to the one of Zachary. He made him dip his quill again in the ink well and he could only recognise the strong tapping of the tip against the silver metal as the one of the deceased Banker within him as he heard him say,

-If you are emboldened enough to lose everything you bestow make it clear my son. Do make a mark even if it is the biggest mistake you do.

The boy gave a look at him, which was full of heartbreaking longing, as his lips whispered,

-Pa?

Vincent Valdi dropped the teenage hand trying to regain some control of his possessed body. He corrected with a knot in his throat,

-No, just Vincent, but wherever your Pa is, I can assure you with certainty that he is watching over you. As I arrived in Wilton Town as a bold twenty year old Italian full of dreams, your father didn't discourage me. On the contrary, he drew a concrete plan for me to be able to achieve them. Everyone can do with some directions at the start of their adult life. In the memory of your father, know that I will always be there for you. I owe it to him for I value his stern guidance he provided over my first steps in Wilton Town that much. It is payback time Zachary Wilton-Cough for both of us. Just sign your name down here, for whatever happen I will look after you.

A signing Zachary had tears in his eyes when he replied to the Doctor putting his heart on the table,

-I must confessed I truly miss Pa. It feels like I misplaced my compass and I am lost in the woods at night. I thank you Sir for what you just said. I will not dismantle your surgery if I win, I will let you get it back sometime, in another wild gamble.

It was Abraham who regained the power over the voice of the Doctor who replied,

-So very kind of you my child, I will bear that in mind when I come in possession of your inheritance and promise that I will try to keep it as whole as I can too. Let's see that warranty. Very good. No spelling mistakes, neat and clear. See an almost perfect copy cat of what I just drew out. I reckon you could be a good clerk in hiding.

The lad saw his paper being displayed in the middle of the gambling table against the one of Valdi, with the smaller stake of the gentlemen and just wondered if he did the right move. But he was not one to back down for it could show a cowardliness which he was very much against. So he just looked at his warranty hopping that the Doctor was not as smart as he boasted and that he was lying when he said that he didn't show him all of his techniques however the last rounds had proved quite the contrary.

Dwelling in his deep uncertainties Zachary lacked the focus required to play such a game unaware that his own ghostly father was peering over his own shoulder working at his undoing one card at a time. When a card disappeared making him lose a little more every time, his hand wanted to find the glass of alcohol but it had been replaced by the one of water, and his cigars were all gone to dust courtesy of Doctor Valdi. He kept playing sweating madly thinking the worst, but thinking better for Mr Brand and Sutton were also losing helplessly just as he was. It was that little bit of pride, that little bit of he was not the only one at that moment in time losing flatly to his opponent. The intense minutes past ever so quickly and when Valdi displayed the killer blow that he had lost his entire inheritance to him, Zach couldn't even utter a single word. He only loosened his pretty scarf around his neck trying to understand what it meant.

Opposite him, Vincent downed the glass a rum in one go, he took the inheritance warranty and folded it carefully with a triumphant smirk to put it in his pocket. He then told him in a very stern manner,

-My dear boy, do not look so forlorn, the end of the world did not happen nor your ruin. I will not spend any cent of that money, I will make you earn every single one of them. You are a Wilton-Cough and I believe you will make it through this challenge. Gentlemen take your money back, the lesson is over. Thank you for playing.

Mr Sutton and Brand shook vigorously the hand of the Doctor who gave them everything they lost to him. This was to the dismay of Zachary Wilton-Cough who complained out loud,

-Why can't I have my own money back, Sir? They have lost like I just did!

Vincent Valdi turned to him with a terrible smile on his face,

-This is when fairness stings my boy. Grow a good considerate heart like them to be treated equally. They showed concern to the fate of Mr Snow when you wouldn't. Hence they get their stake back and you will be shown no consideration in the matter. Anyway grab your coat for we are heading to town. Your mum was hurt tonight in an incident and she will appreciate seeing you earlier than dawn. Life is tough and not everything is about you. Miss White, if you are coming with us, fetch the unguents that may work best for Zach's mother.

The teenager put his coat on immediately,

-Is my Ma alright, Mr Valdi?

The Doctor replied, pleased with Zach's immediate concern,

-She is at the presbytery where I looked after her. She is fine but her injury is deep enough to leave her a physical scar for life but also a mental one about the attack.

Zachary Wilton-Cough was now by his side, not even thinking of his lost inheritance anymore, as he asked bewildered,

-Who could even think of attacking my Ma? Tell me all on the way Doc, tell me all.

Chapter Fifteen

The Eternal White Witch

They all left the gambling room, Mr Sutton and Mr Brand going straight to the bar, very happy about their night and ever so eager to share what happened in the room to the good Georgia Marlow. The Doctor was met by a very drunk Mr Snow who had very thankful eyes and slurred words to offer him,

-Doc, Doc, I, I must tell you how thankful I am by what you did. I, I, I owe you big time. Since the death of my, my, my strict Mrs Snow, life took a turn for the worst. She, she kept me from everything wasteful and without her, I went, went, straight into them. I lost, lost more than her, my job, my small business, and here I am a waste. But, but, I thank you so much with all my heart. I owe you big time, and you can ask me anything, anything, Doc.

Vincent Valdi tapped the shoulder of the man and led him to a couch, enjoining,

-Good, for at this minute I need you to sit down and have a big resting nap. I will come for you tomorrow around noon, so stay here until then. I know how much you lost when the good old Sabrina passed away but I do believe she is by your side watching over you like an Angel. So you'd better sleep everything off until I come back for I will take you to a job interview I have in line for you. I will tell you more about it tomorrow as we walk to town together.

Scott Snow stared at the empty side upon the couch, imagining his dead partner, whispering an earnest confession to Valdi,

-I will do what you say Doc, for I know what my Sabrina would shout if I don't follow your instructions.

Zachary standing by the tall Doctor felt extreme pity for the former milkman for the first time. In a move that surprised everyone in the room, he crouched by Scott offering,

-Mr Snow, I know how you feel. I feel like that too. I want you to know that I am truly sorry about tonight. Do you want me to fetch you a big glass of water? When I go to sleep a bit tipsy in the morning, I always find it helps to calm down any possible headaches.

The old man stared at him before looking for an answer on the face of the Doctor. Vincent putting his hand on the shoulder of Zachary, confirmed,

-Zach, the water is a good idea.

The teenager went to the bar as Valdi confided in a whisper like a secret to the milkman, that went along with a wink,

-We have a reformed Wilton-Cough. His own guardian angel had a good talk to him.

When Zachary brought the glass of water to the table by the old man, he had a very unmistakable apologetic demeanour about him. Scott Snow gave him a smile full of sympathy and opened his arms for a ready hug as he offered,

-Thank you for the tip. I will drink it all in the memory of your father. Trust me when I say that you are not lost when people do love you.

The youngster reluctantly accepted the hug because of the alcoholic stench of the man at that moment in time yet when the arms enclosed him tapping his shoulders gently, he could only think of the distress he had put that man through, of the kindness still displayed by Snow, but also that he was now in a similar position that he had put the milkman earlier on and was wondering if he could be as loved as Mr Snow was by the people of the town. But he had very big doubts about that for he had been an arrogant arse with everyone for a good while. Breaking down, Zachary started to cry upon the kind shoulder while he sobbed,

-I am so sorry, Mr Snow, really really sorry. And sorry for your loss too. I know how you feel because everything went out of the window when my Pa died. I hardly ever want to get up anymore.

From the musicians who had stopped playing to listen to what was happening, the twelve year old Mina White poked the crying teenager with her violin bow. When he tearfully turned to her, she told waving her bow like a school mistress,

-But you must. Ma would say that you must get up for yourself, for the people who love you and the ones that did, like your own Pa.

The possessed Vincent Valdi picked up the crying teenager from the hug of Mr Snow and offered the shelter of his own broad chest to hide Zach's tears as he commented with a positive nod to the young vampire before him,

-Mina, you are ever so right and we will make sure that this young man wakes up every morning from now on. Mr Snow, see you tomorrow.

He walked out of the room with Zachary hanging onto him like a shield to protect what was left of his pride. Vincent felt strongly, at that moment, as he reached the doorway of the hotel like the very father of the lad. He had felt and shared the feelings of Wilton-Cough for a while, and he agreed with plenty of them. He felt strongly in accord with the stance of the ghostly Abraham very deep down now and as he opened the door to head back to town, he could only admit to himself that he was a very willing surrogate dad for the Wilton-Cough's brood of children. He definitely would make sure Zachary would turn out alright, and was looking forward to looking after Abigail.

On the top of the steps, he smiled at the very thought of holding a newborn baby with the aim of raising her entirely. As a man, looking at the stars shinning above the dark forest, he felt ever so ready now to be a father himself, despite having none as a child, he had developed his own confidence by meeting Abraham Wilton-Cough.

Behind him, Miss White put on a cream leather cape, discarding her feather boa in the hand of Georgia, giving her her last recommendations about the hotel. She put a trendy bonnet on, and took a white vanity case before stepping into the night enjoining Valdi and the young Wilton-Cough.

As they left her courtyard, she turned to Zachary, with a very tender look, confessing,

-Zach as much as I like seeing you, and you will still be welcome at my place, I think it is grand time for you to face all you avoid, especially your own family who are grieving as much as you do but in a different manner. Face the morning with your mother and younger brother, embrace them, for you only have them and they only have you. You could tell your mum to eat up her porridge and look after her a little, for she doesn't do it very well for herself at the moment. She is just the shadow of what she was when she smiled happily on the arm of your father. Beside with what happened to her tonight, she could do with your presence because it will reassure her that you are alright. Could you do that for her for a while or a long while?

Wiping off his tears the teenager left the safe sanctuary of the Doctor's chest to consider what was said to him. He then ventured with a disarming honesty,

-I am not sure mum would listen to anything I say. Why should she when I never truly listen to her? She would probably listen to Josiah though because he is Mummy's boy. But I can bully Josiah for him to do what I want so I can force him to talk for me.

Abraham Wilton-Cough reacted by giving a desperate look to the night sky. Still within Vincent Valdi, which he enjoyed the strong body very much but also he must admit talking to, it felt like having found a friend and a partner in crime. Dead, Abraham wished to be alive and well again, to redo and change his steps, for he would not have chosen books of accounts as his most cherished companions, no, he would have chosen the like of the good Doctor, and feel fortunate to have his friendship. But alas, his time to be flesh and blood were over, he was just a mere Ghost, needing a host to feel once more, even just for a night, a little bit alive again. That's when Vincent, with his thirst for knowledge, his extreme curiosity, but also his slight guilt to not have been able to save him, came in with his odd but most welcome proposal. The experiment created a symbiosis between a living man and the spirit of a deceased which somehow both enjoyed: The man benefiting of the advice, warnings and comments of a deceased who could teach him a lesson or two about life, while the Ghost was given the opportunity to have enough physicality to be able to influence and correct his loved ones. And right by him, was the eighteen year old Zachary, which reminded him so much of himself and how wrong he had been most of his life but more importantly he dreaded that the attitude of his eldest son was due to years of his own bad example as a father. Zach was his incentive tonight. If only he could rectify his lessons to his son, where he wanted him to be tough, proud to become a prosperous man. If only he could make him see that those lessons were preposterous, that what made you truly rich, happy and content was simply, love, care and humbleness.

Wilton-Cough shared his thoughts to Valdi's mind,

-Vincent, I know my son is right by you, that we have succeeded in making the boy follow us and listen, that we are taking him back to his mum but please let me remain within you on the way back to talk to him some more for it is much needed. I want him to see you as a father figure from now on. Let me give you that authority over my lad for he still needs so much direction and also correction.

Covering his mouth and coughing in his hand, the Doctor whispered at the attention of his internal Ghost,

-Granted. Use my voice.

Miss White asked with certain concern, tapping on his back,

-Are you alright, Vincent? You are still extremely cold, we need to walk as fast as we can into town and get you indoors.

Valdi gave her a kind smile, despite disliking her knowledgeable touch for he didn't want her to find out that he was quite possessed by the Ghost of Abraham Wilton-Cough. Being invaded by him gave him an edge on things, which he was reluctant to see depart. For one thing, it made him be more inquisitive about Whilhelmina, enough to make him realise she was a supernatural being of a similar kind to a vampire, but not quite. He had known her fairly well for twenty years. In difficult births in the district, they were side by side doing their utmost to save the lives of infants and mothers. He almost considered her like the eldest sister he never had, and if she were a man, a blood brother. They dwelt together side by side, their hands covered up to their elbows in blood trying to save lives yet what he learnt that entire night unsettled him. It raised more questions within his mind about Miss White than ever before. He also had a feeling of dejection for her not to reveal who she truly was for all those years. Her lack of trust was simply reverberated in his will to keep secrets from her. Trust, he didn't think he lost it completely about Whilhelmina, because she showed her care and attention so often, that he knew deep down that she had a good heart. However the old saying of keep your friends close and your enemies closer kept bugging him whenever he thought of her now. He gave a false explanation for his sudden cough, then Abraham took over his voice to take the opportunity to talk to his eldest son,

-I just tried to say I am losing my voice. I must have caught something, Whilhelmina, but nothing to worry about.

Turning to Zachary, and closing the teenager's open coat, he told sternly,

-Let's not have you catch death roaming in the night, for that would certainly worry your mother. So if the only way to talk to your brother is pretty uncivilised in your book, in mine it goes like this, if I ever see a bruise on that boy which is from you, you can expect the same kind of violent talking in the future from me: A bruise for

a bruise. You do not bully your brother. Josiah has been in a
boarding school where he has met his fair share of bullying. Your
father's dying wish was to bring him home to make that stop, to
protect him. So if Josiah is a Mummy's boy or not, as a Daddy's
boy, yourself, you have to respect Abraham's last wishes to the
letter. Your brother needs your respect, your tenderness but never
your fists or bullying. The jealousy between you two stops with
immediate effect. Understood? Now, tell me when did you last
talked properly to your mother?

If Zachary Wilton-Cough felt totally patronised, he also felt again
like a child by that adult which allowed him to ditch any pretence
and just be himself, ready to be guided back home through the dark
forest. Somehow he appreciated that very much, he replied in a very
subdued fashion,

-I kind of do not have any conversation with my mum, Sir. I am in
bed all day when she is awake and I just say 'Bye' at night when I am
leaving. She is so sad since Pa left that it is unbearable. I fear that if
I stand next to her more than five minutes I would just collapse in
her arms and shed tears like the great fountain in the middle of
town. I am pretty sure she will do the same and together we will
never stop.

Vincent Valdi sighed deeply while Abraham acknowledged how
sorely grieved he was by his family, still, months after his death. It
warmed his heart to know that he was loved despite it all. So there
must have been a few things that he did right during his life then for
him to be missed so much. He made the Doctor's arm go around
the shoulders of his boy as he scolded tenderly,

-There is nothing wrong about crying, Zachary. You will not lose
your Wilton-Cough's pride by shading a few tears. Listening to your
heart will only make you a better man. Beside you and your mother
need to pierce that sore blister. Your shared tears can only bring you
two closer together. I can also tell you that you need it as much as
she does. It will bring you both comfort but also a closure for as
hard as it is that Abraham departed, but his spirit will stay with your
family forever.

Looking at the long and narrow path snaking downhill between the dark trees, the youngster enquired,

-Do you believe in souls, Doc? I never thought you did, because you never go to church. Or is it something that you are just saying to soothe me a little from my grief? You know, I don't quite believe in souls or whatever, but it makes me hurt more to think that Pa is just gone-gone like totally gone and that was it. I don't know and it kills me and my mind as a tendency to think the worst on that matter.

The Doctor didn't let Abraham talk for him as he replied with a confident smile,

-You see Zach, my entire life, forty odd years now, I was plagued by lots of questions and lots of doubts, and I can tell you that I went way and beyond to quest for answers. I do not know everything, because you keep learning every day that passes, but there is a few things I know for certain. Spirits and Souls do exist. You do not need to go to church to believe that. The most important thing for you to do once you have that knowledge is to make sure you are a good man with a sound heart. Isn't this right, Miss White?

She nodded positively as she trotted beside him, before adding her words to the stance of Valdi, for she was impressed by the way he was dealing with that young troubled and troublesome Wilton-Cough and she was confident that he was on the right track with him, therefore she was more than happy to validate everything he said,

-Very right. I do believe in Souls and Spirits just as well. You do not have to be religious or overly religious to believe in that. I rather be a good person by acts and deeds rather than going religiously somewhere and pray. Why spending time praying to a higher being to help the sick and poor when I can be by the bedside of one of them and provide my arms to help them, physically, and when my kind words will support them morally? Doctor Valdi and I have hardly got any spare time to go to church but it does not make us believe less or have lesser morals than the others that do. Our religion is the one of our hearts and spreading it simply with our love and care to others.

It was the turn of Zachary to nod and to agree yet he asked deeply interested,

-How do you two know for sure about Souls and Spirits?

Doctor Valdi replied with a sad stern voice,

-Because we saw far too many depart: Holding the hand of a living, watching his or her agony, only to witness the light extinguishing in their eyes, to feel the last movement of their fingers holding desperately to yours, feeling every digit hanging on to yours like they are their last anchor to a bit of life.

Feeling deeply emotional, Zachary confessed,

-I wished I did witness my Dad last minutes. But I knew it would be terribly upsetting but also someone needed to be there for Josiah. He was very distressed by it all that day and night. He never saw Pa so weak and so hurt. But also, Pa never told things to him like he did, that night. I had to retain Jo from coming back into the bedroom because he wanted to hold Dad's hand till his last minute just to tell him, in his silent fashion that he did like our old man after all. We hanged onto each other like proper brothers for hours. In the wee hours of the morning, we were finally allowed back in the bedroom to see his cold body. Josiah couldn't take it all in and ran away from home. I fetched him back with Mrs Bates. We found him crying sitting at the base of the statue of Noah M Wilton. I wished I could have told him about Spirits and Souls then but I couldn't, not knowing myself. Like do they live on after the body is gone stone cold? Where do they go?

Vincent Valdi could feel the heavy sobs of Wilton-Cough within him so he replied for him to the wondering teenager,

-As I told Miss White, I had quite a night tonight. One in which, I sat at a table with Father Theo Odell, your mother, your great aunt

Josephine Cough and the good Widow Bates. Nothing extraordinary about it apart that we talked to the Spirit of your father. They are ways for you and your brother to communicate with our deceased Abraham. To learn them, I refer you to your own great aunt who knows a fair few techniques to speak with the dead. This is why it is grand time that you have proper conversations with your elders for there is much you can get from them that will help you with your own life and that can help answering the many questions you may have. This is why I have been talking to you the way I did all the way through, for I have clear instructions from Abraham Wilton-Cough to do so. You aren't lost any more my boy, you have me to confide into, courtesy of your Pa, who made me fetch you. I can tell you that his Spirit is right here watching over you. I can tell you that his Spirit went to stay right by his loved ones.

His talk had the unexpected effect to make Zachary hug him like if he was hanging onto dear life, crying and smiling at the same times, moaning, pestering yet welcoming,

-I knew you were onto something, I just knew deep down. Blast! You sounded so much like Pa at time, that I could swear I could see him through you. I miss him so so much. Every night I sit by his grave before I go to the hotel, there I am killing my brain asking questions into the darkness until it hurts, until I will either collapse into a snooze or walk to have booze after booze to forget the grief. Valdi, you managed to talk to my dad. Can you still talk to him now? If so tell him how much I miss him and love him.

Scruffing the hair of Zachary, Vincent confided,

-He already knows that for he is within me watching over you. You can hear him and almost see him because his Spirit is simply here.

His revelation made Miss White pale if she could go any paler. Her thin red lips grew into an all knowing smile as she commented, swearing,

-Damn! Valdi! You didn't! That would explain a lot. Oh yes, you caught something! Well someone, I dare say! Me worrying away that you caught death so freezing cold you are, have been all evening, me trying to bring colour to your cheeks with a fair few glasses of my best rum. Onto something you were indeed! Oï, Wilton-Cough don't damage the Doctor, he is far too useful in this town.

Despite despising the honesty of Valdi at that moment in time, the Ghost of Abraham replied through him with his spectral voice in order to validate the truth of what Vincent said,

-I won't. I know how much his good Soul is worth. He allowed me to speak straight to my son.

While Zach started crying again upon the Doctor's chest, Vincent reassured,

-Abraham is ever so gentle with me and my body, Whilhelmina. I know what it can be like otherwise by experience. I am sorry for your worry but you are a friend to me that in my mind didn't share as much as you could have either hence causing maybe as much worry to me as I did to you tonight. Zachary, your Pa is ordering me to tell you to man up, right now, and to blow your nose on Mr Sutton's handkerchief and not on my shirt for I will truly catch a cold then.

This made Miss White and Zachary smile widely to the Doctor but also looking at him like a very strange creature coming out of the deep blue of that Spring night. When the youngster blew his nose like requested Whilhelmina confided,

-For our friendship I owe you an apology, Vincent. It's for Mina that I kept myself so secretive to protect us.

To which the Doctor replied starkly, showing that he felt insulted,

-As if my hands could have stake you both! As if I didn't bestow a damn heart! You mean to this town as much as I do if not more, for you belonged to it since, since, I do not know when, for I am not worthy enough of your trust to know.

Miss White struggled to catch the large steps of Valdi. Yet she felt that she was following a human worth telling all. She had watched him for long enough to know he was one bestowed with a strong steady heart who embraced everyone. Rich or poor didn't made any difference for the Italian Doctor, he would give his full care regardless. Young or old, she saw him strive to save every minute of everyone for every second counted to anyone for him. If he could save one life, she had witnessed his pure smile full of bliss that he did it, but also the tear at the corner of his eyes that would never fail to appear then. So to know that her eternal life and the one of Mina did count regardless of everything in the eyes of Vincent touched her more than she could tell. Yet she tried to as she finally reached one of his strong but ever so cold hand,

-Vincent, please, accept my apologies and let me confide everything for I value your friendship more than I can say.

Valdi was unwilling to slow down however, giving a quick glance at the woman begging him, he realised in the entire eagerness of her composure, mainly the vert-de-gris eyes which were certainly about to cry if he carried on any longer his harsh stance, the distress rising within her. He applied a reassuring pressure on her hand, before letting her carry on,

-I didn't mean to insult you by my secrecy. You are the last person I would imagine to dare to insult. I respect you too much for that. I have seen many, many, lives and you are one of the most descent individuals I ever met. The only other one I knew was Noah M Wilton, so they do not come along that often.

This had the Ghost of Abraham fairly excited as he exulted with fascination to Vincent,

-Blimey, she knew my ancestor! Ask her to speak about him...

But Vincent Valdi only smirked at the Wilton-Cough's great pride for their ancestry woken inside Abraham for he could feel it just as well. He commented with a tone which was more sarcastic than he wished it to be, still displaying his annoyance at having been mistrusted for so long,

-Clearly! Knowing Noah means quite a while then, quite a big long while to be around. Ignoring the flattery you indulge me with, how was that illustrious man? Was he as strong as the legend has it?

In the Doctor's pinch of curiosity taking over that Whilhelmina perceived, she felt that she would now become an object of his forever investigating mind. This frightened slightly her very reserved and secretive nature but she was willing to go under the scalpel of his questions in order to preserve their established friendship so releasing his hand she started with a noticeable timidity,

-I have been there since the beginning of Wilton Town, in fact, I arrived here with Noah Wilton. I am one of the original settlers, the last one truly alive.

Zachary was too stunned about her admission to join in the conversation. With a mouth open which could have caught a moth or two in the night, and a mind racing to comprehend what was going on, he remained in a totally shocked silence. Vincent Valdi gave him an amused glance, wanted to reassure the teenager with a 'It's okay, she doesn't bite' but voted against it for he didn't know for sure himself.

But on reflection he would certainly have been bitten by now for he had walked many times those woods and the countryside with Whilhelmina White questing for medicinal herbs. So his general assumption remained that the strange eternal creature that she was, was perfectly safe, or maybe there was an imaginary safety close just for him. He was safe from her because she had true respect for him. Whatever the situation was, it intrigued him enough to get plenty of clarification. He asked with a point of humour in his voice, as he could sense the clear anxiety of Whilhelmina by his side, and surely it should have been the other way around he thought,

-I won't bite you if you tell me all, Miss White. Tell me more about Noah for I have the Spirit of a Wilton-Cough within me very eager to know more about his ancestor.

This reassured Whilhelmina enough to make her smile as she reminisced about Noah M Wilton out loud,

-He was a very good man. I never saw someone as generous as him until you came along into Wilton Town. He would devote almost his entire time to help restlessly. He saved me and my daughter from the prison we were in among the other prisoners he freed, back where we all came from. I felt very much in his debts from then on especially because he was doing so much for everyone. I used to be a maid, a servant before I was thrown into jail, so once freed I decided to attach my services to Noah to become his servant.

The fascinated Doctor prompted by a very curious Wilton-Cough enquired,

-Did you love Noah, like going in a relationship point of view?

The sadness of the eyes that blinked at him made Valdi regret straight away his question before he heard the answer. The woman wrapped her arms around herself protectively, shivering uncontrollably before she tried to express herself,

-I can't, I can't love, I mean I can like people, but it stops at just that. Something happened to me, something so shattering that I hardly trust anyone anymore since an eternity. Mina is the result of a violent rape. Since, it was never the same again. I was alone when I gave birth to her and it didn't go well. It was one of the worst complicated birth you can imagine. I butchered myself to save Mina and I. Relationships, I simply can't have any loving ones beside I do not know what proper love is, and will never know. I was a devoted servant to Noah who I just admired as a very good person. But he treated me well with no pride or condescension like all the other Wilton-Cough that followed seemed to possess aplenty. He considered me due to my knowledge of herbs, and by then of childbirth like a doctor. Since Mina's birth, I made a vow that no women should suffer so much, so I learnt everything there was to know about birth to help others at that crucial laborious moment. When we settled here, I had twelve years of experience as a midwife. After years of looking after everyone's ailments in town, I saw your coming with a welcomed relief. Four hands are always better than two to help the ever growing population of this town.

Zachary Wilton-Cough seemed to wake up from his daze with his sudden outburst, however he had been listening ever so attentively to understand all of what was said,

-That's what we need in Wilton-Town! We need a hospital with plenty of caring hands like yours to look after all the people that need looking after. Doc, you should create it, draw plans and all and I will help you do it even if I would probably be only good enough to carry stones from A to B and maybe at bricklaying. Bricklaying shouldn't be difficult should it? We would have special sections into it to make it the best place to get treatment from in the entire district, like a maternity ward and we will call the ward in your honour Miss White for you have been here for so long helping this community. We would make all the doctors working in that ward do the same vow as yours, with hand on heart and all. You know, you know I am truly sorry for what happen to you for, for, I had a friend who did that to a girl and the following day she was found by her parents hanged in her bedroom. The guys and I never talked to that lad ever again, for Laura was such a sweet girl, as good nature as my mum is.

His sudden participation in the conversation was welcomed by his ghostly father who shared to Valdi's mind,

-We have a budding Wilton-Cough in him after all. What do you think of his suggestion, Doc? Would you be tempted to attempt that project with my boy? Zach sounds excited enough to be willing to work hard for it and god knows I spoilt that son far too much so he never lifted a finger in his youth.

Vincent Valdi gave a good look at the teenager and could see passion in Zach's eyes like if he was seeing already the hospital in front of him. Day dreaming or as it was still dark, night dreaming, but wide awake, Zachary was the picture of someone struck by a lightning of some sort. Of course not of the type which straightened the hair all across one's body, yet the good Doctor's ones were all raised up at that moment in time, but this was due to another Wilton-Cough, of an entity type, chilling him to his bones. Vincent didn't know how the thought process worked in that teenager, but like his father he welcomed the result. Let's just say, it was a bombshell that left him bewildered and awe struck but it was a nice bombshell nonetheless. Faced with a younger Wilton-Cough which had suddenly woken up from his limbo of having no will at all for months, Vincent went into congratulations and praises as if he was assisting to a birth,

-O boy, that is a brilliant idea you've got there! Miss White, you have to help me here for I am almost lost for words. Do you realise, Zachary, that this project could consume both of our lifetime? We are not eternal like Whilhelmina here. Your father just informed me that you never lifted a finger in your life however he is very pleased as I am with your idea. Let me give you a little circumspection just now, what are you going to do about what you just said? How are you going to go about it?

Zachary, falling under scrutiny, gave a glance at his hands that, it was true, had never worked. He presented them to the Doctor, palms facing the sky, with a poignant and very honest plea,

-I will give you those, Doc, for you to teach me how to use them so I could be helpful. This is how I will go about it. This is what I am doing to bring about this idea. I am afraid I do not know any better than to give you that idea and those to deal with. I am sorry if it, if it is not good enough. My hands are all I have. You know I hide my stupidity with my Wilton-Cough's pride so no one finds out, how stupid and clueless I am about everything.

Vincent grabbed the hands of the boy as Abraham replied to his son,

-Look at me, Zachary, and understand that those, your idea and your hands are the best things you can offer. At this moment in time, I am the proudest father to have just heard you say that. And I am not talking about the Wilton-Cough's pride here, but simply of down to earth human pride. The time for hiding is gone and the time for showing is here, right before you, and all you need are those, just those hands ready and willing to do some work. It is with his hands holding his big axe that Noah M Wilton built this town. You can build an hospital with these, brick after brick, but you can also help with the numbers of the entire operation. For Doctor Valdi and I will show you exactly how. You offer is accepted and you are Vincent's apprentice from now on. Last but not least let me tell you that you are not as stupid as you think you are.

Zachary Wilton-Cough found his smile back and it was such an eager humble one, that Vincent Valdi, only hugged him, tapping his back. Whilhelmina White joined in, with a half truth,

-If I had a son, I would not have minded if it was you at this moment in time, Zach. I am pretty sure even Noah would have been proud of you.

This made Zachary's eyes glisten with joyous pride, yet he asked the Doctor in a very humble fashion,

-When do you want me to work Doctor Valdi?

As they resumed walking, the teenager noticed that the arm of the adult was still around his shoulders protectively, while the Doctor answered,

-The day after tomorrow. I want you to be with your family for the competition of Josiah to support him, with your presence and your applause. After that just take it easy and rest all day. I will expect you at nine in the morning the following day, on the dot at the doorstep of my surgery. You will work from nine until five, six days a week apart for Sundays. We will also talk to your former teacher for those extra night tuitions. Your father knows that Mr Claude could do with a bit of an extra income every now and then, for he took a large credit to drive to school in style in a buggy pulled by a fancy white pony instead of walking the three miles distance from his home. It has all to do with man getting older and wanting to have a gentle woman by his side for his old days. So he is convinced that we could easily get out from your teacher, two hours for three times a week, between five thirty to seven thirty. How does that sound?

In another bout of true honesty the teenager could not hide his gasp,

-Dreary. When do I sleep?

Vincent Valdi laughed as much as the Ghost within him, out loud. It was a gutsy and guttural laughter all at once who kind of scared the pants of Zachary. He could recognise clearly his father's voice now. However he knew for a fact that his father was not one who was laughing much. The voice of Abraham blended ever so well with the one of the Doctor, that it was so hard to distinguish who was talking. Or was it them both, in a common agreement, which was ever so spooky for a naughty teenager to have two adults at once on his case. Zach's mind went totally checkmate at that moment thinking that his dad was back with a vengeance because of how lazy he had been for the past few months. He used to play chess with his dad at night after his homework and school. It was a rather very solemn and silent affair all the time, with for only words the critical comments of his father after his every move. From the tactical experience, if he was getting better, like Abraham told him one day, he did not remember a single win against his father. Zachary felt like doom all over again, like when his dad spelt out the every letter of checkmate when he did lose which was all the time.

However the Doctor recovered from his laughter only to tell him very sternly,

-From now on you will sleep at night, my boy. We are reversing the clocks back to when there was some sort of order and time keeping in your home. If you want to sleep properly, you will only be able to do it in your grave once you have fulfilled your life full of good deeds.

This was clearly his father's talking but then came the last blow, and he knew it came from Vincent,

-Dreary? Wait until I make you work a field with me. Wait until those young muscles of yours rest from pure exhaustion only. You will have the best sleep ever then, for you would not have shunned from hard work in your life.

Zachary couldn't hide his unease and his rather posh upbringing when he demanded,

-What kind of fields are you talking about, Doc?

-Fields of crops that feed people, my boy.

-Surely as a Doctor you do not do that type of work, therefore I shouldn't.

But Valdi's stark gaze told him a different story as much as his answer,

-Unlike you, Zach, I have very humble beginnings. The status that I have gained will never make me forget about them. I know what it means to harvest a few crops. And the sheer sweat to get them is never lost in the belly of the person that consumes them. Imagine one of my patients, Zach, an old farmer who lost everyone, or almost for one daughter who married and lives abroad. The crop does not only mean food on his table but his livelihood. When an illness strikes him so bad, when he breaks his hip, what do you think I would do as a Doctor? Give him a remedy, bandage, a patch and walk away charging him for it? Can you walk away when you see a field ready to harvest and the man who cannot walk to do it for at least six weeks? Do you know how much trauma a situation like that could put on poor Mr Haler? Would you not help out? For I would, I rolled up my sleeves and made sure that man had food on his table to get better. Your father would add with a wink that I would get paid later for my patient didn't end up in a grave. So to answer your question, being my apprentice, you will work in a field or two alongside me.

A mind harassed by far too many questions at the same time, the young Wilton-Cough imagined himself in situ with a scythe in hand.

If he knew he would be proud to help a poor farmer he also wished that none of his friends would see him do so for they would scorn him endlessly. And maybe his father was ever so right in saying that he had the wrong kind of friends. He fell again in a very deep reflective silence. Zachary looked ahead at the winding path which lead to the big clearing. He loved this part of the woods although he knew that the other part was much darker, dense and went right up to the other side of the hill, one he was always scared to cross.

But he could only admit that knowing that he had the strong Doctor by him, he felt safe. He also knew for a fact that no one dared to cross the Sicilian Valdi in town. If everyone had great respect for him, and if it started in a field, Zachary was ready to work out his own muscles and aplomb with a scythe. With larger biceps, he thought he could teach a lesson or two to any of his so called friends who would dare to grin at him if they saw him with a scythe in a field. The teenager's thoughts were running wild across a brief clearing of romantic ideas all at once.

Miss White, seeing the youngster ever so silent, advanced,

-Maybe working in a field doesn't suit Zach? We had humble beginnings, Vincent, we can cope with such things, but him?

Valdi corrected her with the voice of an upset Abraham,

-Of course he will cope with it! He is a Wilton-Cough for Christ's sake. No sweat is spared in our undertakings. You know something about it so teach my boy about Noah and his large axe that felled trees to build roofs over his people's heads. My Zach is not to know plush anymore, he is to learn right. I do not want any of you lot to spoil him for I did his spoiling. Let him earn whatever he can get. Show him right...

Thus scolded, Whilhelmina gave a scrutinising head to toe look at Zachary, thinking that indeed the boy did love his luxury too much but she could not see him for one bit in a field. However she could be entirely wrong. The boy was only a couple of inches less tall than the strong Valdi. If Zach fed himself properly, she could envisage a

emerging man in him. But she could not get herself to imagining
him with a tool, holding it vigorously, with such aim, like his
ancestor Noah. However she did as she was enjoined to, for the
Ghost of Abraham Wilton-Cough didn't sound like one you wanted
to disoblige, very much like when he was fully alive, so she started,

-A true Wilton, Zachary, knows his origins. He does not ignore
them despite their humbleness. Noah was a son of peasants, who
came from a long line of peasants respectively. However he was a
boy and then a man of vision who wanted the best for his own
parents. He wanted a better roof over their heads. So he worked
very hard from the onset but also strived to get an education. He
learnt to build houses from scratch and like no others to build
another one for his parents. But his generosity made him look at his
poor neighbours with their derelict houses, so he built them new
ones, no one could stop him, and it carried on from there. He learnt
to read and write with very with great application too for he saw it
as a means for anyone to get out of sheer poverty and, at that time,
the tyranny we were all living under. As much as he got to know
how to fell a tree, to have planks from its timber, to cover the
planks to make it a rain and winter proof roof over one's head, he
learnt by heart the law, not only of that country but many, articles
by articles. If he recited to you one, it was with so much gusto and
presence that he would silence his opponents right away, sending
them back to their books in order to give him a proper answer.
Your ancestor was so fiercely protective of people that he became
political. As a visionary he freed us to follow him and to go and
create the town of our own desires and dreams. Some didn't follow
but a fair few did take that wild journey into the unknown with him
as our leader. Noah M Wilton did it all with his hands, a vision and
sheer hard work. I dare say he never complained about his sleep
despite having hardly any, once he took us all on the venture that
was the creation of Wilton Town. Are you willing to follow his
footsteps, Zach, as best as you can?

Her account had made Zachary just imagine what he was like back
then, back in the days, where a town could simply be built. But it
also encouraged him greatly, for the vision of a hospital was much
more downscaled than a town. He was very willing to get stuck in

and learn everything about brick laying to build great walls but also to ask his former teacher Mr Claude what skills were needed to become an architect. Because in his mind as the town was already created by Noah M Wilton, he, as a descendant, could just focus on creating useful buildings for it, starting by a much needed hospital. So he replied with some enthusiasm,

-Yes, Miss White. I cannot promise I could be as good because I am only me. I would not be able to learn law things for a start and heavens forbid start to have a clue about politics but I have the desire to build something, like my own Dad with his bank, and Noah with the town. I will get stuck in, in any field Mr Valdi wants me to do, just to get my lanky muscles to some sort of shape and then I want to learn how to make houses from scratch. Not so much with wood as before, like in Noah's time, but with bricks, stones, marble and so on, you know what I mean. I was fairly good at geometry so I hope I could make a wall stand straight. But I would ask Mr Claude to make sure I can for I don't want my walls to fall upon anyone squashing them. No, I want to show them to Ma and Jo and show them that I am good at one thing. O' boy, o' boy, would I be ever so proud to have built a house, let alone a hospital. If the hospital comes into fruition, I would sit on Pa's grave, and I would then smoke a cigar not to just give me an air of importance but proudly, just to tell him, that I did it, that I did something out of myself. Of course, I would chuck the ashes of the cigar onto his neighbouring grave not his, being respectful and all.

If everyone was happily astonished with his answer, the Ghost of Abraham scolded outright,

-You will do no such thing on my grave unless you bring an ashtray with you and be truly respectful to all. Because you would never know what is hiding in a coffin near you so just be mindful of your neighbours wherever you are, before you have a Ghoul ravaging your neck like your mother. But I applaud at what you just told us. I think you found your aim, even if it leads you to sit upon my grave with a cigar in hand, as long as you have a hospital built or a house to show for it, not forgetting the necessary ashtray, I will allow it and I may share your joy and smoke a puff or two within you.

This sent Zachary right back into a wondering silence for a good minute or so before he demanded ever so worried,

-What is going on here? What happened to mum? Do Ghouls exist?

It was a call out loud which was handled by Vincent Valdi, for he went from realisation to realisation throughout the night so much so that he was letting his own guts carry a Ghost. Therefore he started by wrapping his arm again around the anxious teenage shoulders of Zachary before revealing,

-Ghouls do exist as much as Spirits, Souls and Vampires... Do not ask me for I had a right night of it all and the very Ghost of your dad within me to teach me all about the existence of almost all I took for fairy tales.

Zachary tried his utmost to get his head around it all, as he asked again,

-So did a Ghoul tried to eat my mum?

Vincent Valdi rolled his sleeves up to his elbows to show his uncared scars and bites marks from Ghouls to prove his say as he answered,

-Well one or two had a good go at her shoulders and it took all the wit and strength from Father Odell, Josephine Cough, Mrs Bates and myself under such attack to get your mum safely into the presbytery. Like you said yourself your mum is a sweet thing but she doesn't fend nor fight. We had a proper battle in the cemetery, Zachary, and it was against Ghouls, a fair few of them. The thing is your own father warned us about them because he know about a curse which made him very restless because...

The Doctor's voice failed him. He was ever so worried on the affect the rest would have on the teenager. But what he didn't expect was Miss White stopping him on his track, opening her vanity case just to grab one of his arms so he could not move it. He saw her tending to his arm with water and lotions very attentively yet she scolded him strongly,

-Vincent, you can not let a Ghoul's wound fester on you. They eat the dead. Uncleaned their bites can become deadly. This town needs you too much to see you die for stupidities like that. You look after everyone yet fail to look a little after your own self. Now I understand the state of unrest you were in when you came to my hotel. So much to take in during one evening must have been quite something. Show me the other arm. That one is not as bad. So that explains finally all the questions laid at my door tonight.

Looking at the care given to him, Valdi nodded to her affirmatively. However giving a sheepish smile, he decided to be bluntly honest confiding,

-I am still in a state of unrest. I have so many questions to ask to gather a little peace of mind, yet my unrest is nothing compared to the one I feel from Abraham Wilton-Cough. I can't express the level of his sorrow and his anguish. It is so heartbreaking that I will do anything in my power to make sure his spirit can rest in peace.

Cleaning one of his wounds, Whilhelmina offered,

-May I can be of some help to both of you?

Valdi gave her a wicked welcoming smile as he replied,

-You may my dear Miss White as long as you don't bite me for asking far too many questions. Tell me what made you become eternal? Can you reassure me on what you eat? Because I am having a hard time to get my head around that. It is because I do not want to assume the worst especially knowing how caring you are.

The glance given to him was extremely shy while he felt her hands shivering on his arm, so he added firmly,

-Rest assure that I will not harm you.

Whilhelmina, feeling somewhat slightly reassured, showed to the Doctor her left arm, and pointed to her wrist, exhibiting two punctures not far from each other. She started her confession, in a voice full of sadness,

-I do not bite, I get bitten. In prison, attached to a wall, I saw my child being attacked by a Vampire. The fact that I couldn't intervene was devastating. The following night was the one where we were freed by Noah. Without knowing it, Noah Wilton sometimes always seemed to intervene a little too late. I told no one that my daughter was turned to a Vampire because I wanted to protect her. But I had to find a solution fast for her to feed but never to kill. I also needed to be eternal myself because my Mina would forever be a twelve year old. Before we left our former country I managed to find a book of very dark black art. I knew a little white magic before which got me imprisoned and labelled as a witch. My solution was to forever feed my daughter with my own blood. I worked out a way to be partly turned but not entirely. Like that I can look after Mina and make sure she is harmless to all. The only person which she is allowed to feed upon is me. As for me I have an almost human diet, by that I mean I eat normally like everyone, apart that I do eat placenta regularly for my blood to be rich enough for Mina, for her to never suffer from any craving or urges. This is why I keep my daughter more or less a guarded recluse. This is why I worked out ways to render her safe. I also educated her very strongly in order to tame the demon within her. She is a very obedient little girl and our bond became ever so strong ever since. Mina is entirely devoted to me. My secrecy ensured our protection, hers more particularly. This is also why we live at the limit of the district, remotely after this large forest.

If that revelation left Zachary Wilton-Cough with another case of a mouth in grand risk of swallowing moths, with his ghostly father pestering wildly in the mind of Vincent Valdi that he will be damned, on the other hand the Doctor, put the sleeve down on the pale arm of Miss White, covering it along with the young Vampire's bite of Mina, back respectfully before he stated,

-You have not only a friend in me Whilhelmina, you have now a protector. If you come in any trouble due to your very unusual circumstances, you can fetch me and I will give you all my help to try to resolve the situation as best as possible. I want you to know that you can count on me to be there for your daughter and yourself. I truly do admire the way you never gave up on Mina. I have a very spirited parent within me who is fighting to save his son from a curse, and trust me, when I can assure you that I understand you. Always having paternal cravings like I do, is something but feeling so paternal that you can take on board every children in need of help is something else. This is where I am at right now.

Her hand stopped shivering within the one of Valdi. Her eyes shouted her gratitude before her thin lips whispered it,

-I thank you so much, Vincent. You do not know how much this means to me who lived in fear for my Mina for an eternity.

Whilhelmina White never expected that reaction from the Doctor. She could have hugged him like the teenage Zachary had done impulsively before, if she was not so worried and so reserved of any close contact, one of the lasting damage of her rape. At long last, she had found a true friend and she could have cried for how blessed she felt right now, something which rarely occurred to her throughout her long life. However she gave an anxious glance to the younger Wilton-Cough trying to analyse his entire attitude. He looked ever so baffled by her revelation that it was still hard to tell. However she saw him taking his cue from Vincent Valdi, only to give her a long look back, and a presented hand to shake, accompanied by a shy smile,

-I can't spell out protection to you Miss White, because I haven't the muscles that have worked in fields like the Doc has, however I can say: cross my heart, I will keep your secret and shut up about all I heard. Each time I come to yours, Mina is rushing to welcome me like if I was her elder brother. I must say that her greeting cheers me up and makes me do the scary walk through the woods more than the cards are. I must also say that I would not like seeing anything bad happening to her either. It's not that I wished to have had a younger sister more than a younger brother but there is a bit of that.

If Vincent and Whilhelmina welcomed his move with the latter shaking Zach's hand with her slight shiver coming back, the ghostly Wilton-Cough enquired straight away within Valdi's mind,

-I do not reproach my son's handshake but just ask him why would he have preferred a sister to a brother. As for the coming Abigail, just keep my secret from him for the time being. I just fear another underlying issue he has with Josiah. Just dig the dirt for me, Valdi, so I can put it straight.

The Doctor did as he was told somehow as interested as Zach's father when he enquired,

-Why the preference for a sister over a brother?

Putting his hands in the pockets of his coat, the teenager replied with a straight honesty,

-Because I get compared to my bro all the times. With a little sister, any of my lacking may stand a chance with a bit of forgiveness. I mean, I do hear all the time, that Jo got the beautiful blue eyes of my mum but that I have the stare of my father. If Josiah always comes up with a sweet thing to say, I come up with brain failure and nothing to say, and there I get the 'he is either stupid or arrogant' look so I went to play arrogant fully saving me to be labelled as fully stupid. Josiah does shine, for my bro is very bright, very. If you ask him he can play Bach's Toccata backwards, I have seen it, but I would never know if he fooled me either. So, how do I stand a chance compared to such a brother?

Using Valdi's voice, Abraham scolded his eldest son,

-Everyone is special my son, everyone. It doesn't matter if it is boy or girl either. Do not get lost on concentrating on comparison. Your are as special as anyone. Everyone is unique. What you need to concentrate on is bringing your own specificity to this world. What will be your contribution? It might be the one in which you will help to build a hospital. We need everyone to build a world. Do not lose your time on aimless comparison, no, use that time instead in investing on yourself to be a good man which can contribute by your acts to a better world. Remember that everyone is equal in the eye of the above and that the only thing that matters is your heart. In the eyes of my own father Terah, I was no good, with the only reason that I was appalling at hunting. Well I had other skills which meant that I was able to contribute to this town. You, my boy, like I, understand your numbers. Well this is good enough and there is plenty of ways that you can tap on that skill. It is useless to compare. Just be yourself fully and simply.

This made Zachary feel better despite recognising the similar lines which his father had used on his death bed. He usually despised and shunned anyone talking to him in that type of commanding manner. However this was different, this was his father having good talks with him beyond his grave via Doctor Valdi. He could only acknowledge the importance of it but also how precious it was to be able to listen to his dad once more. Also he missed bitterly so much the sense of direction that Abraham provided him during his life.

The boy gave a long silent hug to Vincent Valdi which was supposed to go through to his ghostly father if it could. The good Doctor looked helplessly at the burst of sudden filial affection, his own heart feeling the strong pinch of paternal love. He confided with a certain emotion to Miss White, while messing the hair of Zachary tenderly,

-Whilhelmina, I was at the birth of this chap eighteen years ago. It was during a full moon. Do you believe in the righteousness of a curse which condemns him to be a monster after his life? A distressed Abraham Wilton-Cough is determined to fight off that curse and I am just as well. You, who did know Tristina, how did she do it? How can we reverse it to save the children of this town? You, more than anyone else who has a knowledge of magic can help.

Watching the scene before her did pierce the eternal half human's heart, let alone the stirring words of Vincent Valdi. Closing her vanity case with care yet determination, she replied,

-No more, you three have won your case. Doctor Valdi, you are an excellent advocate and I will help in that fight with all my might. I tried to break the curse myself many times without success. Maybe because I am more of a creature now than a full human. Maybe because the magic I do know is of the harmless type and the one used was different. I only did dark magic on myself once never to touch it again. However I can tell you all I know of what happened then and what could possibly be tried out to break that curse.

The ghost of Abraham jubilated once more in Valdi's mind with a congratulation,

-Fantastic job Vincent, you enlisted the right soldier for our mission. When there's a curse, there's some magic involved and a witch cannot go amiss. Praise her yet quiz her more.

The Doctor was very satisfied with the answer of Miss White but not quite. His constant curiosity awoke once more and yes, he had very much all the best intentions in the world to quiz more the intriguing pale creature who had managed to live for so long. First he tapped on the back of Zachary twice gently, and enjoined,

-Let's move on. I would not like to get Father Odell so worried for us that he starts walking into the forest dragging the old Josephine Cough along with him just for a bit of protection. I tell you what, young man, your great aunt can kick a Ghoul or many alright. She was a right fighter by my side, watching my back as I watched hers. You should have seen Theo using the cross of his church like a sword for this was quite a picture which will stick in my mind all my life. Whilhelmina, you are a very welcomed warrior. Your understanding of magic will be invaluable to us. First tell us what happened back then.

As Vincent Valdi set the faster pace, Zachary Wilton-Cough followed along, with a mind which went wild with thoughts of his great aunt Jo battling it out in a cemetery, but also all the rest. He tried to follow what has been said but that made him wonder far too much, so much that it was hurting. However he understood one thing, one important thing: His father would not rest until he knew he was not affected by any curse. Zachary who had not been the favourite in town for the past few months, felt embraced again and it felt good. Somehow, the teenager had been spurred beyond belief, and, yes, there was a reformed younger Wilton-Cough walking in those woods.

Whilhelmina White followed too but with her mind disturbed in another fashion. She tried to recalled days long gone with precision in order to deliver the recollection of them to Vincent. The call to save Zachary and all children within Wilton Town stroke a cord within her heart. She confessed to the Doctor,

-I truly hope so. Back in the days, the journey we undertook with Noah to those unchartered territories that became Wilton Town, brought us together as very united people. We were very much looking out for one another until we were hit very severely by famine. The one that kept doing the looking out despite it all was Noah M Wilton. For my part, I had to make sure I lived a little away from the town, for my little vampire of a Mina not to sink her teeth to no one but me. However I was working in town, helping out, for with famine striking, they were a fair few in need of care, only making the trip back to my own home at nightfall ready to feed my daughter with my own self. One person I had to tend to quite a fair amount, which was not due to starvation but by the constant battering she was receiving from her husband was Tristina Ogin. I became very slowly but surely her crying shoulder and confident. She became also mine. If she shared what happened to her, I would share some of my deep secrets, not all, but some. She knew about the details of how violently beaten up I was during my rape which made us be some sort of sisters of misfortune. She also knew that I had been condemned to be burnt as a witch in our former country. She was fascinated by that last aspect, always wanting me to do potions and brew for her but also to show her a particular potion.

Vincent commented negatively on that one,

-That doesn't sound good to me. Did you share your knowledge of witchcraft to her?

The eternal creature shook her head negatively yet her sad eyes looked at her feet, before she replied,

-I didn't, but what I did for her repetitively was the potion which would calm down her terrifying husband and eventually make him sleep. I only taught this recipe to you when you had to deal with poor demented and restless Mr Stabe so he would not hurt himself during the worst of his crises. However the effectiveness of that potion increased by tenfold the interest for witchcraft of Tristina. As you may have already guessed the ruins in my garden are the ones of the Ogin's cottage.

The Doctor acknowledged with a stern nod,

-Yes, I did work that one out, Whilhelmina. So the Ogins became your neighbours.

Miss White sighed deeply before carrying on with her story,

-They did, for I didn't keep the secret of what was happening to Tristina almost every single night away from Noah. Their neighbours in town did kind of guess what was happening but I knew the truth from the horse's mouth. I also knew how bad it felt to be under a battering hand. So I confided to the good Noah M Wilton the entire matter. Like most of any Wilton after him, he went straight in to resolve the situation. However the man Ogin would not let himself be scolded in front of everyone like Noah did about the state of Tristina for a second time. No, he decided to move his entire family away from the town. But fearing the unknown beyond it, and at the request of Tristina, they became my neighbours for quite a short while.

She stopped talking to look all around in the woods with her vert-de-gris eyes questing for something, before adding,

-It was too short and yet too long. I would come home to nurse my young Vampire of a daughter which I had yet to properly tame which took years, hundreds of years. In the background, I had the noise of that senseless beating she was going through, and could not intervene as it was impossible for me to leave Mina alone even for the space of a few minutes. My intervention came in the form of my potion. So Tristina had my potion for her husband delivered every morning on her doorstep, as soon as he left for the fields. As I said, the potion worked wonders and after a few shouts the hot tempered Ogin would slumber sometimes at his table. But maybe because of the desperation of Tristina or the desperation of the time itself, she became fixated on wanting the recipe, so much so that if she was not spying at my very windows, she would intrude and step in at whatever time. You can easily imagine that with the heavy secret that my daughter was a Vampire to keep from anyone, I became more guarded against this nosy friend. My fears were that she would witness how my Mina was fed. But if that didn't happen something else did.

She stopped talking and looked again anxiously all around her in the deep darkness of the woods. Vincent Valdi, who had heard the slight noise that made her pose, encouraged,

-It is far too light to be a boar, a Ghoul or a human. Therefore it must be a rabbit, a weasel or a young deer. It is nothing to be worried about beside I am here, and so is Zach.

The teenager felt some pride to be mentioned as a possible protector for if his own great aunt Josephine Cough did fight that night, he didn't want to let down the Cough part of his lineage either. Pushing his shoulders back to make himself look taller, he confirmed,

-I am, Miss White, maybe not a knight in shining armour, but I still intend to do my bit of protecting. So you can be at rest and carry on your story. Pray, tell us what happened?

Whilhelmina saw on the face of both men an eagerness to know, so she continued but with a lower tone of voice,

-There was a night, a night more terrible than all others, a night where the noises next door didn't stop, so much so that I wondered if Tristina had given the potion to her husband, or if he did found out, or else. But that morning, taking the potion from my hands, she warned me as a matter of deep secrecy, that whatever would happen that night to not intervene, for it was a family matter. She told me that she would put an ultimatum to her husband, either he needed to accept the charity given to him of the food offered to them by the town, either to cease farming his fruitless fields and start hunting like Noah did. She said that she would beg him with all her heart for the sake of his children, for she had enough to give them roots which were not even vegetables, which left them hungry and starving. I heard her that night crying that his pride was killing his entire family. That morning when I went to town after her confidence, I could not keep it for myself, because I was deeply worried for her. I went straight to Noah to warn him of the situation. He told me to stay put in my home and do as Tristina ordered me to, to not intervene, but he mentioned it was for my own sake and safety. Noah added to leave it to him.

Interrupting her Zachary asked wildly,

-What did my ancestor do?

Miss White replied to the eager teenager,

-Noah Wilton stayed in the darkness of the woods near the Ogin's cottage with a few men of the town, ready to intervene. They waited until they heard the screams of Tristina, and the noise of crockery being thrown. Then they went in and they took the Ogin father away. Noah was doing his justice in the smaller clearing, with his most trusted men. I know for a fact that Ogin had a good talking to that night in that clearing. Noah did let that out to me as I came for my service the following morning but he also advised me to keep an eyes on that cottage and inform him of everything concerning there. Noah said that if the man Ogin was not subdued for one bit, they had managed to make him consent to learn to hunt until the heaven would break open and that rain could finally anoint the fields of that stubborn farmer giving him the hope of a crop. You see that clearing from here right on the left.

Zachary looked full of interest and begged the Doctor,

-Mr Valdi, pray can we just have a look.

If the Doctor despised the idea like an indulgence being allowed to the Wilton-Cough's pride and a useless sight seeing of where their ancestors once stood, he agreed to it. Reluctantly so, he did give his permission, because he had a noisy Ghost within his mind, just willing to see the little clearing, like his son was, making a racket which if it didn't stop was sure to give him a terrible headache by morning. He led the way across the wet ferns until they reached the clearing which stood under the moonlight. It was only about three to four metres away from the main path which kind of made it all the better for him to conciliate with the fact that they were deviating from it. As the three of them stood still and silent at the edge of the clearing, Abraham warned in his mind,

-I saw that clearing before, on my deathbed. My own father Terah never entered it for he said it was belonging to Ghosts.

Vincent burst in an out loud imprecation,

-You damn Wilton-Cough! Now, you are telling me after forcing us to go there. Zachary, Whilhelmina, I think we should retreat to the treaded path. I have just been informed that the clearing is particularly haunted.

Chapter Sixteen

The Haunted

A heavy mist thickened the grass with water droplets. In the middle of the clearing all could see shadows, almost moving with the breeze. Zachary opened his mouth wide in utter stupor. His trembling hand went to nestle in the strong one of the Doctor. On the other side of Valdi, Whilhelmina nestled her shivering arm under his. Vincent just knew, from those cues, that he will have to manage the situation. He stated firmly,

-Right, we have seen the clearing, everyone is happy, let's go.

But Miss White recognised a Ghost among many, who was gliding slowly with his hand on the head of the Crying White Doe. She whispered ever so faintly,

-That's him. It's Ogin.

Zachary felt his heart thumping in his chest as he spelt out,

-The horrendous wife beater.

Tugging the teenager's hand sharply, the Doctor warned in a mutter,

-Shush! Keep your mouth shut to stay out of trouble, young Man. You do not know what a Ghost can do to you.

The younger Wilton-Cough pouted before retorting, yet having lowered his voice to a mere whisper,

-They can't do anything for they are not physical. If I was not a man and a Wilton-Cough I would pull my tongue to that horrid bastard.

Vincent Valdi corrected him sternly,

-As I said, you know nothing about what a Ghost can do. I can tell you from experience that they can twist your guts, penetrate your body and hurt you from the inside out. So do not pull your tongue and stay very silent by me.

This made the teenager look at the Ghost of Ogin with dread, and yes he fell into a deep silence full of internal turmoil. There he thought that the Doctor had a very valid point which he could not contest because he knew too well that Valdi was the host of his ghostly father. About the existence of Ghouls and Ghosts, Vincent had certainly a more physical experience than him. Zachary also pondered that it would be a good idea to let the good man be even more experienced than him on this occasion, for he was a little scared at that moment. So he retreated behind the Doctor slightly just in case the Ghost of Ogin did hear him. At the increased trembling of his young hand in his, Vincent Valdi knew that his information sank in Zach's mind. It was all the better if the lad stayed behind him out of trouble too for he could have sworn that the Ghost was looking in their direction.

The Doctor wondered, addressing himself very quietly to Miss White,

-Did the final chastising of Noah Wilton-Cough work on Ogin?

Whilhelmina shook her head negatively. Giving her a worried look, Vincent demanded,

-Carry on. What happened when he came back from that clearing?

Miss White confessed,

-I do not know exactly, Vincent. All I can say for sure is that he was not shouting anymore the following evening. I took it as a good sign that the telling off of the men of the town upon him had worked and I told Noah just so that the next morning. Ogin was meant to go and learn hunting with Noah that afternoon. But the man never woke up. It was about mid morning when Tristina came to town, looking devastated. She announced to Noah Wilton that her husband was dead, that he passed away in his sleep. The woman was in such a state of anguish, that it was heartbreaking to see. Noah who asked me to come with him to assess the death, along with about four men who would bring back the body of Ogin to town to be buried. When we reached the cottage by about noon, we witnessed the scene that I described to you earlier. Terrance and Tarquin were so starving that when left unattended they feasted on their own father. It was so horrendous to watch that Tristina fainted in my arms. It revolted Noah Wilton-Cough right and proper.

The Ghost of Abraham commented in Valdi's mind,

-I bet it did! Vincent, observe, that if the Crying Doe possess the Spirit of his battered wife, she is walking with him.

Noting the fact, intrigued the Doctor enough for him to enquire,

-Whilhelmina, did Tristina forgive her husband?

The answer that came in a whisper unsettled him,

-The question could be did he forgive her.

A shocked Zachary blasted in a muted voice,

-What? Scuse-me for saying so, Miss White, but that prick is the bad arse that needed his arse kicked right and proper during his life. Why would Tristina have to say sorry for being brutalised every night?

If his interjection showed that the eighteen year old had paid great attention to the conversation, and felt somehow passionate about it, which was something a little unusual for him, it was also unfortunately loud enough for the Crying White Doe's neck and head to turn nervously in their direction. Her large black teary eyes observed them as the animal stood still like a statue, yet in full alert.

Vincent Valdi swallowed his breath when the movement of the fragile beast had warned Ogin's Ghost of their presence. The floating cadaver with a rib cage ripped apart looked worst than frightening.

Behind him Zachary tapped on his shoulders frantically, repeating the same question to his ears,

-I think he saw us. I definitely think he saw us, he is gliding towards us. What do we do now, Doc? What do we do?

Valdi, fairly annoyed with Zach after advising the youngster to remain silent which he did no do, replied sarcastically,

-Pick your choice: shit in your pants or run for it. Whil', grab your skirts up now. Zach, take her vanity case and don't lose it, for your mum's medicine is inside it.

The boy looked very panicked yet took charge of the vanity case, before asking for confirmation,

-We are running then?

The Doctor gave him a killer glance, with a wicked smirk, along with his directions,

-See, you made the good choice! You aren't stupid after all! Of course we aren't going to stay and see if we will get trashed. Just run, my son, run! Take the other hand of Miss White and don't let go of her. I will be right behind to protect you two. That Ghost can't plunge within my body, if he attempts to do so, your father will give his Spirit the Soul's arse kicking he deserves.

Zachary Wilton-Cough didn't wait to be told another time. He grabbed Miss White's hand and made a dash to go back to the path as fast as they could. He was very aware that he had blown it somehow, and repeated to Whilhelmina who followed him as best as she could,

-I am so sorry, Miss White, so very sorry. Sometimes, sometimes, I would slap myself.

Despite muddying the bottom of her dress, despite jumping over ferns like her life was at stake, Whilhelmina White couldn't help smiling kindly to the sheepish and utterly scared teenager. Since his lost game, since his talk with a possessed Valdi, it was the first night she was seeing Zachary truly showing proper emotions, and finally trying to express himself. At the way, he firmly held her hand and kept looking back to make sure she was alright, she knew that Abraham had managed to dig the dirt his eldest son was hiding behind. She looked upon that younger Wilton-Cough much differently. Now that all his walls and pretences were down, she could only see a shy, anxious young man, full of disharming honesty, needing direction and encouragement. So she did so,

-Don't slap yourself, you are doing good, look here's the path. We made it to the path. Let's not go too fast, in case, in case, Vincent needs us. If he is under attack, I may use witchcraft and intervene. If I do so the Doe may get upset and I will need you to deal with her. The Spirit of Tristina lives in the Crying White Doe. She is a very sorrowful and upset Spirit.

As Zachary engaged in the path with her, his mind went into a bewildered state for how could he talk to a sorrowful Crying Doe? And when they both turned to check on the Doctor, Miss White and him saw the Spirit of Ogin grounding Valdi in order to go inside him. This fighting sight was so terrifying that the teenager just trembled, until, Whilhelmina ordered,

-Deal with the Doe, I will deal with Ogin.

He repeated for himself many times over, when he had absolutely no clue about it,

-Deal with the doe. Deal with the doe. I will deal with the Doe. How do I deal with a doe?

And Zachary went to deal with the fragile doe who looked so sad, so tired, so distressed, that it was just breaking his own heart. He just went to her as clumsily as one could ever do so with a,

-Hi, Pet...

While he was attempting to talk to the Crying White Doe, Vincent Valdi had been penetrated by Ogin with devastating result. The Doctor could feel a terrible pain within his chest. However The Ghost that came in his body left all of a sudden for Abraham Wilton-Cough fought him back. Valdi saw himself levitate like he did in the church. The anger invading him was not his but the one of Abraham so was the voice that vociferated against Ogin,

-Brutalising someone during your life wasn't enough! You want more. Let me give you more. I will drag you to hell with me. Let me teach you what it costs to dare touching that man!

Vincent Valdi lunged into a vicious attack against the Ghost, his strength multiplied by the mere presence of the cross Banker within him. Despite his chest still in pain, somehow he managed to make Ogin collapse and stay still with fright underneath him. Ogin's spectral voice demanded,

-What type of creature are you?

To which Wilton-Cough replied,

-You do not want to know. How dare you dwelling in Wilton's forest for eternity when you couldn't be man enough to go hunting to feed your children? You have no right to haunt those woods. Your only resting place is Hell, let me spell it out for you: H-E-L-L.

He spat the letters upon the Ghost with punches, and at the last punch and letter, a great light poured out of Valdi, encompassing Ogin.

The frightened Whilhelmina, standing nearby, crossed herself, as she saw a winged creature spitted out from Valdi which took the Ghost of Ogin. She could swear it was an Angel, who dragged Ogin across the clearing away from them, who made a circular sign with her angelic hand in the air. The gesture opened a portal in front of the Angel where all could see flames pouring out from. The portal closed behind the Angel and the Ghost who gesticulated in fright.

Holding the Doe, tight in his arms, comforting her, Zachary had another of his catch the moth with my mouth moment as he witnessed the scene. Speechless, his mind went wild with questions, of what was this and that and how.

Vincent Valdi stood up, shaken, yet he dusted his shoulders with a certain nonchalance, indicating falsely to the other Ghosts in the clearing who had been standby spectators that he was used to that sort of thing and was doing it every night. He hoped the trick will make them stay away from Miss White, Zachary and also from him. He walked with great assurance to Whilhelmina, who had fallen on her knees, praying silently, and enjoined,

-There is a time for everything Whil', and this is not the time nor the place to pray. This clearing is full of restless Souls. Let's get out of here before Wilton-Cough has to play proper poltergeist with me again to protect us.

His strong hand helped her up, while he gave a glance to the trembling teenager who had watched everything halfway through the path and the clearing. Zachary was stroking the Doe and the animal was nestled against his young chest. Whatever Zach was doing with the Crying White Doe seemed to work for she looked very tame at that moment in time. Of course Vincent Valdi hoped the Doe will stay long enough with Zachary so he could satisfy his curiosity about that mythical creature haunting Wilton Town's woods.

Following the Doctor, Miss White was considering him with great awe, so much so that Vialdi told her as they walked hurriedly towards Zachary,

-It's me Whil', a possessed me, but it is still me, Vincent.

Then he spoke out loud to Abraham Wilton-Cough within him,

-Thank you, Ab, I am mighty glad you are looking after my guts. What was that? I never felt that powerful in my entire life.

The Ghost within him smiled internally replying to his mind,

-That was something. I can honestly say I never felt that powerful in my entire life either. But I tell you what, you and I share the same Angel, Abigail. She intervened to protect you like I did. The strength, the words, your ability to physically pin down a Ghost, were all hers. She used me as a medium to go within you. Gosh, that was something. The good news is you are angelic property Vincent. Fancy that, possessed by an Angel, I guessed you seen it all now.

While he replied: 'Not yet' to his internal Ghost, Valdi had a wild irresistible smirk drawing on his face at Abraham's confidence. Not only did it make him understood what happened to him, but it was also good to know that he had that 'extra pair of wings' level of protection. He could not resist for one minute to share his news to the White Witch's enquiring eyes,

-According to Wilton-Cough's Soul, I am angelically protected, Whil'. The Angel you just saw is Abigail. She usually appears as a little orb of bright light guiding your footsteps. She lit my path to yours today.

It is fair to say that Whilhelmina White was utterly gob smacked. She could not think of a sentence let alone just a word to say to that. She thought that yes, definitively Vincent Valdi had what he called 'a night', and since he came to her hotel, she was having one herself. For Christ's sake, he caught her praying in a clearing full of Ghosts. But if something was up with this Doctor big time, she was catching it too. She felt compelled to follow him and help him, since a while. She couldn't put a finger on exactly when precisely, but thinking hard, she established it was since the day he arrived in Wilton-Town.

His soft voice pulled her out of her thoughts,

-So you went back for me, Miss White? Staying in the path would have been a better place for you and Zach, much safer than the clearing.

The eternal woman confessed,

-I couldn't stay there fearing for you. I went back in to help you if I could with witchcraft. I attempted to make Ogin a physical Ghost so he could not enter you again. But, but that's dark magic and it's within that book, and I do not know it by heart, for it disappeared from my home a very long while ago. I haven't been practising since ages. I felt like a rusty Witch without any means to help you. I gave the order to our young Wilton-Cough to look after the Crying Doe for we will need her to break the curse. She is the container of the Spirit of Tristina and she is the one that needs to agree to reverse what she has done.

Nodding his acknowledgement to her, Valdi and within him, Abraham Wilton-Cough were satisfied not only that Whilhelmina was committed to their cause, but also was definitely a very loyal friend to Vincent. The Doctor tapped twice her hand he was holding reassuringly,

-Well, never mind about that book and being a black Witch, you can remain a rusty good white one for I can tell you that Ogin felt the punches I gave him. He was getting gradually more physical under my hands enabling the Angel of Abraham, Wilton-Cough and I to control him.

He then started to fetch something from inside his leather satchel. When he found it, he put it in his coat pocket and tapped his pocket twice with a satisfied grin. By that time he was by Zachary. He ruffled the teenager's hair, before pushing the chin of the teenager up in order to close his open mouth. The Doctor ordered,

-Enough time wasted to satisfy your curiosity my boy. This place is badly haunted and we are getting out of here. Introduce me to your friend, first, for she desperately needs to be talked to just as much as you needed.

It goes without saying that Zachary was by now totally in awe of the Doctor. He would obey him and do as he said alright without even arguing especially now that he had witnessed an Angel coming out of his very mouth. He answered in a very subdued way,

-It's Tristina, Sir. She cannot talk but one can nonetheless feel her extreme sorrow. I have been trying to soothe her but I am not that successful for her blood tears are still running thick and fast.

Crouching by the teenager in order to not scare the human spirited animal off, Vincent explained,

-This is because Tristina has a lot to be sorry for. Her tears will not dry until her revengeful heart is laid to rest. We are going to help her to retrieve her peace. We are taking her with us. Hold her still for me.

Zachary stroking the Doe, did as he was told, with his eyes watering. He kept soothing,

-Tristina, it's going to be alright. I promise you. Doctor Valdi is a good man. He knows how to speak to Spirits and Souls. He will help you out. You can trust him.

Vincent took a cord from his coat pocket, and despite the beast struggling to get away, managed to tie the front legs together. He then proceeded to do the same with the hind legs, as he stated sternly,

-There is no more running away from your own deeds, Tristina. It will be for your own Spirit's good but also the good of all the innocents you have condemned.

Now crying for the animal, hugging her desperately, not understanding, the teenager objected,

-What are you talking about Doctor? Tristina is forgiving. She has a forgiving heart. Look we witnessed her walking by her husband.

Valdi stroked the head of the Doe, gazing right through her teary eyes in search of the human Soul stuck within the fragile animal. Before he responded to the unrest of the youngster,

-Yes, I admit that we saw that, Zach. But we will try that very same heart to see if it can apply the same generous forgiveness to the like of you and the many children she has condemned for an eternity in this town. Let go of Tristina, my Son and trust that we are putting things to right before her curse affects you like so many others and transforms you on your deathbed to a flesh eating Ghoul.

Zachary released his hold on the beast, stupefied by the information thrown at his doors. He remained distressed and ever so silent, as he tried to comprehend the entire matter. Miss White came by him. Her kind arm surrounded his shoulders as she reassured,

-It is complicated stuff, Zach. We will fill you in bit by bit along the way. Whatever Doctor Valdi mentioned is ever so right.

Lifting the Doe from the ground Vincent Valdi put her across his shoulders so he could keep her secure with her legs on either side of his neck. He gave a quick glance at the distraught teenager before demanding,

-Just trust, Zachary. We will not hurt Tristina. She had her fair share of hurts all her entire life for us to be unkind to her. We will help her spirit out. Just look at her, do you want her to live forever in this eternal sorrow?

The young Wilton-Cough shook his head negatively as he replied,

-I trust you, Doc. There is so much I don't know but one thing is sure is that I do not want Tristina to suffer like she does.

-Good. Let's hope she can reciprocate the same compassion for as it stands with her curse, from a sensitive young man, you will become an insensitive monster.

The Doctor set the pace which was making them move away from the clearing while Zachary pondered silently what Valdi had said. He could not get his head around everything and trying to keep the stride of Vincent, he asked him puzzled,

-Why would Tristina curse me? What harm did I do to her?

-You didn't do her any harm. You were not even born at that time.

The stern reply that came from Valdi made Zachary question him even more, with an honest confusion,

-Did she know that I would be born a bit stupid and a bit too proud? So she cursed me as an unworthy foolish lad...

Vincent and Whilhelmina glanced at each others before looking tenderly at the troubled teenager who was so full of insecurities. While the Doctor messed Zach's hair up with affection, it was Miss White who reassured him,

-She could not know this type of thing. Beside you are far from stupid, proud, unworthy and foolish. You have only started your life and bestow plenty of time to learn everything, one day at a time. No, Tristina didn't know about you at all, she was so upset that she did curse many in town, anyone born during a full moon, so no one could ultimately rest in peace, so all would have their graves disturbed. She didn't mean to curse you in particular. She meant to affect everyone in one way or another via her curse.

Zachary finally seeing the end of the forest, the walled path leading to the cemetery and the town beyond the church, was rather disheartened. He confided in a shy question,

-So I am not that bad. She just did that to everyone. Did everyone born during a full moon deserve to become a Ghoul?

The Doctor stated sternly,

-This is my point and the right question, my boy. What do you think? I remember all the babies I held at their births and it is with utter sadness that I learnt that lots of them are cursed. If I hate the thought of you becoming a Ghoul in the future, you can clearly imagine the outrage of your father. You can be sure that we will do everything in our power to correct things in order to destroy that curse which affects so many. It is my belief that Tristina was so full of grief at her husband's death that she overreacted in a hell of a big way. I would not be surprised either, Miss White, if she had used your black magic book, that disappeared. When did you notice that it was missing?

Whilhelmina concentrated to remember precisely, then confided,

-It was after the death of Ogin. It was about a couple of days or three days later at most. I came back from town at dusk like usual, and I noticed a hole in one of my windows. Tristina came to me with a very sheepish look on her face to explain what happened. She apologised for the damage, that her restless boys had been throwing stones at each other and that one landed in my window. She confessed that since their father's death, she had not been able to control them. Terrence and Tarquin worried her as much as causing her fears. I reassured her as best as I could then stepped into my home. Upon first sight, the stone used was still there, on the floor, nothing looked damaged or missing, and I went to check upon my Mina who was profoundly asleep in her bed. She was as fine as I left her that morning. Being a worried person, I then went to check my most valued possessions. All were to be accounted for but the book. This gave me great anxiety for it is not the sort of book to be possessed by anyone like that...

Calmly scrutinising her countenance, Vincent enquired at her sudden silence,

-What did you do?

Miss White looked anxious and pale. Her hands twisted one another continuously as she replied,

-Mina woke up. I had to look after her. She didn't drink too much of me that night. I hadn't eaten since Ogin's death. I think my daughter realised and paced herself. The good Noah who had vowed to feed all of his people since seeing Terrence and Tarquin feasting on their father's corpse, wasn't seen for a couple of days. I raised the alarm for it was unusual for him to disappear like that. His trusted men scoured the woods and found him, lying injured and in a poor state the following day. That morning, at dawn, I knocked on Tristina's doors to enquire about my book, just before going back to town. She was tearful as she let me in. She told me that she had no idea of what I was talking about. She collapsed on a chair and went on a proper rant against Noah, who had made a promise yet was not delivering it, the town's people who were eating their own dead when Noah was not watching, almost everyone was blamed and shamed and her own children too. Her fear of them was so great, that she trembled as she spoke about her night. She said she was laying in her bed, when she heard them whispering and contemplating her as a meal. It went as far as them standing by her bed, just looking at her body, thinking she was asleep. Although she faked, she told me, taking it all in of their little plot, which was utterly gruesome. They had described her as skin on bones yet that she was better than nothing despite her starved state. Tristina told me, she just lost all hopes. During her confession I looked everywhere for my book but it was nowhere to be seen. Her children were somewhere and she believed they must have joined the town people who were eating their dead for she couldn't feed them. Before I left she threw her only expensive possession in the fire place in front of my eyes, which was her rosary, stating that god did not exist, that if children ate their parents, they were all cursed to be damned.

A listening Zachary interjected after her silence,

-But, but, but, I didn't ate my own Pa. I would never think of such things. I don't come from that famish time. I don't know what it is to be starving. I've got nothing to do with it. Why did Noah Wilton not keep his promise?

Whilhelmina answered him,

-Noah did but it came a little late. That morning I arrived in town and his house was still empty. Then the men who went to look for him brought Noah back to town. It was noon. His hunting trip didn't go well. His leg had been gored by a boar. Despite his loss of blood your ancestor was conscious although running a fever. His temperature was a warning sign for me that infection must have settled in his body. I could have cried when I saw him in such state for all in Wilton Town relied on him for almost everything. However I rallied all my fighting spirits up and endeavoured to save that man to make him better. His leg was so torn into pieces, so butchered, so infected that he just knew if he kept it, he would die within days, however if it was cut he could stand a chance to survive for the community. He is the first Wilton, and he was such a brave and generous man, Zachary. Selfless even then, he said that he needed to get back up as soon as to go back to hunt. He ordered me to cut his leg, to mend him as best as I could and his men to carve a leg out of wood for him.

The fascinated teenager interrupted again,

-I never knew my ancestor had a wooden leg. Did he survive the operation?

Somehow that question made Miss White thin lips smile at the recollection she gave to that young descendant of Noah M Wilton,

-He did for Noah was strong. It would have taken more than a single boar to take him down. It was a hard operation, for I am mainly a midwife and a carer, a nurse, not a proper Doctor like Vincent is. Noah knew it but he told me that he trusted me to do my best, scolding me to encourage me to proceed. He said that with that leg, it was only a matter of days for him to die anyway. It had to go and he couldn't trust anyone else for the task. I made him drink to numb the process and to make sure he was still with me throughout, I talked to him. I engaged him in anyway possible to keep his mind away from the pain but also conscious. Nothing was better than to tell him about everyone in town and how they were all doing and coping without him for the past couple of days. It spurred him on. It was like talking about his children to their father. He knew almost everything about anyone. During his time he felt a duty to record every event in Wilton Town, along with a death record and a birth one, he wrote a diary about the town and its people. I believe the diary is still in the presbytery which used to be the cottage of Noah. During the operation, running out of news to tell him, as he enquired about me, I picked up the courage to tell him about my lost book. He reassured me that he would look for it, but not return it to me if found, that he would either burn it or keep it safe forever. As I was cutting through his leg, he swore that despite my knowledge of witchcraft, he didn't want me to be burnt in his town by sheer misunderstanding, despite me sawing through his bone giving him tremendous pain, he swore that he would look after my life as much as I was doing to his, which meant to protect it from being cut short. If it meant a parting of some sort, as he put it: 'a leg or a book, so be it'. I very much understood that if anyone found my book but him, I would be in trouble. Till this day I do not know if Noah found my book or not, but I know I am alive and there were no professed black Witch in Wilton Town during all that time. As for the wooden leg, Noah being a Wilton, the first one, had that small pride, to always be remembered as he first stepped into those woods creating Wilton Town. He didn't want to see a glimmer of pity in anyone's eyes looking at him either. Any depiction of him was to be the one when he put two firm feet on this land and no other. In the memory of who he was and his will, it stayed that way.

If Zachary felt proud of his ancestor, if his ghostly father had relished upon the account, Vincent Valdi was eager to know much more as he probed,

-Was Noah M Wilton a confident to you? Did you trust him?

To which Miss White replied straight away,

-At that time, I would not work for someone anymore if I didn't trusted them first. Noah was straight and forward like an arrow. He also wore his heart on his sleeve a bit like you. He would talk openly about everything with a honesty which I can see glimmer of in

Zachary, and saw a lot of in Abraham. Like I said, he was a father figure to all of us in town so, to answer your question, yes I did confide in him a great deal. I never kept anything from him apart that I was eternal and my daughter was a Vampire. I was forever informing him about everyone in town, knowing how they all mattered to him, highlighting anything that could be of concern. On knowing that Tarquin and Terrence were so troubled by starvation, he didn't want to rest, and recover from his operation, he went with his men to hunt. That fatherless family needed to be fed as soon as possible and they became his priority. Their hunt was successful. The men separated after the hunt. While Noah was to bring his catch to Tristina and her children, his men brought theirs back to town.

Her voice failed her. They had arrived at the rusty gate of the cemetery. Valdi opened it, then commented, finishing her story,

-That's when Noah stepped in, a minute late or so, with the murder of Tristina by her children, just having been done, with their hands still on her beating heart, eating it.

Despite the shrieking of the gate, the appalled scream of Zachary wasn't hidden. He opened his mouth twice, then thrice before being able to articulate his thoughts,

-No! How could children do that? No, it's too horrible! It's too inhuman! Their own mother, it's not possible.

As they entered the cemetery, Whilhelmina confirmed sadly,

-It did happen. Terrence and Tarquin ran away, and despite all our efforts to find them, they were lost to all forever.

Somehow the interjection of Zachary made Vincent Valdi think out loud,

-Maybe they were inhuman. Whil' if your book disappeared from your home and was used to do the curse in this town, who are the culprits? I believe there was a mother, Tristina who was fascinated by witchcraft, upset with everything and grieved who desired it for one specific reason or another. She could not control her children without Ogin. She could have wanted the sleeping potion for them but how to demand it from you reasonably now with her husband being dead. Let's not forget that she was scared of them. I believe however that she requested the book from Terrence and Tarquin and that they did deliver it to their mother. She didn't go herself to break into your house. The reason is, and this may upset you, they may have encountered Mina, and your daughter fed on both boys. This is why Mina was not drinking as much as normally from you that evening. She already had her fill during the day. Maybe the black book was bargained, maybe not, maybe the experience may have been frightening enough for the boys to step in, getting what they wanted and step out. But if those boys were turned, they would not have their human inhibitions anymore and restraint. They were already wickedly planning beforehand, now at their first thirsty urge, they just acted making their first victim of their own mother.

An extremely pale Whilhelmina White had trembling lips and tears appearing in her eyes. Whatever the Doctor had just spelt out was her worst nightmare. However she could not ignore its possibility and probability. If it was the case that would mean that Terrence and Tarquin were two young Vampires on the loose for an eternity, but it would also explain their complete disappearance. They would have become creatures of the night, elusive, furtive in shadows and living fully under the moonlight. Their thirsts to quench may have led them far from the starved Wilton Town. She looked desperately at Vincent, searching for any signs of vindictiveness in his demeanour but found none as she apologised,

-If it is the case, and I strongly hope it is not, I am ever so sorry. But I can't help thinking that you could be right, because that would explain so much.

Positively nodding, the Doctor confidently told,

-We will sort it out together, Whil'. You have knowledge of Vampires more than any one else, and we will track our two youngsters down, if it is the case, once the two of us have properly talked to Mina to confirm it.

As they walked through the cemetery they saw Father Odell by a grave who seemed deeply engaged in a conversation with the old Josephine Cough. In fact, they were so engrossed in their conversation that they didn't notice their arrival whatsoever. Theo was holding both hands of Josephine and jumped when his friend standing only a metre away from him, wickedly shouted,

-Boo!

He turned half crossed and half happy with relief, whispering,

-Vincent!

If the Priest's face was full of worries and wonder, it also had a welcoming smile, as he appraised the situation in front of him. He could only acknowledge that the Doctor did bring back Zachary Wilton-Cough, whose demeanour was not the proudest he ever saw. By Valdi, Miss White stood looking like a lost sheep being brought back to the shepherd. To finish off his scanning of the situation, there was, that famous White Doe, a pure local legend, alive, on his friend's shoulders. Theo had thousands of questions but before he could just utter a word, the Doctor told him,

-I can explain my lateness, I can explain everything.

-I am sure you can, you always can, Vince. Zachary, your mother is going to be so happy to see you earlier than day break. Miss White, I didn't expect you. Our last parting made me feel that I was the last man you wished to see and meet.

Vincent stepped in straight away before Whilhelmina could reply for herself,

-Miss White comes to help. She has something to treat wounds caused by Ghouls that is necessary for Mrs Wilton-Cough, but I dare say, for you and Josephine as well. Don't be proud, show her where they bit you. Theo, Miss White is an eternal White Witch which can help us greatly with our matter at hand, aka, getting rid of that damn curse. But she hasn't been able to on her own.

Father Odell took a good head to toe glance at Miss White. Her countenance was a far cry from the one he had witnessed not so long ago. Presented straight forwardly as a Witch before him, she stood like the most frightened person on Earth, like if he was about to stab her in broad day light, or worse, crucify her. Therefore he presented his hand to her in a reassuring fashion, with a few words,

-Miss White, your help is most welcomed. Let me show you to Angela. She had quite a night, a fright and a bite. Vincent did a very good job, however she is growing quite a temperature which is worrying all of us for the past hour. Mrs Bates is attending to her applying cold compress after cold compress. If you need anything just tell me and I will fetch it for you. I don't have any servants, never did. May I offer you a coffee to repay for your help and my deepest gratitude?

The woman assessed the man for a long minute, letting him stand there with his hand right up in the air before her trembling hand shook his. She answered very shyly and softly,

-I could do with a strong coffee as much as Vincent. I will need just some hot water for your scars and if Miss Cough has some, for I know you have been fighting fiercely tonight. I saw Valdi's arms to tell the tale.

-Do not forget to inspect Mrs Bates, just in case.

Reminded Vincent, as he was already inspecting once more the arms of Josephine Cough.

Whilhelmina nodded to him as she followed Father Odell and Zachary inside the presbytery.

The Doctor told with a confident smile to the old Aunt Cough,

-Only scratches. But I can swear I am seeing a tear in your eyes, Jo.

-Fiddlestick, Doc. It's an eyelash.

-You haven't got that many. Doesn't work with me. What's up?

-I've been confessing to Theo about the ghosts that haunt my past, that's all. He probed me about the hate I have carried for so long against my sister Juliette.

-Come, dry your tears, we all have a past haunting us. We are all haunted. Now, let's make it all better together. Let's forget about it and live in the present. All we can do is correct all we can from the past and its mistakes. There is a massive mistake of a curse done in the past that is plaguing us today which needs all of us to correct it. Come on in.

Chapter Seventeen

'A Friend in need is a Friend indeed '

When he entered the living room, Doctor Valdi saw books and maps laid on the table like in a military operation. Mrs Bates seemed to be on top of it all while Mrs Wilton-Cough received, surprised, Zachary who went into her arms in a silent hug. When the teenager finally managed to express his thoughts, his first words were simply,

-Mum, I heard what happened, about the biting Ghouls and all. How are you?

His mother stroked his hair before saying,

-Already better since I've seen you.

This made the boy literally cry upon her shoulder. Angela looked helpless for a minute, trying to find an answer on Vincent Valdi's face, but he explained in a few words instead,

-Wilton-Cough had a good talk with the lad.

Angela nodded positively, and hugged her eldest son even closer despite her pain, smiling ever so tenderly. She asked Zach full of curiosity,

-What did your Pa say?

Drying his tears, Zachary told earnestly,

-I had a right telling off, Ma, so much so that I wished I was buried in my bed, but you know with Pa, you can't hide, you've just got to face the light and the music. But, but...

His voice sank momentarily before he confessed crying thoroughly once more,

-Hearing him again was music to my ears. I felt so so lost without him. I can't explain...

This broke the dam of his mother's own tears as she kept the teenager in a tight embrace. She felt like her son was finally given back to her. She also shared totally his emotions.

Watching the scene and knowing how overdue it was, Vincent felt himself quite emotional. Making the two steps that separated him from Amelia Bates, he went to hold her hand ever so silently. The Widow felt a warmth at that simple gesture and when she dared to meet the Doctor's gaze upon her, she just knew he was moved and that Vincent's impulse was to share it with her. Touched, she left her hand within his, enjoying the strong yet soft grasp of it. She blushed before readjusting her glasses upon her nose with her other hand, only to consider the strange collar around the Doctor's neck. She swore,

-Mr Valdi, for Christ's sake, did you go hunting while we were all worried for you?

Vincent gave her a very apologetic sheepish look. He went to lay the animal by Zachary with an order before returning by Amelia,

-Zach, look after Tristina. Soothe her.

The teenager left his mother's arms, obeying straight away without a complaint. He crouched by the tied animal, stroking her gently while Valdi reassured Mrs Bates,

-I do not indulge in the sport, nor like it. I have enough chicken in my backyard to give me eggs for breakfast and dinner. No, this is Tristina Ogin. Well it is rather complicated but her Spirit is within the Doe, our local legendary Crying White Doe. She is the woman responsible for cursing the children of Wilton-Town. We need her to reverse the curse. Her Spirit needs to agree with it or at least allow it. How's your feet, Amelia? Let me check your arms. Miss

White has a special lotion for Ghoul's bites. She came with me to look after Angela's wounds but also to help us break the curse. She treated my arms already.

Amelia gave Angela a very long look as the two women shook their heads together in sheer disbelief. Then she shared their discoveries,

-We found out that Miss White has been around since the settlers of Wilton Town for she was very much so one of them. But we also know that she was accused to be a Witch and about to be burnt with her daughter. We thought, well assumed, that she was responsible for the curse. The fact that she has been a midwife in Wilton Town for so long led us to believe the worst.

The Doctor staunchly corrected,

-Assumptions will get you nowhere. They cause more harm than good. Look at me, I have helped at so many births during my twenty years in this town that I cannot remember the number yet I remember the name of every single child. Am I evil for helping a woman give birth? Whilhelmina White has helped women in this community for longer than I can say. She is a Witch, she is eternal, but she is not responsible for the curse. I swear upon my own soul that she is far from evil. We fought together to save lives, so many times that I know it for a fact. I didn't even have to ask for her to look after Angela, she simply proposed it out of concern. Ladies, please, correct your assumptions at once and welcome her in your midst. Now Amelia, tell me about that plan and books.

Mrs Bates despite having her fair arms inspected by the Doctor, described proudly to him,

-Well, Mrs Wilton-Cough and I were far from aimless, Doctor Valdi. We scoured the birth records and the death ones, every single entry of them. Then we referred to the cadastral book to pinpoint the tomb of every Ghoul in town. You see them all marked down with a red cross on the map.

Impressed Vincent praised, then giving a good look down to the map, paled,

-Right, that scratch is a little too deep for my taste. We will have to clean that. This sounds like you have been busy bees, Ladies. Jeez, it's worst than I thought! Do not tell me that one in three tombs in that cemetery contains a Ghoul?

Stepping into the room with Miss White, who carried a bowl of steaming water, Theo Odell confirmed,

-Indeed, it is the case, Vince. But for all those there is hope, because from our trip to my crypt with Miss Cough, we were able to ascertain that exorcism works on the Ghouls. Mrs Juliette Wilton-Cough who had been exorcised as a child was a skeleton. She did not turn into a Ghoul. However she was not a perfect one, I mean a complete skeleton, for she was as gnawed upon as was the poor young Miss Pendleton.

Theo put the silver tray holding steaming cups of coffee he was carrying on the table in front of his best friend before continuing,

-As you can realise by that map, there is no chance that any of the graves in this cemetery remained undisturbed. I did an exorcism in the crypt, and all the Ghouls down there, transformed from living dead to skeletons. With this map, I will be able to put to rest the Ghouls of that cemetery, exorcism after exorcism upon their every grave. Then Mrs Bates and Angela worked out the list of all in town, still alive, victim of the curse, like our Zachary Wilton-Cough. Here, have some coffee. Miss White told me that you are harbouring the Spirit of Abraham. If it did some good it also gives you a concerning hypothermia. Wilton-Cough, if you hear me, just let Vincent's body recuperate. Be at liberty in my home, and it kills me to say this, to express yourself with my furniture. But I sincerely rather you ghost write, or if you must, use my own body but just a little. Let spare Valdi from a pneumonia, shall we, and be a good ghostly guest in my presbytery instead?

Abraham blasted through the voice of Valdi before exiting him,

-Jeez, Father Odell, your goody-goody ways can be tiresome sometimes! I was getting comfortable in there. Vincent, it's been an honour and a pleasure. You have all my heartfelt appreciation for harbouring me.

Vincent Valdi felt like if a blanket of coldness was removed from his entire self. He could breathe freely again. His entire body was his once more yet it felt so empty all of a sudden, that he scolded his friend,

-Theo, I was coping perfectly well with the ghostly intrusion of Abraham. You are such a kill joy. It was such an experience, one of a lifetime, I say. Abraham Wilton-Cough, if you want to invade me again at anytime, feel free to be my guest. The pleasure of that deeper acquaintance is all mine. You can rest assure that I will be there for all of your children. I have been sharing your gut feelings for too long to ever neglect them.

If everyone looked worryingly to one another at his speech, Zachary went to hug the Doctor with an honest spontaneity and gratitude,

-Thank you so much, Sir. What you are doing means more than I can say.

Ruffling the teenager's hair, Valdi enjoined,

-Right, let's close the door and free the Doe together.

Whilst Zach closed the door, the Doctor took the ties off the legs of the animal. The freed beast looked ever so lost amongst everyone yet when the teenager went back to her, she nestled against him. Theo considered the Doe with deep curiosity, before commenting,

-So much for a local myth, I am mystified. Can't we keep the beast outside, Vince? I know you are fond of interesting creatures but I am a little less kin on them especially in my home...

But the Doctor ruled it out while standing by the fire trying to warm himself up,

-I don't care if she makes a mess in your home. She stays where I can keep an eye on her. She is essential to get rid of the curse upon the town therefore I can't risk her to be eaten outside in your Ghouls infested cemetery. Miss White, if you have a look at the shoulder of Mrs Wilton-Cough with no further a-do. I will treat the scar of Amelia. Then we need to find a solution to reverse the curse.

Whilhelmina opened her vanity case before bowing to Angela Wilton-Cough who had no sympathetic smile to offer her. The Widow of Abraham was still harbouring the sentiment that Miss White had stolen her eldest son from her so many nights for months. Despite the blond Lady giving her a very shy smile, despite her being gentle as she removed the bandage to inspect her wounded shoulder, Angela was unwilling to befriend her and avoided firmly all eyes contact.

Whilhelmina knew that it would probably be impossible to break the ice with her, yet she tried,

-I am ever so sorry for what happened. Ghouls have no sensitivity, nor morals just that hunger to quench. Rest assure Mrs Wilton-Cough that we will do everything in our power to save your boy from becoming one. Hmmm, at first glance, Vincent did a beautiful job. Your injury is bad but not as bad as I expected. It has been cleaned so well that your risk of infection was minimal. The only downside, minimal, still means there was a risk. It depends on the patient and on their ability to heal. For you, you are so fragile at the present, that there is a start of infection. Now, you have two boys that need you. Losing one parent was already hard enough on them. You must start to look after yourself better than that. Abraham would tell you exactly the same thing. I am sure he is upset to see you like that as I am.

Angela looked at the blond nurse with sheer disbelief but also some slight anger for her cheek to scold her. However before she could even formulate an answer she heard the voice of her husband who did go back inside the tall Doctor in order to join in the conversation,

-Miss White is right, Angela. She had to tell our Zach to look after you, to make sure you eat properly. Everyone in town is seeing you vanishing away. No one wants to see you gone, especially not our boys. One parent to pass away from an untimely death is enough, my Love, enough. Because of it, both boys need lots of nurturing, lots, and I count on you Mrs Wilton-Cough, to be brave, strong, and to give it aplenty.

Thus scolded, Angela had tears in her eyes. The Doctor felt the ghost of Wilton-Cough leaving him again, and this time with his own voice, he added in a soft yet serious tone,

-Your husband is ever so right, Mrs Wilton-Cough. We are all ever so concerned about you.

Zachary came by his mum to hold her hand. He confided,

-I will be there for you and Josiah, Ma. We will be brave and strong together, just for Pa, just for Pa. I won't runaway like I did to hide my grief. I promise you I will get up in the morning, every morning, and we will have breakfast together. But also I will come back for dinner. Doctor Valdi is taking me as an apprentice and I am starting working for him on Monday morning. Then we are going to talk to my former teacher to see if he can give me private tuition in the evenings to catch up on what I missed from school. Pa reckons he won't say no. So I will be able to get myself up to scratch, or so I hope. I won't be troublesome anymore, Ma, I promise. I wanna be a good boy like lil' Jo but I won't write sonatas and music for the ears like him, I will be me, and draw plans to build a hospital for the town, Doctor Valdi's hospital.

Angela looked utterly confused for a moment. It was not to do with her running a temperature, or any bites she sustained, it was to do with her usually grumpy teenager all of a sudden opening up to her. He was honest, simple and he touched her heart more than words could express. She truly had her eldest boy back. She kissed the palm of his hand silently still surprised, that Zachary had finally decided to lift a finger in his life. She could only wonder what his ghostly father told him but she was certain that it must have been one of his most spurring talk seeing the result.

Miss White, tapping gently on her shoulder with her special lotion, couldn't help whispering secretly to her,

-I have been at a loss to try to talk to your boy for months, Mrs Wilton-Cough, only his own father could do the trick. Although Zach is a lovely boy, he shuts himself up in his own sorrow. I welcomed him in his grieving state because I didn't want him to go further than Wilton Town. Vincent even taught him to play poker properly to make sure he would stay interested to come to my hotel at night and not go where we could not find him anymore.

This avowal pacified Angela who finally offered a smile of gratitude to the woman looking after her. She was touched to know that the people had been concerned by her and her children. Since the tragedy that her family endured by the tragic loss of Abraham Wilton-Cough, they have been involved in their own way to help them. She knew that Father Odell had taken a liking for the musically brilliant little Josiah but now Doctor Valdi seemed interested in helping out her troublesome eldest Zachary. He had already done so without her knowledge, for she would have certainly disapproved of Zach learning to play poker however she could see the benevolent intention behind it. Just like she could realise now, that the grieving boy was better kept safe at night at Miss White rather than being an aimless vagrant anywhere else. If the footsteps of her teenage boy had carried him already as far as beyond the woods at the edge of the town, Miss White and her mighty attractive hotel stood in the way of him going any further. She despised the fact that it was a place of addictions of all sorts yet it has been useful in the case of Zachary somehow. The mother always feared that her eldest lacked the intrinsic charm of her youngest, the charm which would allow him to ingratiate himself to anyone, for Zachary had been so full of a revolting attitude, a seeming carelessness all wrapped up with a Wilton-Cough's pride and arrogance. But despite it all, her son had managed to find people who were not going to wash their hands of him, who were concerned by him enough to get involved to sort him out. She couldn't dream of a better position for her boy than working for the respected Doctor Vincent Valdi. Angela was confident that this would do her eldest a world of good. She had no doubts that her ghostly husband's intervention put the teenager in the best of hands possible.

Angela Wilton-Cough didn't realise that she had a happy and satisfied smile on her face while she was dosing off completely lost in her myriads of thoughts. Whilhelmina looking at her as she wrapped her shoulder with clean bandages, asked concerned,

-The poor thing is exhausted, Vincent, shall I wake her up?

Theo and Valdi gave each other a glance then on the wounded Widow of Abraham, before the first one commented,

-She worked very hard with Mrs Bates despite being unwell, Vince.

The Doctor nodded his acknowledgement then ordered,

-Let's make her comfortable on that couch, Theo. We will let her rest and sleep. Miss Cough would you mind looking after her and supervise her temperature. We will wake Mrs Wilton-Cough up only if necessary. Miss White, Josephine just has scratches but it is worth cleaning them and putting some lotion upon them.

Whilhelmina went immediately to Josephine Cough who had been sitting very quietly all along. She put her vanity case by her and started on her arms while the old Lady enquired about her friend Georgia Marlow, who worked at the hotel for Miss White. Their conversation had an immediate amicable turn.

After laying Mrs Wilton-Cough on the couch, the two men discussed out loud all the possibilities facing them.

-It is clear that exorcism works. Doing one in the crypt affected all the Ghouls there at once. So during the day, if Ghouls go back to their respective graves then we have an easy fix. Then it would be a matter of doing an exorcism on all who are alive who were born during a full moon.

But Josephine Cough objected out loud,

-Father Odell, we are talking of far too many exorcisms. They are hardly pleasant as I witnessed and the toll will be dangerously solely on you. I can already predict that you would collapse of exhaustion after doing three in a row. There must be another solution.

Miss White replied fairly shyly,

-There is. The curse was done using a black witchcraft book, my stolen one and it can be reversed. We need to follow the recipe the other way round.

As the Doctor was inspecting the arms of Theo, he asked,

-Right, do you remember that specific curse, Whilhelmina? When you have finished with Josephine, I need the lotion for Theo. He has a nice festering bite on his forearm. I guess he is another one too proud to moan and complain that something was not quite right with him.

Coming to them with her vanity case, Miss White apologised most anxiously,

-I don't remember the curse with precision, Vincent. I only flicked through the pages of the book once to get to the specific formula I was after. But I saw it in there, it was entitled 'how to curse a town via its children.' It horrified me enough to glance at the page a little longer, enough to know that there were many methods and that one of them was about creating Ghouls out of children. But I am so sorry, I didn't read anything properly to remember it. It was so long ago. I never opened that book after what I needed from it. I never endeavoured to learn that kind of magic. I already kick myself to have been in possession of that black book and for it to have been stolen and used.

She handed her lotion to Valdi while checking Father Odell's arms herself. A concerned Theo demanded,

-Vince, can you enlighten me about that book?

The good Doctor struggled for a while about what to say before coming up with an answer which would protect Wilhelmina's secrecy about Mina being a Vampire,

-Well, this lost magical book, Theo, well, not lost, stolen, was used by Miss White to make herself and her daughter eternal. It came from the land beyond the ocean where it was printed...

Vincent struggled under the ever so judgemental look of Theo even if he had just uttered one little protective white lie. Upon his silence, Whilhelmina came to the rescue, understanding that Valdi was trying to advert the Spanish inquisition of the Priest to befall upon her and her daughter, she corrected ever so shyly,

-Well, it wasn't printed... Printing had yet to be invented at that time. It was hand written by generations of Witches, passed down from mothers to daughters, since a very long time. The book is said to have moved from Mesopotamia to Egypt, from Egypt to India then to Tibet for then to move across continents with the barbaric hordes of Attila the Hun.

Father Odell gave her such a killer glance that she feared having said too much and not enough, and just like Vincent before, she fell silent. She could see clearly that the Priest was boiling with retained anger, so her eyes dived down to his arm as she applied more lotion upon it. The Ghoul's bite he had sustained was definitely a very nasty one and she was surprised that he did not have a fever by now like Angela Wilton-Cough. Theo fired out what was burning in his mind,

-In which evil time do you come from Miss White? Was that book passed down from your mother to you? Did you intend to pass it to your daughter? Why did you decide to defy the laws of God to become an eternal living being?

Whilhelmina's hands shivered. Her lips trembled. Her mind recollected her trial for being a Witch. She remembered being attached to a plank and thrown into a river. She felt like she would drown, she choked but the plank did bob above the water, which convicted her in the strange eyes of the justice of the time to being a very malicious Witch. To her great surprise, Zachary who was attending to the Doe replied for her,

-Miss White bought the book, Father. It was not handed to her nor did she want any to touch that book, especially not her daughter. She, herself, only opened that book once.

To Zach's defence of the White Witch, Vincent added with conviction,

-The possession of that book was motivated by the hard time, they were living. When the long famine struck the settlers, when so many were dying, Whilhelmina opened the book to make sure her daughter would not die like a fly like all others from starvation. A desperate mother used that type of witchcraft to save her only child, and upon herself to look after that eternal child. Who can point the finger to that and blame her?

When the face of Theo Odell softened, Valdi knew that they had won the case of Whilhelmina White, maybe with a little edulcorations and a little bending here and there of the truth, but it was worth doing to help a good woman, or creature, or being, whatever she was now, which he only knew for sure was a trusted friend in slight trouble. He gave a connivance wink to the young Wilton-Cough who replied to it by another one and a smile.

If the teenager would have expressed his motivations for being defensive of Miss White, it was only because he was fond of the young Mina which he considered in his heart like a sister. Having been let into the secrecy that she was in fact a Vampire didn't alter the matter for one bit for him. It only made him more conscious of the importance of keeping the secret of Miss White safe and secure from the knowledge of others.

Father Odell, seeing the pale trembling hands applying diligently the lotion upon his scars, offered in a softer tone of voice,

-Although I wear a black robe, Miss White, I am only a human and therefore not a judge. It's beyond my capacity to be one. Also, to be honest with you, rather than making blunders and mistakes, Vince can tell you that I would rather let the tough job being carried upon by the above. Please, do accept my apologies at once and let your caring hands stop shivering. If you may have known the time of Witch hunts and still fear them, let me reassure you that they are gone. Noah M Wilton built this town to be a safe haven for everyone, and I would be the last one to want to destroy his good work. We learnt about you in his records. We know that he valued you enough to protect you from your past. Now, tell me who stole your book? What did that book look like?

Theo met the grateful and about to be teary eyes of Miss White, who remained very silent. He kicked himself internally to have been maybe too harsh and too presumptuous. The watchful Doctor, acknowledging first the look of guilt upon Theo's composure, and then the humble demeanour of Whilhelmina, guessed that he would need to help to get the conversation going a little further, so he replied to the questions himself,

-Our conclusions upon reflecting on what went on back then are that Tristina Ogin, whose Soul is stuck in the Crying White Doe, who performed the curse while she was still alive, had the book. She was the neighbour of Miss White, her friend and knew about her Witch's past. Troubles of her own made her very interested about witchcraft... We don't think she performed the theft herself but had her two extremely naughty boys to do the task. At Tristina's death, a frightful one, the one told by the legend of the Doe, if you are well acquainted with it, her murderous children were never seen again. As for the book, it hasn't been found since it left Whilhelmina's house. Noah Wilton was the only one to know of the existence of that book, for Miss White, a servant to him and a nurse to the entire community, confided almost everything to him and reported its theft. He promised her to look for it but not to return it if he ever found it. He would either burn it or keep it safe.

A deeply interested Theo asked again most eagerly,

-What does the book look like?

Miss White answered,

-It is big and black. The pages are made of vellum. They are full of illustrations and formulas written in all sorts of languages. It is bounded by a dark thick leather which was said to be neither human nor animal. The man who sold it to me claimed that it was made of the skin of a demon. I only thought it was to increase the price of it. Yet he told me that he was the end of a long line of Witches, maybe because he was born to be a boy, maybe because he was no good at magic at all, maybe because he was dreadfully scared of being hunted down as a wizard. His hands were burning to get rid of this book at any price. So he handed it to me willingly, with the warning of never let that book in the hands of whom could never be trusted. He also knew so much about the book's history that I believed I had the genuine article within my hands. There is the picture of a crying eye embossed on the front: the eye of Ra. It is also known as the eye of Horus. It is an Egyptian symbol of protection. The book has been cursed in a certain way by an Egyptian Priestess. If it was ever to be misused, the wrongdoers would bestow the eternally crying eye, with the passage to the After-life denied to them. I never believed that until I saw the Crying White Doe. I tried to guess what my friend did wrong until fifty years or so later, after her death, I met my very first Ghoul in Wilton Town. Then I tried so hard to remember the curse I saw once, I tried endlessly to reverse it but to no avail.

Her desperation was very palpable. Father Odell enclosed her fingers with a comforting hold as he enjoined,

-All may not be lost. We may have the answer to everything right here. The presbytery was the home of Noah M Wilton. I believed he found your book Miss White, for when I inherited the place my predecessor warned me very staunchly, about a book kept here which should be kept out of sight and out of hands. I did keep my word to him, however I could not help looking at the book in question, just the cover of it for I was never that daring, but it does bestow the leather black cover embossed with the eye of Horus.

Everyone in the room, apart for the sleeping Angela turned to Father Odell, with faces full of curiosity and excitement. But none beat the look of eagerness in Miss White's eyes apart Vincent Valdi's whose mind was repeating to him with joyful disbelief that they just may have the recipe to break the curse on all those children. But the Doctor wanted to see now the very physical proof of it, the book itself. Having the book being recognised by Whilhelmina would sanctify the fact for him that they had finally the ability to rectify things. He demanded,

-Theo, how could you hide that type of thing from me? Are you even sure it is the book we have been talking about?

As Father Odell's arm was being wrapped up in a bandage, he replied with a solemn sentence,

-Curiosity kills the cat, and I never knew a more curious cat than you Vince. Forgive me from obeying my orders and trying to protect you. I believe it is the very book for it was handed to me with the presbytery with the same warning that Miss White received when she bought it. I was also told it came from the time of the settlers and a possession of Noah M Wilton. Miss White, I only need your confirmation. Follow me. Is Vince to be trusted?

Tidying her lotions and potions back in her vanity case, the White Witch vouched,

-He is. He has the right mind about him to handle that sort of knowledge.

Valdi was not only satisfied but also somewhat proud by that verbal accolade. If he wasn't particularly interested in magic however he was indeed very curious about how a magic formula could turn into something physical. It simply puzzled him greatly and he wasn't the only one as he felt the Ghost of Abraham Wilton-Cough penetrating his body to announce to his mind,

-Wherever you are going, I am going. This is too good to be true. I want to see it. Finally we are putting our hands on our chance to save my Zach.

Feeling the cloak of coldness invading his entire body, the Doctor, following his friend and Miss White out of the room, alerted them,

-Wilton-Cough is coming with us.

Father Odell looked worryingly at Vincent as he led them to his large refectory, whilst he demanded,

-Do you mean within you?

It was Whilhelmina who answered the confirmation to the Priest for Valdi only offered a bright cocky grin to Theo. She held the hand of Vincent for a brief second. It was icy cold enough for her to acknowledge the presence of the Ghost within the human. She nodded positively to Odell,

-Clearly within.

Theo gave a disapproving glance at Vincent before scolding,

-Right Abraham, I let you stay a little longer within my best friend on one condition only, the promise of your best behaviour. I do not want to see any senseless poltergeist-ing of Vince which could jeopardise our entire mission.

The Doctor entering the refectory after Theo made a gallant gesture to invite Miss White in, while he reassured,

-Abraham promised everything you want, but he also says that you are worrying too much. He rates himself as one of the best Ghosts one can be possessed by. I must admit, if I do not have any point of comparison at this moment in time, I would say so too. It feels like having your best friend within, a partner.

Theo Odell turned to him, his hands on his hips, a frown on his face, visibly offended,

-Partner in crime, I dare say! I am the best friend here! I don't throw you up against a church wall and twist and turn your guts until you believe now do I? Trust you, Vince, to enjoy being possessed like you would do of your next experiment and befriending the dead like no other! I am glad you are having a party in there to which I am not invited.

Vincent started laughing and playfully messed the hair of the Priest as he teased,

-Sounds like someone is jealous! Isn't jealousy one of the seven sins? Of course you are still my best friend although you failed to make me believe in anything for so long. Possession has its good side, I was momentarily possessed and protected by an Angel tonight, the very Angel that you saw, the one of Abraham, Abigail. Now, where's your book? Show us the goods.

Whilhelmina White was amused by their banter. She saw by the large giggle now coming on Father Odell's face as he let himself be slightly abused by the Doctor, the true camaraderie between the two men. It also highlighted to her an aspect of the personality of Theo, she was not acquainted with: his humanity. When she always thought of him as standoffish and all wrapped around an overbearing cloak of religion, she was finding out that it was far from the case.

Dusting his black robe Theo argued back,

-Now I am truly jealous! Possessed by an Angel, I ask, how did it feel? Let me compete before you even start, you, popular Doc, I spoke to the Virgin Marie tonight. Well she rather spoke to me and I just uttered imbecilities so taken aback I was. You can't beat that especially since I have a witness too. Josephine Cough was by me when it happened in the church.

-Boohoo, competing with grand names, are you now? What's next? A visitation from the Holy spirit, maybe? But you are a little too vain and frivolous for that one. You would need at least a good month of fasting and a good year on a humility course. I have a witness just as well, in fact I have two, Zachary Wilton-Cough and Whilhelmina, no three if we count our dead Abraham. The probability of hallucinating together is far less on my side than yours. Beside what happened to me was so extraordinary that it made Miss White pray straight away in the clearing. See I can convert even better than you do. Tell him Whil'. So what did the Virgin want to say to you?

The eternal human couldn't believe her ears at the childish arguments between the two men. She couldn't help smiling widely, deeply amused. Giving her an inquisitive look, Father Odell queried,

-Is this true Miss White? Did it make you pray? If it reforms this incurable atheist of a Valdi as well then I will grant Vince that it was a miracle.

Miss White nodded positively, confirming what Vincent told by adding,

-Vincent was attacked by a Ghost in the haunted clearing. Angel Abigail came out of him to protect him and dragged the aggressor away. It did make me fall upon my knees into a prayer. Vincent, tell me, did you lose your religion?

This made the winning smile of Valdi disappeared. Upon his silence, his friend Theo explained,

-To be able to lose your religion, you should have it first. The reason why Vince never believed in god is because only as a toddler, he saw his parents being bluntly killed by his side. Horrors of the Napoleonic wars made a firm atheist of him. He was brought up by a aunt who, herself, did lose her faith totally during that time.

However she made a good man out of him who only believed in his own steady heart and science to help his fellow men.

As they arrived at the large fireplace within the room, Miss White apologised,

-I am sorry Vincent I didn't know.

Crouching down by the fire, Father Odell took a long iron poker as he said gently,

-Don't be sorry Miss White. Vince is not the kind of person to be an ogre about this type of thing. No, he is just rather silent about his early memories for they were just not pretty nor rosy. I managed to find out myself, digging deep into the dirt during our many debates where I always failed to convert him. He doesn't dwell upon his past to others either, because he never wanted to possess anything that was the result of pity, only things that were the result of his own hands and honest heart. If you gave your friendship to him, because of who he is and not the war orphan he was, he will respect that friendship as untainted by a compassion he does not seek, nor want. Now Vince are you quite recovered to talk to us a little? You have to forgive him, when he goes like that, all silent on you, Miss White, that's when he has his childhood flashbacks. Vince, crouch, so I can show you the magical trick that this house possess.

Miss White watched the Doctor do as he was told and his face being alive again, with eyes full of curiosity and queries. She had no doubts anymore that both men had a very strong and solid friendship which resembled a brotherhood of some sort. She crouched by them eager to see for herself but also to enquire,

-You two know each other so well. One could take you for brothers. It sounds like you haven't got any secrets from one another.

Valdi replied with a kind smile to her, knowing how the shy eternal being had difficulties confiding so riddled with fear for her daughter she was and therefore never had a lot of friends herself,

-True, we have almost none. Our friendship grew ever so strong, a little like ours, Whil', when you are with me at plenty of births, Theo is by my side at plenty of deaths. He is the last call I make when I realise someone is not going to make it. Together we try to help people pass away as peacefully as possible. But sometimes we see the worst when we can almost do nothing than catching someone's last breath, holding their hands tight, together. It was the case for the trampled young Miss Clara Pendleton a few days ago. It was heartbreaking to watch her die so young. While I carried her damaged body to her mother, Theo informed her of the accident. We are staying and helping those who grieve to the best of our abilities. It is a help that doesn't last a night or a week or a month, no, it lasts until it is no longer required. It comes in many forms, like me teaching poker to Zachary Wilton-Cough, to Theo informing you that his mother was worried about him. Lots of people in town had tried to talk to the troubled boy to no avail, you were kind of a last resort after we made sure he would settle his aimlessness at yours. I know you did have a small chat to Zachary afterwards which like ours failed yet also that you resented Theo for coming to see you. But all was not lost because of the unresting Abraham, which I allowed to possess me to do that overdue talk with his eldest son. You see Whil', Theo and I aim to help the people of this town in any ways possible and that definitely brought us together like brothers, just like I consider you like the eldest sister I never had the chance to have.

His speech warmed the heart of Whilhelmina endlessly. Her thin red lips parted in such a genuine grateful smile that Theo commented,

-Well I never had an eldest sister either. As you are yourself such an helping hand in this town, since, well more than I can say, Miss White, I would be very much honoured to bestow your friendship. To let you in, in one of our brotherly secrets, Vince treats me like his youngest brother for I only arrived in town five years later than him, however I treat him also like a younger brother for he is three years younger than me. If we do bicker all the times, we are also always there for each other. I am his crying shoulder and confidant and he is mine. If you ever need another friend as well as bestowing the friendship of Vince, you can count me as a very willing one. And this is not my payment for you looking after my Ghoul's bite it comes from the single fact that friends of Vince are friends of mine. I know him to be extremely selective in his friendships and I am quite fussy too, hence if you see two loners sitting together in a pub sharing the hardship of the day they went through and debating about science, politics and religions, it will be us two.

The White Witch welcomed the Priest's proposal by presenting her hand to hold, impressed by his straight honesty. She replied with a deep shyness,

-The honour will be mine, Father. I only experienced Priests wanting to burn me at the stake before, never wanting my friendship. Heaven's forbid! I am deeply touched and overwhelmed. Just call me Whil' like Vincent does. Just to let you in a little, I have always been a very secretive being, very afraid that someone would want to hurt my daughter who is no Witch at all. She went through the same conviction and ordeal as I back in the days of Witch hunting. Since then I lived with some sheer anxiety sown to my guts. I am only able to trust so very few like Noah and then Vincent. I value friendship like a treasure.

Compelled Father Odell shook her hand firmly, saying,

-That's a damn long while to be out and about for a Soul and only be able to count two true friends because of fear and another one who betrayed your trust. Count me in as your third truthful one, and call me Theo, rather than Father, Whil', if you only will. Now tell me if you recognise this for if so, Noah M Wilton not only hid it very well but also protected you just as well doing so but also the town from more harm.

Theo pushed the iron rod against an iron diamond shape behind the fire, which had an embossed acorn at its centre. His push made the acorn go within the back wall of the fireplace. It triggered a mechanism, rather old, heavy and noisy, which baffled Whilhelmina and intrigued Vincent. At the end of it all, the large flat floor stone, engraved with an acorn in front of the fire lifted itself by a good inch.

Theo enjoined,

-Vince, help me here, this is as up as the lid will go. Behind is Noah Wilton's niche and treasure.

Both men joined their strength to lift the heavy lid. Once opened the cache revealed its contents. The trepidation in the chest of Whilhelmina was great, and matched the one of the Doctor who looked at the dreaded magical book. Whilst the entity of Abraham shouted in his mind,

-Odell spoke of Noah's treasure! Where is it? It cannot be only that book.

Valdi scolded out loud his internal Ghost, while he took the courage to grab the book as his companions were only looking at it in awe,

-Abraham, you were the Wilton-Cough that did sit on a fortune, your ancestor was an educated logger, a humble one, and from humble origins. Don't expect the cavern of Alibaba in here. For me this book is treasure enough for it will allow us to save the town's children.

Lifting it by the light of the fire, the Doctor removed the thick layer of dust from the cover. From anthracite grey the book became jet black with the crying eye of Ra at its centre staring at their bewildered faces. As Vincent was surprised by the smooth softness of the old leather but also its good state of conservation, Theo asked with eagerness,

-Whil', do you recognise your book?

The Witch had tears in her eyes when she replied to him. She was thinking of all the damage done to Wilton Town because the book had fallen once into the wrong hands.

-It is the very one.

The Priest and the Doctor nodded positively. They looked at one another so seriously, that one could have thought that telepathy was going on between the two of them before Theo stated sternly,

-Right, do you agree with us, Whil', that after its use to break the curse this book shall return to the grave where Noah M Wilton buried it? Its cache shall be revealed to none. We must swear to keep this emplacement secret, you, Vince, myself, and you as well, Abraham Wilton-Cough. This becomes our secret. This book is never to leave this place unless there is an emergency in town that requires its help like the curse we are about to tackle. Vince, you can abandon all temptations of doing experiments of the magical kind. We saw one pretty result of mishandling that book, a Crying White Doe in my drawing room with a Soul stuck in it for god knows when. Whil', if I will authorise you to use it in the emergency for the town I was talking about, forget about reclaiming that book in any shape or form. Taken from you once, it had dreadful consequences. All my graves in my cemetery have been disturbed. None did rest in peace in Wilton Town since its creation. As for you Abraham, I don't fancy you haunting my presbytery constantly because we have a problematic curse in town, so keep quiet about that book to anyone you decide to possess, but know that my intentions are as much to save your son from being a Ghoul as to lay your soul at rest. Also know that I appreciated your warnings, keep them coming if you know something from the Spirit's world which could affect us badly but a little less poltergeist actions from you would be...

The deadly guttural voice of Wilton-Cough replied through Valdi,

-Father, be a Ghost first, know how difficult it is to communicate, then scold me. I will definitely bless you if you manage to make me rest in peace however I quite enjoy being with you, my lovely living lot, possessing and helping, mainly making sure that my family is fine. But if you have not my total poltergeist silence, you have my complete secrecy about the book, Odell. I don't want anyone hurt by its contents anymore. Vincent, swear to your friend, it is an order. We know how curious you are. Hence you are the more at risk here. Hence you will cause us all worries if you succumb to experimental temptation. Be warned that if you do I will haunt your damned arse forever. Beside you are duty bound to Abigail, now.

This speech was welcomed by Theo Odell who stated,

-We have one soulful Soul agreeing to the secrecy. Good. Vince, your turn, please appease my concern.

The Doctor gave a beautiful yet sarcastic smile, as he commented,

-My temptations can't be more cornered than that with Theo's constant earfuls and Abraham's gut twisting abilities.

Whilhelmina White corrected him outright with a devilish grin,

-Yes, you can be even more cornered. You haven't seen a caring Witch curse you yet. Theo Odell is damn right, so is Abraham, and you will swear to the oath of secrecy but also to not use that book in so called 'experimental' fashion. I saw shit happening to my friend Tristina for putting her hands on it, do you expect that I will let that happen to you? Give the book to Theo right now and swear to us.

Somehow this made Valdi obey straight away and he handed the book to Theo without any questions. He only knew that the White Witch valued friendship very much because it was all she could bestow, so she was bound to treasure them and be ever so protective of her only friends. Did he feel more cornered? Of course he did. Anyhow he felt much responsibilities now upon his own shoulders. He felt like the very father of Abraham's children. He wanted to care for them with all his might, and it was stronger than opening a mere book. He surrendered and swore,

-You have my secrecy and I will never be tempted upon opening that one, in the name of Abigail, Zachary and Josiah. But also, because of you three, Theo, Whil' and Ab, my dearest friends. Thank you for caring. Upon my heart, that book will be safe and never be opened by my hands.

The Priest and the Witch gave a very pleased nod at the same time, and glanced at each other which drew an all knowing smile on their lips. Theo acknowledged out loud,

-Good. So we have one good useful Soul to stay away from being cursed. Next one, Whil'. Do you need any convincing apart that I will go all Spanish Inquisition upon you if you do not do so?

Despite remembering the effect of the physical threat upon her own body, Whilhelmina, managed to smile and swore very readily. She also was convinced that Theo was one of those friends who will always have your best interest at heart, and if that meant protecting someone from their own self, he was the very man to do so.

-I swear secrecy. I swear that I will only touch that book to protect my fellow humans. We must keep that book safe out of sight for eternity.

Granting her with a pleased smile, Theo handed the book to her with many demands,

-Let's rectify everything then, shall we? Where shall we do the reversed curse? What do we need?

Whilhelmina trembled as she held the book. A tear was running silently upon her cheek. Depositing the heavy manuscript on her laps she tried to find the infamous curse to be able to answer Father Odell. As Vincent saw the overwhelming emotions taking hold of the White Witch, he reassured,

-You do not have to answer everything at once Whil', take your time, there is no pressure. Why are you crying? Take a deep breath for we need you to correct that curse for us.

Wiping her blurry eyes, she whispered,

-Can't help thinking that my own hands brought that damn book to town, and that it did so much damage.

Putting his hand above hers and holding it reassuringly, Theo told,

-Those very hands can repair the damage done with that very damn book. Do not focus on the past, Whil', just the present to build with us a better future.

This had the desired effect for the Witch nodded to the Priest her agreement and regained control of her outpour of emotion. Finally she turned the pages with care and caution, trying to find the curse in question. She advised,

-There is a slight pressure for night is essential for certain type of witchcraft. If we want to get everything done tonight we haven't got much time.

Valdi confirmed looking at the large ancient clock within the refectory,

-We have about one hour, two at most before dawn. Do you reckon we can do it in that time?

Miss White gave him a short answer,

-We can try.

Her face illuminated as she found the very page she was after. She recognised the strange illustrations and read it commenting,

-As I said the perpetrator of such a curse would not be allowed to pass away to the Spirit world. He or she is condemned to stay until, in our case, she, allows the curse to be removed. So we do have one essential part, the Spirit of the perpetrator, Tristina Ogin within the Doe. Now we need an object belonging to the perpetrator and one belonging to the cursed destination. They need to have been there, in this locality, at the time of the curse.

Vincent had a winning smile as he pulled out the rosary he fond in the ruins of Ogin's cottage from the depth of his leather satchel,

-That's one part sorted.

Father Odell enquired,

-What's that?

Whilhelmina explained,

-That's the rosary of Tristina Ogin, probably her most precious belonging. She threw it in the fire in front of me when she lost all hope and faith during the great famine.

Valdi added considering the object,

-Well it missed the fire by a few inches. It fell in a narrow gap between the stone slabs of the fire place. The diamond shone in the moonlight, catching my eyes. That's how I found it. Whil' wanted to give that for your charities. Now, we need to find the last object.

When the Priest was given the rosary, he praised,

-That is a beautiful one. I have seen a fair few in my time. When I was young however not many Priests or Monks dared to flash such a rosary. Wood was the fashion then to display how humble you were. But it was rather a show than a reality. I thank you for thinking of my charities, Whil', however we haven't got the right to decide how to dispose of that rosary apart from using it for getting rid of the curse. The simple reason is, the Spirit of Tristina is still alive and despite her disposing of it in a fire in her depth of despair, she is still the owner of the rosary. If she wants us to put it in her grave, we will do so. Let me tell you two, finding that tonight was not short of a miracle, and your good intentions, Whil' brought us the very ingredient we needed to reverse that curse. Now, Abraham Wilton-Cough, I have in that cache the only prised possession of your ancestor Noah M Wilton. As much as this object represented him, it symbolises the very creation of Wilton Town. This is all we need. Vince, give the honour to Abraham to lift the axe of his ancestor.

The ghostly Wilton-Cough couldn't hide his excitement, as his eerie voice expressed himself via Valdi while the man lifted the axe from its hiding place, while he could feel through the living hands the shaft his ancestor held,

-Father, I thank you to still think of our Souls after they parted from their physical envelops. Oh, it is such a heavy shaft, so used, so smooth. That axe is a treasure indeed. Thank you so much Vincent, to let me live that moment through you.

Considering the large axe, himself impressed, the Doctor expressed with his own voice,

-I have heard so much about Noah M Wilton since I arrived in town, feel so much respect for him that just holding his axe feels like an honour. He is a man I would have loved to know. Whil', I envy the fact that you met him.

The Witch smiled kindly to him before confessing,

-Yes, he was such an individual, I would say bigger than life itself. His axe is the perfect object to represent the town he built with his own sweat and endeavours. You know Vincent, you have an ability to remain yourself, yet establish a close connection with a Spirit, throughout your entire body. You should ask Miss Josephine Cough about channelling. She may help you communicate with Souls long departed.

His eyes lit with the tremendous potential that it could impart him, especially regarding to knowledge, the Doctor gave his most beautiful grin. This was sufficient for Theo to caution him,

-Whenever you want to do such things like not letting a Soul rest properly and bother it with your endless questions, you have to count me in your so called 'channelling' parties. I will make sure you don't get possessed forever. Now, Whil', stop making tempting suggestions to that inveterate inquisitive Valdi. Have we got all we need for our mission?

Giving Odell a sheepish look, understanding his protective stance, Miss White answered positively yet timidly,

-I think so. The last ingredient is one of the cursed children and although on the verge of manhood, Zachary Wilton-Cough is definitely one of them. Now, it must be performed in a place of worship and by the person invested of the charge of that place. The church is the only such place in town, therefore you should perform the reversal of the curse, Theo.

This had Father Odell standing up in a verbal up-row,

-I am not going to perform witchcraft in my church! I am not going to damn my Soul reading that book!

The Doctor confronted him right away, towering Theo, while the voice of Abraham took over his own voice but to say what Valdi wanted to shout with only more power,

-For Christ sake, Theo! This is not the right time to have a crisis of bigotry! How many Souls are at stake? How many in this town, for you counted them all with Amelia and Angela tonight?

The Priest looked confused at his friend who was at that precise moment a perfect blend of himself and the passed away Banker. He didn't know what to say and to whom, mainly because of the fright it caused him, bearing in mind that Valdi was clasping strongly the axe with both hands, but also because he was so unsure of being right.

Whilhelmina White came to his rescue, trying to defuse the situation most humbly, a tear in her eye,

-I will tell you all you have to say because I will read the book for you. I do not know if I have a Soul anymore but I am willing to let it go for the children of this town. But we have to use the church. A place where people worship together only has enough sanctity to ratify the reversal of the curse. I am a very concerned mother who feels for the parents who dread for their children to become monsters, like Abraham within Vincent. I know my Soul will not be able to rest if we do not do this.

If her intervention was not enough, the Ghost of Wilton-Cough added,

-And I know who I am going to haunt for an eternity if he is not a good Father to his flock. I will not let your Soul rest Odell if my Zach becomes a Ghoul because of your own foolish misconception. Why did you think an Angel talked to you the way she did? To see you do nothing? Why did the Virgin speak to you tonight? To see you coward away from the task at hand? In what upside down world do you live where your Soul is going to be saved when you don't help people? I am a Spirit, and trust me when I say you must do your utmost while you can. Do you honestly think that you can lose your Soul saving this town's children? Well let me tell you that you do not live in the same world like those two, you do not even belong to Wilton Town, you belong to La La Land.

After such a dressing down by Abraham, Theo Odell felt piteous and rather mortified. He could remember vividly the former Banker, his presence, his staunch demeanour, and an argument they had one day over charity, an argument which the Priest lost miserably. He tried to tackle the richest man in town over the fact that he never ever gave away a cent to charity. It was countered by the very fact pointed to him, that Odell redistributed the cents he gathered, while the Banker was making them grow for people who were too weak to do so themselves. The killing blow was when Abraham sent Father Odell away with the recommendation to keep making sure that people had a bit of bread on their table while he was making sure they could keep their roofs above their heads but also live their dreams whilst alive. Theo was a very young Priest then and was lost for words easily in the altercation. He recalled the strong laugh of his new friend Vincent when he shared to him that he tried to argue with Abraham Wilton-Cough and the result. Upon Valdi's advice it was something tried and tested by everybody and never attempted ever again, for their nose would invariably be rubbed in the dust verbally. And Theo was standing there, again, totally lost for words.

When Miss White went to hold his hand, applying some slight pressure upon it, asking,

-Are we all in it together?

He replied in a whispered apology,

-We are and I am sorry to have offended you, Abraham, for you are right.

Squeezing the hand back, Theo told with more certainty,

-Whil', if you still have your Soul, you will not lose it either. Wilton-Cough is ever so right. How can we lose it saving the Souls of many? Let's do it.

After putting the floor slab down, the three friends and the Ghost left the refectory, their hands holding an axe, a rosary and a book ready to defeat the curse.

Chapter Eighteen

Broken Curse

When they opened the door of the drawing room, all eyes turned to them but for Angela Wilton-Cough who was dreaming deliriously upon the couch.

Zachary, tending to the Doe, went all gob smacked again at the sight of the large axe carried by Doctor Valdi. Stroking the beast, he reassured her wildly,

-This is not for you, Tristina. I promise, this is not for you, despite having cursed children, it is not. Valdi will not hack your head off. He is not vindictive like that. He is a good Doctor not a butchering one. I swear, everything is going to be alright.

If this made Vincent Valdi grin tenderly at the teenager's anguish, his attention turned to Josephine Cough who called him to the couch where she was looking after the Widow of Abraham,

-Vincent, Angela's temperature has not receded. It is still running high.

Giving Noah's axe to Josephine, the Doctor went to check the sleeping perspiring woman with great concern, greater for the fact that Abraham was pushing him internally to do something, begging him to help his fragile Angela. Assessing her thoroughly Vincent demanded,

-Whil', I need our willow bark potion, now. Abraham, you can help. The potion will start working within half an hour to an hour. But Angela's fever is far too high right now. Possess her body, cool her for us! It will give her a chance to fight the infection. It will give her the time she needs to recover. She is coming to the church with us tonight, so I can keep an eye on her. With that little trip to that cold and windy building and you, Ab, we should have her temperature under control.

Wilton-Cough's Ghost was not told twice to plunge inside the body of his wife in order to help her. If he cherished the idea of spending his eternity with her Spirit somewhere, for him it was far too early for her to pass away by a mere infection. Well he couldn't really call it 'mere' for it was caused by Ghouls so notorious for eating the dead. What if a Ghoul had chewed upon someone who died of Tuberculosis or something equally bad? His Soul's thoughts put him on emergency level 'sky high'.

Abraham was so concerned about his two boys whom he left behind by his stupid death. Daddy's boy, Zachary had been so hard to be brought back from his grief, he couldn't even start to imagine what it would be like to do the same thing for mummy's boy, Josiah. Would that little fellow even listen to him if his mum was gone too to the Spirit world? He could picture the devastation on the face of Jo if he was to be announced that his mother passed away. It was breaking the heart of Wilton-Cough and his Spirit was ready to do anything to keep his Angela alive. So he woke her up from her rather ghoulish nightmare. He spoke to her mind just like he did with Vincent Valdi. Gentle, he was, a thousand times more than with Valdi, for possessing the body of your wife doesn't call for anything else. He spoke Soul to Soul to her, soft words, yet spurring words which would wake her up. He comforted her from her nightmare and brought her back to reality, however harsh, reality was. He made her open her eyes to the room. He made her sit to face Valdi and his inspection. He kept her awake for her to take the willow bark potion given by Miss White. He made sure she was cold enough for the fever to not send his wife to him, for her to stay alive for their two boys, for them to not be orphans.

Despite his great concern about the method used to care for Mrs Wilton-Cough, Theo Odell could only witness the mother rising from her couch with bright blue eyes. Despite her untidy black curls flowing on her shoulders, she looked like a teenage girl about to confess her puppy love for someone. It was something he probably couldn't understand right now, however he admired the results:

possessed by her husband, Angela was ever so compliant to the help given to her, but also looked like she had found inner peace. It was the complete opposite of when they entered the room. He also admired Vincent for coming up with the idea in the first place, but he guessed that Valdi and his experimental approach to everything was to be thanked for it, for it allowed him to experience what it was to be possessed by a Spirit fully. Theo also knew it was not just any odd Spirit, it was Abraham Wilton-Cough, and he could not help but respect the Soul of that man.

It was not before long that Mrs Wilton-Cough stood among them, with fairly rosy cheeks, fluttering eyelashes, announcing that she was ready for the trip to the church. If Vincent seeing her all perked up by her possession by her ghostly husband left her with a knowing wink to tie the Doe again, as he was fully reassured that none but Abraham could do a great deal of good to Angela, a puzzled Theo, Josephine and Amelia couldn't take their eyes away from the suddenly blossoming woman that they saw so unwell minutes earlier.

It was Miss Cough who enquired first,

-How do you feel with my nephew in you?

Angela giggled at her question before blushing as she whispered,

-I feel cuddled from the inside.

Amelia and Josephine couldn't help smiling while Theo questioned,

-I am not entirely sure that Mrs Wilton-Cough is fit enough to go inside the church. She is talking non sense, Vince. Were you cuddled inside when you were possessed by Wilton-Cough?

As the Doctor put the Crying White Doe across his shoulders, he replied firmly with a sarcastic curve at his lips,

-Of course not! I am not his wife. You are the one talking non-sense. Angela will stay where I can watch her progress. Once my potion is taking effect, Abraham will have to stop sweet talking to her and possessing her body. Think of it Theo, two lovers finally united after months apart, or is it too much for you to figure that one out?

Father Odell, pouting, retorted,

-I still think that stepping into my church in that state is inappropriate. She is all flushed like a poppy.

Taking Mrs Wilton-Cough's hand to assess her temperature, Whilhelmina reassured,

-Her fever is being properly tackled, Theo. She is not as dangerously hot as she was. The more we are, the better it will be to get rid of the curse.

Odell gave the White Witch a killer glance, before pointing to Angela,

-Isn't it obvious that a Ghost is making love to her right in front of my nose and that she shouldn't enter my church while she is on cloud nine!? Proprieties, children, proprieties!

His outcry faced multiple reactions. First Miss White looked fairly puzzled, she didn't know what proper love was so she scrutinised Mrs Wilton-Cough's face for signs of it, remaining silent. Amelia Bates just said an out loud 'No!', full of disbelief and curiosity. Josephine Cough shook her head in disapproval to Father Odell, scolding him,

-How could you say that? This is preposterous!

While Zachary trying to catch up on the conversation asked genuinely,

-What's cloud nine?

Vincent Valdi smirked before giving a proper telling off to his friend,

-For Christ's sake Theo! Can't you be more blunt? Beside there's many aspects to love. It is not just physical. Abraham is having a Soul to Soul with her. It's quite different. Although he didn't sweet talk to me, Wilton-Cough spoke to my mind, and that was powerful enough to make me see a lot of things differently. His Soul is talking to hers, right now, and he loves her more than I can say, trying to save her. Right, Josephine bring the axe, Zachary take the hand of your mum, Amelia let me help you walk, Whil' don't let go of that book and bring your vanity case, just in case for Mrs Wilton Cough, Theo, stop being preposterous and lead the way.

Everyone did as they were told. Theo proposed to carry the case for Miss White while she looked after the very dreaded book. His offer was accepted and the Witch and the Priest lead the small procession to the nearby church. They were followed closely by Josephine Cough which was on the look out for Ghouls, feeling stronger for holding Noah's axe. Zachary behind his great Aunt, helped his mum, asking her what it was like to have his Pa inside her... To which the gentle woman never answered to but only kept blushing. Closing the march, was the Doctor, the Doe around his neck and Mrs Bates leaning against him. Vincent, now feeling that life was too short to miss an opportunity after his very close encounter with Wilton-Cough, whispered to Amelia a question,

-So you were worried about me?

The pregnant widow nodded affirmatively yet silently. If her ankle was not so twisted, she would have stepped away from the man to give herself some countenance as she answered. She would have been able to voice something then or maybe just utter two words together like: 'I was' or 'We were'. For both were right and applied. But she was close. His strong arm was helping her, maintaining her. She could feel him breathe, his warmth, his touch. Then she saw his smile at her silent answer, bright, full of teeth and all. She thought she was done and under and that he could scoop her heart out with a little spoon at that moment. It made her very full belly twirl. She could feel the 'Butterflies'. But the butterflies were very much kicking, and when her hand reached her belly to check on its content, another went to do the same. Amelia could have panicked, but she did not for Valdi whispered in her ear at the same time, in the most reassuring tone,

-I am here for you. Let me look after you.

She looked at his honest blue eyes, and her head dived onto his broad chest like someone who have just returned from the most tedious journey, seeking comfort. Valdi smiled confidently looking at the stars. From that moment on, he knew that Amelia was his companion. He took her hand, lifted it to his mouth to apply a silent yet tender kiss upon it which meant so much for both of them.

For Amelia, it sealed the fact that the Doctor had affections for her. In her state, she never thought that she would become the romantic interest of anyone. But she did feel that something was going on and had been for a while. It went beyond their complicity to hide her pregnancy. She could remember him, every morning passing by her door, that she made sure she was sweeping the door step right at that time, while he was going out of town to check his patients who could not come to see him at his clinic. He would lift his hat to her and stop for a small chat. Valdi would give her the newspaper of the day, the one that he just read, and she would give him the gossips of the town in exchange. If the Doctor never entered to have a cup of tea or breakfast with her, it was a morning ritual that both enjoyed and looked forward to, just the simple fact of talking to each other for a few minutes, every morning.

Amelia Bates, never knew there was a strong liking between them, until she was in trouble and confided the matter to the Doctor. From then on his attention rose tenfold as he appointed himself her protector. Amelia, although being a recent Widow, not only appreciated that level of attention, she was very sensitive to it. Respected and handsome, Vincent Valdi had that manly charm about him which rendered him irresistible to women. Falling for him was not something the Widow could resist to. She also knew for a fact that for all his twenty years in Wilton Town the man had never courted anyone.

From gossip to gossip, she knew of mothers throwing their daughters in front of him, and that the Doctor wasn't paying any interest, nor attention at any level of coquetry done to attract him. Everyone trying to attach that man was failing miserably, fathers had even proposed their daughters for betrothal to Valdi for him only to decline politely. It went to some extent that some people were questioning Vincent's sexuality but no evidence could be found.

She remembered herself having dismissed one gossip running in the town once that Valdi didn't like women as the explanation for him remaining a bachelor. She said it was pure non-sense because he was always very courteous and friendly with her but also that Vincent was often seen with Miss White, that they had an excellent working friendship. She had even discussed the subject with the man himself at her doorstep one morning, for it had reached her ear that he had refused a proposal of marriage again from a father for his daughter the day before. She couldn't comprehend it for the young lady in question, not only was extremely pretty but came from a very rich background. Vincent confided to her that beauty and money were not everything. He told her that he simply didn't have the time to consider marriage but if he ever did the lady in question would need to be one he considered a witty soul mate. They had that conversation years ago. But Amelia remembered it like it was yesterday, even more now with Vincent Valdi letting her know little by little his love interest for her. She felt suitably flattered.

To have a man like that, who a lot of women wanted but never succeeded to attract was boosting her ego endlessly. The will to discourage the good Doctor's intentions was far from Amelia Bates, and in her pregnant state, she could guess that those intentions could only be honourable. When they entered the church, she could imagine herself being led once more to the altar one day in her future. Despite the pain given by her twisted ankle, despite the baby she was carrying kicking inside her belly, the Widow had a happy smile on her lips.

Another Widow had blushed cheeks and an elated smile as she was walked by her eldest son to the altar following the Priest and the Witch. Angela blessed Valdi in her heart for having suggested to be possessed by her husband, for Abraham Wilton-Cough not only was declaring his eternal love for her but he also proposed to use possession as a regular medium to make sure that his wife knew that, despite him being dead, he would always be with her or never far away, looking after her and the boys. She felt heartwarmingly soothed from her grief.

Odell brought the stool by the church organ for Amelia to sit within the circle they were forming while Valdi deposited the Crying White Doe in its middle. Considering the smile on Mrs Bates face and her rosy cheeks, Theo suspected than something must have happened between her and Valdi when they were closing the march to the church.

Father Odell knew his friend's intentions for the woman for they had that big sharing talk a while ago in the pub. He had then Vincent's avowal that he was deeply affected by the trouble Amelia was into. Valdi told him how he cared for her more than he could say, that due to her present condition, he was toying with the idea of proposing to her in the very near future. Theo remembered the deep insecurities of his friend as he revealed to him that he believed he would be an appalling husband for the simple fact that he had hardly any time at all to offer to a potential wife, hence to prevent the unhappiness of someone, he had remained a firm bachelor. However Amelia, as a former soldier's wife, was more than used to an absent husband. He had befriended her for long enough to observe that she was more than capable to cope being the wife of a Doctor. He had always loved her cheerfulness in any circumstances thrown at her. Valdi confessed to Theo that the death of Harry Bates compounded with Amelia being pregnant changed the situation in his heart tremendously, that from enjoying his morning conversation with Mrs Bates, he came to consider that he loved her too much to see her struggle on her own with a child but also that he considered her the perfect loving companion he always desired to have but always abstained to get.

Theo Odell had suspected Vincent to have been secretly in love with Amelia for long before her trouble and the death of Harry Bates however. For when they were together in the pub, the Doctor never failed to report to him the gossips of the town exactly as rendered by Mrs Bates. He also knew how religious Vincent was in the morning to meet her at her doorsteps to have that chat which delighted him and amused him before he would tackle his hard day. If Valdi never spoke of any ladies very much, Amelia Bates was often mentioned, praised for her fortitude in her solitude regularly and referred to very highly by Vincent, enough for Father Odell to gather that she had captured the heart of his friend all along. Theo believed that if Mrs Bates had not become a widow, Valdi would have remained that Spartiate Bachelor. Finally, given the opportunity to bestow the heart of the person his friend found the most amusing, he knew Vincent would start courting the Widow as soon as decency would allow him.

Theo, giving a glance to the Widow of Abraham who was rather in the same 'happily in love' state, commented,

-I swear this is not the smile I would pull before doing an exorcism or a 'witchcrafty' curse reversal. I understand your smile Mrs Wilton-Cough but Mrs Bates... What have you done to poor Mrs Bates, Vince?

The Doctor who was untying the Doe took a look at the blushing Amelia. He gave her a beautiful grin before replying to his friend with his natural un-fussed deep honesty,

-Just a big kiss on her hand for she is letting me look after her. Just expect wedding bells in the near future, Theo, for I want to marry Amelia. Can you be my best man as well as performing the ceremony?

Forgetting all propriety, forgetting her ankle, and her state, an excited Mrs Bates lifted from her stool to run into the arms of Vincent Valdi who received her in extremis as she was tripping from sheer pain. The Doctor scolded her as she enclosed him in a hug which revealed straight away to all, her reciprocal growing loving sentiments,

-I guess that is a straightforward 'yes' my future Amelia Bates-Valdi. Shall we keep you alive until then and return you safely onto that stool? Bad ankle: no walking upon it the Doctor said, that also means no jumping nor running.

Voiceless she just nodded positively to him. Her ecstatic smile never left her lips especially since Valdi kissed her forehead, then her nose. But then he finished with her rosy lips in a hungry kiss which revealed to her that he had been a very patiently waiting man all along.

In front of that full blown passionate kiss, Theo Odell feigned disapproval to recall the couple, however, he was deep down absolutely overjoyed for his friend,

-Vince, each time you step into my church, it is decidedly to commit something which should not take place here... Like flying against a wall for your disbelief, and now, and now, losing all proprieties. This can only happen after wedlock, I swear. To all present, we haven't seen what we just saw. Keep their engagement secret until those two can announce their betrothal publicly. But you are all invited to the wedding. I would have loved to be the best man, but I can't, however, I will take great pride and great honour in performing the ceremony.

Taking the not so subtle clues from Theo, Valdi regained control of himself. He walked an over the moon happy Amelia to her stool before assessing on the face of their witnesses their reactions. The old Josephine Cough went to congratulate him leaving him in no doubts of her approval. That matriarch's opinions were so respected in town as some of the most educated ones that he was sure the entire Wilton Town would follow suit in her wake and turn a kind eye onto his choice to marry finally with none but Amelia Bates.

As Angela Wilton-Cough was all over her best friend congratulating Amelia, being ever so happy for her, as he knew that he already had the blessing of Theo Odell, Valdi turned to the younger Wilton-Cough and Whilhelmina White to check their attitudes to the announcement. The teenager who was crouched by the Doe reassuring her, was having one of his typical mouth wide open into a gobbing fly stunned 'O'. Smiling kindly to Zachary, the witty Valdi had just the trick to win the boy over as he proposed,

-Zach, if Theo is to perform the wedding, would you do me the honour of being my best man?

The teenager felt ever so proud to just be asked to do so for he would not have consider himself the perfect candidate, being clumsy and all, he might just mess things up badly, yet he accepted,

-Sir, O Sir, I would. I would love to. I want to. I will. But I have to warn you that I may be a very crap one. I am not that articulate with my words nor with my moves. Would you tell me what you want me to do?

Vincent felt compelled to mess Zach's hair once more before reassuring,

-Well I am not the best church goer in the world. I would have to learn my steps in there myself to be a presentable bow. So we can learn together under the tuition of Father Odell until then.

His friend welcomed his idea, knowing it only highlighted to him another insecurity of Valdi so Theo confirmed,

-I will get you both patched up in time for the ceremony: You've got yourselves a deal. As for finding what to say for the best man's speech, I can write that with you or entirely for you, Zachary.

The teenager replied with some certainty,

-I guess my Pa would want me to learn those type of things, so if you write the speech with me, Father, I will be your most attentive pupil. Maybe one day, I would be liked enough to be a best man again.

His answer touched Theo so much that he fussed with the hair of Zachary exactly like his friend did beforehand, reassuring,

-I am certain that you will. I am going to make sure that you will be the best Best man there is to be in town.

Vincent turned his attention to Miss White who had remained silent,

-Whil', I would love you to be present at my wedding. Would you be my wife's bridesmaid along with Mrs Wilton-Cough? I know you don't appreciate churches very much like I do too but this is a very special event...

Whilhelmina went to present her pale hand to hold. Her thin lips gave him a very bright smile as she confided,

-I am so happy for you. I will be there. You can count on me, especially if Mrs Amelia Valdi-Bates allows me to be one of her bridesmaids.

A blushed Amelia agreed straight away, liking the sound of her future new name pronounced by the White Witch in an inverse fashion to the one pronounced by Vincent,

-Mrs Valdi-Bates would be very happy to have you, Whilhelmina White, to be my bridesmaid with Angela.

Father Odell clapped his hands together as much with happiness as to recall the attention of everyone,

-Right, if no one has got any other emotional announcement to do, let us proceed, for dawn is nearly upon us, and we have only that short window until then to remove the curse. Miss White let's open the book, everyone, in a circle keeping the White Doe within it.

Whilhelmina went to Theo's side and explained to him, whispering, the entire process, referring to the book from time to time. Feeling more confident for it, Odell was preparing himself mentally as much as he was doing prior to performing an exorcism. When the Witch had fully briefed him, he was ready to attack that curse full on. He ordered,

-The removal of the curse will use the energy generated by our common will. Please, hold the hand of the person next to you. Zachary, I am afraid, you have to stand within the circle by Tristina as you are one of the very victims of her curse.

When everyone assumed their positions, the Priest placed the axe of Noah M Wilton within the hands of the teenager. The boy had no idea that it was the axe of his ancestor he was holding until Odell told him,

-Zach, this is the axe of Noah M Wilton. It represents the town at the time of the very curse. You have to carry it during the session. It is just a matter of holding it. You do not need to use it at any point.

The younger Wilton-Cough felt great pride to behold such an object within his hands. The manner he held it was, well, miles apart from how Noah would have. It was clumsy, as Zach was almost hugging the axe of his ancestor. No one present could have said that they were facing a warrior carrying a battle axe, or someone who could have butchered them if he wanted to with a dangerous weapon. The teenager looked so purely innocent and harmless even with an axe to them that it was hard for all of them to envisage the heartless Ghoul he would become if the curse was not removed. However one, who had no problem to imagine that very Ghoul, was his own father who had seen the very monster in his premonitory nightmare before his death.

The ghostly Abraham Wilton-Cough was too moved and far too angry to remain silent in the depth of his wife guts, he harangued in his most guttural voice,

-How could you curse blindly, Tristina? Look at my boy! Does he deserve to become a Ghoul? Does he? Does any child deserve to be cruel monsters? How could you?

It is fair to say that the Crying White Doe was terrified and petrified at that moment in time. But the teenager by her dropped the axe to coax the animal. He crouched to enclose the creature in his arms, and dared to shout back to his father in a desperate plea,

-Pa! Stop it, Pa! She didn't know. She didn't know anything. She was too distraught. Battered all her life. Completely distraught. Tristina Ogin didn't know. She couldn't. With the death of her husband, feeling his tremendous loss. I was so distraught at your own death I didn't know what to do anymore. It must have been the same. She couldn't realise properly what she was doing. It was all bad grief, Pa, all bad grief, not digested and all. And then, and then her starving kids killed her. Pray, Pa, have pity on her.

Father Odell scolded the Ghost, finding it deep down very unsettling to see Angela speaking like a spectral entity,

-Abraham Wilton-Cough, no one is on trial in my church. We are here to resolve the situation, not to hinder it in any shape or form. If you cannot behave, I will demand that you leave your wife's body. Therefore for Angela's sake and health, be tolerant, patient and charitable. Like your son pleaded, I beg you to exercise some pity for that distraught Soul stuck for ages in her sorry state.

The Priest then turned to the Crying White Doe stating,

-As for you Tristina Ogin, if I am no judge, I only hope that you can see here the result of your action. Before you, you have the Soul of a father who will not rest until the fate of his son is solved. Before you, you have the living mother of our cursed boy, who has been grievously attacked by Ghouls tonight. She has one of the sweetest Souls which would not even kill a fly, yet like all of us in Wilton-Town, she is trapped to sustain the injuries of your curse. Beside you, you have Zachary Wilton-Cough, one of the many victims your curse targeted. He is the very one who has been pleading us for pity to your plight. I hope your Soul is fully sorrowful, sorrowful enough to show the same pity towards him and all the children of this town blindly cursed by you. I demand of you to repair this injustice with us. Agree to reverse the curse on Wilton Town. Lay upon the feet of that cursed boy if your Soul wants to salvage all who can still be salvaged and I will do the rest.

Everyone were anxious, waiting for the effect of the apology of Father Odell on the Doe, observing closely her every move. She went by the standing teenager who had only shown kindness to her from the start. Tristina felt extremely compassionate about the boy so much so that she wished he had been her own boy instead of her two murderous children. Her unresting Soul was indeed sorrowful. She could understand the level of her mistake and the outrage addressed towards her by Abraham Wilton-Cough. Trembling she lay at the feet of the descendant of Noah, regretting bitterly the curse she uttered when she was still alive, expecting that the attendants would order the boy to slaughter her with his ancestor's axe.

However she felt her neck stroked gently by Zachary who may have guessed her thoughts as he soothed softly,

-I will never harm you, Tristina, never. You have suffered far too much. Remember, Father Odell said the axe is to represent the town only. It is to remove the curse not your head.

The Crying Doe lifted her head to look at the caring boy closely. It appeased her to know that there were decent children in Wilton-Town and she had a big example in front of her. At that very instant she retrieved faith and hope. At that very instant her Soul felt tremendous forgiveness despite all that had happened to her back in her living days. But also at that very moment extreme guilt grabbed her heart.

Whilhelmina White called Father Odell back by her side and intimated to him,

-This is the right time, Theo. Repeat after me as loud as you can. You have to hold my hand with the rosary of Tristina. This object will allow the total reversal of the curse to happen.

Giving all his trust on what the Witch confided, Theo started. He repeated loud and clear her every word. Not before too long, he could witness the effect on the Crying White Doe but also on Zachary. Both were surrounded by a strange halo of lime green light the more he talked yet he never ceased the recital believing strongly in putting finally things to right.

To everyone witnessing everything, Vincent Valdi, Amelia Bates, Josephine Cough, Angela Wilton-Cough and the ghostly Abraham, all could not help but repeating for themselves in an almost chanted whisper the very sentences being uttered by Father Odell, all hoping that it will free finally the children of the town from that dreaded curse.

Amelia felt increasingly uncomfortable upon her seat, however she remained silent about it. She knew that there was not much time before dawn and that the removal of the curse could only happen before it, so she was ready to wait until the end before warning the Doctor that she didn't know anymore if her baby was just kicking within her or if it was something else. Expecting a child within days, she was determined to remove any possibility of him or her being cursed like the eldest son of Abraham. The Widow Bates had a strong enough character to sustain some level of pain without uttering a single word about it therefore she did so.

What she was witnessing in front of her was powerful enough to make her mind more attentive to what was happening inside the church than inside her belly. Zachary Wilton-Cough and the Doe seemed to be engulfed together within a circle of blue-green flames. The blood tears of the Doe had redoubled so much so that her fore legs were stained up by them until her hooves. The axe shone so powerfully in Zach's hands that the teenager seemed to be alight just as well. The palm of Miss white was burning from the crucifix on the rosary which was digging into her skin, yet from it, and the joint hands of Father Odell and Whilhelmina holding the precious object came a beam of light which could be seen to reach the Doe at the very place her heart was. Whilhelmina and Theo carried on, undisturbed by everything, until the end.

When the last word was uttered by Father Odell, all manifestations of light, fire and beams stopped. The possessed Angela Wilton-Cough rushed to her son, checking that he was okay, alive and not burnt, but he was fine. He reassured her rather shyly,

-I am all good, Ma. Pa, I am okay. I've still got all my toes and fingers and all. The only difference I can notice is that I feel extremely good and peaceful inside. Let me check Tristina.

The Crying White Doe at his feet lay lifeless. A living human heart was beating by her side and did so for a few seconds before it stopped. A tearful teenager looked for answers all around him. Everyone but Amelia Bates surrounded him closer at once. Father Odell offered the explanation the youngster silently needed,

-When she did the curse upon the town's children, Tristina Ogin did curse herself without knowing it. She was not allowed to pass away. She was cursed to stay with the living. Her Soul has finally been released from her own curse. This means that there are no more curses at all that remain.

Trying to understand Zachary asked, getting distressed,

-Did what we did kill her?

Vincent Valdi went to give him a bear hug as he enjoined, ruffling the hair of the lad,

-Of course we didn't, my silly Boy. She was killed by her own children. Her Soul couldn't reach the Spirit world, where your father is, because of what she did. Now, her soul has the ability to find peace, just like your Pa, she may rest. Give us a good cry for you did so well. You helped her more than anyone did, Zach. I am very proud of you.

His back tapped gently, Zachary sobbed upon the offered shoulder,

-What will happen to the Doe and Tristina's heart?

Father Odell depositing the human heart carefully into a beautiful cloth which had been covering the altar of his church answered,

-A proper burial. Tristina Ogin's grave is incomplete without those two and her rosary. Do you want to assist me, Zach?

As the boy replied in the affirmative by a nod, trying to compose himself by drying his tears, Whilhelmina helped Theo wrapping the remains of Tristina Ogin. This is when the Priest noticed the very damaged hand of the Witch. He stopped her actions by taking her hand within his and inspecting it. He could tell she was terrified by that mere closer look for the woman in front of him shivered uncontrollably with sheer fear in her eyes. The damage the rosary did to Miss White's hand was so substantial that he called upon Vincent,

-Vince, check that one out for me.

Valdi coming to them, gave a worried look to Whilhelmina, already knowing the matter at hand, for he did smell her burning flesh all along the removal of the curse. The Doctor could only be impressed with the stamina of her Being's willingness to do good and put things to right despite her pain. Yet he feared Theo's reaction if he knew all the secrets of Whilhelmina. His glance was enough cue for the Witch to gather that anything she would try to hide was in jeopardy. With unprecedented courage she decided to reveal one, whispering straight within the ear of the Priest who kept her trembling hand within his,

-I may be part demonic since I rendered myself eternal.

Theo nodded his acknowledgement very silently. He tapped her hand before presenting it to Valdi, with a very muted,

-Whil' is clearly in sheer pain. Can you make sure this is looked after?

The White Witch corrected him by another confession within his ear,

-It's alright, Theo, this can't heal, it will never do. I need to have a Soul for it to happen.

Looking at the sheepish eternal Being before him, Father Odell felt moved. Knowing she would be hurt and never been able to be mended, she went through the entire process, conscious that she would be injured for eternity. He didn't believe Whilhelmina had no Soul at all despite whatever she did to be eternal. For him, she couldn't have gone through that much pain without one. Maybe a bargain had been done back in the days, maybe Whilhelmina was part demonic but Theo Odell was convinced that he had the best part of what she had become in front of him. Maybe he was very puzzled about her, riddled with questions yet after what they did together and what her Being went through doing so, he wanted to help her but also know her much better that he currently did. Theo realised how frightened the woman was of Priests, how secretive she was and understood that, like he did with his friend Vincent Valdi, he would have to dig deeper in the dirt in order to find out who she was really inside. Somehow he only expected to be pleasantly surprised with whatever he could find out about Whilhelmina White.

Ready to start straight away, Theo proposed in a whisper accompanied by a wink warning her that he would keep any secret she would confide to him,

-Let us try something together, shall we? Follow me, Whil'. It may only cool your hand but it may also do more.

At the compassionate smile at Father Odell's lips, the Witch followed him, worryingly yet willingly but most importantly, somehow she trusted him since he didn't jump to her throat when she revealed to him that she was part demon. He led her by the church's massive doors. Lodged within an entrance pillar was a massive shell of Tridacna. Theo announced in a low voice to keep everything he said between him and her,

-This is a 'bénitier', Whil'. When I arrived in town I made this church have room to accommodate for all faiths our good people of Wilton Town have so far. It certainly did bring more people in but not you, nor my Vince. Well let me tell you all about this special item. That beautiful shell was hard to get. That particular one comes from the Red Sea. It is the fancy recipient for holy water. I just prayed upon that water many times. That's all it takes to keep it simply holy. Your hand is going to dip in there to cool right off. If the water boils, or if you are burnt further, we will know for sure the state of your Soul. I am sure you do not want to spend another hundred years in that state of fear and uncertainty about your own self. Let's find out together.

Although terrified, Whilhelmina White considered the presented hand of Odell as an helping one, and after a long minute of consideration, she put her hand trustingly within his. He did not wait for her to have second thoughts. He plunged her marked hand within the bénitier. As he did, he uttered a prayer addressed to the Virgin, a prayer which was barely audible, however, it made the Witch wonder if the Priest was attempting to exorcise her. If he could see Whilhelmina's anguish, Theo nonetheless carried on his plea for her injured hand's recovery and maintained it within his in the water.

The Witch felt her skin burning initially, like if her hand had been put in boiling water. However the sensation receded to be replaced by its opposite slowly but surely. She could see steam coming out of the bénitier. She didn't know if it was a good sign or a bad sign. She didn't know either if she had to fear Theo or bless him at that moment or indeed if she had to be scared of what she had become. Pearls of sweat forming on her forehead started to run across her face. Miss White was increasingly feeling faint.

But when her hand was released, she was still conscious, standing by Theo, yet shivering uncontrollably. The Priest offered her a bright confident smile before announcing to her,

-Take a good look at your hand, Whil'. I did an intercession for you. If you didn't have a Soul it would not have worked so beautifully.

Considering her hand, the Witch could neither see the wound nor feel it for it was entirely gone. The embedded sign of the cross which had burned right into her palm was no longer there. Puzzled, she blinked at Theo Odell for more answers however, the Priest just cockily grinned to her along with giving her his laconic reply,

-This is my kind of magic, Whil': mysterious ways, just mysterious ways.

Whilhelmina White was suitably impressed. Giving Odell a grateful smile, she not only discovered that she still had a Soul with his help, but also that she had a determined friend in him. He enjoined her, whispering straight into her ear,

-Don't just stand here, my soulful Witch, we have a big bad book to put away into its cache and Tristina to bury.

As they returned toward the altar, both were all smiles. They saw Vincent Valdi occupied to assess Angela Wilton-Cough's progress. He had asked Abraham to leave his wife's body and to go back inside him temporarily. The Ghost didn't complain for he was eager to know how his Angie was doing. But also if he had a positive influence on her by possessing her, he had the firm intention of doing that very often. Now that the curse was broken, Abraham Wilton-Cough was quite reluctant to rest in peace. He was finally rather enjoying being a Ghost for it gave him some means to still be with his loved ones and communicate with them.

Communication had been fairly troublesome for him, however the former Banker could only admit that at the end of the night with the help of the living, he was getting the hang of it. So as long as his Angel was not going to grab him to go to Hell or Paradise, he was determined to follow his family like a shadow to make sure they were doing alright. As they were no signs of Abigail since she took the Ghost of Ogin to Hell in the clearing, he felt that it was the chance of his After-life to stay by all he loved and cared for.

Vincent Valdi gave him the good news,

-Abraham, let me tell you that Angela is taking a turn for the better. Her temperature is simply gone thanks to you and that potion. What she needs now is just a good rest. So after sorting out your son, we just sorted out your wife. Someone must be a happy Ghost.

Abraham Wilton-Cough definitely was, however as he followed the look of the Doctor who saw some water below Amelia's stool, he realised that someone wasn't doing too well at all.

Chapter Nineteen

Abigail's Dawn

Vincent Valdi ordered straight away while he took the hand of
Amelia Bates who was pale with pain,

-Zachary Wilton-Cough, time for you to take charge of your Ma.
Take her to the presbytery to rest while you will help Theo to bury
Tristina Ogin. Whil', I am going to need your help right now. How
is your hand doing?

Watching the concern on the face of his friend, Theo understood
that the Doctor was dealing with a matter of emergency. He also
recognised straight away Vincent's serious taking things into
control's tone when he faced a medical situation, so he proposed his
help,

-Whil's hand is fixed up. What do you want us to do?

The Doctor was only too happy to reply,

-I need you to take in charge of the looking after of the burial with
Zach. Angela is to rest at yours a little. Josephine, follow Whil' to
the presbytery, she will tell you what to bring back with her. I need
everything as soon as possible. Whil', it is an early one, by about
fourteen days.

Whilhelmina White understood straight away and put her vanity
case by the Doctor, nodding to him positively, with her own orders,

-Theo, take charge of removing the Doe immediately. Miss Cough
come with me, bring the axe.

Herself she took the witchcraft book and ran rather than walked to
the entrance of the church. Josephine Cough understood the issue
and followed suit, enjoining,

-Come on Zach, you heard the Doctor, what are you still doing here? Help your mum.

The teenager didn't grasp what was the matter, yet obeyed without a word, taking the hand of his mother and joining the others leaving the church. Theo was following him carrying the White Doe and the heart.

Finally alone with Mrs Bates, the Doctor took his cape off and laid it on the ground. Rolling his sleeves, he asked concerned,

-When did you break your waters?

Amelia looked at him confused, blushing as she answered,

-Was it that? I thought, that the sheer pain made me be incontinent. It was about a minute ago.

Giving her a kind smile, Vincent Valdi shook his head negatively as he announced,

-Your little one has decided to come and say hello to mummy a little earlier than expected. Let's make you comfortable and check.

Guiding the pregnant woman from the stool to his cape, he added,

-Well, being possessed by Wilton-Cough right now, it is fair to say that the baby will say hello to daddy just as well. Abraham has been at the birth of all his children, like I did. Trust him to not miss one of them.

As she took position on the cape, another strong contraction grabbed her. Acknowledging now that she was about to give birth, she felt blessed that it happened at a time when she was by the Doctor but also that he had a very experienced eternal midwife to help him. She had that fright of having the baby on her own all during her pregnancy. No she was confident that it would not be the case. Inspecting her, Valdi offered her a reassuring smile, as he told her,

-Right, my Amelia, it is nearly there. All the signs are good. I want you to control your breathing. When Whil' and Jo are back, I will need you to push for me.

She nodded. To make sure Amelia did not grow anxious, Vincent kept her mind busy making small talk,

-So what do you think our little one will be, a little boy or a little girl? What would you prefer?

As he already knew what it will be himself, he was rather probing his future wife. She came with an answer that pleased him,

-I have no preference, Vincent. I just love children. I waited for so long to finally be a mum. I always had a dream of a big, joyful family. Yet I was always so alone.

Taking her hand within his, Vincent applied a long and tender kiss upon it before confiding,

-You are not alone anymore, my Amelia, you have me and this tiny angel coming to us. We will have all the children you desire. I was deprived of a family when I was only three and ever since my heart harboured the same dream as yours, the one of a big and joyful family. I will make sure we realise our dream together for I want to make you happy.

This warmed the heart of Amelia Bates endlessly. Another contraction took hold of her but despite it, the tears glistening at her eyes were of happiness.

At that precise moment, Vincent Valdi felt extremely cold. He knew what it was as he recognised the sensation. Even if he only had it briefly earlier that night. It was not due to the fact that he had removed his cape nor due to the Spirit of Abraham Wilton-Cough. Valdi gathered immediately that it was the compounded presence of two Ghosts within him. It chilled his spine with fear and worries but an internal voice calmed his fears at once talking to his mind but also to Wilton-Cough,

-Oops, it is slightly crowded in here. Abraham, I didn't expect you to be present at the birth of your illegitimate child. Doc, do not worry, Private Harry Bates here, coming to join the troupes attending to my Widow.

This made Vincent smirked at the irony of his present situation. With the defunct husband of Amelia, and the Spirit of Abraham who put her in trouble the very night of the funeral of Harry Bates, and himself who couldn't wait for the required grieving period of the Widow to end to ask for her hand in marriage, his new possession promised to be somewhat heavily entertaining him. The Doctor decided not to reveal what was happening to him to the poor Amelia Bates. He didn't want for her to have to justify her present state to her late husband. He didn't want anything to trouble the birth of the child either, for births were already hard enough on their own. So Vincent kept preparing her and getting her ready as he listened to what was happening inside him.

His two Ghosts were having an unusual conversation which he found nosily deeply interesting. It started with Abraham Wilton-Cough's deepest apologies to his childhood friend about having philandered with his Widow the very night of Harry's funeral. Valdi was amazed by the honesty and the surrendering of the proud Abraham who didn't hesitate to confide his past mistake to Harry Bates,

-Harry, oh Harry, your Soul is not resting, it must be my fault. It must be my fault entirely. I did something, Harry, I did something that I can not re-conciliate myself with. It's unforgivable, Harry. It's a big unforgivable mistake. I want you to know how deeply and awfully sorry I am. I slept with Amelia, just once, out of my face drunk, and the result, she is having it, right now. You can haunt me forever for it, I will accept it without a word, for I am ever so sorry.

Vincent Valdi was so surprised by the casual answer of Private Bates after such an avowal of Abraham that he thought that Harry didn't really love his wife,

-I know, I know everything in fact, Ab. Night of my funeral, hey, very, very bad of you. But in memory of our childhood's friendship, and considering that you faced a similar death as I, dying from your shot wound, I forgive you.

A stunned Wilton-Cough whose Soul had been agonising because of that mistake couldn't help repeating with disbelief,

-You forgive me? Just like that. Harry, I am so sorry, you were always so noble. I cried so much at the news of your untimely death.

The defunct Soldier confessed,

-I know how much you cried. I know how much my Amelia cried. Both of you were wrecking yourselves with alcohol on my account the night of the funeral, to try to quench your sorrow. I know all that because I was there. I knew you never had intentions untoward my Widow, because the one that really held her that night was I through you. When I saw my Amelia getting more drink in your kitchen where you were so prostrate and crying, I decided to possess you, for she was hardly standing up already, she needed to go home safely. Well, you were hardly in a condition yourself to be quite in charge of her, so I took your body over while you were so numb with grief and alcohol.

The revelation made Vincent Valdi grin wildly. It also restored fully the respect and esteem he had for Abraham Wilton-Cough which had been dented by his affair with Amelia Bates. Having been possessed himself, he just knew how a Ghost could control you like a plaything if their entity decided to do so. Like the Doctor gave the opportunity of talking to Zachary properly to his father Abraham, Private Bates took the opportunity to look after his Widow via Wilton-Cough the very night of his funeral. Holding the hand of Amelia firmly as she was having a contraction, the Doctor vowed to himself that if he would delay the delivery of that piece of information to his future wife to after she delivered her very angelic mistake safely, he would tell her still, at the right time, for he was sure it would contribute to the peace of her own mind.

The calm reaction of Vincent Valdi who was mainly focused on Amelia in labour, was not matched by Abraham's one. However if Valdi could feel internally the turmoil of Wilton-Cough's Spirit, he also could feel his great restraint. What Vincent didn't know was that the very reason of the restraint of the Banker was due to the fact that he didn't want to impair the moves of the good Doctor as he attended to the birth of his third child. The internal conversation became abrasive as a greatly offended Abraham Wilton-Cough blurted out,

-Without my permission, without my knowledge! You used my body to what? Do your wife one last time! Do you know how distressed I was about my actions, Harry? Do you know that the same maybe the case for Amelia for it was your bloody funeral? Do you realise that made me be adulterous to my sweet Angie who never deserved such thing from my part? I feel raped, totally, body and soul.

His outcry was answered by Harry Bates who tried to appease his old friend,

-Well, your body is quite gone-gone, Ab. But your Soul is still here, well, very much shouting it's here. The Soul is the most important bit, and think of it that way that my confession will bring you the peace you needed. Why do you think I am still a haunting Ghost like you? Because I never have been as noble as you or a lot of people believe. I did my share of mistakes which I attempt to correct. Messing up with you is one that needed to be rectified a little. I never thought you would put yourself in front of a bullet and die so soon harbouring that sheer amount of guilt when I made my dying wish. I mean at school I used to be your fists to recover your stolen marbles and your protector in the yard. How could I figure out that you would put yourself in front of many to protect them from being killed in your bank? How could I guess when I was dying that you were the type to tackle a bank robber? I never thought that you would have the same death as I, dying slowly because your guts were torn apart by a bullet. My ghostly self was by your death bed, you know, Ab, and I truly wished that I had been a security guard at your bank instead of a soldier abroad. I would have been near my Amelia too...

As the Soldier stopped talking, Abraham's anger dropped. He was very well acquainted with guilt and could feel that Harry Bates was full of it. In a calmer tone he tried to engage him to talk some more,

-Did you plan to make love to your wife one last time using me? I need to know so I can forgive you.

The Private's Spirit replied mournfully,

-It was not exactly like that, Ab. I was dying slowly on a pile of soldiers who were doing the same thing, with some who were already gone to the Spirit world. I had a dream, well rather a nightmare, slipping in and out of consciousness, where I could see the result of my entire life's actions. While I could be proud of most, neglecting Amelia had well dreadful consequence which I will not describe. I felt like I had stolen away her life selfishly, along with all her dreams. I met an Angel in that nightmare nearly at the end of it who asked me for my last wishes.

Abraham Wilton-Cough interrupted him, recognising what happened to him before he passed away,

-Was that Angel named Abigail? What was your last wish?

Harry Bates confirmed,

-My Angel was indeed called Abigail. I cried on her lap. I told her that my dearest wish was for my Amelia to be happy. I confessed that after that military campaign I wanted to go home to start the family that she always wanted and just make her happy. I told her that after what I saw in my dream that Amelia couldn't be left alone any longer, that my dearest wish was just for her, for Amelia, to have at least a child, a family, the one I failed to give her. Abigail said to leave it to her for I was a hero. I woke up in my dying body, only to close my eyes totally a few minutes later. I stood up from my corpse as a Ghost in this very church a few days later during my funeral. I was guided by Abigail then a tiny light which hid in candle lights. I followed her for she was following the very step of my Amelia. When I possessed you to look closely after my wasted Widow, Abigail lit the way back to my home. It was the last time I made love to my wife, yes, through you, yes, but it was my dying wish that Abigail made to pass, giving a child to my Amelia so she would never be alone anymore.

As Abraham understood everything, he just wept within Valdi, stating,

-I forgive you with all my heart, Harry.

The Soldier continued, acknowledging,

-I knew you would come to it, Ab. See, I am still protecting your marbles. They didn't do naughty things on their own. I did make them do so for a good cause. Your body was so wasted and lanky that I didn't know if you would ever light the angelic spark. But you eventually did.

To which Wilton-Cough replied very annoyed,

-Let us stay friends and not go into details, shall we? You have spent so much time in the army that one can forgive you up until a certain point for your bluntness. So did you come to watch Abigail's birth or to make sure Amelia would be alright?

Harry answered in all honesty,

-I came to give all my blessings to Vincent Valdi. What he said to Amelia just now is what she seeks the most. I want him to know that my dying wish was for her to have a family and that he completes my perfect picture of it. He makes me a happier Soul because I know now that Amelia will be happy, finally I can rest, and rest assured that she is in safe hands.

His voice stopped. The extreme coldness that the Doctor felt left. Valdi was back to a partial one, which Abraham confirmed to his mind,

-Harry Bates just went, Doc. Oh my day, he couldn't have revealed more. The good thing is you are truly blessed, Vince, and I, I was truly played with. I could weep for the entire world for it, you know, for I loved my Angie so much, but also so badly.

When he finished his sentence, the doors of the church flung open. They were opened by Theo Odell who let Whilhelmina White and Josephine Cough enter with their loads. The two women were carrying warm water in deep bowls and clean cloths. Theo, staying at the entrance of the church, asked his friend,

-Vince, I have Angela sleeping peacefully on my couch. Her temperature hasn't returned. I kept Zach busy to shovel the earth from Tristina Ogin's grave so we can place her heart, the Doe and her rosary inside it. What else do you need me to do apart from the burial?

The Doctor could only welcome the arrival of the two women in his heart for Amelia was so open that he knew her last pushes were imminent. He shouted to Theo with concern, grabbing a large crucifix out of his satchel and throwing it as far as he could near to the feet of the Priest,

-Don't let our Zach alone in the cemetery, for Christ's sake, Theo! Grab your cross and stand by him to protect him from Ghouls.

If Theo Odell went to pick up the cross he thought was lost somewhere but was all along with Valdi silently, when he reached the mid aisle spot where it landed he enquired,

-Did you feel you could do with some protection on the way to the hotel tonight, Vince?

The Doctor gave a staunch scolding glance to the Priest, as he replied,

-Not the right time to query if I started to believe in something, Theo. Not when we have Zachary out there. Wilton-Cough will haunt your Presbytery forever and I would make sure you answer to him if something happen to our lad out there.

Theo was about to walk out when he pointed to the sky, which colour was purple with strips of orange and pink before he answered, holding the cross,

-We made it till the end of the night, Vince. The sun is about to appear. All of us held it together throughout. There are no more Ghouls to be feared. None. Our Zachary is safe. How's our Amelia?

Vincent, looking at the woman before him, told,

-Just beautifully giving birth. She is fine so far, coping strongly. I can see the baby's head.

As Whilhelmina rushed by Valdi's side ready for the birth with bowl and cloths, Theo Odell, watching the sky, stated,

-This baby isn't cursed for sure, for I can see sun rays in the horizon, Vince.

Vincent wasn't able to answer for he just focused on the beautiful baby girl coming bit by bit into his strong hands. As he held her, finally, entirely, tears glistened into his eyes. Voiceless, he looked upon his friend standing by the open church's doors, as he held the baby closed to his chest. The Doctor could see the sun rising behind Theo. It was the end of his own night for him for Vincent felt strongly that he had finally been given a family.

Whilhelmina cut the umbilical cord announcing to all,

-Well, we have a gorgeous girl. Although quite early she looks so healthy and strong that she is just perfect. Amelia, you have a very beautiful baby girl.

If the mother felt relief that everything went fine that she had finally her most awaited first child, the ghostly father, Abraham Wilton-Cough, holding his last child through the hands of Vincent was emotional beyond belief. Deep down he acknowledged that this little girl of his was blessed from the start. If this beautifully blatant mistake was not conceived, he would have remained too proud to admit any mistake at all during his life. He would not have eaten humble pie and changed for the better. He just knew he was beholding an Angel. As much as Valdi's heart was swelling with gratefulness, Wilton-Cough's one was doing so, just as well.

A smiling Amelia saw Vincent letting her hold the little mistake she had been carrying for months. When her arms held her, she thought she was her best mistake ever. She asked her future husband,

-How shall we call her?

To which Vincent Valdi replied with certainty,

-Our little Angel's name is Abigail.

Amelia looked upon her child and tried to see if the name fitted her little baby face or not, but couldn't find nothing wrong with it. She nodded positively,

-Our Abigail, it is then. Such a pretty name for such a pretty little one.

As the Doctor had returned tending to Amelia's welfare, he only commented before giving a fire of orders,

-I know it is a lovely name. We will be able to count our blessings by it. Josephine, I need you to rush to get a horse and small buggy from old Tom. Tell him it is for me. He will not ask for any money, nor question you whatsoever. His coachman is mute and helpful to a fault. When you are back with them, I need you to take Amelia to her home, mentioning just her ankle injury all the way through.

Whil', Theo, the task of depositing our little Abigail upon Amelia's steps befall upon you. Make it fast but don't be caught red handed doing it. As for me, I will be back to my surgery, answering to the knock on the door of Miss Cough telling me that I need to attend to Mrs Bates's ankle's injury. As Miss White and Theo will keep an eye on Amelia's doorsteps like eagles, I will be the first to pick up our Abigail. I will be the first to warn her that a little one was left on her doorstep.

Theo Odell intervened as the sun started to rise behind him,

-I will do the first knock and announcement. Come just half an hour later, Vince. As your are about to marry Amelia, this will avoid suspicion. It will protect you two from the worst of people who think they know better but do not understand true love.

Whilhelmina who was washing the new born infant carefully, before wrapping her up in a white blanket, commented,

-I can only agree with Theo. Let us give that little Angel, Angel Abigail, the best start possibly on Earth.

The White Witch gave the baby girl back to Vincent Valdi who was only too proud to behold her once more before she attended to Amelia. Whilst Miss White was cleaning the mother attentively, the Doctor presented the new arrival to the old Josephine Cough,

-Aunt Jo, meet the last of the Wilton-Cough brood of children: my little Miss Abigail soon to become Abigail Valdi-Bates. Yes, you can all be sure that Amelia and I will give her the best start in life for that tiny mistake is our angelic treasure.

Aunt Josephine considered the child with great curiosity. She had been let into the secrecy of her somewhat shameful conception by Amelia Bates and Angela Wilton-Cough at her return to Wilton Town for the funeral of her nephew. She remembered her utter disbelief at the announcement but also her own words that there must have been a mistake, that Abraham would never had done such thing. However Miss Cough only faced the confirmation of the matter by whom were present at the death of Abraham Wilton-Cough and heard his sorrowful confession.

Presently looking at the result of her nephew's errors, Josephine was searching for the Wilton-Cough's family air in the little baby face. If she found the presented Abigail utterly beautiful, she could not help commenting,

-She has the dark blond hair of the Wilton-Coughs alright. But I could swear at the colour of her eyes that she was Harry Bates's daughter. They are Sapphire blue like his... I mean... I mean... Harry was the best school friend of my Abraham. I took him with us to see the Northern Lights in Norway... It cannot be... but... but... look at that smile... That's all Abraham... and those dimples that's all Amelia... It cannot be...

The Doctor taking a good glance at the giggling baby within his arms which had not been crying whatsoever since her arrival, confided,

-Jo, if I could tell you what I know, trust me it can be possible. This baby is no mistake, it is a tiny miracle. Come let's act fast. You know the plan.

Putting her hand to her head in a military fashion, Josephine Cough winked to Valdi, before announcing,

-Miss Cough, at your service. I know the plan by heart. How could I not if it protects the pride of the Wilton-Cough and our good Amelia in one stone's throw? I am off and shall be back very shortly.

Vincent winked and smiled back. He watched the matriarch leave the church in a hurry before baby talking to Abigail,

-Someone is sussing you out my little Angel... A right little miracle you are... Shall good Aunt Jo be your godmother? I think it would make her very very happy. She doted on little Abraham, you know, like if he was her own son. Seeing her reactions, I am sure she will dote on you.

The Doctor was so lost in his conversation with the infant that he was totally unaware of being observed by Amelia and Miss White. The latter recalled him,

-Vincent, I guessed everything about Abigail. Shall we let her mother know? Are we allowed to let her know, before we rush her back to her home according to the plan? Amelia had the most perfect birth. She is well enough to sustain the trip. Josephine will look after her all the way.

The good Amelia was as usual all eyes and ears, trying to pick up cues from every word and everything. When Vincent met her querying grey eyes, he went by her. Putting the little Abigail into her arms, then putting his own arm across Amelia's shoulders, the good Doctor revealed softly,

-My Amelia, your arms are carrying the last wish of Harry Bates, his dying wish was only for you. He wanted to be back by you to give you that family you always wanted. It was his plan for after his last campaign which unfortunately claimed his life. He didn't want you to be alone anymore. He knew how desperate you were to have children and confided all to an Angel who was receiving his dying Soul. She made his wish come to pass. You are holding in your arms that very Angel, Angel Abigail.

Feeling blessed, Amelia Bates, unaware of how instrumental Abigail had already been in bringing people and Spirits together to break the curse plaguing the children, contemplated her beautiful baby in her arms wondering what Wilton Town's future would be like with an incarnated Angel walking its street.

The End

A Ghost Spell:
A W-C's Haunting Return.
From the Wilton Town's Spooky Tales Collection

By Cordelia Malthere

From the depth of his grave, Abraham Wilton-Cough rises again. He cannot rest in peace. It has nothing to do with his senseless death at the hand of an armed robber while the Banker was protecting his customers. No, Abraham can not rest until he knows his loved ones are fine, all of them, but one is cursed, like many children in Wilton Town. Now a ghost, if A W-C will have no rest, no one will for he will haunt them until he brings everyone together to defeat the curse condemning the children of the town to become ghouls. It is fair to say that Abraham Wilton-Cough is a Ghost on a mission.

From the same author:
Hair Rising, Heir Raising, Erasing.
From the Wilton Town's Spooky Tales Collection

A vibrant beyond the grave tale which will chill your bones while warming your heart. When the deadly serious is delightfully hilarious, you will know you have just been acquainted with Abraham Wilton-Cough. His skeletal hand will drag you from grave to grave, under the moonlight of the night where many dead are rising...

Could it be the apocalypse?

From the It-666's Saga:

Finding It-666: The Beast.

Book One of the It-666's Saga.

Born on the 06/06/1996 in London, the young It is a sweet sixteen supernatural Being of a special kind, one meant to bring the end of the human world: the Beast incarnated, the Antichrist.

Fall 2012, the Beast was found. From the deep darkness of her hole, she is raised up to the light. From her closed cage below a pentagram made of blood, she is freed. The human who found her, Walter Workmaster, is a firm atheist, a private investigator and former human rights lawyer who becomes her staunch advocate. Adopting the lost It, the man released her to his world to make her face humanity and unknowingly much more.......The advent of the Beast has started. Step one, she is found.

Raising It-666: The Teenage Beast.
Book Two of the It-666's Saga.

Adopted by the human Walter Workmaster, the Beast is being given a fair chance to live and learn almost like a normal teenager. 'Almost', for normality does not apply when It-666 is concerned.

Trained to be a Soldier by the Angel of Death, monitored by Archangel Raphael and looked after by Archangel Gabriel, It is raised as a Being with full open opportunity, which her own heart can chose, for the Angels will protect that heart unless it turns bad.

Trips to Hell and fighting demons make her earn her true colours within the Angelic Army raising her up in their midst.

Coming soon:

Cordelia Malthere's

Compendium of Characters.

Second edition.

Take a guided tour in the Author's fantastic stories' world, from the It-666's Saga to the Wilton Town's Spooky Tales. Switch gears from Earth to Hell to the unknown... Meet the characters, their pasts, their presents, and maybe their futures... This Codex is the ultimate companion to Cordelia Malthere's universes.

This edition has all the update of the new characters and the old ones.

Saving It-666: The Archangelic Beast.

Book Three of the It-666's Saga.

The young It-666 is a determined Being who will do everything to prevent an Apocalypse in order to protect the ones she loves. Raised by the Workmasters, taught by Angels in the magical tree house of Archangel Gabriel, the Beast dedicates herself to them with a loving devotion. They are the ones who gave her a chance, a hand and a welcome that touched her heart.

To protect them, the courageous soldier that she has become goes on a mission to close Hell for good. Follow her footsteps in the hellish flames as she fights demons for her survival, hoping that her three Angelic Masters, Raphael, Azryel and Gabriel, will be able to rescue her.

Considering the teenager very much part of their Army, the Angels embarks on a huge mission: Saving It-666...

<<<<>>>>